PENGUIN BOOKS

CHAIN OF HEARTS

Maureen McCarthy grew up the ninth of ten children on a farm near Yea in Victoria. After working for a while as an art teacher, Maureen became a full-time scriptwriter and author.

Her novels include *Ganglands*, *Cross My Heart* (shortlisted for the 1993 NSW Premier's Award, the 1994 Victorian Premier's Award, the 1994 SA Festival Award and the 1994 Multicultural Children's Literature Award) and the *In Between* series, which was adapted from the scripts Maureen co-wrote with Shane Brennan for the SBS TV mini-series. Her bestselling and much-loved novel *Queen Kat, Carmel and St. Jude Get a Life*, was recently made into a four-part mini-series produced by Trout Films in association with the Australian Broadcasting Corporation.

Maureen lives in Melbourne with her husband and three children.

PRAISE FOR *QUEEN KAT, CARMEL AND ST. JUDE GET A LIFE*:

'*Realistic, gutsy and challenging*'

the *Courier Mail* (Brisbane)

'*Few books have the power to bring tears of rage or laughter the way this does.*'

the *Age*

maureen mccarthy

chain of
hearts

PENGUIN BOOKS

Penguin Books Australia Ltd
487 Maroondah Highway, PO Box 257
Ringwood, Victoria 3134, Australia
Penguin Books Ltd
Harmondsworth, Middlesex, England
Penguin Putnam Inc.
375 Hudson Street, New York, New York 10014, USA
Penguin Books Canada Limited
10 Alcorn Avenue, Toronto, Ontario, Canada, M4V 3B2
Penguin Books (N.Z.) Ltd
Cnr Rosedale and Airborne Roads, Albany, Auckland, New Zealand
Penguin Books (South Africa) (Pty) Ltd
5 Watkins St, Denver Ext 4, 2094, South Africa
Penguin Books India (P) Ltd
11, Community Centre, Panchsheel Park, New Delhi, 110 017, India

First published by Penguin Books Australia, 1999

1 3 5 7 9 10 8 6 4 2

Text copyright © Trout Films Pty Ltd, 1999

Designed by Ellie Exarchos, Penguin Design Studio
Cover photograph by Maikka Trupp
Digital Imaging by Ellie Exarchos, Penguin Design Studio
Typeset in 11.5/13 Apollo by Post Pre-Press Group, Brisbane, Queensland
Made and printed in Australia by Australian Print Group, Maryborough, Victoria

National Library of Australia
Cataloguing-in-Publication data:

McCarthy, Maureen, 1953- .
Chain of hearts.

ISBN 0 14 028153 3.

1. Title.

A823.3

Song lyrics on pages 57 and 60 by Peter Townsend, reprinted by kind permission
of Fabulous Music/Essex Music Australia

Song lyrics on page 52 by Bob Dylan, reprinted by kind permission
of Special Rider Music/Sony ATV Music Publishing

The publisher gratefully acknowledges the Rippon Lea Estate National Trust,
for access to the cover location

The author gratefully acknowledges the support of the Literature Board
of the Australia Council in the writing of this novel

www.penguin.com.au

Simply for Chris. There is no one else.

ACKNOWLEDGEMENTS

For giving up their time to talk to me of their experiences of the Vietnam War from the Australian soldier's point of view, I want to thank Eddie Place, Peter Norton and Tony Rogalsky.

And for an insider's view of the Vietnamese migrant experience I wish to sincerely thank Mr Truc Lee and his family.

The warmest thanks to Erica Irving who has always been so enthusiastic and supportive of my work. Thanks also to Kay Ronai, Laura Harris and Natasha Treloar from Penguin for their more recent input.

The few weeks I spent up there in that town with my Aunt Fran proved so important to my eventual recovery, it's hard to realise that at the time I had only a very hazy idea of why I was there. On the other hand I don't remember saying that I *didn't* want to go – I was seventeen at the time and anywhere seemed better than staying at home with my parents – but I wasn't enthusiastic. Not by a long shot.

'Your Aunt Fran will have you for a few weeks.' I remember my mother's voice coming at me through the bedroom door, which I'd locked from the inside. 'So pack your bags, Sophie. You're going this afternoon.' I never thought to wonder how desperate my mother must have been, or how much it would have cost her, having to ask for her sister's help.

Fran had made a name for herself as an illustrator of kids' books. Not a big name, but big enough to annoy the hell out of my mother. I enjoyed rubbing Mum's nose in her sister's success whenever I could. My mother was just a nurse who'd married well. Very well actually. My father is a bowel surgeon and rakes in the cash. We've always had everything. Beach

1

houses and boats. Fancy schools, clothes – you name it.

'Your sister has got a new book out,' I'd say, faking innocent enthusiasm. 'Look, there's a photo of Fran in the paper, Mum. She's won an award.'

My mother would look at the photo with this tight blank look on her face and turn away. Jealous, I assumed with smug satisfaction. At the time jealousy seemed to fit in well with the rest of my mother's character traits – she was obsessive, mean minded, controlling and vain . . . just to name a few. Back then I had her all worked out. Although I remember being interested in the fact Mum and this sister didn't get on – we hardly saw my aunt and her family, except at Christmas and big family occasions – I had assumed that my aunt must have had the good taste to reject my mother. I had no idea then that it might be the other way round.

I look back at that time and see myself, just seventeen, bloated with all the crappy food and fizzy sweet drinks I was stuffing into myself, sour mouth, a stripe of bright blue across the top of my hacked-off hair, studs in both nostrils and angry. So absolutely mad at the world that I was virtually jumping out of my skin. I remember imagining them all dead as I lay on my bed one particularly horrible, very hot afternoon, refusing to go to school as usual, refusing their healthy food, refusing to see doctors and counsellors. Mum and Dad could go first and then my older sister, Lauren. I could picture her lying in her coffin, eyes closed, as perfect and cold as a long dead fish. Next would be my former best friends, Jessica and Alana . . . and then that wheedling little troublemaker, Truc. Let them all have a knife, down some back street. Even Mihn could go because, after all that had happened, what was the point of having him alive? Hell! What use were any of them?

While I was lying there weighing up the various advantages of poison, knives and guns, the music that drove the rest of my family mad bounced off the walls, the ceiling and floor and pounded away in my head. It felt then as though the whole world, the whole impossible world with its deep secret oceans and lush green forests, its crazy violence and rivers of pain, was just outside. Hammering away at my door, wanting to get in. Just waiting to rush in and get me.

I can hardly bring myself to read my diary entries of the time. The words almost jump out from the page, like spits of fat from a burning pan. I'm glad I wrote them though. And in certain moods I *can* read them and it puts me back in touch with who I was. Who *I am*, I guess. After all, it was only three years ago. It's important to remember, to take stock and recognise how far I've come.

Reading my rantings from that time does make me wonder where that fury came from. There was the Big Event of course, the cataclysmic incident around which everything else hangs. Sophie Douglas before the Big Event and Sophie Douglas after it are like two completely different people. But the Big Event doesn't explain everything. Why blame my mother? What about the total contempt I had for my father? The indifference I felt towards my sister and all the others who were trying to help: teachers, counsellors, even a clairvoyant that my mother dragged me along to, in the crazy hope that something would connect up with my black mood and make me change?

I try to pinpoint when things started to improve and I find myself thinking of that painting hanging in the front living room above the fireplace at Fran's house. It was a sort of child-like dreamscape of masses of rich swirling colour. But there was an undertow of mystery and sadness in it, too, which was not child-like at all. Fran had done the painting when she was seventeen, the summer after she finished school, and just before she went off to the city to study art. I never understood why I found it so evocative. It was just a river surrounded by bushland. And down in the left-hand corner of the painting, a girl with long fair hair in a red dress, floating in the water. All of it under a multi-coloured sky.

As a little kid coming up to see my grandparents every Christmas and Easter, that painting was always there along with the old scratched window sills, the dull coppery green taps in the outside wash house, the delicious smells of shank and barley soup cooking on my grandmother's stove. Until I was seventeen myself – and in a complete mess – I'd never thought to ask what it was about.

When I told Fran that I used to feel the sadness and mystery in that painting, I think her attitude to me changed. It was a kind of turning point in my time with her. She stopped seeing me as just another bored, sullen, spoilt teenager that she had to put up with and cajole. Me telling her that I'd always been able to feel the ghosts in the painting made her think differently about me, I'm sure. In fact, I like to think we became friends around that point. After all, Fran had a past of her own to deal with.

Fran put the phone down. Her hands were shaking and her mouth was dry. She slumped, shocked, onto a nearby chair and stared in front of her, elbows on the table, waiting for her beating heart to slow. She was still holding the little trowel that she'd been working with outside and her hands were grimy. She put the trowel down and picked at the dried mud on her fingers. Caught off-guard. Absolutely. She'd come running in to answer the phone, puffing a little and picking up the receiver, saying brightly, 'Hello! Fran speaking,' thinking it might be Amy asking her down to the main street for coffee, or maybe one of her boys ringing from the city to see how she was going. Damien was in the middle of exams but Peter's were finished, and he'd landed himself a job in a pizza shop. And darling James, overseas. She was worried about him. If only *he'd* call. But it wasn't any of them. It was . . . her sister Geraldine. *Geraldine!* Who hadn't spoken willingly to her in twenty years. Ringing to ask if she'd have her seventeen-year-old daughter to stay. The girl was *troubled,* whatever the hell that meant. And Fran, so stunned, had mumbled that she would. *Oh God!* She'd said yes as Geraldine knew she would.

'For a few weeks only, you understand, Geraldine,' she'd mumbled weakly at the end of the short, tense conversation. 'I'm here to work in solitude you know.' Then there had been a few brief moments of silence between them. A silence in which Geraldine was telling her to remember that she had no right to lay down any conditions. A silence that reminded Fran just who stood on the moral high ground here. Oh hell . . . *Why? Why do I buy into all that stuff? How come she still has that power over me?*

Fran got up and went over to the sink, turned on the tap and stared out the window. The sky was clear blue, the air crisp. A breeze was making the fronds on the peppercorn tree sway. She'd been back here only ten days and already all her apprehensions about coming home had disappeared. She loved it. It was exactly what she needed. Basic solitude most of the time and company when she needed it. Amy, her best friend from her schooldays at Sacred Heart, was still running Robbertson's haberdashery. And her brother, Jimmy — after a painful, acrimonious split with his wife of nearly twenty years — had moved back to Ballingo the year before to run the town's oldest pub. He too was now only five minutes' walk away down in the main street. *Too good to be true*, Fran had laughed after the first few days. It all felt so absolutely right.

But now, now that she had dared to accept her good fortune as fact, it had suddenly come undone. Right first time, she thought bitterly. *Too damned good to be true!*

Even as she stood there she felt the quietness of the old house settling around her like a comforting cloak and a sob rose in her throat as she washed her hands at the kitchen sink. This wasn't fair. She was forty-seven and she'd done her share. Worked on causes all her life – Vietnam, East Timor, once-a-week volunteer in a women's refuge, for years. There was looking after her sister Trish for the nearly two years of her dying. Then she'd lost Daniel, her own husband, so suddenly last year. And before she'd had a chance to even let that sink in, her 85-year-old father had got sick . . . so she and her three sons had looked after him until he went. *And managed damned well!* Nobody could say they hadn't! (And where the hell was Geraldine through all of *that*?)

This was her time now. She wanted, *needed*, quietness and solitude. A year was all she was after. A year to get back inside herself, to make sense of things, to see if she could find a new direction in her work. No, damn it. She wanted to start painting seriously again. After that, the house could be sold, she'd move back to the city and . . . This year was owed to her.

I don't want anyone, least of all the teenage daughter of my enemy-sister! I'll have to ring her back. Tell her in no uncertain terms. She hates me anyway, so why not?

Fran remained where she was for some time and when she eventually moved, it wasn't to the phone to ring Geraldine but over to the open fire to pile on some more wood. The light outside was fading fast now, but she didn't feel up to the bright fluorescent in the kitchen. Her sister had left her no time to think about it. No time to get used to the idea. The girl would be arriving the next day. *My God!* Fran squatted down, poking small sticks back into the flames and thinking that fate – *other people's fate when it came down to it* – was destined to stymie her again. All her plans would come to nothing. The year would be ruined. She might as well pack up her bags, move back to the city and become the bourgeois widow that she was.

Hours later, when Fran was cleaning her teeth for bed, the phone rang again. She almost didn't answer it. It was just on midnight. No one she knew would ring at that hour. It was probably a wrong number. Then the image of James over in London, in some kind of trouble and trying to get through, came to her and she found herself running down the hallway in her nightie, hoping to reach the shrill noise before it rang out.

It was Geraldine's husband, Robert, making sure that Fran was 'okay for their arrival' the next day. What could she say? A flame of pure fury sprang to life in her chest. Hadn't she told Geraldine hours earlier that she would expect the girl the next afternoon? Bloody hell! What else did they want? But there was some other agenda under all this polite blather about it being very good of her, and if it was too much then . . . Blah blah. Fran waited, knowing it would come out sooner or later. What the hell *else* did they want?

'Yes. Everything is ready,' she murmured through clenched teeth. In fact she hadn't even decided which room she would put the girl in, much less got it ready.

'I don't know how much Gerry told you, Fran.' His easy, low, totally confident doctor's voice made her want to slam the phone down in his ear. 'About Sophie I mean.'

'Not much,' she said shortly. Geraldine would have told him every detail about their conversation, so why pretend?

'Well, she has just become impossible,' he went on, 'hiding away in her room all day. Won't go to school. She's eating very badly and putting on a lot of weight.

She's cut her lovely fair hair and dyed it blue. Screaming at her mother whenever she's asked anything . . .' He gave a dry, mirthless laugh. 'You could say she's turned into the teenager from hell! And the psychiatrists have been worse than hopeless.'

'I see,' Fran said, and then didn't say, *So you thought it would be a good idea to dump her on me, did you?* 'So there wasn't someone . . . er, a favourite teacher maybe, who she could talk to?' she asked weakly.

'Actually there was one fellow she agreed to see,' Robert said, 'a history teacher I believe, but by the time she told us, he was away overseas on long-service leave . . . unfortunately.'

'I see.'

'Look Fran, Gerry just needs a break and we're hoping, of course, that the break might do Sophie some good too.'

Oh really! And what about me, Robert? Does my life even come into your set of calculations? I needed a break when I was caring for Dad a few months ago, but I didn't notice either of you offering any help. You pompous jerk!

'Right,' Fran murmured, 'but just for a few weeks, Robert. I'm up to here with work, you understand.'

'Yes,' he cut in, 'I . . . *we* know that. It's just that . . .' He hesitated before going on. 'I understand that your brother, Jimmy, is now living up there?'

'That's right.' Fran almost laughed. *Here we go. The real reason for the call!* Their brother, Jimmy, at nearly fifty was still wild enough to make people nervous. His last serious bout of trouble was about two years ago when he'd got drunk with a couple of other Vietnam vets, then took himself off alone into the centre of the city with a loaded shotgun. He'd landed up in the Botanical Gardens, standing on the roof of some

9

rotunda and firing randomly into the bushes. No one had been hurt so he was let off. His name *had* been in the papers though, and her other sister, Monica, had told Fran that Geraldine had been mortified. But Jimmy had been in all sorts of scrapes since he was twenty-two and the rest of the family were used to it.

'Do you plan on spending much time with him?' Robert asked lightly.

'Oh, we see a bit of each other,' Fran said coldly. How dare he. Not only were they going to dump their daughter on her, they wanted to start controlling her social life as well.

'As you know, Geraldine thinks the world of Jimmy,' Robert continued, 'but . . . we thought he might not be the best influence on Sophie at this time.'

'I see my brother whenever I feel like it,' Fran snapped, 'and if you want your daughter up here and she wants to see him then I'm not going to —'

'Of course,' Robert said quickly, 'we're not expecting you'll control her movements. She's too old for that. But perhaps if she starts spending a *lot* of time with Jimmy . . . or any other unstable or . . . unsuitable person for that matter, you could let us know?'

'All right,' Fran agreed grudgingly. 'Jimmy actually works very hard, you know. The pub is successful.' It was annoying to be so often in the position of defending her brother. Through the years she'd often thought darkly that it was her chief role in life: defending Jimmy.

'Of course,' he went on, as though he hadn't heard her, 'we'll keep in contact.'

In bed at last, Fran switched off the bedside lamp and lay in the dark thinking. She suddenly saw herself at twenty-six, just after she was married, coming back from travelling through northern and central Australia, with three dozen paintings under her arm. Cheeky and confident enough then to agree to a one-woman show when one was offered.

No one, least of all Fran, had expected much to come of it but the exhibition had been a sensation. The people who mattered declared themselves stunned and the reviews, without exception, were raves. The first one to appear was in the arts sections of the *Australian*, by Malcolm Benning, one time senior curator at the National Art Gallery, sometime critic with *Time* magazine, the most respected and, it had to be said, toughest and most scathing reviewer in the country. After all these years Fran still knew the review by heart!

This young women has the mind and heart of a true artist . . . The works are stunning; simple and yet so highly refined that I was speechless for a good hour after viewing them. In my humble opinion she has a long and illustrious career in front of her . . .

. . . landscapes full of poignancy, of a dreamlike and lyrical quality that makes it quite possible to talk of her in the same breath as Drysdale, Arthur Boyd, Fred Williams . . .

I am very aware that this is a huge statement to make and that my making it may very well may have ramifications on my own reputation, but I am an old man. I have seen much. In her case I throw caution to the wind. Some things have to be said . . . Along with only a very few other truly talented landscape artists in this country, she is both within the European tradition and yet she is saying something totally fresh about it – and in a deeply moving way.

I salute you, Frances Mary Kathleen O'Brien. Your work is truly magnificent. If this is what you can do in your twenties, then I pray I'm spared until you are thirty, thirty-five and forty . . . I sincerely want to be around to see what you will do for the rest of your life.

After that, other papers followed suit and the crowds came. The paintings were all sold for good prices. The gallery owner was thrilled. Fran was interviewed and celebrated for nearly a year afterwards. At the time it seemed that everyone in the world was waiting breathlessly for what she was going to come up with next.

Outside, the night is very black. Low clouds have blocked out the bright stars that had dotted the sky earlier. Fran turns over in her bed and reaches her hand over to the other side, where Daniel, had he been alive, would be lying. She remembers how he used to lean over, still asleep, and pull her into his arms when she'd come up to bed after him. How quickly the two of them could warm up a bed! And she wonders if she will ever get used to sleeping alone.

She remembers her birthday when she was pregnant with Damien and she can't help laughing as she curls her legs up under the woollen blankets. James was home, sick with the chickenpox. Peter was in a tantrum about not being allowed into the bedroom to play with him and she was feeling sick herself. Her mother and Trish came around with a cake at about three o'clock in the afternoon when she'd just managed to get Peter asleep and had been looking forward to putting her feet up. She didn't want cake and didn't want to see her mother or sister. She wanted only to be left alone.

She hadn't picked up a brush in three years.

She remembers too the day, maybe a year after she turned thirty, reading that Malcolm Benning had died and the feeling of relief that had overwhelmed her. Meeting him in the street, a toddler on either arm, and him asking what she'd been working on lately – this was the stuff of her nightmares.

She slips off to sleep thinking of her sister, Geraldine. And she decides that now, niece or no niece, it is time to begin again.

Fran 1968

If only the rest of us didn't have to wear clothes, Fran thought grimly as she stood in front of her easel, eyeing the nude model draped across the grimy pink velvet settee in the middle of the studio. Life would be so much easier.

The model was a woman with long grey hair. Probably in her mid-fifties, she had her head thrown back and eyes closed and might have been asleep, with one arm lying along the back of the chair and the other resting gently near one of her large, pendulous breasts. The daylight coming down through the oblong windows at each end of the studio played across her shoulders and heavy buttocks, making her as solid as a piece of heavy white marble.

Fran rubbed both blackened hands down the checked artist's smock that her mother had made her, and thought miserably how even *that* was wrong. Cheerful, multi-coloured, with a round gathered yoke and two big machine-embroidered pockets, it was . . . too obvious by far. Not the thing a serious artist would wear at all. The other female students wore huge over-sized men's shirts that they'd got from op-shops;

14

overtight dirty jeans and paint-splattered cowboy boots. But what could she do? Loyalty to her mother stopped her throwing the thing away even though she was tempted to do it every day.

There were fifteen first-year drawing students in the studio, all working industriously. Fran picked up a fresh piece of charcoal. Might as well stop dreaming and get on with it. The lecturer, Dominic, a handsome bearded man in his fifties, the epitome of a *real* artist in ragged jeans, frayed jumper, tattered and oil-stained red beret and smoking a pipe, was talking loudly to one of the students on the other side of the room. He would be around to her side soon and so she'd better have something to show him.

Dominic had given them a sharp talk earlier about purity of line. No one was to attempt any shading or trick angles or anything else *but line* for the whole three hours this evening.

'Concentrate on the line,' he'd yelled. 'And for God's sake, open your eyes!'

Line. Line. Line, Fran muttered under her breath as she lifted her right hand to the blank paper, staring at the model. Trying to think, this isn't a person. This is a shape, a mass and a subtle interconnecting line and . . . form. *Use your eyes.*

She'd had one of her drawings held out to the class as an example of how *not* to approach drawing earlier in the year.

'Prissy,' Dominic had said scathingly, 'and lacking in any overall *vision*. You're drawing the parts of the body as though they are separate from each other.'

In front of the whole class he'd done that! Then he simply dropped her drawing on the floor as though it was a piece of rubbish and had gone up to the model and waved his hands around her body, trying to get them all to see the human form as a whole, an integrated unity.

'We're not making decorations here people!' he'd yell lustily. 'We're making art! So I don't want to see any more prissy *nice* drawings to hang on grandma's wall, okay?' Around her everyone had grinned and nodded as though they understood what he was talking about and Fran had hung her head in shame.

That had happened only three weeks into the first term and how it had stung! The fact that he'd pulled out three or four other people's work and given them the same treatment meant nothing. He'd done hers first, and even now, at the end of the year, she hadn't gotten over it. From that time Fran had avoided his every look in case he decided to single her out again for another attack.

'Our time is almost up, people,' Dominic suddenly called out. 'Five minutes then we'll call a wrap.'

He usually got around to every student once during the three-hour class. Fran hadn't stopped dreading these individual interactions even though he'd not humiliated her again. The longing for him to stop talking to her and get on to someone else was so strong that she usually missed most of what he said.

'I like what you've done there,' Dominic said slowly. It took Fran a few moments to realise what he'd said.

'Oh . . . do you?' she said. She resisted a strong impulse to put both hands over her drawing so he couldn't look at it any more. If he looked longer he'd surely see all the faults.

'You've come on in leaps and bounds, you know,' he

said, taking two steps back and squinting thoughtfully at her drawing, then he moved forward, putting one thick, hairy arm up on her easel and faced her full on. Fran didn't know where to look. She could smell the nicotine on him, and that other faint smell of wool and paint and old jeans. A male smell. She was pleased of course, but had no idea what to say.

'You think so?' she mumbled hoarsely.

'Oh come on,' he replied, smiling at her laconically. 'You must know it. Feel it yourself?'

'Er . . . yes,' she stammered, 'a bit.'

In fact she didn't. She had hoped that she was getting better but she really hadn't known it at all. A wave of uncertainty rushed in at her, and then crashed into a thousand tiny drops of delight. *My God*, she thought . . . *I'm getting better*. She was. Maybe . . . *maybe* she would be able to manage after all. Dominic was pulling her drawing from the easel and walking with it to the centre of the room.

'All right everyone,' he yelled, 'come in here. Let's take a look. What Frances has done here is bloody terrific. Have a look at this.'

The other students clustered around and Fran wondered what she would die of first — embarrassment or pure happiness. Was it really her drawing he was commending?

'Something important is happening here!' Dominic shouted, pointing to the thin black line that joined shoulder to breast to hip. 'See this line here. And this space.' His fingers clenched into a ball, emphasising the hollowed-out round space on the paper. 'Frances O'Brien has stopped messing around!' He was beaming at her warmly, nodding his head and holding the drawing this way and that so they could all see. 'She's beginning to see like a fair dinkum artist,' he exclaimed. 'Bravo!'

'You coming down for a coffee, Fran?'

It was the boy who'd lent her some paper the week before. She was heartened by his friendliness. The whole class was packing up now. Dominic had gone and the students were chattering to each other as they packed up their cumbersome folios and boxes of charcoal and pencils.

'I can't tonight,' Fran replied a little longingly – so many times in the past few months she'd waited for such an invitation – 'I have to catch a train home.'

'Where's home?'

'Ballingo,' she said, hoping he might have heard of it. Or even be vaguely interested where it was. But he only shrugged and smiled and said he'd see her the following week.

Fran walked out with a group of about four or five young women and men and stood at the lifts with them. They lit up cigarettes and flicked the ash carelessly onto the lino floor as they waited, talking in desultory tones about all the work they had to do. The folio of paintings and drawings they had to have ready by the end of the year was just the beginning. Fran listened, smiled and groaned in the right places but didn't dare contribute to the conversation. There was a sharp, witty edge to their talk that she wasn't confident enough to join in with.

'You got anything on this weekend, Fran?' Sally asked, turning to her suddenly. She was an older student – in her late twenties – and very talented. Dyed blonde hair in a bun, short, with thin, even features and a loud laugh. Fran was in awe of her ability but also of her sharp tongue. Once she'd heard Sally tell the painting lecturer that he was 'talking bullshit'. It was hard even imagining being game enough to say that to a teacher.

'Yeah.' Fran couldn't help the note of pride and excitement in her voice. 'A family wedding . . . my sister's actually.'

But instead of expressing some surprise or even a little interest, Sally immediately shrugged, made a face and looked away.

'Poor you,' she said quite unselfconsciously, blowing out a long tight line of smoke. 'Hope you survive.'

'Weddings!' someone else groaned derisively. 'Isn't it amazing the way people *keep* getting married!' There was a titter of amusement, then a loud creak as the old lift doors opened. Fran followed the others in, praying that no one would look at her. Like just about everything else that year, she told herself, she'd got it wrong . . . *again*.

Sally's reaction epitomised what had been her problem at art school from the beginning. Nothing intentionally nasty but the others were just . . . different to her. A bit older, most of them, but different, so much cooler, thought-out, sophisticated. They talked about avant-garde artists in America as though they were the people next door. Raushenberg. Andy Warhol. Lichtenstein. Names Fran hadn't even heard of when she'd first arrived. On the weekends they went to exhibitions down grimy little cobbled streets, into spaces where there was hardly any room to exhibit the strange, dripped and splotched, raw-toned paintings, much less anywhere to sit. The plastic cup of red flagon wine someone had thrust into her hand when she'd arrived at her first exhibition had tasted like kerosene. Fran had made herself go to a couple of these events but she found it hard finding her way there by public transport; no one had made her feel particularly welcome, and she didn't understand the art or know what she should do or say. And so she'd made an excuse when someone had announced the next one. Needn't have bothered of course. No one cared if she turned up or not.

And now, buoyed up by Dominic's positive comments, Fran had momentarily forgotten to shut her mouth. Amongst these people a family wedding was something to be avoided at all costs. If it couldn't be avoided then one spoke of it as something that one simply couldn't get out of, like a jail sentence. When, in fact, Fran and her whole family had been preparing for and looking forward to Geraldine's wedding for months. Her older, married sister, Trish, would be matron of honour. Fran was to be chief bridesmaid with the groom's little sisters, Lizzie and Jane, the flower girls. Her mother, an expert seamstress, had at last finished all the bridesmaids' dresses – the material alone, a deep fuchsia satin, had cost a fortune – and the bride's dress was being made by the local dressmaker in Ballingo, who – the whole town was proud of this – supplied one-offs to some of the top fashion houses in the country. Fran had been home every weekend for the past three months, having dress fittings, and helping organise everything.

The one blight on the whole proceedings was that their eldest sister, Monica, wouldn't be there. Mum and Dad had written a special pleading note to the

Mother Superior in the convent that Monica lived in, down in a seaside suburb of Melbourne, but within the week they'd had the decision in writing. 'None of our Sisters attend family events such as weddings or funerals,' came the cold reply. 'We are sorry if this disappoints you. God bless your whole family.' How her father had fumed. Why had Monica entered that bloody place? It was so damned unnatural!

'Yes dear,' her mother had cut in before he could go too far, 'but remember, it's what Monica wants . . . we have to accept that.'

But the rest of the family had agreed with Dad. It was such a useless, stupid disappointment that she couldn't be at her own sister's wedding.

And it wasn't just their family who were so involved in this wedding. Geraldine was marrying Paul Healey, the captain—coach of the local football team and maths teacher at the high school. A handsome, very popular young man from a local family of good standing. The whole town was involved.

But how could she explain any of that to these city art-school people? How hard it had been in the early days to read those hard, wry, superior looks of incredulity when she'd joined in the conversation with scraps of information about her life. So many times she'd felt her face heat up and her voice go high, wondering blindly what it was that she was saying wrong. Now she'd learnt to shut her mouth.

All the mistakes in her first year in the city might have been bearable if she'd made even one good friend. But there was no one. Not amongst her fellow art students, who were a race apart, too intimidating by half. Nor had she made friends with anyone in the Education

Department hostel in South Yarra. There were about thirty girls, in all, who shared the large 1930s converted mansion. And she'd teamed up with none of them.

Thinking about it all often reduced Fran to tears so she only allowed herself this indulgence late at night, or when she was on her own and there was no way she'd have to explain herself. She desperately missed her best friend Amy, not to mention the ease she had felt with the rest of the matriculation class at Sacred Heart.

Fran followed the rest of the students out through the wide doors of the building and down the front steps on to the street. She shivered a little in the nippy wind, put her bag and folio down on the pavement and rummaged around for her windcheater, quickly pulling it on over her tee-shirt. She would get a tram down to Spencer Street, get her bag out of the locker and then wait for her train. Around her, the others were calling goodbye.

'See you then!'

'Yeah. You going to the Albion tomorrow?'

'No, I'm going to work all weekend.'

'Bye Fran.'

Fran returned their smiles and waves and, picking up her things, turned away, guilty that she would be doing no work at all over the weekend when the end of the term was so near. She began to walk, suddenly longing to be on the train, on her way home. It left Spencer Street at six every weeknight and would arrive in Ballingo at nine-thirty. Her father would be there to meet her. His tall, slightly stooped frame standing out from the rest of the people milling around. The grave eyes lighting up when she came in to view.

'Fran!' he always said, pretending to be surprised. 'Fancy meeting you here.'

Half an hour later, taking her seat in the crowded carriage, Fran couldn't help smiling as she thought of the chaos her family home would be in tonight. Her mother had told her on the phone that morning that Geraldine was in a frenzy because her dress still wasn't completely finished – the dressmaker was sewing a thousand pearl droplets onto the bodice by hand but had to stop the day before because she'd cut herself when she was peeling potatoes.

And the dozen or so older ladies from the church who were setting up the hall for the reception were in a tizz because Geraldine had insisted that all the table napkins be folded in a new, special way. Mrs Maguire had led the delegation up to the house the night before. Geraldine's way was just too complicated for them to master at this time in their lives, and five of them had complained of headaches.

Three sets of uncles and aunts were arriving that night from interstate and were staying with various relations around town. Most of the contingent from the city would be arriving that night, too. Already some of the cousins' noses were out of joint because they'd had to book into a pub and hadn't been asked to stay by a relative when others had. Fran could tell her mother was tired but enjoying herself immensely. A very practical, capable woman, Mary O'Brien liked nothing better than organising a big event. Trish's wedding four years before had been the talk of the town for a year afterwards. Everyone said in their thank-you notes that it was the most enjoyable wedding they'd been to.

Fran couldn't see her father on the platform when the train at last pulled into Ballingo's old red-brick station. Although she was surprised, it didn't worry her. They were probably just running late. Visitors might have arrived as he was leaving. Geraldine was probably having kittens over something to do with the dress. She pulled down her little case and stepped onto the platform. Around her people were huddling into groups, greeting each other and calling goodbye. The foggy voice of the stationmaster blared out that the train would be leaving in five minutes.

Night-time, and the big fluorescent station lights made deep dark shadows as she walked towards the wooden gate. Fran knew just about everyone on the platform. There were the Miller girls, Anne and Sharon, come to meet their mother who always went to the city on Fridays. There was Mrs Phillip from the library being met by her husband. And Paul and Jim Baker seeing off their little brother. Fran smiled and nodded to them all. The conductors and stationmaster as well. She'd been to primary school with some of them. A long, loud whistle blew.

'No prizes for guessing why you've come home!' Larry Sommers leered at her as he took her ticket, clicked it with his little silver puncher and handed it back. 'Big sis tyin' the knot, heh?'

'Yes.' Fran tried to smile as she picked up her bag and went through the gate. 'Thanks, Larry.'

'No worries Franny,' he called after her, 'see ya around.'

She hated being called Franny and she loathed Larry. His two brothers were bad enough, but Larry was a sleaze. Once when she was about thirteen he'd held her under the water at the swimming hole and felt her up. When she'd told her older sisters they'd confronted him and he'd denied it. Every time she saw Larry she thought of what it felt like, not being able to breathe, with his hands running over her body. Why didn't he get himself another job? She hated seeing him every time she came home.

Fran looked around. Still no one here for her.

'They forgotten you, Fran?' came a pleasant voice behind her. Fran turned and tried to smile.

'Yeah. Looks like it.'

'Oh well, there's a lot else on their minds, I dare say.'

It was pudgy little Mrs Collins from the post office, one of the ladies who was helping her mother prepare the hall for the wedding reception. Nosey parker *par excellence*. Fran tried to act unconcerned as she peered into the dark street.

'We can give you a ride home,' Mrs Collins said. Fran hesitated. Getting a ride would save lugging her bag all the way up the hill but the ride with Mrs Collins would involve answering all kinds of inquisitive questions about her life in Melbourne.

'Thanks a lot, Mrs Collins,' she said quickly, with an attempt at a sincere smile, 'but Dad will be here soon. I only spoke to Mum this morning.'

As soon as she walked through the front gate, Fran knew something was wrong. You could see into the kitchen from the path leading up to the front door, and instead of people, her family, milling around, there was . . . no one. A bare table, the light hanging down above it and . . .

The big kitchen was where everyone gravitated to. There was always someone around, shifting about from the pantry to the stove, peeling vegetables, walking through to the outside with a bucket of scraps for the chooks that lived down the back of the garden. Except now. The car was in the drive and the kitchen light was on. Fran tried to shrug off the feeling. *So? They're all in another room. Maybe trying on their dresses one last time. Dad has been called away by Father Doyle to go through the ceremony . . . anything.* But there was no noise. The front door was open as usual but the house was still, as though it had been deserted.

Fran stood just inside the gate looking at the house, waiting for a couple of moments. *Waiting for what?* She didn't know exactly. Maybe for the sudden cold feeling that had just washed through her to fade away? Maybe. Or maybe she was hoping that the whole house would suddenly switch on to 'normal'. That the lights would start blazing, that her sisters would dart to life, yelling to each other. Her brother would materialise. That her mother would come bustling out the front door in her apron, hair in rollers, a smile of welcome on her lined face. *Oh Fran. Sorry to forget you, love! But everything has just gone crazy with getting ready for tomorrow!*

And Fran, weak with relief, would accept her warm embrace.

It doesn't matter, Mum. Only a short walk up the hill. Is Gerry's dress finished yet?

The pace of her heart began to quicken. Had someone died? *No. Surely not.*

She was filled with the strangest feeling. For the first time in her life she actually *saw* it. The old house that is, where she'd lived with her family for every one (bar this) of her nearly eighteen years. A moment later and she was being overwhelmed with a wave of pure love for it. The jumbled roof-line, the deep veranda that went right around, the cream, peeling weatherboards. It was like a slightly battered old ship. Her dad had lived there as a little kid. Although it wasn't a big house, it was comfortable in its own rough way.

How she'd loved those creaks and groans at night, especially in the winter. Her three older sisters had the biggest bedroom, down the end of the house, and she and Jimmy shared the smaller one, opposite the bathroom, until he was twelve, when they built him a makeshift room on the back veranda. Jimmy and her lying in their beds in the dark listening to the sound of rain on the red tin roof. Dad had once told them that those noises were little messages from their taciturn grandpa who was up in the sky, glowering down at all the yelling and shouting that had invaded the place with their big family.

Fran and Jimmy had taken the theory to heart. Somehow it made sense. 'There's Grandpa,' they would murmur to each other as they were going off to sleep, the joints in the house grating and complaining in the wind, 'and *he doesn't sound too happy*!' Often they'd break out laughing and shout out rude things to their ghostly ancestor.

'Get lost, you old killjoy!'

'Yeah, go and bite your bum, sour mouth!'

'Stop whingeing, Grandpa!'

Getting louder and louder till their mother came in.

'Be quiet you two! You'll be heard in the street!'

The house was perched up on the biggest hill in town, just opposite the Catholic church. (The next day, all they would have to do was get dressed up in their finery and walk across the road. No cars. And no excuses for being late, Father Doyle had joked lamely to Geraldine.)

But along with this new feeling of love Fran felt a kind of longing, almost a panic for what had been. The house, just for a few crazy moments while she stood there, seemed to rise up and hover in mid-air before melting away into the encroaching darkness. An awful vision: as though all it had ever contained, all those years and months, weeks and days, the *hours* that her family had lived in it, were being sucked away into thin air.

Fran hoisted her bag up onto her shoulder and willed herself up to the front door.

'Hello!' she called gamely, walking into the hallway. 'Anyone home?'

There was no answer. She kicked open the door leading into the kitchen and looked around. It was the same as ever, basically clean but untidy. A big square room painted canary-yellow with a stove and sink down one end, an enormous table in the middle, with a matching heavy, old-fashioned dresser opposite the window. Down the far end was a big open fireplace. There was a formal lounge room on the other side of the hallway, but the kitchen was warm in the winter, with a big wood-burning stove as well as the open fireplace, and cool in summer, shaded from the heat by the trees outside the windows, and this was where everyone would congregate.

There were, as usual, all kinds of bits and pieces stacked in corners and piled on top of the benches. Half a dozen wedges of chopped wood piled on the hearth alongside three pairs of high-heeled shoes set out on newspaper to be cleaned. A large faded sun umbrella stood in one corner. No one had moved it since last summer. The table was roughly set for a meal with knives and forks, pepper and salt. A crystal dish of potato salad sprinkled with parsley had been placed squarely in the middle. Two hat boxes sat on one of the chairs. Remembering the conversation she'd had that morning with her mother, Fran was tempted to peer in. Mrs O'Brien had been having difficulty getting the right hat to go with her mother-of-the-bride outfit, but she'd told Fran that one of the big city stores had sent her up a selection by train, one of which had turned out to be just the thing.

Fran took a couple of steps further in and put her bag down. A tea-towel was spread over a joint of cold lamb on the dresser. Seeing it, she realised she hadn't eaten for hours and was hungry.

'Hi ya, Fran.' Jimmy had come in behind her and was leaning against the doorway. Fran turned quickly.

'Oh, Jimmy,' she said, relieved. 'Hi! What is . . . ?'

Normally they would have rushed towards each other for a quick hug. He would have begun joking and teasing her immediately. But her brother was frowning and moving from one foot to the other, not meeting her eye. Something *was* definitely up.

He was absurdly handsome. It startled Fran all over again to realise how much he'd changed in the last year. No longer a skinny, gangly, dark-haired kid with spots. Every time she saw him now, something was different. Almost nineteen, he was just over six foot, his shoulders broad and his waist slim. His chest had really filled out, too. The spots were gone. Dark bristle covered his chin. But it was those big, deep, blue eyes, which no one in the family had ever even noticed, that set him off. Jimmy had turned into a heart-throb in a matter of months. Not that any of his four sisters let on. Not in front of him, anyway. Even if they mentioned it to each other in private, they always guarded against him getting a big head. As far as his three elder sisters were concerned, he was spoilt already. They had always pestered him about leaving his smelly clothes everywhere, his dirty fingernails and bad school marks. But Jimmy was Fran's big brother. He was the one she'd shared her childhood with when the others were busy being teenagers. She could hardly ever bring herself to seriously criticise Jimmy. They were very different in their views and aspirations, but she quite simply adored him.

'What is it, Jim?' Fran said. 'What's happened? Where is everyone?'

'Well, I don't know, Fran,' he said, looking genuinely bewildered, slumping into the nearest chair. 'I dunno what's going on. I just came home from cricket practice and everyone was sorta . . . running around.'

'What do you mean?' Fran snapped. 'Did you ask what was up? Where's Mum?' She took a deep breath. Sometimes he was so thick it drove her mad. Her premonitions and worries were ridiculous. There would be a very simple explanation for this.

'She's with Geraldine.'

'Where?'

'Well . . . In the bedroom I think.'

'I'll go and see,' Fran said hurriedly, dropping her bag to the floor. 'Where's Dad?'

'He's around,' Jimmy said. 'I saw him walking down the side of the house with Paul. I was gonna go and talk to them about the team for next week but they more or less told me to piss off.'

'*Paul!*' Fran repeated. Geraldine's fiancé wasn't meant to be there. Mum told her that they'd decided to stick to the tradition of not even *seeing* each other for the week before the wedding. 'Why would he be here?'

Jimmy simply shrugged. Then, as though losing interest completely, he got up and began cutting himself some bread.

'Want a sandwich?'

Fran shook her head. Her father walked into the room, his face very grave.

'Fran,' he said, 'how are you?' No smile. No apology for forgetting the train. No coming over to her for one of his quick dry hugs.

'Dad, what's going on?' she said curiously. 'Where's Mum and Geraldine and . . . have Trisha and Gavan arrived yet?'

'Trisha and Gavan?' her dad repeated, absent-mindedly, turning away suddenly and going over to the stove, putting on the kettle. 'No . . . er, that is . . .'

'For the wedding tomorrow?' Fran said loudly and sarcastically. God! First her brother and now her father acting like complete zombies! Her father turned around and faced her, his big bony hands hanging awkwardly on either side of his thin, tall body. Now that he was standing in the light Fran could see he seemed upset. His expression, usually mildly serious, was strained.

'There's not going to be a wedding,' he said softly, and then turned to Jimmy. 'I am sorry but there isn't going to be a wedding tomorrow.'

Fran stood there dumbfounded. Jimmy looked as though he'd been struck by lightning, mouth open and holding a butter knife in mid-air.

'Why not?' Jimmy asked in a hoarse whisper.

'Well . . .' Fran's father had never been good at explaining things. He did his best but he was a reticent man by nature and often joked with outsiders that his wife did all the talking that needed to be done in the family. Fran could see him floundering inside for the right words, wondering how he could best explain. 'The thing is, Fran . . . and Jimmy. Well, the thing is, Paul has decided that it's not the right thing to do. That he doesn't want to marry . . . your sister.'

'God!' Fran's voice came out like a demented squeak. 'You mean?' She was silent for a few moments. 'He's just told her *now*?'

'That's right,' Dad said, 'just over an hour ago. It's unfortunate but . . . well, there we are.'

Fran could feel the beginnings of panic stirring up inside her chest. Mixed with fury. *Now? The evening before the wedding?* She wanted to hit someone. Tears sprang to her eyes.

'But Dad! How . . . how could he do this to . . . *Gerry*?'

Her father only shrugged. Fran tried to calm herself. No one ever got anywhere with him by being overly emotional. And there had to be some sensible explanation. Geraldine and Paul were devoted to each other. Everyone knew that. They'd been saving for years for a house, finally buying a beautiful little cottage out on Laughing Waters Road, about four miles out of Ballingo. Mum and Geraldine had been collecting nice old pieces of second-hand furniture and had made the curtains and cushion covers. Paul and his father had taken two years to make a beautiful oblong table with six chairs out of the best blackwood timber. Everyone loved Paul.

He was so good looking and funny and . . . easygoing. He played guitar and had a great singing voice. As well as being the head maths teacher at the high school, he taught small groups of local kids guitar out of school hours, without being paid. For five years Fran had been secretly in love with him herself. But then, so were most other girls in the town.

'He might be just having pre-wedding jitters,' Fran said suddenly. She vaguely remembered hearing jokes about that kind of thing. But the suggestion made no impression on her father at all. His face remained grave.

'That's what we all thought,' he sighed. 'I suggested that he go and speak to Father Doyle. But it turns out he's been with him all afternoon . . . before he came to see us —'

'Oh, Father Doyle!' Fran spoke sharply. 'What would he know!'

'Yes, well . . .' Her father shrugged and looked away.

'If only Father Cleary was still here!' Fran said frantically. 'He'd be able to *do* something!'

'Hmmm,' her father sighed in agreement.

But Father Cleary, the down-to-earth old priest who had been immensely popular in the district for over thirty years, was dead. The good-looking, young, shy Father Doyle, sent as his replacement, was considered weak and uninspiring in comparison.

'Paul is quite determined,' Fran's father added, looking at her seriously. 'Said he'd been thinking it through all week . . .' Her father's voice faded and Fran was left staring at him. The three of them stood in shocked silence.

'But what about Geraldine?' Fran whispered in a choked-up voice. 'What else, Dad?'

Her father looked as though he was about to walk

out of the room. Never one to utter an extraneous word, he'd delivered the news and so as far as he was concerned that was that. Fran sighed in frustration. 'I mean . . . what did you *say* to him?'

'What could I say?' her father replied sharply. 'It's his decision. He's a fully grown man in command of all his mental faculties.'

What the hell do mental faculties have to do with this? Fran fumed. She decided that getting more details from her father would be like extracting teeth.

'Is Mum in there with her?' she asked. 'I want to go and see her.'

'Yes,' her dad sighed, 'but I think you should wait a while, Fran. They're . . . both terribly upset.'

Fran shrugged and walked out anyway.

'I just can't believe it! I just *can't*! He can't do this to me!'

Geraldine was lying prostrate on the bed, sobbing, when Fran tiptoed into the bedroom.

'I'll kill him! I will! He deserves to die! I'll . . . I'll get a gun!'

Their mother, sitting next to her and patting her shoulder, tried to smile at Fran but couldn't quite manage it. Tears were running down her face. She was dabbing at them with a handful of tissues but they kept coming. Fran went up to the bed and sat down glumly next to her mother. So it was true. Her mother took her hand and squeezed it. Fran understood it was the best greeting she could give.

'I'm so sorry, Gerry,' Fran whispered eventually. Geraldine sat up a little and turned at the sound of Fran's voice. Her face was red and wet and swollen.

'Where did you come from?' she demanded hoarsely.

Fran was startled by her aggressive tone. 'I . . . er, I've just come home,' she managed weakly, glancing at her mother, 'on the train. For the wedding.'

'Well, I wish you had knocked,' Geraldine said through gulping sobs. 'I don't want everyone to see me like this!'

'Geraldine,' her mum said kindly, 'this is your sister here. Not some stranger.' Geraldine pushed her face back into the wet pillow and howled even louder. Mum squeezed Fran's hand again sympathetically. Don't be offended, her touch seemed to be saying, Geraldine doesn't know what she's saying. Fran nodded and looked away. What could she do? What could anyone do? She sat listening to her sister cry, feeling the blunt sense of disappointment grow steadily inside as the news sank in. Apart from everything else, so much energy, not to mention money, had been devoted to it. Was all that really going to come to nothing? She had been so looking forward to this wedding, just thinking about it had kept at bay all kinds of other miseries that she hadn't wanted to deal with.

'How could he?' Geraldine cried again. 'How could he do this to me! *To me?*'

But Fran and her mother could only murmur meaningless sympathies. It was the one question they couldn't answer.

Fran had never been as close to Geraldine as she was to Trisha or, strangely enough, Monica, because in a way they were opposites. Gerry was always so neat, so on top of everything, her whole life worked out from a really young age. She'd started going out with Paul when she was eighteen. After the first date – she told her sisters later – she decided she would marry him.

Whereas Fran, naturally dreamy and a little vague, now at the same age as Geraldine had been when she'd decided on Paul, wasn't in cooee of even having a boyfriend, much less someone she was intent on marrying. Geraldine was very practical and well-organised and although she did admire her younger sister's ability to draw and paint – had even framed a watercolour Fran had done at school the year before for her new house – she didn't approve of Fran's vagueness and often told her that sooner or later she was going to have to 'wake up' to the real world.

If you don't want to be an art teacher, then what are you going to do, Fran?

Of course, this kind of lecturing made Fran furious and there had been some terrible rows, especially over the last couple of years. But apart from all the irritations and differences, they were sisters and the love between them was real.

'Darling, we are going to have to ring people,' Mum said eventually, very gently, 'and let them know.'

Geraldine gave a loud groan of pure agony.

'It will be around town like wildfire!' she moaned. 'How Geraldine O'Brien has been ditched the night before her wedding. Won't they be *sooo* pleased.'

'Now darling,' Mum said soothingly, 'it doesn't help to think like that. Most people . . . will be very sad for you and –'

'No they won't,' Geraldine snapped fiercely. 'Maybe a few. But the others will love the gossip. It will just take over!' She burst into a fresh bout of sobbing. 'Oh God, Mum. I just don't think I'll be able to stand it!'

'Did anything seem . . . wrong these last weeks, Gerry?' Fran asked tentatively. Somehow it still seemed unreal, sort of impossible that the wedding wouldn't take place. 'I mean . . . did he give any sign that –'

'*What?*' Geraldine screamed, sitting up, her eyes streaming, and facing Fran furiously.

'Well . . .' Fran stammered, 'all I mean is, did you have any inkling that . . . he was . . .'

'Any inkling that he was going to do this to me?' Geraldine spat sarcastically. 'Any inkling that he was going to ruin my life? Oh sure, Fran! *Sure!* That's why I've spent all year getting ready for this wedding! Why Mum and Dad have spent a fortune on my dress and . . . yours! Why we've got hundreds of people coming here tomorrow . . . why the church is packed with flowers . . .' She began to weep again and banged her clenched fists on her raised knees. 'Why . . . all the presents have been bought and why the honeymoon has been booked and –'

'Now, now,' Mum interrupted her diatribe, 'that's enough. It doesn't help to get so angry. It's not Fran's fault.'

'Well, what a question!'

Fran decided to retreat. She was hurt by her sister turning on her but tried not to take offence. It was Geraldine's way. She couldn't help it. Fran quietly shut the door behind her and headed for the kitchen again. Geraldine's grief, immense and wild and furious as it was, was being made a million times worse by the fact that everyone would have to know sooner or later. All the people she worked with. Paul's colleagues. The guys on the football team. All the friends and relations. Gerry and Paul were *the* popular couple around town. Both of them good looking and personable. Geraldine was not used to being humiliated.

The kitchen was empty so Fran simply fell into a chair, wishing her brother would come in and talk to her but not having the energy to go and find him. God! She thought, how could this happen? What must have been going through Paul's head this last week? Geraldine was right. There would be people in the town who would pass the news around with glee. People who found meaning for themselves in other people's heartaches and misfortunes. It was oddly humiliating.

'So.' Her father was back in the kitchen. 'Everything still . . . ?' He didn't bother finishing the sentence. Fran knew what he meant and nodded.

'Dad, we're going to have to contact people.'

'Yes.' He sighed and looked at his watch. 'It's getting on for nine now.'

'Why don't you and Jimmy go down to town,' Fran suggested 'and let all the people staying know and I'll start ringing around.' She suddenly remembered Patsy, an old friend from school. A lot of the guests coming to the wedding from far away were staying at Patsy's family's hotel. Fran tried to swallow the bitter thoughts that were swimming up but they wouldn't go away. It was as though she'd eaten a lemon whole. On top of everything else it would be awful, having to put up with Patsy's patronising sympathy and inquisitiveness.

'Good idea.'

Her father went into his little study off the kitchen and found the invitation list. The names were alphabetically ordered, with neatly written telephone numbers and addresses next to them. Typical Geraldine. Fran waited for her dad to leave before making the first call.

The responses were predictable. Disbelief, shock and then a flurry of questions.

Oh no, Fran. But *why?*

Had he got some other girl into trouble?

What was Geraldine going to do?

Were they both going to stay in the town after this?

Poor Geraldine.

The heartless brute.

Poor Geraldine.

After the first half-dozen calls Fran was on the point of screaming. If someone said *Poor Geraldine* again she just might throw the phone at the wall. She took a few deep breaths and decided to cut the calls back to the basics; simply relay the information that the wedding was off and that the family would contact them soon with more details. A lie. But she had to get through those calls somehow – and remain civil.

Gerry and her mother stayed put in the bedroom. In between phone calls Fran could hear their murmuring and the occasional bouts of crying but she didn't go back in. In a way she was pleased to have a practical job to do.

Her father got back at about 10 p.m., looking cheerier.

'Where's Jimmy?' Fran asked.

'Oh, he went off to see his friends,' her father replied. 'I didn't think there would be any point making him come back home. No point in us *all* being unhappy.'

'Well, I think he should be here,' Fran sniffed. *Typical.* Jimmy basically did what he liked. She and her sisters and her mother would bear the full brunt of all this. It wasn't fair!

'Anyway, it's done,' her father said, rubbing his hands together and looking hungrily at the leg of lamb that Fran had put out on the table. 'I can't tell you how much I was dreading that. Now, with all this business, I didn't have anything to eat. Put the kettle on, would you, Fran?'

'Who did you see?' Fran asked. She'd already got herself something to eat in between phone calls, so she watched her father, half-amused to see the way his mind was already on something else. Always a fussy eater, he was methodically getting everything together for his meal.

'Ted and Marie of course,' he mumbled in reply, beginning to cut thin slices of meat, 'and all Mum's brothers and their wives.' Fran's mother had four brothers and they all came from Hamilton, about a six-hour drive away. 'I also ran into Mrs Collins from the post office, in the street outside the pub, so I told her.'

'Oh, Dad,' Fran groaned, 'why'd you tell her for?'

Her father looked up in surprise.

'Well, she'll know soon enough,' he said shortly, 'and she's sure to tell everyone. Save us having to.'

They caught each other's eye and both laughed half-heartedly.

'Oh God, but I just hate her knowing,' Fran groaned.

'Fran, this is nothing to be ashamed of,' her father said suddenly. 'I know Gerry feels that it is. But it isn't. It's not a tragedy. She's a beautiful girl with a good job. She'll meet someone else. If I was a betting man, I'd put fifty dollars on it being within the next year.'

'Dad! How could you say that!'

'Two years at the most. She's what, twenty-two? It's hardly a catastrophe, is it? Er . . . apart from all the wasted time on preparations, of course.'

Fran shrugged uncomfortably. What could she say?

What he said was probably true, but so what? *Now* was so bloody awful, especially for Geraldine.

Father Doyle came around at 9 a.m. the next morning, with Paul's parents. The priest was probably only thirty, with clear light-brown eyes and sandy-coloured hair that kept falling onto his forehead and that he kept pushing back nervously. He had a quiet, almost respectful air to him that immediately made everyone more nervous than normal. Fran liked the priest's gentle manner, even though she wished with all her heart that Father Cleary was still around. She ushered him and the very subdued Healey couple into the kitchen.

'So Father, you've spoken to Paul?' Fran asked politely.

'Er, yes I have.' The priest met her eyes seriously. 'Yesterday. For a number of hours.'

'Father couldn't talk him into it, love,' Paul's mother burst out, her eyes brimming over with fresh tears. 'He tried but –'

'Well, not strictly true, Mrs Healey,' Father Doyle said hurriedly. 'I didn't see it as my place to *talk him into it*. I . . . er, tried to help him examine what his true feelings were.'

'Yes.' Fran nodded and tried to smile. *Damn it.* Father Cleary would have definitely tried to talk Paul into it.

By 10 a.m. people began to arrive en masse. The news had circulated through the town. The phone began to ring non-stop. Fran couldn't believe how stupid she'd been, thinking that she'd dealt with everyone over the phone the night before. Of course, no one was satisfied with the simple information that the wedding had been called off. They wanted to know why, they wanted to offer help, they wanted to be part of it. Neighbours, hordes of relations, family friends, friends of Paul and Geraldine, everyone in the town, it seemed, quietly and sorrowfully made their way to the O'Brien household to offer their plates of scones, bottles of drink, sympathy and help. Just as though it were a funeral.

Geraldine wouldn't come out of her room – sent the message that she wasn't up to seeing anyone – so it was Fran, her father, Trisha and Gavan who greeted the visitors. Occasionally someone special was permitted to creep in to see Geraldine, to commiserate. But only one at a time.

Fran and Trish found themselves tied to the kitchen for close on three hours, making tea and offering cake and biscuits, being pleasant to them all and seething underneath about the way Jimmy could just walk out of it when he felt like it. Fran knew she couldn't leave. Her mother was depending on her.

'I'm afraid I'm going to have to leave you.'

'Well, thank you for coming, Father,' Fran's father said courteously and that was the cue for everyone to stand and farewell the priest.

'Goodbye, Father! Thank you for all your help, Father.'

'Not at all, not at all!' The priest was at the door. 'And tell Geraldine I'd like to see her when she feels . . . a little better.'

'We'll do that, Father,' Trish murmured.

'I'll be praying for you all.' He looked pointedly over at Fran's mother, who was sitting looking completely exhausted with two of her sisters. 'We've all got to pray for the grace to accept the things we can't change.'

'Thank you, Father.'

'Our Lady is very helpful in these kinds of situations.'

'Yes, Father.' Fran saw him to the door. He turned to her before she had a chance to open it.

'You'll be a great help to your mother and sister, Frances,' he said gently.

'Yes, Father.'

Behind his back Fran grimaced.

Just at the point when Fran thought she could take no more, rescue came in the middle of the afternoon with the arrival of Amy, her best friend from school.

'Go on,' Trish said when she saw Amy coming in the gate, 'go and have a spell from all this.' She gave Fran a push. 'Go and hide somewhere or go for a walk.'

'Oh thanks, Trish!' Fran hugged her sister and went to grab Amy before she got waylaid by all the other visitors.

'I've heard the news,' Amy said quietly, eyeing Fran warily. 'Want to go for a walk?'

'Yep.' Relief flooded Fran. 'Somewhere quiet, where we won't see anyone.'

'Bet you're sick of talking about it.' Amy said as she followed Fran down the path.

'Right again.'

'You haven't told me anything,' Amy complained, as they wove their way slowly along a little crooked path through the graves of the Ballingo cemetery. Both girls were in tee-shirts and jeans. It was a perfect, still, sunny day. Tall grass grew up so high in places that some of the headstones were completely hidden. 'What about the hostel? Is it getting any better?'

Fran shook her head and smiled wryly at Amy.

'I hate it.'

'You've said that before,' Amy said mildly, 'but tell me *why*! Why do you hate it?'

'You want the gory details?' Amy nodded immediately. Fran laughed. 'Okay, I'll try.'

She thought of the hostel. What *was* wrong with it? What was wrong with a lounge room on the ground floor that was fitted out comfortably with couches and record players and an old black and white TV? And the small kitchen where they could make cups of tea and snacks? The dining room where they all took breakfast and dinner was around the corner, at a similar place only five minutes away, filled with more female students. The big, light bedroom at the front of the house that she shared with five others was awful. A dormitory! How her heart had sunk when she saw it. But she'd already told Amy all about it in her letters. No, it wasn't the place. It was the girls that she had to live with.

'Have you made friends with anyone yet?' Amy asked quietly, as though reading her thoughts.

'Nope.' Fran shook her head and then added, a little defensively, 'I'm not sure exactly . . . why not.'

But she did know why, didn't she? At least in part. The girls she lived with in the hostel were, in the main, country girls like herself, and had been friendly, loud and helpful when she'd first arrived. But . . . Fran couldn't fit in with them somehow. A lot of them smoked and swore and talked crudely about the boys they were going out with. They hated the city, and spoke longingly of finishing their training so they could get back to country towns to teach. Although Fran was also on a teacher's scholarship, she wasn't looking forward to teaching and she didn't want to go back to the country even though she knew she didn't fit in there in the city. It was all so complicated. There was no one at the hostel doing her course either. Most of them were studying to be primary school teachers.

'They think I'm a snob,' she said to Amy suddenly. 'That's it. They really think I'm a snob.'

'You?' Amy said incredulously.

'Yeah,' Fran replied with a dry laugh, 'me!'

'Well, that's stupid,' Amy said matter-of-factly. 'I mean . . .' She turned to Fran, her face quite serious. 'You've got nothing to be snobby about.'

'Thanks, Amy!' Fran laughed immediately, pretending to hit her over the head. 'Thanks so much. With friends like you . . .'

They had come to the little nest of O'Brien graves that Fran could never resist visiting.

'Hang on, Amy!' Fran said, nudging her with a wry grin. 'Just want to check on my relatives!'

Amy smiled an okay, and sat down at the end of a grave on the opposite side of the little path. 'Give 'em my regards,' she called lazily.

Fran went to the big family plot first, the one with the big stern angel on top. Here was her great-grandfather Con and his wife Brigid, all the way from County Kerry last century, and a couple of their children. When she moved along to the next narrow grave a shiver ran down her spine, the way it always did. *Ruby Mary O'Brien. Aged seventeen. Died by drowning in the Ballingo river in 1924.* Her father's only sister.

'Everything changed after Ruby died,' her father often said when Fran pestered him to tell about his own childhood. 'When I was ten all the life went from our house . . . because Ruby was gone.'

Fran shuddered, thinking of the painting she'd done the previous summer. Ruby in her red dress drowning in the river. She'd not spoken to her father about it, but figured he must like it to let it stay there – pride of place in the lounge room. Once she'd caught him examining it up close when no one else was in the room; squinting thoughtfully as though he was trying to understand something.

Bringing home her huge folios and canvases didn't go over well with those girls in the hostel. From the beginning they'd treated the fact that she was studying art with incomprehension and then when they saw some of her textbooks and drawings they were incredulous.

'You call that art? My little brother could do better!'

When she'd stuck a small reproduction of Van Gogh's *Starry Night* onto the cupboard near to her bed the girl next to her had asked her to take it down.

'I know this might sound crazy, Fran, but it's the first thing I see in the morning,' she said in her flat, nasally twang, in front of all the others who obviously felt the same. 'And it kinda makes me depressed.'

'Depressed?' Fran had exploded without thinking. She'd got very good at being quiet and not taking offence but this was outrageous. 'You can't be serious!'

'Yeah,' the girl had continued serenely, confident that she had the rest of the room with her, 'it's so . . . *so* ugly.'

'You're right, I *do* think you are crazy,' Fran had said coldly. Her lip trembled even as she knew it was also curling with disdain. They were probably laughing behind her back. She took the print down, trying to tell herself that she didn't care. She didn't care one bit about any of them.

A week after the wedding fiasco and Fran was getting off the train in the middle of the city, having travelled all the way back from Brighton where she'd spent two hours visiting Monica. Her parents had asked her to go. After the tumultuous week, Fran's mother had not felt up to making the trip down, and her parents had been worried that Monica would have no visitors. They'd written and told her the news, but her mother was anxious that Fran should go and fill her sister in on all the details. Mrs O'Brien didn't want her eldest daughter feeling left out of the family crisis.

'Oh Fran, for goodness sake! He did the only thing he could do in the circumstances!'

Monica was standing by the window in the stuffy little convent piano parlour thumping her fingers on the sill and looking impatiently out the window on to the convent's rose garden. The eldest in the O'Brien family, she'd always been the fiery one. People were forever asking after her and saying they remembered her as the most un-nun-like person they'd ever met. It sometimes got quite boring fielding questions about Monica.

'What do you mean?' Fran shook her head.

Monica was dressed in the full habit, long black serge dress caught in at the waist with a plain wide leather belt. From it swung a large black rosary and crucifix. Her pretty face and neck were surrounded in cardboard-stiff starched white coif and wimple. Because she hadn't yet made her final vows, a short white veil covered this instead of a black one, folding down into a point in the middle of her back.

'Why should he tie himself down to someone who was going to bore him to tears?' she went on passionately.

'How can you say that?' Fran shot back. She was sitting in one of the uncomfortable high-backed chairs, looking back at her sister, stung but not exactly surprised. You could never predict what Monica would think about anything.

'But what about . . . poor Gerry?' Fran managed to stammer.

'Poor Gerry!' Monica snapped, turning around from the window. 'What do you mean, *poor Gerry*? She deserves this.'

'Monica!' Fran was genuinely outraged.

'Well, Paul's *interesting*,' Monica went on furiously. 'I mean, as soon as I met him I thought that. He's got ideas about things.'

'Like what?'

'Well . . .' Monica made a broad sweep with her arm. 'Vietnam. Did you know he's got an anti-war group going in the town? He's a progressive thinker!'

'Gerry is intelligent and . . .' Fran countered loyally, 'she's —'

'I'm not talking about intelligence!' Monica cut in sharply. 'She does nothing. Takes no interest in the outside world. Look, I'll tell you straight, Fran, I don't blame Paul at all for not wanting to marry Geraldine!'

Fran was flabbergasted.

'When was the last time you heard Geraldine say anything that wasn't to do with herself or her own little boring world?'

'Yes, but —'

'I mean the *real* world.' Monica pointed vehemently out the window. 'It's in turmoil! Think of what's happening in America. The European universities! The situation in South Africa. We're sending all these young boys off to get killed in Vietnam and the big decision of Geraldine's life is whether to make blue or red cushion covers! I really can't see what choice he had.'

Fran handed her ticket to the collector and joined the small throng making their way through the iron gates and out onto Flinders Street. She stood on top of the steps for a few moments, trying to decide what to do. She wondered if she dared miss dinner at the hostel. The matron got angry if students didn't let her know well in advance that they wouldn't be there for meals. Sometimes ridiculous punishments were meted out for such infringements: no late nights for the week, or washing up all the dirty crockery every night for three days. Stupid childish things. But it was still early on a Sunday evening and Fran couldn't bear the idea of going straight back to the hostel. She wanted to walk around for a while and think about her afternoon with Monica. Sift through it, see if she could work out what she thought.

It was warm and, being Sunday, not particularly busy. The streetlights, even the traffic lights, were beginning to glow in the fading light and they made Fran suddenly feel light-hearted, filled with a new exciting sense of her own anonymity and freedom. Damn that horrible place and other people's rules. What did she care! She would wander up Swanston Street, look in the shop windows, get something to eat. Take her time.

She began to walk up the Collins Street hill towards Parliament House, looking into the beautifully lit shop windows as she went.

Of course Monica was partly right. Geraldine was a

bit self-satisfied, but she had good points, too. She was kind. Would do anyone a good turn. Everyone who'd ever been a patient in the hospital said she was a wonderful nurse. And she was petite and beautiful in a way no one else in the family was. Geraldine had personality. Everyone always said that. She was vivacious and stylish and . . . a fabulous ballroom dancer. Anyway, weren't sisters meant to stick up for each other? Fran shuddered to think how upset her parents would be to hear Monica talk the way she had.

There was some kind of large gathering at the steps of Parliament House, but because Fran was deep in thought, and also half-looking for somewhere to buy a hamburger, she didn't take any notice. But as she got nearer she saw that the crowd was in fact large; at least five hundred people. And they were making a lot of noise. About four women were standing at the side of the group holding a large painted sign, 'Save Our Sons'. Other more roughly painted placards bobbed up and down in the crowd: 'Stop the War' painted in red over a skull and crossbones, and 'Do something for your country. Don't Register!'. A young, fair-haired woman was singing through a crackling loudspeaker system on a makeshift wooden stage but Fran couldn't hear the words. Curiosity got the better of her hunger and she moved closer.

Some people were holding lighted candles and others were handing out yellow leaflets to anyone passing. Two rows of very grim-looking policemen stood in stiff lines some distance away, on either side of the crowd. The singer finished and a rather good-looking, roughly dressed man with wiry dark hair got up.

'This is an immoral war!' he yelled into the microphone. And the people around Fran cheered and whistled and called out.

'Right on!'

'A war that will never be won by the West,' he continued in a slower, deeper tone. 'So my friends, we have to ask, *why is it being fought?* The answer? For America's imperial interests! Certainly *not* for the people of Vietnam. We must join with other like-minded groups across the world and together fight Australia's involvement!' He raised one fist and pumped it up and down in the air.

'Say no to conscription!' he called out. 'Say no to war!'

Loud applause broke out, filling the air as the man leapt down from the stage and joined his friends below. Three people, a man and two women, all with guitars, immediately took his place. The crowd talked loudly amongst themselves as they waited for the guitar players to tune up, then someone called out loudly, 'Bring our boys back home!' The call was taken up by two or three others, then by the crowd. En masse, hundreds of people began to chant, 'Bring our boys back home!' To her own surprise Fran moved steadily closer, deeply fascinated. She could see the musicians' faces now. The two men were scruffy in old jeans, desert boots and long hair. The girl standing between them had a red and black band tied Indian-style around her head and she wore a long, multi-coloured caftan. Her face when she smiled was bright and excited and . . . so involved, so *part of everything.* Fran felt a pang of pure longing as she watched her cue the others in, *One and two, three!* They launched into a loud song that Fran couldn't name but knew she'd heard somewhere before.

'Please get out of the new one
If you can't lend your hand
For the times they are a-changin'!'

Fran took a leaflet from a girl her own age who was smiling as she wandered though the crowd. She moved nearer, right in amongst the people, strangely excited and moved by the loud rousing song.

She thought of her brother, Jimmy, his handsome face laughing at her that last night at home. They'd gone for a walk down to the river, and she'd let fly with some of the anger she'd stored up against him over the weekend.

'How come you think you can just get up and leave any situation when you like?'

'Fran!' He'd laughed, perplexed. 'What are you talking about?'

'You think I *liked* making tea all day for all those old busy-bodies? Huh?'

'Well, you should have just . . . left.'

'Don't bullshit me, Jimmy! You know someone had to be there! Why couldn't it have been *you* just for once?'

Nothing had been resolved. He really *didn't* know what she'd been talking about. Even so, after the fight they'd walked home together in the dark, friends as usual. There was something about Jimmy that went way beyond any kind of rational explanation for Fran. She admired all her sisters. From the time she'd been small she'd never been able to decide which one she admired the most. The pretty, happy mother and housewife, Trish? The strong-minded Monica? Or the vivacious and talented Geraldine? They all seemed so successful and wonderful in their own particular way. At different times she wished to be all of them. But the way she felt about Jimmy was something else. Sometimes it felt as though her very soul was talking back to her when Jimmy told her something.

At the end of the year Jimmy would be required to enrol for National Service. The army. She'd heard her parents talking in hushed voices about it last Christmas but she'd simply refused to think about it. It was just too *outside* anything any of them had ever thought about. *But what if he actually did get called up?* A shiver of fear went through her. *War!* There actually was a war on. Why was Australia involved in it? It shamed her suddenly that she'd taken so little interest and that she was so ignorant. *Where the hell is Vietnam?*

After standing more or less in the same spot for nearly an hour, Fran turned around noticing that the crowd had grown much bigger, and that some people were now sitting a little further away on the steps. She decided to join them. It had been a long day and her feet were starting to ache. Edging her way slowly backwards towards a place to sit, she suddenly found herself staring straight into the face of Paul Healey.

'Fran!' he said.

If anything, he was more surprised than she was.

'Hello.' Fran's eyes dropped and she felt herself flush. She glanced around for a means of escape but the crowd milling around made it impossible to move anywhere quickly. She looked up again into his face. He looked no different. Tall with strong, broad shoulders and a pleasant, handsome face, his clear hazel eyes staring directly into her own. They stood for a few moments, looking closely at each other in the semidarkness. Fran remembered the conversation she'd had with her mother only that morning. Geraldine had hardly eaten for a week and her face had become swollen and puffy from all the crying. How dare he look so fit and well!

'What are you doing *here*?' he said at last, genuine surprise in his voice. Fran bristled. Why did he think he was entitled to put her on the spot with questions?

'What are *you* doing here?' she snapped back angrily, trying to sound sarcastic, but it came out wrong. Her nervousness showed through.

'I'm on the committee organising safe houses for people refusing to comply with the draft.'

'Ah well . . . bully for you!' Fran said and turned away, suddenly afraid she would cry if she stayed any longer. But she had only moved off a couple of steps when she felt a hand on her arm. It was Paul. She tried to shrug him off but his grip remained firm.

'Fran,' he said, 'I've got to talk to you . . .'

'I don't want to talk to you!' she replied heatedly, this time managing to shake him off. 'I don't want anything to do with you! Excuse me please,' she said, pushing her way through the crowd, annoying a few who were trying to see the speakers, but so anxious to get away she didn't care. 'Excuse me! Please could I get through?'

At last she was free. Another speech was starting but she didn't look back. She headed off blindly, heart pounding, towards the lights. She would cross the road, walk back down the way she'd come, and get the tram back to her hostel. Breathing heavily she waited for the lights to change and then saw to her dismay that Paul was standing right next to her. He'd followed her out of the crowd.

'What do you want?' Fran demanded angrily.

'I told you, Fran,' he said, his pleasant face clouded with a frown, 'I want to talk to you.'

'And I said that I didn't —'

'Please!' he cut in. 'Only a few minutes?' Somehow his face didn't seem as complacently ordinary as she'd first thought. He was frowning, and she saw that he too seemed nervous.

'Okay,' she relented stiffly, 'just for a few minutes.'

They went to a nearby cafe and sat down.

'How's Gerry?' he asked simply, as soon as they were seated.

Fran shrugged and to her dismay a huge lump rose in her throat and tears came to her eyes.

'Bad, eh?' he said softly.

'What do you expect?' Fran said through a strangled voice. But when she looked up she saw that he was close to tears. This disarmed her a little. Her curiosity was ignited.

'Why?' she gasped. '*Why* did you . . . ?' It was the question she and her mother had been asking each other all week. Why had he treated Geraldine so shabbily? But Paul only nodded slightly, to show he understood what she was asking, then sat quietly for so long that Fran had the feeling he wasn't going to answer her at all.

'It was weak and pathetic and hopeless of me not to . . . tell her sooner,' he suddenly said in a low, passionate voice, 'but you see I wasn't sure. The feeling had been growing in me for weeks but . . . I wasn't sure . . . thought I might be just feeling nervous about getting married. Even when I knew I shouldn't, I felt as though I . . . couldn't call it off.'

'So you waited till the last night before the wedding?' Fran whispered, 'Paul, that was so cruel.'

'You think I should have gone through with it?' he asked simply. There was no sarcasm in his voice. No reproach or defensiveness at all. Just a simple question.

It startled Fran. In a flash she knew that of course the answer was no. She bowed her head.

'So when *did* you know?' she whispered, looking down at her hands twisting around miserably in her lap. 'I mean for sure? At what point . . . did you know that you . . . couldn't marry . . . her?'

Paul brought both hands up to rub his eyes. He groaned.

'Ah shit, Fran!' he whispered. 'Shit. Shit! I'm so sorry. I'm so unbelievably sorry.'

'Yeah, well,' she said, feeling for him in spite of herself, 'sorry isn't enough, Paul.'

The cafe was filling up with young people from the rally. Most were dressed in rough, shabby clothes and many were holding rolled-up banners, leaflets and placards. They talked excitedly, the mood between them triumphant. Two young men in jeans and long orange Indian shirts and shoulder-length hair noticed Paul. They stopped and smiled, one of them patting him on the shoulder.

'G'day.'

'Oh hi,' he muttered distractedly, looking up without smiling. Fran glanced at him swiftly, noticing for the first time his bloodshot eyes and the drawn skin around his mouth. She could see that he actually looked quite haggard.

'Good turn out, heh?'

'Yeah.'

'It's growing, man,' one of the young men said, smiling, punching the air with a gleeful gesture. 'Opposition is really mounting.'

'Yes.'

Sensing they were intruding on a private moment, the friends passed by. But others coming in nodded and called hello to Paul. Fran was fascinated, in spite of herself, to see evidence of Paul's other life. He was known by these people, was part of their group. It couldn't have all happened in a week. How much of his involvement in the anti-war movement did her sister know about? Why didn't she ever mention it?

'My Generation' by The Who began to play on the juke box. Fran closed her eyes, listening to the song.

'People try to put us down . . .'

She forgot about Paul for a few moments, allowing herself to sink into the song's beat and rhythms, letting it feed the emotional hunger she felt lying just below her skin.

'Do you remember that big family lunch we had three weeks ago?' Paul suddenly asked. Fran looked up and saw that he was looking at her intently.

'Yes,' she nodded, waiting and thinking back.

Both families had got together under the huge peppercorn trees out in the Healeys' backyard for a pre-wedding family party. The weather was sunny and everyone was in such high spirits. Bottles of beer and sparkling wine were opened to toast the soon-to-be-married couple. Silly speeches were made and dumb jokes told. Some of the older ones organised games of cricket and keepings-off for the kids. The two families, who before this day hadn't known each other well, got on famously.

'Vietnam came up,' Paul went on slowly, meditatively, one finger slipping lightly around and around the rim of the cup of coffee in front of him. 'Gerry said something about the anti-war protesters having too much time on their hands. I mean, she knew about my involvement, so I knew that she was having a shot . . . but that's not the point. Then you said . . .' he hesitated, as though unsure whether to go on or not. Fran froze as she watched him. Something odd was happening. She felt her breath go short; it was as though someone had suddenly clamped two arms around her, squeezing her chest. What was he going to say?

'You said,' he repeated, emphasising the words clearly, 'that she was being ignorant and narrow-minded . . . as usual.'

'I was joking, Paul!' Fran cut in, strangely panicked. 'Gerry and me. All of us . . . we're sisters! We're always teasing and criticising each other! Don't try to blame *me*!'

'Oh hell, Fran!' Paul smiled wearily. 'I'm not *blaming* you. Far from it.'

'So what . . . are . . . you . . .?' Fran stammered. The air around them had definitely thickened. 'What are you getting at, Paul?' It was becoming harder and harder to breathe in this place. She clearly remembered the moment Paul was talking about, but now it seemed so much *darker*. Every look, every small gesture, every word fraught with meaning. It wasn't fair to look back on it like that. At the time it hadn't meant anything . . . *had it*?

'Anyway, Fran,' Paul went on slowly, 'I looked across all those other people, at you sitting there at the end of the table, dressed in blue.' He laughed harshly, not looking at her. In fact his eyes were flitting about the now crowded cafe like trapped birds. And you looked so beautiful and thoughtful, with your long hair pushed back from your face. Your eyes,' he went on relentlessly. 'So . . . lively, so impatient with Geraldine's *smallness*. Exactly how I was feeling. And our eyes met, didn't they? Across all those heads, across Geraldine's head and . . . we sort of smiled, I don't know. We looked at each other, didn't we?'

Fran, looking down at her hands, said nothing.

'Fran?'

'Yes,' she said in a quiet voice, head jerking up. She stared at the wall behind him determined to stop whatever was happening, but unsure quite what it was.

'Well,' Paul sighed. He was looking at her now. Steadily, right into her eyes. 'In answer to your question. I knew then that I *absolutely* shouldn't marry Gerry . . .' He stopped again, then the words tumbled out in a rush. 'Because at that moment I was looking at you and thinking, I wish it was Fran. She's the one I really love. I wish I was marrying Fran. But it took me another couple of weeks to bring it to a head and tell her because I didn't trust myself and I . . . I really didn't want to hurt her. Oh shit, Fran, I know I've made a bad mess of it. A very bad mess. I just hope that one day you'll be . . . that all of you will be able to forgive me. And that you and I . . .'

She's the one I really love . . . Fran is the one I really . . . love.

'You told Geraldine that . . .' Her voice died away to a whisper. 'Told her you . . . loved me?'

'Well, of course not,' he sighed. 'Of course I wouldn't do that, Fran.'

They sat mute for a few minutes, loud music thumping out from the juke box. Fran looked around the cafe, one thought jumping over another in her head. Over in one corner a group of people were screaming with laughter. Someone had mistakenly lit a paper napkin with a cigarette lighter. There were shouts and excited squeals.

'My Generation. This is my Generation.'

'Well I'd better go now,' Fran said eventually, getting up. He stood up immediately and followed her to the front door of the cafe.

'Bye, Paul,' she said, turning to him and holding out her hand. He took it in both of his and hesitating for only a moment, put both hands on her shoulders and drew her to him, kissing her on the mouth. It was not exactly a long kiss but there was so much pent-up passion in it that Fran's breath was literally taken away. She stood there, unable to stop herself trembling.

'Bye, Fran,' Paul said without smiling. 'See you around.' He turned sharply, and hurried outside into the darkness.

When Fran was out in the cool air she began to run.

She got back to the hostel well after ten and had to knock on the door to get in.

'A message from Matron,' said one of the two pert girls standing near the phone and pointing at the rack where mail and notes were left. 'She's mad you didn't let her know where you were.'

Fran took the small envelope, opened it, read the message and, without a word or look at the girls who were waiting for some reaction, screwed it up and threw it into a bin. She walked quickly into the bedroom where half-a-dozen of the girls she shared with were sitting about talking, dressed already in their pretty dressing-gowns, ready for bed. A couple of them turned and greeted her with forced smiles.

'Oh hi, Fran,' said the red-head from Yarragon. 'You're late. Did you get your note from Matron?'

'Hmmm.'

'Had a good day?' she added inquisitively, cold eyes taking in Fran's rumpled appearance and edgy manner.

Fran ignored the question, and with her back to them, slipped her shoes off. She was exhausted, her head thumped and her feet ached. She threw the sandals into her cupboard and then dumped the contents of her bag out on her bed. A purse, comb, brush, three tram tickets, a lipstick and a few inky biros that didn't work. The leaflets she'd been given at the rally. She had only three more weeks to spend in this rotten, uptight, foul, blasted hostel! Three more weeks of college and then . . . next year she'd make sure she was living somewhere else – in a flat alone or with someone . . . But who? *Damn everything.*

Her hands were shaking, she wanted to cry, but somehow she couldn't. She was so confused, she didn't know what to do with these sudden surges of rage and longing that pulsed right through her. Didn't understand where they were coming from at all.

Monica is right. There is a big world out there. And I'm going to be part of it. I'm going to paint, I'm going to think, I'm going to try everything, say whatever I like, I'm going to . . . go places. I'm going to live.

Five separate leaflets in all. A couple of them were covered with finely written paragraphs of background information: the history of the war, the real reason for the West's involvement. These she would study more carefully later. The bright yellow one, the one that had 'Stop the War Now!' as its headline, she taped to the door of her cupboard with sticky tape, right where Van

61

Gogh's *Starry Night* had been. *This is the least I can do for Jimmy.* Without even looking at the other girls, who were now curiously watching her, she went out to the foyer and pinned up on the hostel noticeboard the large pink leaflet that advertised the next big demonstration in the city.

'Protest Australia's Involvement in the War! 12th of December'. And underneath the headline, 'Six Reasons Why You Should Demonstrate'. Pinned now between a College Christmas Ball poster and a notice about rules for swot vac. She turned to the two girls who were still standing by the phone, eyes wide and mouths open, about to protest.

'I don't care what you think,' Fran said very coldly. 'You take this down and I'll put another one right back up. If it's okay to have church timetables and sports news here, we can have this!'

From there Fran went out to the little kitchen at the back of the hostel. Thankfully it was empty. She made herself a cup of cocoa and sat alone at the long table thinking about Paul's words, *I wish I was marrying Fran . . . Fran is the one I really love!*

She knew he meant it. She could still feel the dry, rough prickle of his two-day beard, his strong kiss on her mouth. Fran had never kissed anyone like that before. It was like he was claiming her . . . letting her know he really did want her.

By the time Fran had finished her drink the lights were out in her room. She could hear the other girls murmuring as she undressed, but there were other things to think about now. She slipped thankfully between the stiff white sheets and made the sign of the cross in the dark.

Hail Mary full of grace. The Lord is with thee. Blessed art . . .

Would it be a sin to pray that she would run into Paul Healey again? She wanted to ask him about Vietnam. How had the war started? Who was for it . . . who was against it. He could fill it all in for her. Tell her what books she should read. Maybe they would sit in a cafe and drink coffee. Maybe they'd talk for hours. Then, later, he would hold her by both shoulders and pull her towards him again. Kiss her? She didn't have to be told that she had no right to hope, much less pray for, anything like that to happen. But how could she help herself? It was what she wanted more than anything else in the world.

SophieSophieSophieSophieSophieSop

Dad brought me up here. The dragon, *that bitch* commonly known as my mother, didn't come. When I found out she wasn't I thought there was a chance, a tiny weeny chance, it might turn into an okay trip. I imagined myself just sitting back with my headphones in, with him driving, and me listening to my music. But no. He insists I sit in the front with him. *Shit!*

'Take out those bloody things, Sophie!' he demands, as soon as we are out on the highway. I take them out **slowly**. God, he is a joke! Acts so tough. As though he **knows** what's going on. The gut specialist with no guts of his own! She's got him wrapped around her finger. I decide not to care if I don't have music. I'll just look out the window for the whole two hours.

'Do you know why your mother didn't come?' he asks, trying to sound reasonable. I shrug and don't answer. But I know. She hates her sister and doesn't want to see her. So I figure that is about the one thing going for me at the moment. The fact that they hate each other might mean that the sister is an okay person. There is a slim chance I'll get on with her.

'Your mother is actually getting sick,' Dad says.

I look at him to see if he's joking. He's not, and so I give a little snort of laughter to let him know what I think of *that*. My mother has to be the most healthy person on the planet. She never even gets a cold.

'Sophie! *You* are making her sick!' he goes on and then when I make no reaction he starts droning on about what a good person she is. How everybody has their faults, but we all have to try and understand each other. That families are this and families are that. Blah blah! I tune out and try to think about what it would be like to be a tree or a cow. Apart from the cold at night, just standing around in the open fields all day would be okay. Well, I suppose there are all the horrible humans you'd have to deal with. Coming out at you with their whips, electric prods and chainsaws. But then humans have to deal with horrible humans too. My own situation being a case in point.

Then I try to imagine my favourite teacher ever, Mr Schmit, on his long-service break. No way he'd go somewhere crass like Surfers or Noosa like we did last holidays. I'd bet big bucks on that. Oh no, old Schmity would be somewhere like Venice or Istanbul, soaking up all that stuff in the museums and libraries. Maybe he's on an archaeological dig in Turkey. Once he told the class about doing something like that in Afghanistan. I smile to myself, trying to imagine portly little Schmity keeping up with the others as they traipse into some harsh, hot landscape looking for broken remnants of past civilisations. God, I wish I was with *him*.

Mr Schmit would have to be the ugliest man I've ever seen, alive, dead – I've actually seen two corpses, so I *do* know – on TV or film. Think Danny DeVito and then go down about a hundred notches, right into the extreme end of gross. Bulging eyes, fat bum and belly. White, damp skin that sweats at the mention of a two-minute walk. Short loaves for legs. But so what? The uglier he gets, the more I like him. And I like the way he laughs too. Sort of throws his head back like a horse and opens his mouth wide, as though he wants you to throw something into it, like a clown at the show.

'Sophie, are you listening to me?'

'Yes!' I say loudly, thinking, *No! Because I don't listen to dickheads if I can help it.*

'So what do you think?'

'About what?' I snap back.

'About your mother being sick for starters!' he says angrily. I knew it wouldn't be long before he started yelling.

'Well, she makes me sick too,' I snarl back. And that, thank goodness, shuts him up for awhile. He sighs a couple of times and then groans as though he's in pain. I take a glance at his face and I know I'm meant to feel sorry. For him, for my mother and for the terrible person that I am. I don't though. I don't feel sorry about anything. I didn't ask to start the stupid conversation. Let him stew in the mess he's made of it.

I don't think we spoke for another hour. By that stage thinking about being a cow or a tree was wearing a bit thin. I was actually dying to get there and really dying for my father to get lost.

In the past I've found my mother's sisters reasonably nice. (Bad luck for me that I got the one that wasn't, heh?) But on the other hand I don't exactly know them very well. Aunty Trish died of breast cancer about three years ago. That was pretty sad. Then there is

Monica who is religious. Or was. She used to be a nun and now she's got herself a new job as a lawyer in some grungey inner-city practice. I don't know much about her except that she moves around a lot into different jobs and has never married. Then there is Geraldine, my mother the champion ballroom dancer, and completely abysmal human being. Then my uncle, Jimmy. Apparently he was everyone's favourite until he came back from Vietnam *changed,* whatever that means. (Changed, touched, affected, *damaged* are the words they use for poor old Jimmy!) And then there is Fran, the kids' book illustrator. One boy and four girls! No, five actually. I forgot the *ring-in*. That's what Mum used to call her. The girl that came to live with them when she was twelve, for two years, because her mother had pissed off when she was a baby and whoever was meant to be looking after her couldn't for some reason. Amy − Fran's best friend, who married the boy next-door and never moved out of Ballingo. My mother is always so scathing about her.

There were seven of us in this little three-bedroom house. And our parents took in another one just to make it completely impossible. Nowadays the health department would crack down on that kind of situation.

Always so generous, my mother!

She is always telling me how lucky I am because I only have one sister and one brother and such an incredibly swish house with my own bathroom and about a million CDs. Give her half a chance and she'll be raving on about *when she was a girl,* how badly off they were, how they didn't have anything except an old black and white telly, because there was so many of them. (Was I meant to start sobbing at that stage?) Oh shit, that stuff she goes on with is so boring, I refuse to write about it! I figure that even if this little visit to my aunt's place turns out terribly, it won't be as bad as staying at home.

I wish I had the guts to really piss them off completely. I hate myself for not being braver actually. Before the Big Event I was doing a project on the late-sixties and seventies with Mr Schmit. I loved reading about the protesters and all that hippie, counter-culture stuff and I loved the music. The whole idea of people just pissing off their families and joining communes really appealed to me even before the BE. (I have decided to refer to the Big Event from now on as the BE. Much quicker and it means I don't have to think about it as I write it.) I love thinking of all those young people gravitating to cool places like Nimbin and San Francisco and just *hanging out*. Not thinking about their futures or jobs or anything except having a good time. The Summer of Love. Hmmm. That sounds so great. Of course I never let any of that on to Mr Schmit. He might have thought I wasn't taking the subject seriously.

I once asked my beloved mother about that time. But she was so dumb, she didn't know what I was talking about. Then when I'd spelt out what I wanted to know — basically, what her experiences of that time were — she still didn't know what I was talking about.

'Oh, that was just for a very small group,' she says in this utterly dismissive way, 'most young people didn't get into all that silly business.'

'But Mum,' I said, hardly able to believe my ears, 'you would have been about twenty then. Didn't you get into the music and everything?'

'I was studying to be a nurse,' she said, 'and I had

my dancing. That took up all my leisure time.' Seriously, that is what she said. 'So I was very busy. And I was engaged to a nice boy, preparing to be married.'

Oh God! So all this really cool stuff was happening. All the music and drugs and people trying out new ways of living, all those bell-bottom jeans and Indian beads and long dresses, and my mother was back in her little home town being a bloody nurse with a diamond on her finger, foxtrotting around in her spare time. My teeth just grind thinking about it!

At last we're there and I begin to feel nervous. I realise that I don't really know my Aunt Fran. In fact I haven't even seen her since last Christmas, when we would have said about two sentences to each other. Also, the sight of the old house brings memories up for me. Coming up here to see Grandma and Grandpa. Shit, I really loved Grandpa. Both of them actually. Oh God, I wish they were alive and I was going to stay with them! I wish I was little again. That would be really cool. I wish everything that has happened could be changed. I'm also hoping now that my aunt won't mind me bringing up my CD-player, because I won't be able to live without my music.

I've always loved that old house. My best memories of being a little kid were all tied up with it. Arriving to see my grandparents at Christmas and Easter, laden with presents, all the calling out and laughter. Seeing Gran in her apron, her blue-rinsed hair set for the occasion, smiling and hugging everyone. So pretty. I never could have imagined then that she'd ever die. Feeling my grandfather's thin arms around me and breathing in the faint whiff of strong pipe tobacco on his jumper. There was the smell of the place too, toasty warm and sometimes sweet. Of cakes and clean washing just in from the line and flowers in vases from the garden. The open fire in the kitchen and the stews and casseroles and roasts that always seemed to be cooking. We never had that kind of food at home. The big tangled garden, the line of peppercorns along the fence, the vegetables growing out the back. There is a veranda all the way around too, and when there is a strong wind the weatherboards creak and shake and the tin roof rattles.

We hardly saw Grandpa at the end. (Another thing I'll never forgive my mother for.) Because Aunt Fran was caring for him in her house in Fitzroy, Mum wouldn't go there. (Maybe she went a couple of times, I don't know.) I was really cut up about this because we'd been told that he was fading fast and that he mightn't last long.

'But, Mum!' I remember crying. 'I really love Grandpa. I want to see him again. And he's your father.'

'I've already said my goodbyes,' she snapped at me. I could tell she wasn't feeling too comfortable about it. 'You can go by yourself!'

I did go once by myself, by public transport. Aunt Fran was pretty nice to me. Brought me in and gave me a drink. I had quite a long time sitting there with Grandpa. My cousins, James, Damien and Peter, were there and I enjoyed talking to them. But Aunt Fran's house was right on the other side of the city. It took over an hour to get there by public transport and I guess I just didn't make the time to go again. I'm not proud of the fact that I didn't go more than that. That probably means I'm gutless too, just like her. I shouldn't be living with them, *living under their roof,* as my mother so sweetly puts it. No. I should piss off and find some other like-minded souls and set up my own commune. Like in the sixties. I wish I'd been born then.

I see she's in the garden when we get out of the car. She gives a wave and comes out the front gate to greet us.

'Sophie!' she says, friendly enough, taking my arm, but she doesn't kiss me. I see that she both looks like Mum and she doesn't. She's slim, but bigger than Mum, and fair-skinned, but her hair has streaks of grey in it and it's long, tied-up loosely in a bun. She's got rubber boots on, old cotton slacks and a big, brightly coloured shirt on over a black polo-necked jumper. She smiles at Dad and they awkwardly peck each other's cheeks.

'Geraldine didn't come then?' she says, careful not to make it sound too serious.

'No,' he says, not looking at her.

I also see that she doesn't want me. That she is trying like mad to be nice. Shit, I've had enough of this already. I almost pull Dad's arm on our way into the house. 'Let's go home,' I want to say. Then I remember that I hate Dad and home and I think, oh stuff it! They don't want me there either; I might as well hang around here for a few days at least.

Dad picks up a couple of my bags and I grab the other one and we go through into the old kitchen. I want to stop to look around, notice the things that are the same as I remember from when my grandparents were alive. The fireplace and the old wood stove are both alight and the smell is nice. But the place is sort of darker than I remember, and my eyes have a hard time adjusting. And she's leading us through the hallway and down a

71

couple of little steps to the back bedroom, which was built on in the fifties.

'This is where your mum used to sleep, with Trish and Monica,' she says, opening the door for me. I step past her into this poky little room with a low, slanted ceiling and look around. I'd forgotten what this room was like. There are two single beds, each covered in faded pink cotton bedspreads, with a little wooden dressing table between them and, above that, a big gory crucifix complete with nails and crown of thorns.

'There are only two beds,' I say stupidly, looking away abruptly. I find religious icons ridiculous and embarrassing. 'Where did they fit the other one?'

'Just behind the door.' She smiles at me and I can't make out whether she is trying to tease me or not. Behind the door now is a big heavy wardrobe. The dismal picture is completed by white net-lace curtains, faded floral wallpaper that is peeling off in places, worn lino on the floor, and a mat beside each bed. The room feels like a step back in time, into the fifties. It really does look like no one has slept here for about forty years. But I don't say anything. I don't really care. What does that matter? I tell myself. It will do. But I am a bit unnerved. My memories of this house are of cosy rooms full of comfortable, homely furniture. This is so cold and sort of stark.

'I'm up the front of the house in Mum and Dad's old bedroom. I put you down here because it is the furthermost room from there,' she says, smiling a bit so I know she doesn't mean it as an insult. 'I imagine you've got music . . . a CD-player or whatever?' I nod and she nods, an anxious smile around the corners of her mouth that reminds me of my mother.

'Well, Sophie.' She smiles. 'Have the music in your room by all means but I don't want it so loud that it is heard all over the house.'

'Okay,' I say, looking away. I know they are looking at each other but I don't care.

'It's really very good of you, Fran,' I hear my father telling her outside. I've been left standing in the kitchen looking at Grandma's old faded coat hanging on the back of the door, wondering if I'd be ever game enough to put it on, seeing now as she's dead. How creepy would it be, wearing a dead person's clothes?

'I really appreciate it very much and . . . of course Geraldine does too.'

Oh yeah! Such a friggin' hypocrite! I hear them walking down the front path towards the gate and I can't believe he isn't going to say goodbye. Suddenly I remember something *I've* forgotten. I slip quickly into the front lounge room – it smells musty and closed up – and breathe a sigh of relief. Yes. It's still there. Thank goodness. Every Christmas when we'd arrive at this house, it was the first thing I'd do. Check the big river painting hanging above the fireplace before going out to see the chooks or climb the trees, or even eat some of Grandma's Anzac biscuits. And here it is, in its spot, like always. Good.

I move to the middle of the room and half-close my eyes. (When I was ten, I worked out this was the best way to look at it.) The title, *Ruby's Point*, at the bottom is the only part of the painting that stays the same for me. I know that sounds mad, but that painting seems to alter slightly every time I see it. Maybe it's only that I notice different things about it. Anyway, sometimes the colour of the water changes, or the foliage of the trees. At other times the sky seems to have a shining blue tinge to it and then next time I don't even *see* the sky at all. Aunt Fran was about my age when she did it and its spookiness has always fascinated me. I wonder if I'll get up enough nerve while I'm here to ask her about it.

My father does come back. He sticks his head in the lounge doorway and gives me this look. Shit! What am I meant to have done?

'Goodbye, Sophie,' he says, as though I'm some stranger he's just met. 'I've left your CD-player outside the front door so I'd advise you to get it in before nightfall.' *Yeah? Well I love you too, creep!* I feel like screaming but I just mumble 'bye' then I turn away.

I come back into the old kitchen and look around. This is weird. The same and yet different. Lots of things have gone. Gran used to have a heap of old baskets up on the top shelf of the dresser. Gone now, but I recognise the three canisters on the wall above the sink. All kinds of different birds on them, hardly visible now, all brown and faded with age. The big table is still here but it's bare and I wonder why she's got the fire going when it's quite warm outside.

What the hell am I going to do here? What do I know about country towns? I don't know anyone except her and . . .

Through the window I see Aunt Fran coming back down the path towards the front door and I get an attack of the jitters, and rush off to the bedroom thinking how I'll unpack my stuff. It will give me something to do.

But she follows me. I hear her footsteps coming down the creaky hall and so I lift the case up onto the bed, open it and begin fiddling around to stave off my

embarrassment. She taps on the door and I start hauling armfuls of my stuff towards the big cupboard.

'Sophie, you're welcome here,' she says again, standing in the doorway. I stop, not knowing what to say. I
see that she is making what looks like an enormous
effort. 'But please, no smoking, and no music too loud.
Unless I'm out of the house . . . which I will be quite a
bit of the time actually.'

'Where will you . . . I mean, what are you planning
to do?' I ask, surprised and suddenly curious in spite
of myself.

'Well,' she smiles, a genuine one this time. 'I'm going
to be working out the back in the studio Dad made for
me when I wasn't much older than you. At least for
some of the time. And, I'll be out and about a bit too.
Sketching and . . .'

'I didn't know there was a studio here,' I said, and
then immediately remembered the shed down the back
of the garden with the skylights in the roof. Grandpa
used to refer to it as Fran's shed. We weren't allowed to
go in there when we were kids – I don't think I'd ever
been inside – it was all locked up. And Grandpa said
there were things there that might be dangerous.

'It has been locked up for years,' she said. 'I've spent
the last week cleaning it out and getting it ready.'

'Okay,' I say weakly, wanting to ask her more but
unable to find the words. 'Sounds . . . pretty . . . good.'

'Yes.' She grinned suddenly. 'If I can get it together,
it will be good. Listen, I'm going to be eating soon.' She
began to back out of the room, reaching for the door
handle to close it behind her. 'Just bread and scrambled eggs . . . why don't you come back down to the
kitchen when you've unpacked?'

'Er, no thanks,' I say. 'I don't want anything . . . like that to eat. I've got stuff. I'll just er . . . hang about here for a while and then maybe go for a walk.'

She shrugged and then slowly left the room.

I choose the bed under the window and then flop on it awhile, hands behind my head, thinking about what I can do now. I'm waiting for the fluttery feeling in my stomach to leave. This is no good, I'm thinking. No good at all. It won't work. She doesn't want me here. Probably hates me already. I resist lighting up a fag and instead get up, poke around in my case for my jacket. Maybe I'll feel better if I get out for a while. Have a smoke, get something to eat.

I slip out of my room and through the back door and then around the side of the house, deciding to go check out the town for fast-food joints. The walk down the hill past all the small, quiet houses on either side of the road only takes five minutes. In the front rooms I see the brightly moving screen bubbles, the shadowy out-lines of people sitting glued to their seats, and I wonder what I'm missing on TV. A squirt of something a bit like panic hits me. *Does my aunt even have a TV?* What am I going to do in the middle of the night when I can't sleep? I'm used to switching on the movie chan-nel whenever I feel like it, from my bed. The fading light in the evening sky is nice, but the quietness unnerves me. Feels so odd to be the only person around. The streetlights flicker on. Like the eyes of sleepy children waking up one by one. That, and the cool breeze that has me pulling my jacket hard around me, makes me momentarily feel better.

Once down the hill I'm virtually in the centre of the town. On one side of the grassy median strip is the swimming pool, the town hall, post office and community park. On the other side, about four blocks of shops with a pub at either end. I cross the empty road and begin to walk along, past estate agents, banks, a chemist and big double-window haberdashery store, heading towards the lit 'chicken' sign. I see through the multi-coloured plastic strips that they arc packing up. Already? I look at my watch and see it is only eight o'clock. So this is Friday night in Ballingo. There is one more winking neon cafe sign, further up towards the bridge. I'll take a walk up there, see what's on offer.

I'm in luck. Deep fryers, fish and chips, hamburgers down one end and ice-cream, lollies and all that other kind of junk up the other. And a deafening noise from the small portable telly set up on the counter.

'Wadaya want?' An old bald man emerges from the doorway behind the counter, widely yawning and glaring at me belligerently. A bell had rung when I entered and it obviously pissed him right off, having to see to it.

'Hamburger with the lot,' I say. 'And chips.' It annoys me that he doesn't turn the noise down as he begins to cook the food. I turn away, take a can from the fridge and pick up a magazine.

'You want salt?' he shouts at my back. I've been sitting on a nearby stool waiting for it to cook, trying to avoid looking at myself in the grotty mirror in front of me.

'Yeah, thanks,' I yell back. He grunts and then proceeds to shake this huge metal container over my chips, dumping about a kilo of salt before I have the sense to call out.

'Enough!' I yell over the television noise, thinking the whole thing would be funny, except I'm hungry and I want to eat the stuff. I walk over. His bald head is tanned and shiny, there are hairs growing out of his ears and all over his trembling liver-spotted hands. He must be eighty.

'You said you wanted salt,' he snaps accusingly, then, sighing and grunting, he proceeds to wrap my order in butcher's paper. I hand over my money and he sourly nods goodbye. Two take-away food joints in the whole town as far as I can make out, and I've already alienated one of them.

The buzz of men's voices cheers me a bit as I walk under the hotel's low veranda and on towards the little park at the end of the street. There are maybe a dozen cars parked around here so I guess someone is having a Friday night. It gives me a shock to remember that my uncle runs one of the pubs. But I'm too shy to poke my head in to see if it is this one. He probably wouldn't want to see me anyway. I haven't spoken to him since Grandpa's funeral.

I sit myself on the park seat away from the light. When you're my size you don't want to be seen eating this kind of junk — so down here in the semi-dark I feel nicely concealed. I open my piping-hot package and begin to eat greedily. First the hamburger and then as many of the chips as I can stuff in. I suddenly start thinking of Mr Schmit and the way he'd come bustling into class. Excited. He was always just a bit excited about something. Had we heard that General Pinochet may be extradited to Spain to face a war-crime tribunal? Did we know that the whole Russian Parliament was to be reconvened? Had we watched *Hitler's Henchmen* on telly the night before and wasn't it extraordinary that . . . And then it's like I can hear his voice in my head. *Questions*. Always asking questions.

So when did this whole thing begin?

As though you don't know, Mr Schmit! Every person in that school read about the accident in the paper. It was on the news. The ninth of April this year. Eight months ago. Mai's name. Mihn's name. Mine too. I was the driver after all. Shit . . . as though I could forget.

A more thoughtful, honest answer please!

Okay, I'll be honest. After the Big Event everything changed completely but . . . I had started to change before then.

How do you mean?

Over the last year I often had the sensation that I'd been stuck on one of those escalators that was going up and up and up . . . with no way of getting off.

That explains nothing. Just a feeling, a vague and virtually meaningless impression . . .

Think background!

Think key elements . . .

Think actual events!

I lie back on the grass and look up into the sky and grin to myself. It really is like I can hear Mr Schmit's voice.

There are layers of truth, girls. And we should set each layer down one on top of the other like geographical overlays until we get a clear picture of the . . . the piece of time we're talking about . . .

Okay, Mr Schmit, but how far back do I go? To the beginning of this year when my friendship with Alana and Jess was starting to unravel but I didn't want to admit it, even to myself? To becoming friendly with Mai, meeting her family? Mihn? That momentary illusion I had of happiness before the BE? The feeling that I could actually have a life – me – apart from my mother and father and sister and brother and my so-called best friends? But no. I have to go back further still or it won't make any sense. Back to being fifteen, so desperate for my mother's approval that I nearly starved myself to death over one summer. *Earlier still?* Oh shit, does it serve any purpose going over this stuff?

Yes . . . it will help you understand. It is part of the history.

How about being eight and not being allowed to start ballet like my sister, Lauren, had at the same age, because I was 'lumpy' and 'uncoordinated' and really would be more suited to some kind of sport? It was so unfair. I was dying to do ballet. I'd been watching Lauren, who is four years older than me, and the rest of the class go through their paces twice a week, for years. Mum always took her and picked her up on Saturdays and sometimes I was allowed to go with her and we would stay to watch. Sitting down the back of the room along with a few other mothers and little sisters, I was always transported. The clanking, vibrating piano music in that empty room with the wooden floor and the high windows, the repetitive commands from the teacher, a small, elegant old lady with a grey bun, who walked up and down the rows of girls, smiling a lot, her eyes darting about like dark little sparrows, looking for imperfections. The rows of girls in soft pink toe-shoes, pink tights, black leotards, their hair scraped back into tight buns. Some of them willowy, like my sister, others shorter and chunkier and a couple even plump. I longed with all my heart to be part of it.

'Couldn't I just try!' I managed to whisper, my throat thick with jammed tears, when she first told me that all that magic was not for me. Tears of shock, completely unbidden, had rushed into my eyes. I was trying desperately to hold them back because my mother hated whingeing of any description. But after the shock came disappointment, like a blow to my chest. I could feel the pain just sitting there like a stone. Disappointment and humiliation. I'd told all my class at school that I'd be starting ballet that year. None of them had expressed any surprise. It was a private girls' school. Half the class took lessons. They were not all thin and wispy and talented like my sister. I'd never even dared dream that I'd be as good at it as her. (She always got the leading roles in the end-of-year productions.) I only wanted to be part of it. In the corps de ballet. I saw myself as just one of the girls in the back row, dressed up and made up, smiling sweetly, helping to create the magic that the soloists would intensify.

'Darling, you're just too big,' my mother said matter-of-factly. 'It would be . . . ridiculous. You'd look like a elephant clumping around in there. Some people are meant for dance and some aren't. But I'll talk to Daddy and we'll see if we can find you a suitable sport.'

Sport! My mother wasn't just completely disinterested in sport of any kind, she loathed it. It was dance and music, ballet and theatre that she adored. I'd often sat with her and Lauren in coffee shops after a Saturday matinee of an Australian Ballet performance, listening to them going over what we'd just seen in great detail: the artists' technical expertise, the interpretation, the costumes and music. I loved the performances and I loved listening to them. Just sitting there quietly watching Mum's eyes sparkle, her whole face animated, glowing with excitement. She and Lauren knew all of the dancers in the leading roles. They could tell if an individual's performance had been breathtaking, ordinary or lacklustre. I figured that once I started learning, I'd gradually be privy to this secret knowledge too. I'd be able to use the same kinds of words. As it was I simply loved each performance for the web of magic it weaved inside my head. It always took a good hour for me to come back down to real life.

When I was presented with a new tennis racquet the next month for my birthday, complete with a whole year's subscription of lessons, I'd burst into tears.

'What *is* the matter with you?' My mother was immediately angry. 'You ungrateful girl!'

But I couldn't stop. The tears just kept coming. There had been Lauren and Dad, me and Mum for breakfast. My brother, Peter, was away on camp. They'd just made a big fuss of coming in with their presents behind their backs; teasing me that they'd forgotten. Asking me if I remembered what date it was. It was the way it was always done in our family. Presents at breakfast for each of our birthdays. My heart simply dived when I saw the shape of the wrapped present from my parents. *Surely not a . . . racquet*? I smiled and accepted their kisses and gamely pulled open the paper. I suppose a small part of me had hoped that this too was some kind of joke.

But no. There it was in front of me. A tennis racquet. I heaved involuntarily and then let out a deep, wrenching sob. Then I couldn't stop.

'What is it, Baby?' my dad said kindly, genuinely mystified. Ignoring my mother, whose face was tight with fury, he pulled me onto his knee, holding me against him. 'If you don't want to learn tennis, that's okay, honey. Tell us. Is that it?'

But I couldn't speak. I couldn't explain because I didn't rightly understand what I was feeling.

'Well, she has to learn something!' my mother spat out loudly from the sink. And then to me, over her shoulder, 'If you don't want to do tennis, *fine*. We can return the racquet and get a refund on the lessons. But you have to do something. You really do, Sophie. You're getting quite . . . lumpy. And you need to do something to improve your coordination.'

'Oh darling, that's just . . . uncalled for.' Dad began his protest at her unkindness angrily but his voice by the end of that small sentence had petered out. He must have been genuinely shocked because he hardly ever questioned her. She has that kind of power over him. Although he was always kind and encouraging to me, he never stood up for me against her. Lauren must have been shocked by Mum's attitude, too, because it is one of my few memories of her being nice. I saw her give Mum a dirty look, then she lent over and grabbed me by the leg.

'Tennis would be good, Sophie,' she said fiercely. 'I reckon you'd be really good at it.' The actual words weren't important at all. It was the way she said it. As though she was on my side.

So you weren't allowed to learn ballet?

I know! I know what you're thinking! So what? Where is the big deal in that? All right. I can see it is nothing.'

Let's move on, shall we?

But maybe we have to go back even further. To my birth and even before that! My mother already had the two perfect children that she wanted. A boy and a girl. I was unexpected. An unwanted surprise. And big. She always let me know that the first two were easy births but I was 'a huge baby' and very difficult. Apparently she had all kinds of complications with me; tearing and so many stitches that she was immobilised for weeks. It was after my birth that she finally had to give up competitive ballroom dancing for good. By the time she was back on her feet after having me, her partner of six years had found someone younger and more reliable. She was furious at his disloyalty, but in the end she had to accept it.

'So when did you stop dancing?' I can still hear visitors asking as they looked admiringly at all the cups and ribbons and trophies lining the long shelf in the sun room. And my mother always gave a light little laugh as though it was nothing.

'Oh, when Sophie was born,' she'd say. 'I never quite managed to get back on top of things. With two, it had been just possible to keep going but three children somehow overwhelmed me. By the time I was ready it was too late.'

So she was a horrible mother?

A horrible mother? Oh God, *no!* Not at all. I've probably given the wrong impression altogether. I adored my mother . . . and so did my friends. In fact I often suspected that the reason they spent so much time around at our house was because of her. Alana and Jess were both fascinated by my mother. She was so elegant and I know she adored them too, especially Alana. She talked and laughed with such energy that . . . well, I know Alana and Jess thought she was wonderful. Their own mothers were normal, harried, hard-working women who looked their age and who never thought anything or went anywhere much. Alana was a scholarship girl from a poor home. She was jealous of everything I had. I can see that now. But most of all she was jealous of me being Mum's daughter. It became part of . . . part of what happened later.

Just picture Alana, Jess and me slouching in front of the telly, sipping cocoa and mumbling on about some school assignment. And then Mum would burst in from down the street. Maybe even carrying a couple of bags of shopping. My friends' eyes would simply swoop on her, devouring all that cool style.

'Hello, girls! What a lovely surprise!'

'Hi, Gerry!' they'd chime. Mum had told them last summer that they knew her too well to have to call her Mrs Douglas forever.

A little black straw hat with a tight-beaded red top over loose-fitting black jeans maybe, with high-heeled blue snake-skin boots. And always as though she'd just thrown the look together without a thought.

Can we jump a few years?

To when?

This year? You said that change was beginning to happen before the Big Event. What kind of change? How would you describe it?

I remember one day very clearly when something snapped inside me. It was the Sunday directly after Grandpa's funeral last March and I suppose six weeks before the BE.

Picture this. Our perfect household at lunch, sitting around the beautiful round, polished rosewood table in the front dining room. Dad, the big-time surgeon, is pouring wine. Mum, the beautiful, svelte, ex-champion ballroom dancer, wife of the big-time surgeon *and* the mother of two more big-time doctors (or at least on their way to being doctors), is smiling at the wife of our important visitor and telling her about the trees in the

Botanical Gardens. My 23-year-old brother, Peter, is sipping his wine and listening to everyone politely. He lives in a flat with another medico near the university where he is studying his specialty, dermatology, but he comes home for lunch most Sundays. And my sister, Lauren, in her fifth undergraduate year, and still living at home, is there, sitting next to Dad and smiling at Mum's enthusiasm. The important guest is an American named Tex who is dressed in a loud orange shirt and striped tie. He is a surgeon too and has been doing a few weeks of special high-tech work at Dad's hospital. He is a tense, polite man who had been telling us before how delightful it was to relax and meet *a real Australian* family at last. I remember thinking, *Is that what we are?* The conversation moved on to the management of infectious diseases in public hospitals. After this had gone on for some time Tex turned to me with a smile.

'When you're at med school next year you're going to know what us guys are talking about,' he said in this friendly, slightly greasy way. I smiled back at him blankly, my mouth full of food. I'd heard my mother telling him before we sat down that I would be doing medicine.

'She's doing brilliantly,' she'd gushed. ('Brilliantly' is Mum's favourite word.) And I was too. I'd chosen all the hard sciences and I was doing very well. Soon she was going to have three children *doing medicine brilliantly*.

'I don't think I'll be at med school next year,' I said. 'I'm going right off the whole idea of it.'

This is completely crazy but I hadn't known until I'd said those words that it was what I'd been thinking for some time. By the end of the sentence I felt even more strongly about it. *I don't want to do medicine. Full stop.*

It had taken looking across the table at this rather nice medical specialist from the other side of the world for me to realise it. But I did realise it. It was as though a powerful cracker had gone off in my head. My heart was suddenly racing.

'Oh, but I thought . . .' Tex looked at Mum and raised an eyebrow. Everyone else simply stopped talking and looked at me.

'Well . . .' I said coolly, bringing another fork of food to my mouth. 'I've changed my mind. That's all.'

'Oh.' my father said carefully, after a swift glance at my mother. 'You could do dentistry, I suppose'.

I almost choked on my food but then saw he was actually serious. *Dentistry? Is that all he can come up with as an alternative to medicine?*

'Why would you think that, Dad?' I asked.

'It might be something to think about,' my father muttered weakly.

'No,' I said. I was enjoying myself by this stage. Enjoying the attention and enjoying the fact that I'd shocked them all.

'But darling,' my mother began lightly, smiling at me and then at the two guests, trying to put over the idea that these kinds of little arguments happened every day, and that they didn't mean anything. 'You haven't finished school yet. Don't make any hasty decisions. Don't rule out anything.' She gave a little laugh. 'I actually think dentistry might be a very interesting field to be in.'

'Orthodontics is very lucrative,' Lauren said suddenly, quite seriously.

I looked at her, so blonde and perfect in her blue silk singlet and matching scrunchie in her hair. Then I looked around at the others, thinking that they'd all gone completely bonkers. What was it with bloody *teeth* all of a sudden? Why wasn't anyone saying I could be a space scientist or a marine biologist if I didn't want to be a doctor? This was surreal! I felt like I was in a *South Park* episode.

'No,' I said again, and then, because I couldn't think of anything else to say, 'dentists have the biggest suicide rate of any profession.'

That shut them up. The Americans, determinedly positive and optimistic since they'd arrived, shifted in their seats uncomfortably. Any further mention of suicide would make him go green, I could see that. Mum and Dad exchanged a hurried look. They were having trouble coping too.

'Well,' Mum said, smiling coldly. 'Let's leave it, shall we?'

After a few awkward moments the conversation began again.

But it was later, out in the kitchen, that the shit hit the fan. I got up and took everyone's plate out after the first course. I was scraping the scraps into the bin. My mother came rushing in and I knew immediately she was angry. She hadn't wanted these guests. I'd heard her giving Dad an earful that morning about all these damned overseas hospital types that we had to entertain because of Dad's position at the hospital. I thought it might be about that. At least I hoped so. She took a bottle of wine from the fridge, let the door slam shut and stood waiting for me to look up. When I did I was shocked to see just how angry she was.

'What were you were on about in there, Sophie?' she whispered furiously.

I fought inside against the usual initial reaction I had, to apologise, explain, make her happy again. Why should I feel completely intimidated and reduced by her? What had I said, after all? That I didn't think I'd do medicine. It wasn't exactly a criminal offence.

'What do you mean?' My voice was not as steady as I'd have liked. She gave a deep exasperated sigh and looked at the ceiling.

'So what *will* you do next year?' she said nastily. She was out of control. I could see that, even if I didn't quite understand why.

'I thought I would . . . study history,' I said. Once again, it just came to me. Off the top of my head. I hadn't thought about it at all. Of course I'd loved my twentieth-century history classes that year, but I hadn't told my parents. As far as they knew, taking that sixth subject was just for me to have a little light relief from the *real* subjects I was doing. But as soon as I'd said it, I knew it was something I would like to do.

'*History!*' she spat. It was like I'd said I was going to work in K-Mart. 'And then what?'

'What do you mean?' I stammered.

'When you've finished studying history,' she hissed. 'What will you do?'

'I don't know,' I said lamely and shrugged.

'There *is* nothing but . . . *teaching*,' she said dismissively. 'You know that and —'

'So I'll be a teacher,' I snapped doggedly. And it didn't seem such a bad idea at all as I said it.

'Sophie!' She jumped in wildly. 'Besides the fact they earn nothing, face some facts about yourself! You would be a disastrous teacher. You are *not* good with people. You have no personality to speak of! Teachers have to be inspired! You don't know how to be inspired about anything. You have a . . .'

But I didn't hear the rest.

You have no personality to speak of . . .

She was ranting at me in this furious whisper. And I understood finally that this was more than talk about my future career. This was about *me*. Who I was deep down. My actual being. If I refused to fulfil some half-baked dream she had about being the mother of three successful medicos then she would have no use for me. She would try to destroy me. All the years I'd wasted trying to get my mother's approval. Now I knew it was useless to even try. I walked out of the room while she was still talking to me. (A first ever.) And I went to my room without apologising to the guests. I lay on my bed, suddenly devastated.

You have no personality to speak of . . .

Unable to stop going over those words in my mind. What did they mean? That I was nobody? A blank page that anyone could write on? Did everyone think this about me?

I sat up slowly and then walked over to the window. Elbows on the ledge, I watched the puffs of breeze make the leaves in the huge golden ash opposite shudder and rustle. Every nerve in my shoulders, my neck and arms, right down to my hands, felt exposed, somehow.

Of course until this year I did want to do medicine. It was a family thing. Dad's two brothers were medical specialists and his sister was a GP. I think more than anything I wanted the kind of easy respect doctors get. I wanted to be part of their cool, friendly fraternity, and I was attracted to that easy, gracious way people had of assuming that if you were in medicine then you'd be doing things worthwhile as well as slightly mysterious. (A nice combination.) Oncology was going to be my specialty. I'd often imagined myself talking to someone who'd developed terminal cancer. How cool and professional and . . . *nice.* I'd be playing God. 'Yes Mrs Smith, there is a good chance with this treatment you will live . . . Mr Clarke, you have a fifty-fifty chance of making it till the end of the year. I suggest you call your family, Miss Brown, you're going to need a lot of support.'

Like years before with dance, I was attracted to the secret language of medicine. I was jealous of my older sister, so slim and busy coming in from her long hours training at the hospital, gushing on to Dad about some case that had the registrar in casualty baffled.

'Dad, you wouldn't believe it. There was a peritonitis of the . . . and the registrar didn't have the slightest idea.'

And him smiling and looking up at her proudly as she flounced around the room being beautiful and intelligent, explaining how everyone else was getting it wrong.

So you consider this incident the beginning?

Yes . . . but I agree it's pretty banal. Other seventeen-year-olds have real problems. They're homeless, hooked on drugs, illiterate and unable to cope because of terrible poverty. The big crack in my life opens up when I decide I'm not going to be a doctor! I mean . . . it isn't exactly World War Three, is it?

Don't apologise! There is much more to uncover! You have taken the first vital step.

You think so?

Yes.

You see, I can trace so much back to the day I told

91

them I wasn't going to be a doctor. It was the day things began to seriously go downhill between my mother and me. We'd never been really close in the way she was with Lauren but we'd sort of managed, up to that point. And it was the beginning of the end, too, for Alana and Jess and me although none of us knew it at the time.

But that day was sort of on the edge of a lot of beginnings as well. Within a week I'd met Mihn. Within two weeks of that day I knew for the first time what being in love meant. And within a month my life as I'd lived it up to then had turned upside down.

The girl looks wretched. What in God's name has happened to her? It's not the blue hair or the rings in her nose. I've always thought that kind of thing looks rather terrific on kids. But she has put on so much weight and her face is so sullen. She looks *dead*. So totally lost. Her skin is sallow, and there is an ugly splotch on one cheek. The hair looks as though it's been hacked off across the top, the rest falling in rats' tails around her face. She looks for all the world like a bikie's moll! No wonder they're worried.

I have to admit to a tiny feeling of intense pleasure in all this. Geraldine is having this trouble with her daughter. Oh my God! Wow. Mrs Perfect has to come down and deal with the real world for once. *Oh I mustn't. I mustn't be like that . . . can't help it though. Can't help . . .*

I've offered food three times now and she's knocked me back three times. Do I try again, or what? If she dies of malnutrition I suppose it will be my fault. Then again, she's not likely to disappear overnight. She's very hefty. Oh hell. I don't remember her being so miserable looking. When did I last see her? Must have been last Christmas. No. Dad's funeral in March.

Nearly eight months ago. And she was this gorgeous thing with big grey eyes, shining healthy skin, in a tight-fitting blue and cream dress with brown, shapely legs, the feet all strapped up in the most wonderful pair of Italian sandals I'd ever seen. And a smile like summer. Not fat. Rounded. I remember looking at her in church alongside the rest of them and thinking what a peach she was. A ripe peach. Geraldine and Robert's youngest child. So how wrong was I? Oh damn my tight-mouthed, arrogant, disapproving sister who has thrust her onto me without giving any proper explanations, or, more importantly, any proper instructions. What do I do if the girl is on drugs? Or if boys come sniffing around? I'm not used to daughters. And I'm buggered if I'm going to have this place become the country retreat for a whole lot of bored, spoilt city teenagers. One is more than enough. Better tell her that in the morning: along with no smoking and no loud music there are to be no visitors.

It's ten o'clock at night now and I'm sitting in front of the kitchen fire scribbling into this big beautiful book that Amy thrust upon me last week. My first morning back in town. I'd walked into Robbertson's for some insecticide and a comb (damned if I'm going to go to that new bloody supermarket!), and Amy comes up to me from behind the lingerie counter and hands me this huge, beautifully bound, shiny black book with a million blank pages in it.

'For you from me,' she says, putting it into my hands. 'Just go with anything that comes into your head,' she said. 'Whack it down. At least once a day. It will help.'

'But I'm not here to write!' I wailed. 'I'm trying to paint.'

I'd told her the night before over dinner how terrified I was of picking up a brush, or of even looking at those blank canvases out in the dusty studio. How the night before I'd dreamt about squeezing a two-inch squirt of cadmium red out onto a wooden palette, and I'd woken up sweating. It had all come rushing out with the first sip of wine. How ridiculous it was at my age to be going back to something I did as a girl. That it was pathetic, unseemly, and that everyone was probably laughing behind my back.

'It doesn't matter,' she said, refusing to take the book back. 'It will help get the creative juices flowing. You're only scared because you haven't done it for so long.'

At that point I just burst into tears. In the shop, in front of everyone. But it didn't matter. There were only a few old ladies. Most didn't know me. And the one that did – Mrs Hillsop – had been a friend of my mother's and she pretended she didn't see.

Fact is, I've felt so damned scared on every front for over a year now. Of living without Dan, of leaving my lovely city house, and of being so far away from my sons. Coming back here has meant stepping away from everything I've built up around me over the last twenty years. All my work at the refuge, my illustrating work – I was offered a lovely contract to illustrate a series of six books for ten-year-olds by a wonderful author who is internationally successful and who had asked specifically for me to illustrate his work. Quite by far the most interesting job that had ever come my way. And I turned it down! I'm leaving the whole publishing world and all the different friends who've been so good to me since Dan's death. It feels eerie, as though I've been blindfolded and am taking these giant steps backwards into my past.

But Amy, of course, understood. I hardly even had to explain things to her, my soul mate since we were twelve. She is not, nor has ever been, an artist in any shape or form and yet she cottoned on to what I'm about straightaway. All my artist friends back in town said it would be *easy*. That because I'd been an illustrator for years, I'd be able to slot back into serious painting without a worry in the world! I could tell by their faces that most of them thought it was a pretty crazy idea though, that I was mad to be doing it, and I'd be back before they could all shout *mid-life crisis*.

Within a week of putting my grand plan into operation this *troubled* kid gets dumped on me. I might have known that I wouldn't be allowed to have the kind of space and solitude I know I need. (God, that sounds such a bitter, snitchy, old-woman-kind-of-thing to say – I'd better watch myself.)

She's been here three full days now and I've only seen her for brief moments in passing, except for one half-hour at breakfast-time when I did most of the talking – the very thing I swore I wouldn't do. I remember that pretty smile at the funeral and realise that I haven't seen her smile once since she's been here. Maybe once. When I told her a little about the painting hanging over the fireplace in the lounge. Too bad if her mother thinks it inappropriate. The girl is almost grown-up. That's one thing I've decided. I'm *not* her mother. And I'm not going to hold back on what I want to say . . . or pry into her psyche.

That particular morning I got up early, before daybreak, made myself a flask of tea and took off with my pad under my arm and about six sharp pencils in the pocket of my jacket, feeling . . . well, feeling excited actually. Nervous and excited. So far, so good, I kept thinking as I walked out the door. *Just let your feet take you, girl*. I was at the front gate before I realised that I wanted to turn right, walk up the hill, through the old cemetery and then further out along Heany's Road. I remembered seeing some nice old sheds out there last Christmas. I could take a look at them as the sun rose. The sky was relatively clear. Maybe the eastern light would make the collapsing sheets of iron blaze with gold for a minute or two. I had a sudden desire to see it. All the time I was telling myself to relax, that it didn't matter at all if I did nothing. It was enough just to be out there, letting the early morning soak through me. I had to learn to *see* again, and that would take time. To lay myself open to whatever was about me. Let the images fly in, settle, crush around me in the way they used to, making me excited, sad and full of wonder.

I'd been coming up with clever drawings for other people for the past twenty years and I didn't need to do another. I decided that I wouldn't even open my sketchbook if it didn't feel right.

As it happened that first morning went rather well. I didn't make it out to the sheds but got waylaid in the old cemetery on the hill and got so busy there that by the time I'd finished I was too hungry to venture further afield.

It wasn't so much the headstones that interested me. More the long grass growing up around the neglected graves. I haven't thought about grass for so long! And in this early morning light, to see it trembling slightly in the breeze was sheer joy. I sat on one of the graves (my great-grandmother's actually), and watched the golden light start to spread through the green rushes, the thistles and coarse brown tussocks. Robins and finches jumped about, feeding on tiny seeds and worms in the cracks of the old concrete pathway. By the time the sun was up the magpies were out in full chortling chorus. Almost without thinking I opened the sketchbook and began to try and catch some of what was around me. A lovely oval shape between two clumps of long bent grass. A crumbling marble angel lying forlornly amongst some green weeds. Two tiny plump birds swooping little rings around each other in front of the peppermint gum.

I hadn't listened properly to magpies for years. I felt the old familiar surge of delight as my hands began to think of their own accord. As I concentrated on the cracked wing and placid face of the fallen angel I saw my sister, Trish, lying in her bed those last few days, her skin and flesh pared right back to her bones and her eyes wide open and blue as the sky that was opening up in this pristine morning light. *Oh, Trish. Darling. Your cold, cold hands so waxy yellow and thin. Had you left us already by then?*

My fingers reached into my pocket for a heavier lead. I turned the page and let my hand skid across it in short hard strokes, looking for a horizon to break up my white square. Jagged tombstones and scraggy branches, one corner of the old brick wall.

Her children had been with her right to the end. Along with Mum and I. We'd both dropped everything in the last few months and become her nurses. We washed her and emptied her pan, tended her sores and tried to make her comfortable. Mostly it was impossible, her bones were just about breaking through the skin. We gave her slugs of the morphine cocktail and tried to moisten her cracked mouth with Vaseline-coated cotton wool. Poor Mum, beyond crying, beyond exhaustion, ragged with sorrow, sitting at the end of the bed, almost lost in the mountain of pillows, combing her dying daughter's dull, broken hair.

I change positions, leaving great-grandmother and moving on to one of my uncles' graves, deciding that I want to see the whole stretch of broken brick fence that runs along the far end of the cemetery and the one tired little tree that sits in front of it. I wanted the oblong of sky above and a mass of shapes below. Grass, gravestones, and that pretty little wooden rotunda with the latticework walls. My father had told me once that it had been built so that the old people at funerals wouldn't wilt in the sun.

Oh Dad. I can hear you saying it, as though it were yesterday, with that smile around your eyes when I asked whether people looked like flowers when they wilted.

I had no idea how long I'd been there. Hours, by the way my stomach was growling away. The sketches were not very good but I didn't care. I was rusty as hell and this was a start.

I was making a fresh pot of tea, my mouth full of toast, when she came into the kitchen. I was surprised. She'd obviously been out walking, too. It was ten o'clock and I'd thought she'd still be asleep. She was dressed in horrible green pants, and an ugly bright-blue parka.

'Hello Sophie,' I said. 'Cuppa?'

She nodded and unzipped her parka, letting it drop behind the door. I didn't at all like the way she did that, immediately sensing that she was going to be leaving her stuff about for me to pick up after her. But I held my tongue.

'You make yourself whatever you want,' I said, reaching for another cup, and waving at the bread and jams on the table. 'At any time of the day or night, won't you?'

'Okay. Thanks,' she mumbled, sitting down at the far end of the table. I had a sudden stab of panic. What the hell is this girl going to *do* here exactly? I was on the point of asking her if she'd brought any schoolbooks with her, if she had any plans at all, but I managed to hold back.

'So you've been out?' I said, and then chided myself. Remember. No intrusive questions. Let her say what she wants to say.

'I've been down to the river,' she said, staring out the window blankly. I took a quick glance at her but couldn't tell if the river had pleased her or not. 'The old place over the other side,' she went on, 'the big house and the bridge. It is the same house as in the painting, isn't it?'

'Yes,' I smiled. 'Grandview.'

'I've looked at that painting every Christmas and Easter for years,' she said, almost accusingly. 'I didn't know it was a real place.'

'You should have asked,' I said lightly.

'So what is it now?' she asked, frowning, accepting the cup of tea I'd poured for her. 'Is it some kind of hotel or just a house?'

'I'm not quite sure right what it is now,' I said. 'It has been a lot of things in its day. Originally a very grand guest house. Then a private hotel. It was derelict for years. Then much later it was renovated and turned into a kind of camp for talented musicians. But I'm not sure what's going on there now . . . did you see anyone about?'

She shook her head and looked away, as though the subject suddenly bored her. I handed her the tea, and took a sip of my own.

'Is the girl in the painting *real* too?' she asked bluntly, with a sweet kind of rough innocence that had my heart going out to her. *So under all this grouchy sullenness you're a curious girl?*

'Yes,' I said uneasily, not knowing how much she knew about Ruby. 'When I was young, we had a party one night on the river. It was the first time I met my husband Daniel and I decided that night to do the painting.'

'But what about the girl in the red dress?' she cut in. 'Who was she?' A lump rose in my throat before I had a chance to ward it away. I swallowed quickly and got up, brushed down the table stupidly, thinking that there was no way I was going to burst out crying in front of this blasted teenager with blue hair. No bloody way in the world! But I was remembering Dad telling me the story when *I* was only seventeen and it somehow seemed sad to be telling another seventeen-year-old from the next generation. 'Well . . .' I managed to go on. 'The girl in the red dress lying in the river is Dad's . . . your grandfather's sister, Ruby.'

'Really!' She smiled suddenly, transforming her face completely. It was as though a light had been turned on inside and she'd become totally different. 'So the Ruby of *Ruby's Point* is . . . was a real person? I saw the sign, Ruby's Point. I had no idea that it was called after a real person.'

I nodded, wishing she'd go on smiling but the blaze had disappeared abruptly. 'So the place was named after her?'

'Yes,' I said, surprised she didn't know it. 'Your great-aunt.'

'So,' she began shyly, 'I've always wanted to know, is she . . . is Ruby floating or drowning?'

God, what a question! I almost laughed. *Floating or drowning?* A sudden gust of chilly air seemed to rush through me.

'Ruby jumped off the bridge when she was seventeen,' I said shortly. 'When your grandfather was only ten, in 1924, his big sister Ruby jumped off the bridge and drowned.'

'Oh,' my niece said softly. She was staring down into her cup.

'Of course it was hushed up at the time.' I went on more gently. 'Everyone was told that she'd simply drowned but it was . . . well, she meant to do it.'

'Suicide?'

'Yes.'

The phone rang just at that moment. It was Amy. As I picked up the phone, out of the corner of my eye I saw Sophie quietly edge her way out of the room with her cup of tea. I breathed a sigh of relief.

'Amy!'

'So how did it go?'

'Well, good.' I laughed a little. 'I actually made a few sketches and –'

'Great!'

'Amy!' I lowered my voice and looked around to make sure I was alone. 'What is this niece of mine going to *do* here? Even if she does keep out of my way? I mean . . .'

'Well, you've got to get her out of the house for at least a few hours a day,' Amy said practically and very firmly. 'Otherwise she'll go mad and so will you.'

It is the thing I love most about Amy: she always sees clearly where the problem is and she doesn't beat around the bush.

'But how?' I groaned.

'I'll think of something,' she said calmly. 'Don't panic.'

'Amy,' I said, feeling the tears rush into my own voice but needing to go on anyway. 'She was asking me about the painting above the fireplace.' My voice broke and I went on in a hoarse whisper. 'And it got me thinking about Daniel.'

'Oh, Fran!' Amy said softly, with such warmth and kindness that I was immediately filled with self-pity and really started to howl. No one had lost the number of people I had in such a short space of time. A sister, a mother, a husband and a father. All in just over three years! But it was Dan I missed most. My husband, best friend, comrade, colleague, father of my children. The kindest man to ever walk the earth.

Attacks of grief sneak up on me at odd times like this, usually with no warning. I can be fine for days and then choke up over some small thing. I searched around for a hanky in my trouser pocket.

'You want to come down for lunch today?'

'Sure,' I gulped.

'Why don't we go to Jimmy's bistro, and really eat well?'

I laughed through my tears.

'Amy! I've come up here to work! Your know what Jimmy is like! He'll ply us with wine and cognacs and we'll be lying under the table by the end of the afternoon. How can I justify having a huge lunch after my first three hours?'

'Easily,' she said. 'A celebration! And it's on me.'

I put the phone down as Sophie came back in the room and went straight to the fire to warm her hands. When she saw that I'd been crying she immediately began to edge back towards the door.

'Don't go,' I said, waving her back. 'Come and have your breakfast.' My crying had somehow relaxed me a bit. 'I was just having a cry about Dad and Daniel . . . and everything,' I explained, and then smiled to let her know that it was all over. 'There is nothing wrong, really.'

She sat down tentatively.

'I'm glad you like that painting because it has great sentimental value for me too,' I went on calmly. 'It was just after Dad told me about his big sister that I decided I was going to be an artist. I walked down to the river that very night and came back knowing it was what I was going to do.'

'Really?' my niece mumbled as though genuinely awed. Then, more thoughtfully, 'Did you just *know* you were going to be an artist or did you *decide* to be one?'

It was a interesting question and one I had to think about.

I suddenly saw myself at her age, sitting there listening to the night sounds. My legs tucked under me and my long straight dark hair pulled back from my face. I had just that day finished school and I could almost feel myself floating away on that story about Ruby. I'd stopped thinking about my friends and family and school. What did any of it matter? The full moon was flicking gold along the top of the moving water. How would I paint the scene. *How could I?* A heavy, deep wash of inky blue first, for the sky. Then the river, and the little backwater where her body was found, with its overhanging trees in sombre greys and blacks, touches of dark green. Glittering tips of silver from the moon and stars on the leaves and branches, then flashes of it streaking across the water. And *Ruby* lying in the water with her masses of fair hair spread out around her like a veil. She was known for that hair, Dad used to say, and her lovely voice.

Seventeen years old, bold and full of fun. *Everyone's favourite.*

Dad's older sister. The water. How do you paint water? I had longed for a huge square of pristine white canvas. I wanted to pick up a pencil and stand by myself in front of a piece of the big white unknown and feel the world around shrink away as I carved out my own version.

'A combination of the two,' I said finally. 'I wanted to be an artist and I felt . . . that I was one.'

'So you knew what it was you wanted to do for the rest of your life?' my niece said, staring out the window wistfully. There was such innocent hope and enthusiasm in her voice for this idea that I hated having to dash it. It was the first time since she'd arrived that I'd seen her look even vaguely animated.

'Oh hell, not really.' I laughed uncomfortably, getting up and putting the lids on the honey and jam jars. 'I had to go off to art school and get humiliated like everyone else. Learn from scratch all over again, about a dozen times. And I had . . . boyfriends who gave me heaps of problems, before Daniel! Deciding I was going to be an artist was just the tiny first step.'

She was sitting down one end of the kitchen table now, and after putting the things away, I moved across to the window. Fat wattlebirds were balancing themselves upside-down on the bottlebrush branches. It was almost a shock to suddenly come back to where I was. And *who* I was. Back in the old kitchen. In my girlhood home talking to this sad seventeen-year-old niece who I hardly knew.

'It's a fantastic painting,' Sophie said reverentially and I smiled. The painting is actually very rudimentary. Some sections of the foliage were all right but the figure of Ruby was rough and so was most of the sky. The whole thing, I suppose, has a certain childlike, naive quality to it, but that is all.

Sophie suddenly turned to me. 'When I was little I used to look at that picture and make up things about it,' she said quietly. 'I never knew there was a *real* story behind it.'

'Well, there you go.' I shrugged and picked up my plate and cup and brought them over to the sink, thinking that the girl surely wasn't as *troubled* as my sister Geraldine made out. In my experience, seriously troubled people took no interest in other people's lives.

'I'm off to work in the studio now, Sophie.'

I'd finished wiping down the old sink and was wondering when the best time would be for me to tell her that she must clean up after herself. 'Have you got any plans for today?' Her face immediately reverted to its former wary and sullen expression.

'Not really,' she said, getting up. 'I'll just go and listen to some music.' She was out of the room before I could say another word. I turned on the tap, trying to quell the hope that had risen inside me. *Maybe* . . . I was thinking. Maybe we'd be able to just get on. She'll do her thing and I'll do mine. We'll meet over a few meals, have a bit of a talk, but apart from that keep to our own sides of the fence. Before long, it would be time for her to go home.

'Why did she do it?'

I turned around with a start. My niece had come back in and was now standing in the doorway putting her jacket on. I caught a faint, sudden smell of cigarettes and I nearly groaned aloud. There is no way I'll put up with a house that stinks of cigarettes. With some effort I decided to ignore it.

'Oh, Sophie.' I turned back to the sink. 'Who knows *why*? Who knows the pain that other people suffer?' I was fobbing her off, I knew. But I was extremely uncomfortable. Maybe the girl was more disturbed than I realised, and feeding her Ruby's story would just put morose ideas in her head. Oh, what a nightmare it would turn out to be if . . . Shouldn't I at least wait a few days? Check her out a bit? I glanced up and she was still there, waiting for me to go on.

'No one really knows,' I said shortly. 'No one is absolutely sure why she did it.'

'Did you know Daniel then?' she asked quickly, as though sensing my reluctance to talk and wanting to sneak another question in before I shut up shop completely. 'I mean, when you found out the truth about Ruby, did you know your husband, Daniel?'

What an odd question! I smiled at her and tried to think back. So much of the past is like a murky blur in my head but of course some things do stand out. Meeting Daniel for the first time was one of them.

'I did!' I said, pleased that I could remember. 'School hadn't finished for the year when I met him properly. I'd been in dancing class with him all year but . . .' I shrugged, slightly embarrassed in front of this nineties kid. *Dancing class!* How did you explain the importance of a country town *dancing class* to a city kid who has probably gone to sophisticated clubs from the time she was about twelve?

'Dancing class?' Sophie frowned, as though mimicking my thoughts.

'Hmmm,' I sighed, pulling off the rubber gloves. I stared out the window. 'I met Daniel properly just after the last dancing class for the year and I think . . . and it was around that time that Dad told me about his sister.'

'So you and him were . . . together from that night?'

'Oh no!' I laughed at her innocent assumption. 'We didn't start really going together for years. We were always tap dancing around each other.'

By the time I got down to lunch that day Amy had a plan and although I wasn't at all sure Sophie would come at it I decided it might be worth a try.

I walked down to the main street after spending a couple of hours in the studio sifting through old work – most of it terrible – and waited for Amy, as planned, outside Jimmy's pub. As I saw her running across the street towards me from Robbertson's I had a rushing sense of my own good fortune. How lucky I was to have these two: my one and only, slightly cracked-in-the-head brother and my best, eminently sensible close friend. Both of them living so close by.

After we left school Amy stayed in Ballingo, living with her two unmarried aunts and working in Robbertson's clothing and general haberdashery store. At the time I was so appalled by that decision that I nearly wrecked our friendship. Much of my outrage and angst was for myself, although I didn't admit it. I was lonely and sad and so I wanted her with me, in the city, even later on when I was freaking out over men and poetry and Vietnam like I was.

'For God's sake, Amy!' I remember screaming at her. 'You're smart, you've got to come down, study, you've got to get involved, see the world!'

'But I like it here,' she said. And staying back in her home town was truly what she wanted. She married a local farmer and has lived happily since then. What's more, she owns Robbertson's now. The two bachelor brothers whose father had passed it down to them left it to her in their will.

Soon after Jimmy's marriage folded for good, he had a serious heart attack. This convinced him to come back to Ballingo for an early retirement. But within a month he was bored witless. He'd owned and run city pubs since his mid-twenties so when Nolan's, the main pub in the town, came up for sale, he bought it and spent a lot of time and money restoring it to its former glory. The two main bars had polished wood counters throughout, open fireplaces, stained-glass windows – and a warm and relaxed little bistro out the back that served lunch and dinner.

'So, Sis,' Jimmy said, taking my left arm, and Amy's right, and leading us to the nicest table in the room, the one that overlooked a side garden filled with the purple blooms of a jacaranda tree. 'You settled in yet?'

'Oh yeah,' I said. 'It's been well over a week now.'

'Painted any masterpieces yet?'

'Get stuffed, Jimmy!' I laughed.

'They tell me you've got yourself a boarder.' He grinned in sympathy and I made a wry face. 'So our dear sister, Gerry, is calling in past debts, is she?'

I smiled ruefully, thinking that Jimmy was about the

only person in the world who I would take that kind of jibe from.

'It wouldn't be right to let an old lady like me live alone, would it?' I quipped back. 'I might get up to mischief.'

'Well, that's right!' Jimmy wagged his finger and hurried off to get the menus. Although he'd put on weight, he was still handsome. His hair, streaked now with grey, was thick and wavy and his grin was as warm and infectious as ever.

'So . . . ?' Amy began.

'So . . .' I replied. And we both laughed as we looked around us.

There were only three other tables in use. The bistro was painted out in cream and blue, the floors were of polished wood. The whole thing was restful and easy. I was filled again with a sense of my own good fortune.

'Well, Fran, here we are again,' Amy said softly. I nodded, knowing exactly what she meant. 'Sitting opposite each other like we were sixteen again.'

'Or twelve,' I said, taking the menu from Jimmy. 'I remember you coming to live with us like it was yesterday.'

'I'll have whatever,' Amy said, waving away the menu with a laugh. 'Spuds in their skins if you've got 'em and anything else you think I'd like.'

'Oh me too.' I sighed happily. 'Anything. I don't care. And give us a bottle of something too, will you, Jim?'

'Jeez!' Jimmy groaned in mock frustration. 'I spend hours slaving over menus and wine lists. Can't you two get a bit fussier?'

'How's Blue?' I asked, watching him pouring us a

glass of white wine each. His daughter, Blue, was a favourite of mine.

'Just great.' He smiled. 'Exams all finished. She's coming home tomorrow. Going to help out here over summer.'

'Oh how wonderful.' I was genuinely pleased. She was a beautiful girl, and smart. And – my mind raced ahead – she might actually take Sophie off my hands for a bit. After all, they were cousins.

'So, Amy has told you all about the secondary college fete?' Jimmy said, giving Amy an enormous wink. 'Four weeks away?'

'Yes.' I nodded warily. I knew these two were dying to get me involved in their bloody fete (the headmaster was a Vietnam vet and a mate of Jimmy's), and I was equally determined not to be roped in. After all, I'd been back in Ballingo for ten days. What would be the point of leaving my life back there in the city, work, family, friends and commitments, only to take up a lot of silly new ones here? It was exactly the kind of thing I *didn't* want to get involved in.

'Listen you two,' I said with a smile. 'I want to make this plain. I'm not getting involved, okay?'

'Sure, Fran,' Amy cut in innocently. 'We don't expect . . .'

'You're running the art and craft stall,' I said, turning to Jimmy – deciding I was going to nip all this speculation in the bud right away.

'Yep.' He grinned sheepishly. 'The biggest and the best this town has ever seen! I've got all the ladies in the bowling club knitting me jumpers and –'

'Right,' I cut in determinedly. 'I'll donate a few drawings. Might even frame them if I get time.' I turned to Amy. 'And I'll bake a cake for your stall *and*

I'll come on the day and buy things. Heaps of things. But . . . *that's it*!'

'Okay! Okay!' They were both laughing, getting the message. 'That will be fine!'

'Get Sophie to come down and work for me for a couple of hours each morning,' Amy said, after we'd clinked glasses and raised them to the success of my time in Ballingo. 'Does she know anything about music?'

I shrugged. The discordant sounds I'd heard coming from her room had sounded completely awful to me, but that didn't mean anything.

'I'm opening a small CD section,' Amy went on. 'There would be some modern teenage stuff but mainly middle-of-the-road, for people around here. I'll pay her of course,' she added. 'She can help me sort through the stock.'

'But, Amy,' I said quietly, 'I don't know if she'll come at it. She doesn't need money. You should have seen the size of the cheque Robert left with me. She's probably never actually worked in a mundane job in her life and wouldn't want to.'

'Hmmm.' Amy picked up her glass. 'How about putting it to her that she'd be helping me out. That I haven't managed to get anyone and that if she could just come down a couple of hours in the morning then she'd be doing me a big favour. Even just for a week?'

'Well, I'll try,' I said thoughtfully. 'Serving in the music section might seem a bit more glamorous than stacking shelves.'

I picked up a pile of letters from the box when I arrived home. It was only when I got inside that I saw one was from Geraldine. My heart immediately began to race even as I was muttering, *Well, well . . . about time.* I hurried inside, glad to see that Sophie wasn't about. I got myself a cup of tea and headed out to the studio, oddly angry that my hands had begun to shake.

Dear Fran,

I realised, after Rob got home from dropping Sophie off to you on Wednesday, that you still might be feeling somewhat in the dark, so thought I'd better drop you a line and explain a few things. Put simply, for the last three to four months Sophie's been impossible to deal with. Rob and I just don't understand. She has always been an excellent student, although quiet compared to her friends. Yet over these last months her school work has ceased to the point where she's given up school for the year, no friends ring or come around and her eating habits have become bizarre to say the least. (You will have noticed her enormous weight gain?) Naturally, we've tried to have her assessed professionally but because she won't open up at all, so far all opinions have either been so vague as to be useless, or so contradictory that they are totally confusing. Things remain blocked.

So why call on you for help? Last Christmas I overheard you speaking to Monica about looking after Dad. I remember thinking that I would never have the patience these days' for such a really intensive job. (As you know, I actually thought he should have been in hospital.) But you obviously do have that kind of patience and I commend you for it.

At the time I envied you your do-gooding instincts but lately I began to think that, seeing you did it so well with Dad, then you might be able to help Sophie.

You probably already know that not long after Dad's death (two months approximately), Sophie was involved in a very unpleasant incident with a few of her friends. I imagine you are aware of all the details so I really don't see the point of dredging through them here. Could I emphasise that in no way was she found responsible for what happened. Neither the police or the coroner blamed her. Therefore, if this is the cause of her present problems, we don't understand why.

Thank you for agreeing to have her, Fran. Going to you was our last resort. If she remains unchanged and you are unable to keep her for some reason (i.e. if she becomes impossible for you too), then we've decided to have her hospitalised for a period, to see if that helps.

Your sister,

Geraldine

Oh you uptight, self-satisfied, condescending horrible . . . bitch! You commend me for my patience, do you? And my do-gooding instincts! Oh thank you so much, Geraldine! I'm so grateful. No, you wouldn't have the patience, would you, because . . . because, well, your hair might get messed up, you might miss lunch with one of your dickhead friends. Shit, anything might happen!

I'm stomping around the studio at this point, unable to keep still, wishing she was here so I could slap her face and mess up her shiny, perfectly dyed $150

Brighton bob. I stop every now and again, clench my fists and howl at the sky in pure fury. She has no right to put it on me to be *the last resort* for her daughter! If I can't manage Sophie, she is more or less telling me that the kid will get thrown into a mental hospital and presumably get hooked up to a drip of psychotropic drugs – or have electric shock treatment. Oh come on, Geraldine! You knew exactly what you were doing when you wrote that . . . didn't you? You know all the right buttons to press with me.

I sit down and pull out the letter and read it again. Maybe I missed something. It can't have been that bad. I could have missed some note of warmth, some sympathy for or interest in my situation. But no . . . of course not. They all wrote to me when Dad eventually died. Of course Trish was gone, but Monica was working with an Aboriginal community in the Northern Territory. And although she flew home a few times, she was unable to give sustained help. Jimmy's marriage was cracking up so he was unavailable. Dad had a brother and two sisters still living and they were kind and supportive. *Thank you, Fran*, they all wrote, *for looking after Dad so well. You had your own grief about Daniel to deal with and yet you were able to make such a great effort for him. Thank you.* But not a word from Geraldine. *Not a word from her.* Married to that rich, boring stuffed shirt, she had heaps more time on her hands than me.

Not that I'm sorry about what I gave to Dad. Oh no. I'm glad. I did do a bloody good job too. My boys and me. *Now* she writes to me, because she wants something.

It didn't take *patience*! (I'm screaming aloud at this stage.)

Oh, Geraldine. You are so far off the mark, I almost feel sorry for you. But not quite. I fantasise about seeing you lying in a bed, really sick, humiliated because you've just dirtied yourself and there is no way you have the energy to get up and clean yourself. I'd like to see you wracked with pain, unable to even say good morning to a visitor because it's hurting so much and the nurse with the injection is ten minutes late. One day I'll make you listen to some of those stories about your father, Geraldine, because then you'd have to realise that the last bloody thing you need is patience, *you complete twit*! Try kindness. A bit of genuine interest. A little empathy. A few practical skills, like how to lift someone without hurting yourself and being able to think of something completely different when the smell of shit and vomit gets too bad. (But I forget, you *were* a nurse. So back there in the deep recesses of your brain, presumably you know all those tricks!)

And by the way, Geraldine, I'm no saint. And although you imply I was sitting there blowing my own trumpet over Christmas lunch, I wasn't. Monica asked me how looking after Dad was going and I told her. I didn't ask you to listen in.

Oh God! What am I talking about? It does take patience. *Of course* it takes patience. Sometimes so much that you think every part of you is just draining away. But what was the alternative? He didn't want to die in hospital. I wanted to do what I could for him. I didn't promise anything. We both knew that it might prove too much. But in the end we managed. I couldn't have done it without my boys. And I'm glad we did too. *Why the hell does my sister still have this effect on me?*

I'm afraid this girl doesn't seem to know about cleaning up after herself. She leaves mugs and plates on the sink. Yesterday I washed four, none of them mine. And three small plates. What can she be eating? None of the food I buy seems to be touched. I did find three sauce-smeared hot dog wrappers in the bin when I emptied it this morning. But . . . she can't *live* on that kind of stuff, can she? I actually *smelt* her room when I went down that end of the house to put things away yesterday. The door was closed but there seemed to be a sort of dank smell emanating from there. Maybe I'm imagining it.

I was about to enter the bathroom this morning and then I stopped. I heard throwing-up noises. *My God!* The girl must be pregnant! Why else would a seventeen-year-old be heaving everything up first thing in the morning? That or some bizarre eating disorder. I rang Amy. She says I've got to confront her. But I don't want to. I don't want to hear about her sordid love life. About some awful boy who did her wrong. How can I talk to her when I can't even bear to speak her mother's name without my teeth locking? I'm tired of other people's troubles. I'm actually tired of other people's lives.

I suppose I'll have to. Damn. I'll have to talk to her. What I really want is for someone to come and take her away. I wonder if her mother knows . . . I wonder if her mother actually knows she's pregnant! Well, my dear sister Geraldine, you are going to have to come and get your girl methinks, because I will not be responsible. Should I ring straightaway? I shudder just thinking about it and then tell myself to stop the theatrics, I've got to pull myself together and *think*.

Sophie

I wake up sweating. Those lights were in my eyes again. Blinding me. I thought . . . well, I was hoping that the dreams might have finished, played themselves out maybe and moved on. But no. It was the same as always. In fact worse. More vivid. Me gripping the steering wheel, thinking what a baby our little car is compared to the big thing that has come up so suddenly behind me. Then the roar of it alongside me. The panic when I realise he isn't going to make it. I can see the lights of the oncoming car and I just know that the truck isn't going to make it.

Those unreal, almost dreamy moments wondering about what was going to happen, as though I wasn't part of it at all. I can't remember putting on the brakes. I suppose I did. I can remember seeing the back of that great truck so close and me jerking the steering wheel 'cause I didn't want to slam into it.

Then the screeching sound of tyres and crashing metal. So loud and terrible. And we go flying off the road down the embankment, flipping over and then over again. That part seemed to go on forever. We land right-side up and there is a hot smell in the car and the

118

squishy sound of air bursting out of tyres. Then an eerie quietness. The horn is sounding even though I don't have my hand on it. But it sounds a long way off. I wonder as I sit there how it can seem so quiet when the horn is blasting non-stop. I turn my head around and, although it is dark in the car, every now and again a blue and red light from up at the road shines in so I can turn and see the two of them, sitting up in the back. Truc and Mai look back at me blankly. I think then that this is what it might be like to be dead. Just stillness, and darkness, and no time ticking forward at all.

Truc raises his hand to his eyes and says 'fuck' in this low guttural voice so I know he is alive and then Mai, who is sitting by the other window, starts to whimper. Truc puts out a hand and makes as if to pat her knee and says, 'It's all right babe, don't cry.' And I'm touched because I've never heard him sound so gentle.

Beside me Mihn has both arms around his skinny knees; he is shaking his head from side to side, muttering, 'We should get out, come on Sophie, let's get out.' I can't think what he means. After the initial shock of thinking I couldn't move, I stretch my hand over and try the door but it won't open. My hand in the revolving red and blue light looks quite beautiful. I am filled with wonder at my ability to make this simple gesture and am about to comment about it to Mihn but I see his eyes are closed.

'Can you open the door?' he whispers to me. I see him trying his own but he can't open it either. At this stage Mai slumps forward against the front seat, moaning a bit.

'You okay, Mai?' Truc asks but although she is breathing heavily, she doesn't reply.

She seemed to be more or less sitting up like the rest

of us although I couldn't see her face. None of us at that stage had seen the blood at the back of her head.

We all stay there like that for so long it feels like we live there, that there really is nowhere else to be. It is as though we are stuck in a little groove in history that everyone one else has forgotten. But eventually someone comes. A torch-light moves across the darkness towards our car. As the figure gets closer I see it is a man. Perhaps it is a policeman, I think hopefully. *He'll know what to do.* I am suddenly overwhelmed by everything. I am not used to policemen. I see the silver buttons on his uniform and I begin to jabber.

'I'm sorry guys!' I say, turning around to the back seat again. 'I'm really sorry for this.'

I'm thinking of Mihn's car. The little Morris he's saved up for and loves so much and I feel terrible that I have crashed it. No one answers me. No one says anything. No one puts an arm around me. I begin to weep. Then the torch shines in my face.

'Everyone okay in here?' a man's ghostly voice calls through the closed window. Always the joker, Truc gives him the thumbs up and starts giggling. Then two men come up to us on the other side of the car. They begin pulling on the doors, trying to open them. I'm filled with panic that we'll all just have to stay here, forever. But eventually they manage to drag open the back door on the other side to me.

'Okay kids, don't panic,' a normal voice says. 'We'll have you out of here very soon.'

I see Mai then, she almost falls out on top of the man who has opened the door and I think the others see her too. The matted hair at the back of her head, dark with blood.

'This little one is hurt bad,' one of the men mutters quietly as they try to pull Mai from the car. That's when Mihn starts to shout and I freeze up inside.

My mouth is open and very dry. There seems to be a faint sound echoing around the room. Have I been screaming?

I'm fully awake now, shivering slightly, even though I'm covered, lying on my back in bed watching the early morning light filter in through the nylon curtains. Calming down. Calming right down. My fifth night up here in this hole of a town. No point letting myself get tied up with . . . It *was* just a dream.

I prop myself up on the pillows and take a gulp of water, thinking that I need to set myself some goals if I'm to stay in this place without going completely troppo. The town is so small and quiet, you can hear bees buzzing in the front gardens as you walk by. More than three cars moving down the main street at the same time is an *event*. A couple of days ago I thought the old guy in the fish and chip shop was going to drop dead on me when he was wrapping up my order, he took so long. The place is full of old people. I don't think I've seen a single person my age yet. They must be here somewhere though. There is a secondary college and a primary school and a video shop with a Leonardo DiCaprio poster in the window.

Number one goal is to make sense of my life. I must go about this systematically. Points covered under this goal would include:
• Mum
  (Why exactly she bugs me so much and what I can do about it.)

- Alana and Jess

  (Do I even care about them any more?)
- Mihn

  (Do I still love him? If so, then how to stop?)

Not necessarily in that order. Oh shit. I actually have no clear idea *how* I'm going to attack this goal. But there must be some kind of way of getting things straight.

Number two: I want to make some kind of record of Mihn and me before the BE. (A history?) The good times are fading so fast that soon they will be gone forever and it will be like it never happened. Only the BE will be there. Like a great stinking boil on my shoulder! Sore and tender and there – for everyone to see. When I'm old I want to be able to look back over the words and say, yes, that happened to me once. It *was* real, therefore it is very important to have some kind of *documental proof.*

"It is not enough just to rely on a heap of feelings or vague impressions, girls,' Mr Schmit used to say to our Year Eleven European History class. 'You've got to have hard proof. History work is like detective work. *Details: dates, times, places . . .'*

Okay then, so that will be another thing for me to do: write down all my memories of Mihn, just in case I come across him again, and the past comes up and he has forgotten everything. (Or worse, tries to deny it.)

Number three: find out about Ruby. My Aunt Fran doesn't want to talk about her, so I'll have to find out some other way. She *was* my grandfather's sister, but it's more than that. I look at that painting and I feel connected to her in other ways, ways I don't understand. All that long blonde wavy hair. Like mine before I chopped it off.

And another thing. I will not go on living here with my aunt if she turns out to be like my mother. Damn it! We haven't spent much time together yet but if she starts seriously hassling me then I'm leaving. After all, I'm seventeen years old. I *can* just leave. Get a job. Get some youth allowance. Whatever.

'Sophie,' she said to me yesterday, all cool, just like Mum. 'Could I ask you to please wash your own things?'

'Oh sure,' I said, surprised and a bit pissed off. I was on the point of reminding her that I'd washed everything from the night before. All the bloody saucepans she'd dirtied cooking this fancy meal that I didn't even like, although I pretended to. Also, I wanted to say that I'm not used to these primitive conditions. No dishwashers, and no paid cleaner. She told me that I'd have to share the housework with her for as long as I'm here. Would I mind taking on the bathroom, on the weekends? Shit, I've never cleaned a bath in my life.

'It would be easier all around,' she said, as though reading my thoughts, not looking at me, 'if when you use plates and mugs during the day, you wash them up straightaway. And there seem to be a lot missing. Have you left some in your room?'

'Yeah okay,' I said, getting up, completely pissed off. Just that morning I'd been lying in bed counting eight coffee cups on the side table. 'I think I've left a few in there.'

In the bedroom I lined up the cups, about to take them back to the kitchen, then changed my mind. I opened up the window and lit a fag. My aunt had sounded like my mother back there. I took a few drags and then decided not to get too carried away comparing them. As horrible as this town is, at least it's better than home.

I look around the room, the blankets right up under my nose. I've got to find a way of *thinking* my way out of this mess. Trouble is, though, as soon as I think I've got a hold on some new way of looking at it, some *old* thought sort of slides in from underneath and sinks me again. The only thing that gets me away from it now is music. A fag, a few slugs of vodka. The Beastie Boys or the Smashing Pumpkins banging away, and me, curled up in bed or on the floor like a fat worm or walking by myself along the river. That's all I want now. It feels like that's all I am. Sometimes I feel as though I never want to see anyone again.

Not true exactly. *Nothing is absolutely true.* Shut up, Mr Schmit. Who asked you in here!

I haven't done a thing to the room. My case is still on the other bed and my clothes are still in it. I don't know how long I'm going to be here anyway. My marvellous mother might decide all of a sudden to come and drag me home. It would be her style. *Come on Sophie dear! There is some new shrink I want you to see. He's sure to do the trick!* But I don't have to go. I must remember that. I don't have to go. All I want is to be left alone.

Not true. Not true again!

My sound system is sitting up on the little dressing table between the beds. I've taken down the crucifix and a dopey picture of some angel holding flowers that was above my bed. And that's about it. On the first morning I woke up and thought, *Oh, what kind of a shitbox have I come to?* I hated the room. So pokey and small, full of faded, old and ugly things. But now, I'm getting used to it. It is starting to feel like me. (The ideal room for a fat worm!) And the window is good. It looks out over the back garden. I can watch my aunt moving to and from her studio during the day. I make sure I time my visits down to the kitchen for when she's not there.

I remember with a start that this will be my first morning down at my aunt's friend's shop. Amy. That little grey-haired woman who smiles all the time and looks like a mouse. Why did I agree to *that*? A new knot of tension slips in just below my rib cage. They caught me off-guard. Fran and Amy acting as though I'd be doing a great service to humankind to agree to a few hours' work in her shop. I've never worked in a shop before. I've never worked before, full stop, although I didn't tell them that. I mean for money. What if I can't do it? It's nearly eight already. I groan and push the warmth aside and head for the bathroom.

I slip out of my nightie, avoiding the image I see in the mirror, and step into the old bath. Turn on the taps. God, I love showers. The heat pounding my back and neck. The noise and steam, the *enclosed* feel of it. Or I did. Here the hot water runs out after five minutes. At home I'd stand under the shower for at least half an hour every morning.

I dress in my best jeans, which are thankfully a little looser than they were five days ago, and a clean shirt and then make my way warily down to the kitchen. I heard the door slam a few moments before so I figure that Fran is already at work out in the studio or out walking. I'm curious about what she does on her walks. I've seen her sometimes walking along – she looks cool in a way, with that big artist bag over her shoulder (guess she's got her pencils and sketch pads in there), long hair up in one of those plastic things. I wonder what kinds of scenes she stops to draw. But I'm too scared to ask her.

I go down to the kitchen and turn on the kettle and put a piece of bread into the toaster, wondering if artists mind people asking them about their work. I have exactly fifteen minutes to eat something and get there. Amy called in briefly the day before to tell me what she wanted me to do. Tapping serial numbers into a computer and putting prices on CDs for two hours every morning this week. Shouldn't be too taxing. But she didn't say anything about clothes. Maybe I'm meant to dress up in a skirt. Fact is, I didn't bring any of my good clothes from home. None of them fit me. Anyway, they'd look ridiculous with my blue hair.

Two days ago my body finally decided to rebel. I'd been so hooked on that stuff, chips and hamburgers, pies and fried chicken, that the thought of even a day without some pack of fried food or a tub of ice-cream was almost unthinkable. But after getting so sick the other morning, somehow . . .

I've felt myself stacking on the weight over these last months and I've often found myself wishing I had a more normal addiction, like alcohol or heroin. At least you wouldn't get to be like a side of a house on that stuff. Of course there was the added attraction of freaking my mother out with my increasing body size – that gave me a sick kind of pleasure. My mother is never *ever* more than two kilos over her ideal weight.

But it's not her I thought of. My thoughts were of the actual food, how good that hot, tasty, salty fish would taste in my mouth. Those spicy kebabs and hot dogs smothered in mustard and sauce! My favourite sweet is a big bowl of Peter's extra creamy vanilla ice-cream, covered in half a litre of smooth pure cream and topped with caramel or choc-mint sauce. I could eat three big bowls of that in one sitting.

At home I was sleeping most of the day and up all night listening to music, watching movies on TV and eating. But here somehow that rhythm got mucked up. The last few days I've actually felt like getting out and walking around during the day. It is such a small place and so quiet. Yesterday I walked along the river under the trees for quite a way. There was no one about. I stopped every now and again, closed my eyes and listened to the sounds around me. It got a bit spooky actually. I felt like, with a little push, I could have drifted off into some other realm altogether.

Anyway, the other night I stuffed myself on fish and chips and ice-cream as usual, and then came back to the house and instead of sitting up all night listening to music, I fell asleep at about eleven listening to the Toy Boys. Bad mistake. I awoke at about three with the most incredible pains. I got up and put on my jacket and went outside for a while. Had a smoke, which only made me feel worse. Then at about six I came inside. Half an hour later I was spewing my guts out in the bathroom. Felt a lot better after it was over but really hope she didn't hear me. Or smell it. I opened the window.

My aunt *did* hear me puking that morning.

'Sophie,' she says to me the next day, 'are you pregnant?'

I was sitting at the kitchen table drinking my tea and reading the paper.

'No,' I said, a bit stunned, drawing a complete blank on why she would think this. 'No, of course I'm not pregnant.'

'Well.' She smiled, a little embarrassed, but relieved too, I could see. 'I'm sorry to intrude but I had this idea you might be and I really had to know.'

'Why would you think . . .' I began and then remembered puking the day before and it was my turn to be embarrassed. 'You heard me being sick, right?' When she nodded, I felt my face go scarlet. 'I'm sorry. I just ate too much crap.'

She nodded and said nothing. I thought for sure she would start lecturing me on what were the right things to eat and I decided that when she started I was going to walk out. Mum is the original expert on food so I know it all. *Don't eat this. Don't eat that*. Years of diet and kilojoule talk. My aunt would not be able to tell me anything new. Before I went troppo Mum watched what I ate like a hawk.

'Now, Sophie, you've had two slices of bread already and dinner will be in an hour! Darling, did you know that dry biscuits are actually full of hidden fat? Blah Blah!'

But my aunt didn't say anything. In fact I spoke next. 'I crave all that stuff,' I told her a little nervously. 'I've only been eating like this for a few months and it often makes me sick. But I think I'm sort of addicted to it.'

'Well, I know what you mean.' She smiled. 'I *love* steamed dim sims myself. Once I ate a dozen all at once.'

'A dozen!' I said, a little flabbergasted. Wow. *That* was me, more or less, on a bad day.

'Yeah.' She grinned. 'I was starving and feeling awful about something. I can't remember. Anyway, I bought six, wolfed them down and then went to the shop over the road and bought another six. I was too ashamed to go back to the first shop!'

I laughed, liking her for telling me.

'Look, Sophie,' she said, suddenly getting up. 'Why don't you eat here more . . . I mean, while you're staying with me. You've hardly had a proper meal since you've arrived.'

'Okay,' I said.

And the weird thing is that I've had two full days now without any garbage. That very night I had toasted sandwiches and soup. It tasted good, and even better, when I'd finished the meal and I didn't have that stuffed feeling. Relief set in. And it was like I'd never been hooked on the other stuff at all. It sort of lost its attraction overnight.

My first morning down at Amy's shop was okay. I found it easily enough. In the main street opposite the old bank, with 'Robbertson's Haberdashery' in big gold letters across the double windows. I walked in and had to wait for a moment while my eyes adjusted. It was a bit like walking into another world. Soft yellow light. Little wooden counters everywhere, filled with stuff. I stood for a while waiting. No one seemed to be about. I heard a noise and walked over to the back corner. Amy was on her knees unpacking boxes. She looked up with a smile.

'Oh hello, Sophie!' she said warmly. 'Great to see you.'

'Er . . . thanks,' I said, feeling absurdly nervous. She was pulling out packets of men's flannelette pyjamas and stacking them in sizes onto the shelves behind the back counter.

'Hang on a sec,' she said easily, 'and I'll show you where I've set the computer up.'

It wasn't like any other shop I'd ever been in. There was so much stuff, so much variety. And all in together. Things like saws and hammers and nails just across the aisles from clothing for men and women. Well, I suppose some of those huge chain stores do that but this place felt so different to those kinds of joints. Sort of dark, and jumbled and peaceful. There were kids' clothes and workmen's clothes and a big range of underwear. There were bolts of material and patterns for dressmaking, plus all the packets of needles and scissors, and all kinds of kitchen stuff. Pharmacy items and cheap paperback books. Then there were the odd-bod things like pot plants and gifts. I had fun looking at all the stuff when I'd get up for a drink or to go to the toilet. Some of it looked like it had been there for ages.

The work itself was a bit boring but I got to meet a few people on the first day and that was all right. Uncle Jimmy came in and was immediately really friendly, which was a relief because the only thing I'd heard about him was that he was unstable and liable to fly off the handle at the slightest thing.

'Hey!' he said, pretending to fall over at the sight of me. 'My favourite wayward niece! Welcome to Victoria's hot spot.' Then his daughter, Blue, my cousin, who I hadn't spoken to properly for about five years, came in looking for him and I backed right off. What a knockout. Tall and slim with long jet-black hair. What a cool name! She's doing some uni course and obviously thinks she's pretty shit-hot. She hardly even glanced at me when her father asked if she remembered me. I suppose I did look a fat disgusting dag, just sitting there at the computer.

But I don't care that much. I've had my share of those ultra self-satisfied chicks. That's what my friends turned out to be, Jess and Alana. Both of them. And they remind me of my mother.

At about midday, Amy came up and told me it was enough for one day and to go home, that she'd see me tomorrow. She acted so grateful that I was helping her out. Said she'd see me the next day. I don't figure it though: why can't she find someone else? I thought country towns were full of unemployed teenagers.

On my way home I saw Fran sitting outside Jimmy's bistro in the sunshine, drinking coffee and laughing with people I hadn't seen before. I felt jealous. I know I used to be like that with my friends. But now it's hard to even imagine being that easy with another person. Instead of walking past and saying hello I turned around before they could see me and headed off home in another direction. My friends, at least the ones I used to have, sit like rocks on my shoulders, weighing me down. Mai and Mihn, Jess and Alana. I start wondering if I'll ever be free of them.

I make my way up the hill towards the house. There was a small crowd of people outside the Anglican church. *Funeral*, I think automatically. Then I actually *see* Mai. Or think I do. This little figure is walking away from the rest of the group, her back to me, waving goodbye, laughing, dressed in a tight short skirt, black sandals and a pink shirt. My breath goes short. The shape and tilt of the head, the quick stride. *It is her!* I think. I'll catch up with her. I quicken my pace as I follow, feeling my throat constrict with dryness, knowing this has happened before but unable to stop myself believing that this time is different. I am excited. My heart starts to beat hard and my hands even get clammy. Then whoever it is turns around and I see that it is not Mai. In fact this person is nothing like her. Everything subsides again and I am left with what happened.

When I get home there is a note from my aunt on the table, saying she's gone out to lunch and would be out for the rest of the afternoon but would see me at dinnertime. I suppose that pleases me, that she would think to write. I head over to the fridge for a cool drink, wishing I'd been game enough to approach her in the street. Wishing I was sitting out on the pavement drinking coffee with other people instead of back here alone.

So tell me about Mai.

You must remember Mai, Mr Schmit! She was in your history class. You and her had some arguments about Vietnam and . . .

Of course I remember her! Who wouldn't. But I want to hear how you became friends with her. And why.

I sat next to Mai for six weeks in maths at the beginning of this year without even noticing her. I was so bound up with Alana and Jess that I hardly even saw this quiet little Asian girl sitting right next to me. I hadn't noticed she was pretty, with cropped jet-black hair and this clear, very pale ivory skin. I knew nothing about her. I had my own friends.

Then this embarrassing thing happened in class. I can't quite remember how it started. I think Mrs Murray began explaining how some mathematical theory was essential to engineering. Just a little aside. Something about the way heat reacts with metal being so important to many industries. Anyway, she was about to move on to a new topic when the absolute idiot of the class, the original lame-brain, Melissa Fry, pipes up.

'We don't have any industry left in this country because migrants take all the jobs.' Something really idiotic like that. No sense to it at all. I could see the teacher thinking that it was too moronic to even comment on. She just raised her eyebrows and started to move on.

'Melissa has a point,' my best friend, Alana, suddenly chimed in. I turned around. Alana and Jess always shared a table down the back of the maths class. Because my eyesight is not good, and I refuse to even think about getting glasses, I always sat near the front. I waited, thinking that Alana was going to make a sarcastic comment that would put dopey Melissa in her place. Actually I think the whole class was waiting. When Alana spoke, people listened. As the most gorgeous-looking girl in the whole year most of them hung on her opinions about everything. Having Alana as a friend had given me automatic status for the last four years.

'What are you getting at, Alana?' Mrs Murray said, frowning.

'Just that I don't want this country to be *Asianised*,' Alana said with a pouty little shrug. Then she looked around at the rest of the class. 'Do you? I mean every time you walk down an Australian street, do you want to see Asian people?'

The silence intensified. I was suddenly aware of the Vietnamese girl sitting next to me. I looked down at her book. *Mai Duong* was written neatly on the top right-hand corner of the front cover, *Yr twelve C*. At the same time, I was willing Alana, with everything in me, to shut up. Didn't she realise how insulting she sounded?

'What do you really mean, Alana?' The teacher sighed quietly.

'Where my mum works in Richmond,' Alana said, flushing slightly, 'she says that no one speaks English there. I mean . . . the shops and restaurants are all run by . . . them.' She looked around, challenging us all to disagree. 'There are parts of this city where there are no Australians at all. You might as well be in an Asian city!'

Silence again. The teacher was staring at the board, frowning.

'I've got nothing against them,' pipes up the brainwave, Melissa. 'Just want them to stay home and stop taking our jobs.'

Our jobs. Melissa's father was the head of some enormous plastics manufacturing company. They were so rich that she had a chauffeur pick her up from school if Mummy couldn't make it. As though she would ever be out of a job!

'No, all I'm saying is that they should be able to speak English before they get here,' Alana said quickly, as though she didn't want to be associated with Melissa. I could tell, too, by her slightly wavering tone that she hadn't thought out what she was saying, that she'd unnerved herself by speaking up like this. Alana very rarely got involved in any kind of serious discussion.

I also knew that if I contradicted her, in front of the whole class, then it would be seen as a betrayal. She ruled our trio. But I knew about her family and I just couldn't shut up.

'Could your parents speak English when they came

here?' I found myself asking, a odd cramped feeling gripping my chest. *What was I doing, questioning Alana?* But I knew her father's family were originally from Hungary. It was an important point to make.

'They were born here actually,' she said coldly, staring straight back at me. I remember thinking, This is going very badly. I shied away from her indignant look. But I still couldn't shut up.

'Well, your grandparents then? Could they speak English when they came here?'

'Well . . . no.' I'd never seen Alana seriously flush before. But to my surprise and, I have to say, intense satisfaction, she turned bright scarlet. 'They still can't but things were . . . different then. They came in the fifties.' Her voice petered out.

'What does that matter?' I persisted doggedly. 'I mean, the fifties verses *now*? What does it matter?'

'They were Europeans!' she snapped defensively. 'They looked the same as Australians . . . even if they couldn't speak English. They fitted in.'

Then Mai stood up. There was a kind of communal gasp when she did, as though people were genuinely surprised to be reminded of her existence.

'My father could not speak English well when he came here,' she said in a clear, even voice. 'Because after the war he'd spent nearly six years in a re-education camp. Five years of living in the jungle with many others. Starving. They ate rats and cockroaches. Anything on top of the one cup of rice they got, just to stay alive for that day. When they let him out he was a "non-person" because he'd been in the South Vietnamese army. Australia was his only chance. And my mother . . . she still can't speak English but we . . . we are a family here.'

Then she sat down as abruptly as she'd stood. There was a strong murmur of approval from the other girls in the class. Even a few claps. But I could see that it had taken its toll. Her hands were trembling as they twisted in her lap.

'Thank you, Mai,' the teacher said, smiling at her. 'Now everyone, I really do think we should get on with our maths topic.'

Once again there were murmurs of approval and the teacher began to teach maths again. I sat there for what seemed like ages, pretending to listen, but really trying to think of something to say to her.

'Were you born over there?' I eventually whispered.

'No.' She smiled at me and I saw that I shouldn't have felt nervous of her at all. There was a real, easy friendliness about her. 'I was born the second day my parents were in Australia. My mum was rushed from the hostel in Nunawading into hospital. Just in time.'

I returned her smile but didn't know what else to say.

At the end of the class I packed up my things slowly, not at all looking forward to meeting up with Alana and Jess. I had history next and they had a free session in the library. Part of me knew I should go and face Alana directly, apologise before she had time to turn against me. But I wasn't game. And I was also interested in Mai. There was something tough about her that drew me in. She looked up from putting her books in her bag, surprised that I was still there.

'Listen,' I said, feeling absurdly shy, 'I'm sorry about before.' I waved my hand to where Alana had been sitting. 'She doesn't mean anything . . . doesn't know what she is talking about.'

'Don't you be sorry,' she said seriously. 'I don't care.'
Her pretty face suddenly broke open into a dry smile.
'My parents didn't sell everything they owned, risk
being out on the high seas in a flimsy boat, get attacked
by pirates, robbed and left to die of thirst for me to be
thin-skinned. I can put up with dumb stuff like that.'

'God!' I said, stunned. 'Did they really?'

'What?' We were walking out of the room now.
Following the teacher. The last students to leave.

'Get attacked by pirates?'

'Yeah,' she said, her face closing over. 'But not as bad
as some. They were just robbed. No killings and no
rapes. They were lucky.' She smiled at me. 'Like me.'

'What have you got now?' I asked, pretending I
needed to look down at the timetable taped to my
folder.

'History,' she said. I could hear that she was surprised by the question. 'Like you.'

I nodded and we walked off together to Mr Schmit's
class, me feeling ashamed that I'd never registered she
was in the history class until now.

'Do you like history?' I asked, for something to say.

'I love it,' she said. I turned and saw her eyes were
shining. She really meant it and I warmed to her even
more.

'Yeah. Me too.'

'Come home with me some time,' she said, gaily,
smiling. 'Have a Vietnamese meal with us.'

'Okay. I will,' I said, hoping she'd ask again soon
because I really did want to go. Alana and Jess hardly
ever invited me home with them. They loved coming to
my house because their families and houses were boring to them. I always felt that they were slightly

embarrassed, so I never pushed it. But I got sick of always getting together at my place.

From that day Mai and I sat together in history as well as maths, and although there was a kind of truce worked out with Alana, underneath I think we all knew things had changed. Mai and I had become friends.

Why do you think you sided with this girl you didn't know rather than with your friends?

I don't know the answer to that. It puzzles me sometimes.

Think!

Get stuffed.

I sighed, got up and washed my glass and then went into the lounge room for another look at the painting. The few hours down in Amy's shop had made me restless. I didn't feel like curling up in my room listening to music. I wanted to do something with the afternoon.

It still changes every time I go in to look at it, but subtly. It seems somehow deeper and more intense because I know that the floating girl is actually my great-aunt and she's dead.

I walked out into the back garden. The sun was shining. Quite hot really for November. I suppose I knew beforehand what I was going to do, but told myself I was just going out for the sun. After standing on the back steps for a while I went around to the far end of the studio and stared in the big window, but I couldn't see much. There were just a couple of big tables, an easel, and pieces of paper stuck roughly to the walls. I wanted to go in there and take a proper look around but I knew I shouldn't. I knew this studio was my aunt's private space and that trespassing would be totally unjustified. Knowing that didn't stop me.

On my way back to the house I tried the studio door and it was locked, as I thought it would be. But I'd seen where she'd hung her key – on the nail above the fireplace. I tried to tell myself that she wouldn't mind as I went back into the house for it.

Well, there wasn't that much to see, at first anyway. I wandered around staring at things. The sketches pinned up on the walls were interesting but there weren't that many of them. I guess they were just little sketches from around the town and district. Birds sitting on fences. A pair of old rubber boots. Quite a few of grass and trees. I don't think any of them were completed but the more I looked the more I saw that there was something lovely about each one. One I really liked was kind of rough but I could sense the breeze running through the grass just by the angle of a few lines. On the easel there was a more detailed drawing, of objects that had been set up on a pedestal a few feet away: an old black kettle, some dried grass and a couple of apples.

Over in one corner was a foot-pedal wheel for making clay pots. I had a sudden memory of being about twelve and slapping lumps of clay onto the spinning wheel, shaping it with wet sloppy hands. Up and down, high and thin. Flat and wide. Me controlling it. Now thick and then fine as paper, enjoying the attention of a crowd of classmates who were standing around watching me in admiration. It had been a two-week elective in pottery at our school and no one else had been able to get the knack of it like I had. Odd that I hadn't thought about it since then. Bending over the clay, feeling the slipperiness of it gliding through my fingers, thinking with my hands. I had a mad desire to sit down right then and see if I could still do it. But this old wheel had seen better days. It was rusty, there was no clay, and more importantly, I shouldn't even have been in there looking at it.

Although I liked the drawings, I was a bit disappointed. I suppose I was hoping to see paintings. But the only bit of colour in the whole place was a print hung up on a wall near the window. A night scene. Lights falling across water and two huddled figures clinging to each other in one corner. The more I looked at it the more beautiful it seemed to me. Beautiful and very sad. At first I thought it was hers but as I got closer I saw that it was a print and that it was by the artist Van Gogh. I tried to remember what I'd learnt about him at school but all I could think of was that he chopped his ear off! After looking at it for some time I went over to one of the tables, which was covered in more drawings. Piles of them. Although I was tempted I didn't dare move any of them. I stared down at all these drawings of fruit and fence posts and hills and sheds, not touching anything.

A couple of times I thought I heard a car door slam nearby, then a door creaking, and my heart immediately started racing. But nothing happened, she didn't come back, so I stayed there, just snooping about. Was I after something in particular? I don't know. I suppose I am a bit intrigued by her. My mother's sister, and yet she seems so different to my mother.

Then, pinned to the far wall, a detailed drawing of a bridge. A narrow bridge crossing a river. The paper was yellowish, definitely older than the other sketches on the table and around the walls. There was a young woman in a long dress, with fair hair, standing on the bridge, one hand shading her eyes. She was frowning and looking into the distance. *Ruby*. For sure. I just knew it. I suddenly felt confused and at the same time a thin spiral of excitement coiled up inside me. I didn't dare to reach out and touch this drawing even though I wanted to. Ruby's face looked familiar. Then it hit me. *Me*. Ruby looked like me. Or how I used to look before I put on all the weight and cut my hair. I felt almost faint suddenly and I wished I hadn't come into my aunt's private place. I had no right to be here.

Then I am back in Mai's room, the neat little room above the family cafe in North Melbourne that she shared with her two younger sisters. She is pulling down a big folio from the top of the corner cupboard. Three watercolours of trees are pinned just above her desk. I peer closely at one, marvelling at the pink and purple colours that fade out into almost nothing. She has just told me that it is all her own work. That she does these watercolours for a hobby. It is perhaps a week since the incident with Alana in the classroom. My first time at her house. I am a bit nervous because I've just met her parents, working down in the kitchen directly below Mai's bedroom.

'Hello, hello!' Her father, a small round-faced man with a shining red face, turned around from where he was gutting fish with a small sharp knife, flicking the lumpy bloody waste down into a plastic bucket on the floor and filleting the fish so easily and quickly that it hardly looked as though he was moving his hands.

We'd just walked in through the front of the restaurant, past all the laminex tables and the red and gold Buddhist shrines. I was shocked. I'd never been in a restaurant kitchen before. I'd imagined them to be large, pristine places with cooks walking around in high-starched hats and white aprons. This place wasn't exactly dirty but it wasn't sparkling clean either. It was small and cramped, jammed full of stuff. There were two huge cookers down one end, an enormous pot of bones boiling away at the back, a fridge, shelves of crockery, and heaps of boxed vegetables all over the benches and floor.

The strong smell of boiling oil and lemongrass, mint and cooking meat was overpowering. Mai's father, dressed in a grubby tee-shirt and black pants and plastic flip-flop sandals, was obviously very busy. Beads of sweat ran across his upper lip and forehead and there were wet patches under his arms. Still holding the knife, he smiled and bowed, muttering to Mai in Vietnamese, then he washed his hands under the tap before coming over and holding out his damp hand to me.

'Hello,' I said, taking it in my own. 'Nice to meet you.'

The room wasn't light enough. Only one yellow bulb hung from the centre of the room. The rows of dried herbs slung across the window blocked out light.

'Yes, very good to meet you.' He seemed to want to say more to me but didn't, just stood there smiling and nodding. Then Mai's mother bustled in through the back door, carrying six plucked ducks in newspaper, their long skinny necks and tiny feathered heads lolling like grotesque toys. She dumped them on top of a pile of leafy green vegetables and stood smiling at me. Plump and round and small, her face red like her husband's. Mai spoke rapidly to her in Vietnamese. Probably telling her who I was, although I didn't hear my name. Her mother suddenly stepped forward and took both my hands in her own.

'Sophie,' she said warmly, squeezing her eyes shut, as though she already knew me well and had been waiting for me to come. 'Sophie! Many welcome I give you!'

'Oh . . . thanks,' I said, smiling awkwardly back at her. 'Mrs Duong.' Then she reached up and touched my blonde and curly hair, looked at her husband and laughed delightedly as she gave it a sharp tug.

'Dreamboat hair,' she said.

I smiled, immediately embarrassed. Then the father began laughing. I looked at Mai and she too was laughing. The three of them were looking at me and cracking up. I think it was about then that I began to sweat.

'She likes your hair,' Mai explained, suddenly sensing my discomfort and pulling my arm. 'Come on, I'll show you my room.'

We walked out the back door of the kitchen and then up some wooden back stairs and into the rooms that the family lived in.

'Did you do all of these?' I asked in awe. I'd been spending quite a bit of time talking with Mai over the last week and she had never said anything about being into drawing or painting.

'Uh-huh.' She was flicking through the pile from her folio, pulling out different pieces to show me, pleased that I seemed so impressed.

'When do you do them?'

'Sometimes, when everything is finished downstairs,' she said, frowning a little, 'I come in here and do a painting. Especially if I'm angry, it calms me down!'

'But they don't look like angry paintings,' I said. It was true. Each one was done on quite a small piece of white paper. Peaceful, delicate studies of trees and grass. One of two little children sitting on a seat under a lamp post. A couple of rice paddies, and peasant figures in coolie hats bending low. I took a quick look at her, trying to imagine her getting angry.

'You should be doing art at school, Mai,' I said seriously. 'The facilities are great. These paintings are really good.'

'Bah,' she said with a quick grin, waving one hand dismissively. 'I'm going to be doctor like you.'

I nodded, not bothering to tell her that I'd decided not to be a doctor.

'I've got an aunt who illustrates books,' I said. 'I think she does okay. You should think about it.'

She shrugged airily, completely disinterested.

'Choose one to keep if you want,' she said, bouncing down on one of the nearby beds. 'Then let's go down and see if my brother is home.'

'You mean it?' I was delighted. I would get it framed and put it up over my bed. 'I can really have one to keep?'

'Yes.' She smiled at me. 'Choose one for yourself.'

I began to flick through the drawings. *Which one?* Each painting seemed to have something more special than the last. Then I came to one that she hadn't shown me. Quite different to all the others. It was a watercolour, but in very dark tones: black and grey and brown wash. An overcrowded boat being tossed on the high seas. Above the boat and all around it a turbulent, dark, foreboding sky. Mai saw me staring at it, got up and came over.

'See,' she said softly, pointing to the top left-hand corner. 'The spirits.'

'Oh!' I hadn't noticed the strange little ethereal faces poking out from under the clouds. 'What are they?'

She didn't tell me immediately but began rifling through the folio again, pulling out more drawings on the same theme. Until the whole desk was covered in perhaps eight bleakly coloured boat pictures. In some of them the boat was tiny and there were lots of full-bodied spirit figures in the sky, and in others the boat almost took up the whole paper, and the spirits were just little faces.

'This is after my parents had been attacked by pirates,' Mai said. 'They were left without food or fuel or money. And because the pirates had stolen my father's navigating equipment, they had no way of knowing which way to go, except by the stars.'

She pulled out a slightly bigger work. It was better than the others. The water was calm and the people on the boat were drawn with great detail. Children, old people, women and men of all shapes and sizes. Above the boat, surrounding it on all sides, were watery grey and yellow spirits – like angels I suppose – floating in a dark, ominous sky. There was so much detail on this ordinary piece of paper that I was dumbfounded.

'That night my father and his father were filled with despair,' Mai went on. 'Around them, all the others had fallen asleep. So they began to pray to the spirits of the ancestors. To keep the water calm. To hold off the rain. They prayed for hours. Just the two of them, begging for help and mercy. My father and his father. And just before dawn they heard singing.'

Mai stopped and looked at me. Very seriously. I

guess she was looking for any flicker of disbelief or amusement. I stared back into her lovely, clear almond-shaped eyes and nodded.

'And . . . ?' I said.

'When they heard the singing they knew that the spirits were looking after them,' she went on. 'And the very next day they came across an American oil rig. They were taken in, given food and water and then taken to the refugee camp in Malaysia. Two years later my father was in Australia and . . .' She smiled at me. 'We . . . our family was saved.'

I nodded, staring at the painting. Not knowing what to say. The story might have been a fairytale. It was so outside anything I'd ever known or thought about.

'My mum got pregnant with me in the refugee camp,' Mai said a little more brightly, and then pointed to the figure of a little boy on the boat standing next to a slightly older boy. 'This is my older brother. He was two when the pirates attacked.'

I stared into the painting, and nodded. 'Can I have this one then, Mai?' I said, picking up the one with her brother in it. Some of the prettier, lighter studies would look better in my room, but I knew it was this one I wanted.

'Of course,' she said. 'But leave it up here until you're ready to go home.'

Her brother, Mihn, was sitting with his back against the fence, catching the last rays of sun, when we came back downstairs. The backyard was very small. Just a square of concrete really, with a few big bins and boxes of soft-drink crates. He was squinting up into the sky, smoking a cigarette.

'What's up with you?' Mai said sternly, walking over to him. 'You should have started work by now.'

'I've got a few minutes.' He squinted up at us, taking a drag of his cigarette. Then he gave me a sudden grin. 'Who are you?'

'Sophie,' I replied shyly, immediately liking his friendliness. He was very thin and quite tall, with badly cut, long, coarse hair. But his features were fine, like Mai's. A long face with high cheekbones and warm brown eyes. It crossed my mind that neither of them seemed to fit with their parents, who were both short and stout. Mai parked herself down next to her brother and indicated I should do the same. Then, to my surprise, she pinched one of his cigarettes, lit up, took a deep drag and blew the smoke up into the air in a very thin stream. She delicately tapped the ash onto the cracked concrete and grinned sheepishly at me.

'I'm giving up,' she said.

'Right,' I replied.

'I'm sick of work,' Mihn suddenly grumbled, bringing his knees up, wrapping his arms around them and looking straight ahead. 'I've been in lectures all day. Now I've got to come and work in this joint all night!'

'Oh poor baby!' Mai teased, ruffling his hair. 'You have such a hard time!'

'Shut up.' Mihn smiled, then turned to me. 'You got a job?'

'Er no,' I said, feeling slightly embarrassed. 'I should but . . .'

'Why?' he said, smiling at me again. 'If you don't need to?'

We sat together in comfortable silence for a while.

'What do you do at uni?' I asked Mihn.

'Dentistry,' he said, frowning. 'Second year.'

'Oh God no!' I grimaced, remembering the lunch when everyone said I should do dentistry. 'That must be so . . .' I was about to say boring but caught myself just in time.

'What have you got against dentistry?' Mihn was looking at me with frank amusement now. It was an odd moment because while I was beginning to blush, thinking I'd put my foot in it as usual, and wondering how I was going to explain myself, little electric shocks were going through me because I was also thinking, *This guy is really gorgeous!* In an odd sort of way. I'm not talking Brad Pitt here. But then I've never liked those prissy, perfect oh-so-cute guys anyway. This brother of Mai's was good looking in his own wild way. Sort of intense and quick but with a grin that really lit up his face. He was *interesting* and he was making my breath go short.

'Nothing . . .' I squirmed. 'Nothing at all. It's just that my family all think . . .' My voice faltered and I shrugged. 'Sorry, it's just a family thing. Doesn't make sense telling it all to a stranger.'

'No, come on!' he cut in, laughing at my embarrassment. 'You think everyone should have false teeth. Is that it?'

'No!' My flush went deeper. 'Look, there is nothing wrong with dentistry. I'm sure it would be . . . interesting.'

But even as I said it my voice petered out. I knew I sounded completely unconvincing. How come Mai hadn't told me she had an incredibly attractive brother? If I'd known he was going to be there I'd have worn something decent, gone to a bit of trouble. Put some make-up on. The situation was saved because for some reason both of them found my awkwardness very funny. Mai began to snort with laughter and Mihn, started teasing me about not working. Eventually we were all laughing together.

A few minutes later we were called inside. The restaurant would be opening in half an hour and had to be got ready. No one asked me if I wanted to be part of it. Nor did they thank me or think it special when I started helping. I simply sat down next to Mai at a table and helped fold the hot, newly washed cutlery from the dishwasher into red paper napkins. After we'd done about three hundred of those Mihn showed me how to set the tables. Then I washed rice out in the big plastic buckets in the backyard and helped write the specials up on the outside board.

We had fun that night – Mai, Mihn and I. The three of us joking and jostling with each other as we brought out the dishes of steaming food, packed up the dirty plates and wiped the tables down. The place was crowded from the moment it opened at six, right through to ten-thirty. As soon as one table emptied, it was immediately filled with more people. Groups of students, families, people on their way home from work – they all came in for quick cheap meals: soup, chicken, fish, rice and vegetables. They seemed to expect fast service too and usually left within half an hour. I'd never even imagined what it might be like being a waitress. But that's what I was that night, taking orders, bringing out food, scraping up the dirty dishes and bringing them out to Mihn in the stuffy little dishwashing room just down from the kitchen.

'Hey, it's the woman who hates dentists!'

Every time I came with a fresh lot of dishes he'd make a joke. I suppose that was the real fun of the night; the feeling that this incredibly attractive, tall guy liked me. Every now and again he'd come out to the main part of the restaurant and tell me things too, while I was working.

'See that guy over there near the window? He breeds pigeons.'

'Really? But . . . he looks like a pigeon!'

'I know.'

And we both burst out laughing, because it was true. The man had a beaky little nose and eyes that darted around like a bird's.

'And see that one? He used to make perfume in the old country and he called his daughter Lan-Huong, which means "fragrance".'

He joked about the people in the restaurant, his friends at uni, his parents and himself. I didn't dare think he might find me attractive. At that point I simply told myself I'd made a friend. I liked Mai a lot and now I was getting on famously with her brother! And that made me feel good.

Alana and Jess both had boyfriends on and off over the years. Mainly boys from other leading private schools, who they met on the trains or in the clubs they went to. But nothing like that had ever happened for me. Sometimes I'd get envious. Their scenes with guys never seemed to get serious or last long. Even so, I enjoyed their accounts of dating. We giggled and chatted together about the details. My shyness with boys bewildered Alana and Jess. They were always giving me pep talks, telling me what to wear, how to lose weight, flirt and push myself. But although I tried, I was never much of a success.

But that night in the restaurant, working alongside Mihn and Mai brought out an easygoing, witty side that I never even knew I had.

Most of the patrons were Vietnamese and I think a few found it strange, my working there. Mrs Duong stayed behind the cash register, taking the money as the patrons left, and her husband stayed in the kitchen and did the cooking. Mai and I waited on tables. By eight I was hungry myself. Just as I was about to ask Mai if I could sneak a couple of the delicious-smelling spring rolls, she motioned me towards an empty table.

'Come on,' she said. 'Let's eat.'

Mai, Mihn and I sat down at the table nearest to the kitchen, and their mother brought us out piles of freshly cooked dishes. Stuffed chicken wings, fish soup, chilli beef on sticks. Rice and noodles. Two younger sisters appeared from upstairs – twelve-year-old Cuc and fourteen-year-old Thu – and took over the waiting while we ate. The changeover went very smoothly and efficiently. The two younger girls knew exactly what they had to do.

When my father came to pick me up at eleven, I was waiting for him on the street, Mai's painting under one arm and a bag of spring rolls under the other, feeling tired and oddly happy. Mrs Duong had insisted I take the spring rolls home to my mother.

'You had a nice time?' Dad asked wearily. He'd come straight from the hospital and hadn't been home yet. I offered him a spring roll and he wolfed it down greedily in two bites.

'God, that was good, love. I've been in the operating theatre for four hours.'

By the time we'd got home Dad had eaten them all. I

didn't mind. I told him a bit about the Duong family and we talked about this and that. Sometimes I get an attack of the jitters when I think of Dad. I start wondering if maybe I've imagined everything. Dad and me in the car late at night, winding our way home through the lit suburbs, through the semi-empty city streets, the radio going softly between us.

'Thanks for picking me up, Dad.'

Him switching off the engine, turning to smile before opening the car door.

'Oh, you're welcome, honey.'

The next morning at school Mai came up to me at the lockers, her eyes shining.

'My brother really likes you!' she whispered.

I immediately blushed and she laughed, obviously delighted with this development. The bell went and we both went off to our different classes. But those few words of hers filled me with a new, deep kind of pleasure, one that lasted all day.

I felt slightly sick as I closed the studio door behind me and locked it. What is the point of happy memories if they end badly? If everything just winds up weird and sad and hopeless? What is the point of even trying to remember? Especially when so much of it has become as vague and misty as ocean spray. But I went to my room and pulled out my book, lay down on the floor on my stomach and tried to pin it down. Doing that sometimes feels like my only hope.

The following Sunday was one of those perfect days that come along every what . . . five years? What makes them so? Everything kind of flows without anyone having to do much at all. I went down to Queenscliff with Mihn's family. They'd shut the restaurant for the day because it was some Vietnamese holy day. Mai told me later that it had been her and Mihn's idea to get their parents out of the city for a break and Mihn had suggested inviting me. I'd already arranged to go to the city with Alana and Jess to see the new big Spielberg blockbuster, but I had no qualms about pulling out. Dad drove me over to North Melbourne and we went in the family's beaten-up van that smelt of vegetables from the market. Mai and Mihn. Their parents and the two younger sisters, and me.

Once we got to the beach their parents seemed overwhelmed. Mihn told me later that they'd hadn't been to the beach before in Australia. They immediately parked themselves on two rugs under one of the big pine trees and simply sat there, staring warily out at the blue ocean, at all the bright, happy, suntanned people who were picnicking and playing cricket games around them. I could see that it all looked so alien and strange to them. After lunch Mihn tried to get them to go for a walk along the water's edge but they were determined to stay in the shade, under the tree.

'Too hot,' they said, smiling at me apologetically. 'We happy here.'

In fact it wasn't hot at all. Almost no one was in the water. It was a perfect day for a walk. The younger girls went off to the swings and Mai, Mihn and I went right down along the pier and then on to the rocks. After a while Mai took off on her own, collecting stones and shells in a makeshift little holder she'd made with her scarf. I guess she did it deliberately, but it didn't feel all that obvious at the time. Mihn and I walked along together behind her, our feet in the water, talking easily,

153

as though we'd known each other for ages, but there was an undercurrent there too, which I found very exciting.

'I really like your family,' I said, suddenly and passionately. It was true. I suppose I really meant his mother. And Mai of course. The younger girls were sweet and friendly and the father seemed okay too. But their mother was funny and warm. And although she couldn't speak much English, she was so accepting of me. It was like she thought it was really special that I'd come along. My own mother that morning had declared herself shocked that I was going to let Alana and Jess down by going to the beach with my new friend, Mai.

'I think there is a certain amount of loyalty you owe to your real friends, Sophie,' she sniped. How did she know who my real friends were? As though it was any of her business! Quite weird really. Maybe she was having fan club withdrawal symptoms. Alana and Jess hadn't been around to gape at her clothes for about two weeks.

'Your parents really talk about everything, don't they?' I said. 'I mean they are so easy. Laughing all the time.' I wanted to go on about it but then thought it might be annoying, having an outsider gush on about your parents. Mihn just looked at me and smiled.

'You know what I like about you, Sophie?' he said.

I shook my head and looked away, out across the bay to the other side, the tiny strip of sand between the sea and sky. The sky was so blue. And the water in front of us so vast and glittering and perfect.

'The way you jump to conclusions,' he said, looking at me directly. I looked up, knowing there was a small sharp barb in there somewhere, but one that I didn't understand.

154

'What do you mean?'

He shrugged and we kept on walking over the rocks, every now and again stopping to look into the rock pools, me frowning to myself, wondering if I'd said something wrong. We both had our shoes off and would occasionally squat down, put our hands or feet in and marvel at the warmth of these small pools of water.

'I've got an older brother,' he said quietly. 'He's in jail. No one ever talks about him. His name isn't allowed to be mentioned in the house.'

'But why?' I said, stunned to my core at the very idea of having a close relation *in jail*, and at the same time trying desperately not to show it.

'My parents are too ashamed,' he said. 'He has disgraced the family.'

'But . . . why is he in jail?'

'Drugs.' Mihn sighed. 'What else? He got involved with the wrong people. The usual stuff . . . He didn't like school.'

'When does he get out?' I asked.

Mihn was sitting cross-legged on the sand now, one hand scooping up a fistful of sand then letting it drain through his fingers. He was staring out to sea, his face creased into a frown.

'He's been in for eighteen months,' he muttered. 'And will be out soon. I've got to try and help him this time. My parents . . .' A hard look came over his face. 'Don't want to know him.'

'Is he an addict?' I asked, barely breathing.

Mihn shrugged.

'I don't know,' he said, suddenly jumping up quickly. 'But he was dealing, which is worse.'

Everything I heard that afternoon could have brought the mood between us right down, but it didn't. I was flattered that he had confided in me. And the brother? Well, he wasn't real to me. He was out there in the great beyond somewhere. His situation didn't touch me.

'So what is his name?' I asked at one point.

'Truc,' he said. 'He is the eldest son. Called after my grandfather.' He looked at me seriously. 'It is a terrible shame for my parents.'

'Yes,' I said, 'It would be.'

'And yet I wish . . .' He looked away, frowning. 'I hate them for giving up on him.'

After a while the conversation changed back to an easy one about school and university and my plans for next year. We were leaning against the cliff face and laughing at the antics of two little boys skidding about on the sand when Mihn suddenly put his arm around my shoulders, pulling me to him a little. We both looked resolutely out to sea, as though this new development between us wasn't happening. Up to that moment we'd been acting like friends. The new turn of events thrilled me but I didn't know what to do next. *What now? Am I meant to do something?*

Very tentatively I slipped an arm around his waist and he responded by drawing me in even closer. Standing like this, with both our bodies touching all the way down one side, was the most excruciatingly wonderful sensation I'd ever experienced. The parts of me that were touching him, even through my jeans and shirt, suddenly went very hot. It was as though someone had switched on electric plates right down one side of one of my legs, another on my hip, still another across my shoulders where his arm was resting.

The rest of me had gone jittery, my heart felt like it was lurching along like a city tram in traffic and my mouth had gone dry. I wanted to laugh and ask if he could feel the heat from my leg. But I was as embarrassed as hell. *Chill out*, I kept telling myself. Stop acting like this has never happened to you before! But instead of diminishing, the heat and excitement steadily built. In the end I just couldn't stand it any longer and started to move away.

But before I could, he reached out and grabbed me back. Before I knew what was happening he'd pushed me against the cliff face and, with one hand gripping my long hair pulling it back, and the other arm around my waist, he began to kiss me. His mouth on mine was hot and sweet and hard. *God!* Whatever had been inside me until that point simply exploded. Heat like molten lava began to run through my whole body, igniting my hands and breasts, my belly, arms and legs. I began to tremble as I kissed him back. Hungry! That's how I felt. I wanted to devour him! Every part of me was suddenly on fire.

Mihn was much taller and skinnier than me but I loved those thin hands, the way I could feel his bones under the skin. I wrapped both arms around him wildly and bit his neck about four times down from his ear to his collarbone. I had never done anything even remotely like that before. Truth is, I'd hardly even kissed anyone! Later I would have time to be shocked with myself. But by then it was too late.

'You're sexy,' he mumbled, laughing, kissing *my* neck and ears and pressing his body up against me, touching my breasts through my clothes. 'I want to touch you all over!'

The words made me shudder. On some level I was almost appalled and yet those words were . . . *true*. I felt powerful and desirable and out of control. My nipples were like hard little buttons, begging to be touched by bare hands. As though they could hear, Mihn's hands dived under my shirt, unclipping me at the back. I gasped as my breasts fell free into his hands. When he gently began to rub the inside of my leg with his knee I let out this low moan that came from a place way down inside I never knew existed. Certainly I had no control over it. I began to moan softly as he continued to kiss and touch me. By this point I was beyond embarrassment. I didn't care. I had become a mass of desire and longing.

We were there for ages, pressed up together against the huge cliff face, arms wrapped around each other, neither of us wanting to be the first to pull apart, both of us breathing hard. I remember thinking: *I will never have enough of this. Never! I want it to go on forever.* If it had been possible I would have ripped off all my clothes there and then and lay down with him in the sand. *Me!* Who was so contemptuous of the girls at school who went all dreamy-eyed when they talked about their boyfriends and about how *far* they'd gone.

Oh! All that stuff used to drive me nuts. They were the dull girls who had no ambition apart from catching a guy. Why don't they just get a life? I used to think. *Do* something, *think* about something interesting, for God's sake. What a joke now! What else was there to think about but this? My only thought at that moment was for us both to fall down together onto the soft sand, for our jeans and underclothes to somehow disintegrate and for him to actually push himself inside me. *Oh God*, I was moaning. *That's what I want. Come on, let's* . . .

But of course he didn't. We couldn't. There were people on the beach. Kids playing. And I didn't even really know him. And anyway, what if he already had a girlfriend and was simply mucking around with me? Did I even *know* this guy? Perhaps I was using him? Oh shit! Besides, we had no condoms. At least I didn't have any and if he had then . . . I would have been suspicious that he was doing the same thing with someone else.

At last, when we saw Mai making her way towards us along the beach, we pulled away. My mouth and neck felt tender and sore, as if they had been bitten by a swarm of strange insects. Watching Mai at the shoreline we began to laugh a little – suddenly shy with each other – as we saw her wade out. Little Mai. I knew suddenly that she'd seen us and was giving us plenty of warning before she walked up to where we were standing. Sighing, Mihn slipped both hands under my chin and looked down into my face.

'You have got the prettiest eyes,' he said softly. 'Are they grey or blue?'

'You're the one looking at them!' I giggled, lifting my hands and running my fingers through his coarse, thick hair. 'What do you think?'

'Smoky grey,' he said, 'like two beautiful little rain clouds.'

His almost sad tone set me off again. Heat began to flicker away in the pit of my stomach and my thighs felt like they were melting. I thought if I didn't get to kiss him again within the next thirty seconds I'd faint. I stared brazenly right back into his face as he looked at me, neither self-conscious or shy. I felt like about ten huge boulders had been lifted from my shoulders. Over the last half hour I had become a completely different person.

We walked back along the beach with Mai to where their parents were sitting under the trees, this time Mihn and I holding hands. At the back of my mind I was already beginning to plan our next meeting. My mother and father would be out Friday night. Only two days away. I'd heard her arranging some dinner party on the phone. I would invite Mihn around. We would have privacy and I'd make sure there were condoms. Everything would be right. Low lights, nice music; perhaps I'd pinch a bottle of my father's wine to make everything relaxed and easy. God, I couldn't wait!

Okay! So this is it. This is what they write songs about!

But I didn't really believe it. It didn't seem then as though anyone else could ever have experienced such lightning flashes of desire or this bubbling rush of happiness that was spilling out like water from a spring.

'You know,' he said softly as Mai walked on ahead, 'I meant it before. I do like the way you jump to conclusions.'

'Yeah?' I laughed, desperate to kiss him again but knowing I couldn't. I had no idea what he was talking about but it didn't matter. Mai and her parents were turning towards us, smiling. Unclasping our hands, Mihn and I walked up the sandbank to where they were waiting for us.

It rained last night. I was awake till long after midnight, not playing my music but listening to the rain crashing onto the tin roof. All very well, having clear-cut resolves about working everything out, I was thinking, but completely different trying to actually do it. Mihn and his relationship with his brother Truc, for instance. Part of me just baulks at writing about that. Maybe it would be a better idea to try and forget the whole bloody thing, even the good times. Ditto for Alana and Jess. Maybe I should re-set my goals. The truth is, I'm not finished with my mother. Not by a long shot.

'Your mother is so . . . exciting!' my teachers were always telling me after parent–teacher nights. 'Aren't you lucky, Sophie?'

Her vivacity charmed the pants off everyone. It was only me that caught the underside of it. But even when she'd been really shitty to me, I often saw a look immediately after that told me she regretted it. Without actually apologising she would often try to make it up afterwards. For example, she was kind for days after the tennis racquet fiasco.

'Come on, Soph,' she said when I got home from school that afternoon. 'Let's go and get you something lovely for your cousin's wedding.'

'But I thought I was going to wear the green dress,' I remember saying shyly, still embarrassed about my tears that morning.

'Nope,' my mother said, pulling one of my plaits playfully, letting me know she'd forgiven me completely. 'You are going to have something brand-new and lovely because it's your birthday.'

The tennis lessons were never mentioned again.

I woke for my third morning in Amy's shop and I saw that the sky was black with heavy, low clouds and the wind was whipping the trees around. I wondered about my family back home. What my father would be doing. Probably at work already. Mum would be at the gym. Lauren would be up, and making herself beautiful for another fabulous day.

I got up, had a shower and wondered what I should do. I hadn't brought any wet-weather things. Would my aunt give me a lift down the hill? But when I went down to the kitchen I saw that the light in the studio was on, that she was already at work. I felt too shy to interrupt her.

It was while I was fossicking around the porch for a pair of rubber boots that my aunt surprised me by coming in behind me through the back door. I'd already donned an old raincoat that had been my grandfather's.

'Oh, Sophie,' she said, holding out a letter to me. 'This came for you yesterday. I'm sorry I forgot to give it to you.'

The handwriting was my mother's and so I didn't take it immediately. In fact I just stood there, rigid, staring at it.

'Come on,' she said in this wry tone. 'It is for you.'

I shook my head.

'It won't bite,' she said softly, more sympathetically.

I took the letter then without meeting her eyes. 'Okay, thanks,' I mumbled, stuffing it into the pocket of the old raincoat. 'I'd better go or I'll be late.'

'Do you want a ride?' she asked kindly. 'It would be no trouble for me to run you down to Amy's. It's damned wet out there.'

'No, I'll be fine.' I turned and walked back into the kitchen before she could say anything else.

I sloshed my way down the hill to Amy's shop, deciding that I would give myself an hour. At exactly fifteen minutes to ten I would either read the letter or cut it up into tiny pieces. But either way seemed somehow too drastic. To actually destroy a letter before I'd even read what it had to say was . . . *just plain crazy.* On the other hand, if I did read it then it might destroy *me.*

Okay, living with my aunt wasn't brilliant, but it was definitely better than home. Sometimes I even had the feeling that things were slowly improving. At least my mother wasn't breathing down my neck. I'd stopped binge-eating. I didn't have murderous thoughts any more. Well . . . hardly ever. I was sleeping better. One sentence from my mother could end all that.

'You look like a drowned rat,' Amy said to me lightly as I stepped inside, trying to pull off the raincoat without making puddles on the floor. 'Come and get dry by the heater.'

'Thanks.'

I worked quietly in my corner. At exactly a quarter to ten I pulled the letter out of the raincoat pocket and brought it over to my desk. Then I pulled the scissors out of the drawer. I picked up the letter in my other hand, about to begin cutting, but suddenly stopped. *Okay . . . I don't really want to do this so . . . that means you have to open it!* But I didn't want to do that either. Feeling like an absolutely ridiculous piker, I slipped it into the drawer with the scissors and went back to work.

The work itself was boring and mechanical but I could look out into the quiet rainswept main street of Ballingo, listen to the wind and the sloshing noise of the running gutters. I enjoyed thinking back to what I'd seen in my aunt's studio. I wondered about her bridge drawing, thinking that in a way its origins were as dramatic as Mai's boat sketch.

The work had almost run out after only three days. I was hoping Amy would find me something else to do. I'd liked coming down to the shop these last few mornings. It gave a kind of structure to my day.

Because of the rain, this morning was particularly quiet. In fact, only one customer in two-and-a-half hours. An old man dressed in a floor-length Drizabone, wanting new batteries for his radio. Even as I was wondering how the shop was doing financially – there had probably only been a couple of dozen customers in the mornings I'd been there – I was enjoying the peaceful, almost sleepy feeling of being there. There was no radio on, no blaring voices, just this quiet stillness. Me tapping away in my corner and Amy gliding around the counters and shelves doing whatever – dusting, putting things away and tidying up.

Just after midday she went out, letting in a gust of cold air, and came back a few minutes later carrying a couple of take-away coffees and bags of hot food.

'Have some lunch?' she called to me on her way past.

'Okay,' I said, pleased. I got up and followed her down to the little lunch enclave at the back of the shop. The food smelt good and I was hungry. The idea of not going out into that squally weather, up to my aunt's house to eat lunch alone, was attractive too. Amy and I had hardly spoken since I'd been here. I don't know why I liked her but I did. I felt more easy with her than I did with my aunt. Sometimes I'd catch my aunt looking at me and I'd get the sense that she was trying to work me out. But Amy had barely asked me a question since I'd met her. Odd to think I would normally dismiss someone who looked like her. So small, with an ordinary little face and grey hair, boring clothes.

'You know I've more or less finished typing all that stuff in,' I said. 'Have you anything else . . . I could do?'

'Oh, have you?' she said, sounding surprised and pleased as she switched on the jug and took a couple of plates down from the rack above the sink. 'Do you want the chicken or the lamb?'

'I don't mind,' I said.

She tore open the brown paper, dumped the pies onto the plates and then sucked her burnt fingers. 'I went over and sneaked these from Jimmy's kitchen.'

'Thanks.' I smiled, taking the plate she offered, disappointed that she didn't pick up on my hint. A pang of loneliness hit me, unannounced. This would probably be my last day here. Ridiculous, but this little job was something. How could I just stay on at my aunt's without doing anything? What was I doing in this place with strangers? What about my friends, school, my future?

I noticed a framed photograph on the fridge. It was a sharp black-and-white image of two girls in their late teens standing in front of a flowering bush. Above and around them the woodwork of an old wooden house.

'Who is this?' I asked, picking up the photo for a closer look. It had obviously been taken some time ago. The fashions were very seventies.

'Have a good look,' Amy said with a smile and then sat down, taking up her knife and fork.

'Oh God!' I said, delighted, now recognising Fran. She was the tall one on the left, one hand on her hip, frowning into the camera. Thick, straight, dark hair pulled around to one side of her face, a peaked fake-leather John Lennon cap on her head and bangles coming up almost to her elbow. Dressed in a tight, horizontally striped tee-shirt and flared jeans, she looked the epitome of cool.

'And this is you!' I said, laughing, pointing to the smaller girl.

Amy nodded, laughing too. In the photo her hair was also very long. Dressed in a short-sleeved spotted blouse, mini-skirt and platformed shoes, she seemed more demure than Fran.

'Two friends,' I said, staring into the photo. 'Why do you both look so serious?'

'Oh, it was fashionable to be serious then,' Amy said and pointed at my pie. 'Don't let it get cold.'

I put the photo down and picked up my knife and fork.

'I remember that photo being taken actually,' she went on. 'It was early summer, before Christmas, and it was taken out the front of my aunt's house.'

'Had you left school?' I asked.

'Oh yes,' Amy said. 'I was about to turn twenty.'

She stopped eating and stared out the window, frowning deeply. 'That day was a big day for me. For both of us.'

I waited, hoping she'd continue. But she just went on quietly eating. I couldn't contain my curiosity after a few moments.

'So why?' I said. 'Why was it a big day?'

'Well, I'd been invited over to the O'Briens', to Fran's place, for my birthday. Everything went wrong. There was a scene over dinner. Daniel Readon arrived in the middle of it. Fran and him fell for each other.' Amy smiled.

'And . . .' I looked up briefly at Amy. 'What about you?'

'Oh well.' Amy blushed a little. 'That was the day I got the letter from my mother.'

What? A sudden rush of coldness went through me before I could tell myself I was being ridiculous. This was crazy. I pictured the letter from my mother sitting innocuously in the desk drawer, a bit like a little bomb ready to explode, and I had a sudden mad desire to tell Amy everything. Ask her advice. The lot. *The day I got the letter from my mother . . .*

'I'd never met my mother,' Amy went on, oblivious to my confusion. 'Up till then I didn't even know if she was alive or not.'

'Really?' I said. 'That's pretty . . . bizarre?'

'Yes,' Amy said simply. 'You might say that.'

We moved back into the main part of the shop just in case a customer came in wanting something. But no one did. The weather remained foul and the people of Ballingo remained at home in droves. I told myself that when Amy had finished talking I would know what to do with that letter sitting in the drawer.

Amy 1970

It arrived by post, addressed in scrawling black ink. To Amy Johnston, care of Robbertson's Haberdashery, Ballingo. After she'd opened it and read it through, heart pumping and hands shaking, Amy turned the envelope over and saw that there was a New South Wales coastal address on the back. Some place she'd vaguely heard of. None written on the page itself.

So she could write back *if* she wanted to, which she didn't. Not really anyway. *Did she?*

Amy stood in the back storeroom of Robbertson's for ages, staring out the window at the drops of rain dripping from the leaves of the huge jacaranda. Time seemed to be standing still. She wondered, quite seriously, if life as she'd known it up to this point had been in fact just a dream. Had any of what had happened before this been real at all?

It had begun like any other ordinary Friday morning. Amy had been standing behind the hosiery counter listening to Mrs Celia Mason moaning on about the cricket club. How they hadn't made enough to run the end-of-year ball, and wasn't that a complete tragedy. Underneath her polite demeanour Amy was thinking about the dinner she'd been invited to that night. She would be turning twenty in a week, and Fran's mother, Molly, wanted to give her a special dinner. Fran would be coming home from the city for the weekend and she'd already invited another girl, Patsy Nolan, who they'd both been friendly with at school. Jimmy was away in the army and Geraldine was nursing in Ballarat.

Amy had been delighted with the idea. She really missed Fran and they both liked Patsy.

That morning Molly had rung to say that Fran had decided to bring a male friend home with her for the weekend, and then Patsy had apologetically rung to say she had the 'flu and so couldn't make it. To top everything off, Geraldine had a couple of days off and had decided to come home. Should they call the whole thing off? Amy thought that a very good idea but heard the disappointment in Molly's voice and so decided not to say so.

'Let's just go ahead with it anyway,' Amy replied, taking a deep breath. 'We can still have a good time.'

'That's what I think too,' Molly had said, pleased. 'I've had the beef in wine all night and the soup is already made. You and Gerry and Fran and her friend will have a lovely time.' Then Molly started to worry that the fellow, Fran's friend, whatever his name was, would feel uncomfortable being the only male. Fran's dad was going to be out at a council meeting for most of the night. Maybe she should invite someone else as well. 'What about that nice boy who lives out on the farm next to you, Amy?'

'Daniel Readon?'

'Yes.' Molly was pleased. 'I'll ring and ask him along.'

Amy thought that was a good idea. Daniel had become a good friend over the last couple of years. They were the only ones from their year at school who'd stayed in the town.

Amy listened to Celia Mason politely for exactly ten minutes before deciding she was entitled to give a few hints that she had other things to do. The ladies' underwear table could do with tidying up and the new cardboards of buttons and elastic had to be sorted out. Also, she had to cut sixty-five blue ribbons for the primary school sports day.

Fran had sounded more like her old self when she'd rung the week before to tell Amy about her new boyfriend. Although they hadn't seen much of each other over the year, they'd kept in pretty close contact through phone calls and letters.

'Oh, Amy,' she'd burst out in the real old Fran style, half shy, half embarrassed, but excited. 'His name is Raymond. You'll love him. He's the most wonderful guy!'

'Is he a student?'

'Oh no,' Fran said breathlessly. 'No, he's passed all that. He's a *real* artist. A conceptual artist . . . so talented. So clever and he really . . .' she giggled. 'He really likes me!'

'A conceptual artist?'

'Well, it's art concerned with process and ideas rather than the end-product,' Fran said, slightly uncomfortable. 'He's helped me change my whole attitude. I'm learning heaps just being with him!' Fran hesitated, as though suddenly hearing herself gush. 'Can I tell you all about it when I see you?'

'Oh sure. Yeah. It sounds interesting,' Amy agreed

hurriedly, vaguely suspicious. She'd seen some of Fran's work and had been amazed. Beautiful, mainly small pastel portraits of people, some little cityscapes no more than a few inches square, framed in white, but rich in colour and detail in a way that made Amy feel very proud of her friend.

So who was this guy, that he could change the way she worked?

'I'm going to bring him up soon so you can meet him.'

'Can't wait!'

Being Friday, what Amy really needed to do was go out the back and check through the latest order from the city fashion wholesalers and think about how some of it might be displayed. Since Amy's rise to the position of assistant manager, the window displays were changed every week. But Celia, the arthritic wife of one of the town's prominent councillors, was still there, and not used to taking hints.

Seeing her stuck, Wally, the older Robbertson brother, intervened, holding out the slim white envelope for Amy.

'Excuse me Mrs Mason, but this is for you, Amy,' he said deferentially.

'Oh, thanks.' Surprised, Amy took the envelope. She hardly ever got letters, and certainly never before at the shop.

'I think you'd better go and see to it straightaway,' Wally added sternly, raising one eyebrow rakishly to let her know he was joking. 'It could be serious.'

'Oh yes.' Amy tried to keep a straight face. 'Yes, I'm expecting news from a . . . er friend in England.'

'That isn't from overseas,' Celia Mason sniffed, looking at the letter. 'No fancy stamps.'

'Perhaps I could help you, Mrs Mason,' Wally said, nudging Amy.

Within a minute Amy was out the back slitting open the envelope with a kitchen knife and thinking that it was what she loved about both the Robbertson brothers. Wally and Leo. Both bachelors and in their sixties. Under their old-fashioned suits, their circumspect manners, white shirts and dreadful striped ties, they were quick to see the funny side of most things. Amy had been working for them for nearly three years and, as well as liking them more than ever, she couldn't imagine being as happy in any other job.

My dear Daughter,

Soon you will be twenty. I've decided that the best present I could give you for your birthday is to let you know that not a day has passed since I signed those papers when I haven't thought about you, and wondered how your life is turning out. I know receiving this will probably be a shock, but I can only hope that the shock of it is offset by the knowledge that you do have a mother and that she has always loved you . . . and desperately wants to meet up with you again.

When I gave you away, I felt so totally alone in the world. It was the worst feeling, and one I hope you never experience. I can't bear to think of the deadly boring existence you'd be having with those two old aunts. They were always so conservative and never approved of me.

In case you're wondering, I live in a beautiful spot about two hours out of Nowra. Rainforest all around. Kangaroos, wombats. Beautiful birds.

We've got chooks and grow our own vegetables. There are even peach and avocado trees in this year. There is the river to swim in, only five minutes' walk. And of course the coast is only a few hours away. I've always known in my heart that I would get you back one day. It was just a matter of waiting for the right time. Now feels right to me. How about you? I really want you to come and live with me up here. But why don't you come up first for a visit and see how you like it? Let's make up for all the years that we've missed.

As always, I remain your loving mother.
Sylvie

Somehow Amy got through the next few hours. She decided not to make any decisions but to sit with the letter for a while and see what she felt like doing when she'd had a chance to digest it.

At lunchtime she went out walking, down to Ruby's Point, the letter sitting like a hot potato in her shoulder bag. She had the strange sensation that the people she smiled at and called hello to in the street were somehow aware of the letter, too. It was like something *alive* in her bag, wriggling around, demanding attention. Strange, she knew, but she couldn't get rid of the idea that she was carrying around something slightly dangerous; like a little snake. The pages might strike out into the air, any minute, poisoning everything, wreaking havoc.

Squatting down out of the wind in her favourite spot under two river gums, she had a good view of the old guest house on the rise opposite. Still sitting there. Still hiding all its secrets. Alone, she at last felt confident enough to bring out the letter. Her hands trembled as she read it through again.

My dear daughter . . .

Just those words on their own were enough. They held a kind of hypnotic power that made her almost swoon. *My dear daughter* . . .

Again and again she read the two pages of black scrawled words until she knew each line and phrase by heart. But instead of everything becoming clearer, she became more and more confused. Her mother had started her letter talking of *I* then it was *we*, without telling anything further about who she lived with. Did she live as a couple with a man or with a group of people? And how would they feel about a long-lost daughter coming to stay? There were all sorts of ways to interpret each line. Some of the phrases could have half-a-dozen meanings.

Amy had grown up hearing only vague snippets about her mother. She'd treasured them and, without ever telling anyone, she often thought about them when she was in bed.

'Your mother looked well in red, Amy,' Aunt Harriet had said once, a propos of nothing, with a small, disapproving frown, when Amy was only ten. 'Don't you think, Kath?'

'What's that?'

'Sylvia looked well in red?'

'Oh yes,' her other aunt had said in a non-committal way. 'All that dark hair and nice, fine skin. Red brought her colour up beautifully.'

Amy had asked questions of course, and the aunts didn't refuse to answer them, but as the years had rolled by and Amy had tried to ask more questions, she became aware that Harriet and Kath, usually so good-humoured and easygoing about almost everything else, from friends to talk about sex to current pop music, were tight-lipped when they answered questions about her mother.

'Not a bad person by any means,' Harriet had said sharply once. 'But nothing solid about her.'

'How do you mean . . . nothing solid?' Amy asked timidly.

'She was a selfish, giggly sort of a girl,' Kath had added. 'With silly opinions about things she knew nothing about.'

'You take after your grandfather, Amy,' they never failed to emphasise. 'Not just physically. But you're sensible like he was.'

'And a hard worker,' Harriet would add with a smile. 'Don't be worrying yourself about things you can't change, love.'

'I'm not worried,' Amy would say softly. 'I just want to know.'

'Of course you do,' Harriet would say heartily. 'And that's only natural. But really there isn't that much to know. She got pregnant to some young fellow who was passing through town when she was only seventeen — he was never seen again. But although she tried for a few months, she couldn't manage looking after you herself, so we, Kath and me and her father, offered to adopt you. Your mother, Sylvie, signed the papers, making it formal and then moved back to the city. The plan was that she'd come and visit when she could.'

'But she never did,' Amy said softly.

'No, well . . . dear,' Harriet said awkwardly. 'She was young and probably very busy with things.'

'She left within six months for overseas,' Kath said. 'And we've never really heard of her since.'

'Never? Did she . . . did she ever ring and see if I was all right?'

'No.' Harriet looked over at her sister, who was staring into the fireplace. 'She never contacted us, did she, Kath?'

'Not that I can remember,' Kath said. 'Maybe a Christmas card?'

'Yes,' Harriet said. 'That first Christmas we had a card I think but we never knew where she was. You see, her father died within a year of us taking you on. She didn't come home for the funeral.'

'In a way it was probably the sensible thing,' Kath added, kindly, tousling Amy's hair. 'She had to get on with her life I dare say, and she'd be wanting you to get on with yours.'

The only other thing to go on was the black-and-white photo sitting up on the piano along with baby portraits of the aunts and one of their parents. A formal head-and-shoulders portrait shot. Her mother's dark hair was pulled up at the back with a fringe at the front and large, expressive dark eyes shining underneath. She was smiling, looking up coyly into the lens as though she thought it funny to be having her picture taken. She looked young and excited and . . . brimming over with life.

How Amy had stared into that photo through the years, sometimes for up to an hour at a time, hoping to come across some little clue that would tell her more.

As the years wore on, Amy still wondered privately about her mother. Where did she live? And now that she was getting on with her own life, did she ever think of the baby she'd left behind? At around thirteen she went through a strange stage of thinking that she saw her mother all the time; in shops, in the street. The aunts became so concerned, they wanted to take her to a city doctor. Then the whole thing stopped suddenly, of its own accord. But she continued to wonder about her mother: what would she look like, was she still pretty like in the photo? And would she be disappointed if she came across her small, plain daughter by accident?

Although she never told anyone, Amy still sometimes had the dream that she'd often had as a child. Of being about ten years old, waiting on the road between the farm and Ballingo with the little suitcase that she'd had for her first day of school. Waiting for her mother to come and pick her up.

'Oh hi, Amy!' Geraldine opened the door smiling brightly, her dark curls bouncing in the fading light. 'Happy birthday for next week! How are you? Come in. This a nice idea of Mum's, isn't it?'

'Yeah.' Amy kissed Geraldine's cheek, thinking that the original idea had been nicer when it hadn't included having Geraldine and Fran together in the same room. 'How are you, Gerry? Fran arrived yet?'

'Yes.' Geraldine shook her head and then gave an impatient toss of her head. 'She and the boyfriend just went for a walk to get Mum something at the shop. You met him yet?'

'No, not yet.' Amy tried to ignore the acerbic tone. 'I haven't seen Fran in ages.'

Geraldine wrinkled up her nose and shrugged. 'Come on in,' she said, taking Amy's arm. 'And tell us what's been happening with you.'

Gerry looked lovely, as usual, in a bright sapphire-blue long-sleeved cotton tunic that had a deep fringe along the bottom with tight jeans underneath and high-heeled blue sandals.

'Not much!' Amy laughed.

Gerry's eyes were dripping in eye-liner and bright blue shadow. Her lips were bright pink and her cheeks blushed to perfection and yet she somehow managed to look totally natural. Even a little make-up made Amy feel self-conscious and silly. She knew her pale features actually needed it more than Fran or Geraldine's and yet she couldn't bring herself to use it.

Will I tell them about my letter? No. Not yet, and not Geraldine. She would wait for a moment over the weekend when she was alone with Fran. She quite liked Geraldine but didn't trust her with such precious news.

They walked through to the kitchen. The round table was beautifully set with candles and flowers in green and red. Molly was at the stove putting the finishing touches to the delicious smelling cream-based soup. Plates of dips and dry biscuits were already on the table. She looked up with a smile.

'Amy, darling. How are you?' She beamed. 'And don't you look a picture as usual!'

'Hi, Molly.' Amy blushed, pleased. When she was twelve and one of her aunts had got very sick, she'd ended up living with the O'Briens for a couple of years, and she had loved Molly unreservedly. Had always secretly considered her the mother she was meant to have. 'So what are we eating?' she asked, accepting the older woman's kiss. 'Smells good!'

'Crab soup and beef.' Molly waved proudly at the rest of the sumptuous dishes that were lining the bench, very pleased with herself. 'Gerry, why don't you take a bottle from the fridge, and take Amy into the lounge room with a bowl of dip or something from the table while I finish off here.'

Amy followed Gerry into the front room, aware of a desperate feeling growing inside her chest. She'd forgotten how . . . *full-on* the O'Brien's en masse were. How was she going to last all night without speaking of the one thing that she couldn't stop thinking about?

Only minutes later Fran and her friend arrived at the front door. Fran was dressed in a long white silky caftan, that was pulled in at the middle by a purple macramé belt. Her hair was pulled back from her face and tied at the back with a wide purple scarf. The last time Amy had seen Fran was the previous Easter and she'd been . . . hyped up somehow. Friendly of course – Fran was always friendly – but talking non-stop about Vietnam, about how everyone in her house in the city was involved in organising a moratorium against the war. So many different people were going to be involved. She'd got herself arrested at some demonstration too, and now she had to find the money to pay the fine without letting her parents know.

Amy hadn't known what to say. The things Fran was saying seemed exaggerated, wild even, although Amy supposed they might be true. She didn't read the papers that often herself. It was on the news every night of course, the war and . . . all the things Fran was talking about. That is, if you bothered to watch the news and didn't find something else to look at while they were showing you the terrible bits. Nixon was dropping megatons of bombs on Vietnam. Burning villages. People were dying every day. But Amy wasn't all that sure where Vietnam was.

'Amy! How are you going?' Fran hugged her warmly. 'Happy birthday for next week. I've got you a present but I'm going to send it to you so you get it on the day!'

Fran turned to introduce the man who'd come in behind her.

'I'd like you to meet Raymond!' Fran said proudly. He was tall and thin with long dark hair and brown eyes set deep into their sockets. Probably in his late twenties. He had prominent cheekbones and a full red mouth. 'This is my old school friend, Amy,' Fran said excitedly.

'Yeah!' Raymond said drily, looking away as though bored with the company already. 'Hi.'

Amy took the limp hand that was offered and tried to tell herself not to judge too quickly. The man was tall and dark and handsome. He was wearing tattered jeans, sandals and a collarless white shirt. It was the eyes, really, that made her feel uncomfortable. They slid all over the place instead of looking at her as they were introduced.

'Good to meet you, Raymond,' Amy said gamely.

'Well thank you. I'm sure.' He was surely mocking them all with this southern American drawl. 'And they tell me you're having a birthday?'

He had struck completely the wrong note. Fran looked uncomfortably at the other two as he wandered off to check the bookshelves.

'Raymond is an artist . . .' she began boldly. 'He's working . . .'

'How about a drink?' Geraldine cut in coldly, heading for the trolley in the corner. On top of the silver tray was the opened champagne bottle and half a dozen crystal glasses. Underneath, a collection of spirits: whisky, gin and vodka.

'Champagne okay for you, Raymond?' By this stage he was over at the window thumbing through the gardening books.

'Oh yeah!' He looked up, seemingly unaware of the tension he'd created. 'Fantastic. Oh but . . .' He grinned as he spied the spirits. 'Could I have a whisky or is that out of bounds?'

'No, no,' Geraldine said demurely. 'Nothing out of bounds here, Raymond. How do you have it?'

'A double thanks, with ice.'

When Gerry went out of the room for the ice, Raymond turned to Fran with a short, incredulous laugh, pointing back at the rows of books about gardens and plants and cookery.

'I always wondered who bought this kind of crap!'

'Mum is a wonderful gardener!' Fran said defensively.

To Amy's complete surprise he leapt up suddenly and wrapped both arms around Fran's shoulders, burying his face in her hair. She tried to shrug him off but couldn't quite manage it.

'Of course she is wonderful, Fran!' he said. 'Like everyone else in the whole world, according to you!'

Geraldine came back with the ice to find Fran trying to push Raymond off, grimacing with embarrassment. The slight tension that Amy had felt since she'd walked in the door tightened and then moved up a notch or two. *This is going to be a disaster. Why didn't I just tell Molly to forget it?*

'What have I said, sweetie?' Raymond said, all mocking baby-voice now, oblivious to the others, who didn't know where to look, trying to lift her chin up to kiss her. 'Come on baby . . . tell me.'

'Please, Raymond,' she pleaded. 'Just don't . . .'

Geraldine looked on with sneering contempt and Amy looked at the floor. Raymond suddenly pulled away from Fran.

'Do you have any idea how very talented your friend is?' he said loudly to Amy, then he turned to glare with narrowed eyes at Geraldine. 'Your sister? Next weekend she will be making *great art* in the city square. Together we are going to turn that whole city on its head! Are you going to be there to support her? Or are you both going to be back here making chit-chat over nice little country dinners?'

Amy stared at him speechlessly. Lost for what to do or say, she took the double whisky with ice from Geraldine, who looked like she was going to throw it in his face, and handed it to him.

'Well,' Geraldine said with a cool smile, 'that doesn't sound all that exciting to me, really, Raymond and . . .' She turned the full blaze of her beautiful blue eyes on him for a couple of moments. 'For your information, Amy is the manager of a highly prestigious local shop! And I'm a fully qualified nurse! Neither of us just sit around having dinners all day.'

There was a moment of silence. Amy saw that now Fran's ire was up.

'He was just telling you about the art, Gerry!' she protested furiously. 'There is no need to give a lecture!'

'I'd like to come,' Amy murmured trying to smooth things over. 'What is it exactly, Fran?'

'A sort of installation,' Fran mumbled nervously. 'It's about . . . *time* . . . and . . . the way we are programmed to get hooked up in other people's ideas of it and –'

'Sort of *nothing*!' Raymond cut in sharply, ignoring Geraldine and pointing belligerently at Amy. 'We will have *twenty-four* people in the middle of the city, climbing ladders at exactly the same time. Incidentally, Fran is the one making sure this happening is in sync. That's her job. And it's a key role. At exactly the same time as the men reach the top of the ladders, a case filled with a dozen live ducks will be released onto a specially erected stage outside Myer. Then I shall personally be ushering them up Bourke Street towards the Melbourne Club with an electric cattle prod. Into the very heart of the establishment! There I will be met by five musicians on stilts . . . plus the ladder climbers who will be walking in to this central point with their ladders from all directions around the city.' He was gesticulating wildly with one arm as he talked taking slurps of whisky in between sentences. 'Together we shall then invade the Melbourne Club . . .'

Geraldine was staring at him open-mouthed.

'It's a statement about privilege,' he said, 'and about time, and all the useless hype around it.' He looked around covetously. 'Who owns this joint, by the way?'

'My parents,' Fran said through clenched teeth. And then, in a low voice, 'Who do you think?'

'Hmmm.' He nodded knowingly a few times, as though this was a very difficult piece of information to digest. 'They inherited it, I suppose?'

'Amy and Gerry, you don't have to come,' Fran cut in, flushing deeply. 'It's not exactly . . .' Her voice petered away.

'Yes they do,' Raymond said forcefully. 'It's very important that the whole thing is witnessed by as many people as possible.'

'But it won't be to everyone's taste,' Fran butted in again.

'Oh Fran, Fran!' Raymond sighed deeply and took another deep gulp of whisky and shuddered as it slid down his throat. 'When did *taste* have anything to do with it? The thing will be a knockout!' He almost shouted the last sentence, and then suddenly seemed to lose interest. 'Look, why don't I just take myself outside for a while before it gets dark? I'll have a smoke and have a prowl around. You gals probably need to have a talk.'

Geraldine gulped, shook her head, then met Amy's stunned look with one of her own. As far as they were concerned it was the most reasonable thing he'd said since he'd arrived. He headed outside and Fran collapsed onto the comfortable chair near the door.

'So Amy,' Fran said gamely, ignoring her sister. 'What's news?'

Feeling shy, Amy made the mistake of beginning to blab on about Jimmy, who was about to begin his stint in Vietnam; how pleased she'd been when he'd come to see her just before he'd left. He'd wanted to know if she thought he was doing the right thing going there.

'And what did you say?' Fran snapped, immediately alert and staring at Amy intently. With a sinking heart, Amy knew this was exactly the wrong topic to bring up.

'What could I say, Fran?' She shrugged uncomfortably. 'He was in his uniform.'

'So what *did* you say?' Fran insisted. 'He asked you.'

'I said I didn't know,' Amy said defensively, trying to ignore Fran's incredulous look. 'Which I don't! But it was his decision and I wished him luck.'

'Oh God, Amy!' Fran picked up her wine glass, took a big gulp and looked away. '*My own brother*. I can't believe he is going. Is that all? You wished him *luck*! What? Luck in dropping bombs on innocent peasants or . . . luck in getting to kill lots of people?'

'Fran!' Geraldine cut in warningly. 'Put a sock in it! You promised Mum and Dad you would not mention that topic in this house again. This is a dinner, okay? No one wants to discuss the war.'

Fran took a deep breath. 'Right.'

'Dinner is served,' Molly declared breezily, oblivious to the tense atmosphere. 'Please come to the table! No, don't bring your glasses,' she called, her back already turned. 'Wine is open on the table!'

At the point when Mrs O'Brien was proudly carrying across the bowls of delicious-smelling soup to the table, Raymond declared himself a vegetarian and, no, he didn't eat fish either and so he couldn't possibly partake of the crab soup. Eyes lowered, Fran picked up her soup spoon and gulped.

'Oh dear.' Molly was momentarily flustered.

'Raymond,' Fran whispered as her mother carried the bowl of soup back to the stove, 'you're *not* a vegetarian!'

'I am,' he declared, gloating at her discomfort.

'Since when?'

'From last night,' he said, and then added loudly, 'I saw a film about the way they kill the animals on television and I decided there and then I would have to quit.'

'I'm sorry, Mum,' Fran said, trying to keep calm. 'I should have let you know but I . . . er, forgot completely.'

'No worries, darling!' Molly replied, genuinely seeming not to mind. 'Our fault entirely. We should have asked. Now, we do have a meat dish to follow, so, how does my lovely mushroom omelette sound, Raymond? I got the recipe when I was honeymooning in France twenty-eight years ago. I'll be able to whip it up in a few minutes. Everyone always loves it.'

'Thank you, Mrs O'Brien,' Raymond said grandly, gulping down his second double-Scotch and reaching immediately for the wine bottle, 'but I'm a *vegan*, which means no dairy products at all. Eggs are definitely out. Same with cheese and milk.'

Molly managed to look bemused rather than cross, although Amy could see the glint in her eye which usually meant something else was bubbling along underneath as well.

'Well!' she said calmly. 'I'm not sure what we can do. There's bread and . . .'

'Bread will be fine,' he declared.

'And there's lovely salad.'

'I'll be fine.' He threw back his head and gave a harsh laugh. 'Hope no one objects to me smoking?' Amy and Fran shook their heads. Geraldine simply stared. No one said anything. Raymond lit the cigarette and blew the smoke over the table. 'Go ahead,' he said sourly. 'Eat your murdered animals and . . . *enjoy*!'

The dinner was ruined. Who could possibly enjoy the perfectly judged crab soup, the crusty rolls and pâté? The home-grown tomatoes and beets and beans. The new potatoes. The locally slaughtered, perfectly cooked beef. The apricot pie made from the previous summer's heavy harvest from the tree just outside the back door. The whole thing was wrecked.

Amy got quieter and quieter. As the conversation lurched from one awful topic to the next, Raymond becoming increasingly belligerent and rude, battling with Geraldine, who refused to let him get away with all his posturing. For Amy it was a new, oddly interesting sensation.

Had any dinner ever gone as badly as this one? Poor Molly, after all her hard work, had been bewildered, wondering what she'd done wrong. Amy sat at the table getting angrier and more upset than she'd ever been in her entire life. It was scary really, and that was why she let the raucous chatter and sarcastic comments go on around her without saying anything. She didn't trust the feeling, kept thinking it would die away soon. It was frightening too, to think that she, little Amy, mild and easygoing, *plain* little Amy, was imagining picking up a meat knife and stabbing this guy in the back with it.

'Shit! Where did she get *him* from?' Geraldine hissed at Amy on the way back from the bathroom, in between courses. 'Listen, Amy, I didn't know he was so awful or . . . honestly, I would have insisted that Fran not inflict him on us!'

Amy shrugged, tight-mouthed, leant up against the hallway wall and closed her eyes.

'It's not your fault.'

'I know.' Geraldine caught her arm. 'But it's horrible for you,' she said with unusual warmth and force. 'And for Mum of course. This was to celebrate your birthday. I'm really sorry.'

Amy gulped. She felt her mouth beginning to tremble but managed to fight it off. She hadn't cried since she was twelve and she wasn't about to start now.

'I think we should get rid of him,' Geraldine said urgently.

'I agree,' Amy said, surprising herself. 'But how?' She

had never sided with Geraldine before but this . . . this was different. Fran seemed to have taken leave of her senses.

'Leave it to me,' Geraldine said. 'I'll think of something.'

'The thing is not to hurt Fran in the process,' Amy said loyally.

'I don't care if we do hurt Fran,' Geraldine shot back fiercely.

They went into the kitchen where Fran was sitting opposite Raymond. He had a pack of cards on the table and was showing her how to play patience. Fran was trying to act charmed and amused but Amy could tell she was freaked out.

'So, do you two usually go take a piss together?' Raymond asked without raising his eyes from the cards. 'Or were you just having a little meeting by yourselves?' Obviously drunk, his words were slurred and loud.

'We were just talking things over,' Geraldine answered quickly.

'Oh?' Challenged by her hard tone, Raymond looked up.

'Have you got a car here, Raymond?' Geraldine asked, all fake sweetness and light.

'Yes,' he said, every trace of drunkenness suddenly gone.

'Well, I think you should get in it and take yourself back to the city. In fact,' Geraldine went on coolly, looking at her watch, 'Dad will be back from his council meeting soon. You better be gone by the time he gets back. Because if you're not, I'm going to ask him, and the man next door, to physically throw you out.'

'Geraldine!' Fran gasped furiously. 'How dare you say that!'

'I do dare, Fran,' Geraldine snapped. 'It is really quite easy. You should try it some time.'

There was a chilly silence as the two sisters stared at each other, the animosity between them almost palpable in the smoky air. Amy looked from one to the other and wondered, not for the first time, if there really was something to those rumours that had flown around town a couple of years before. Rumours about Fran and Paul Healey. But her friend, who told her everything, hadn't said a word. At the time Amy had refused to insult Fran by asking directly.

But these two used to talk and laugh and get on like normal sisters . . . something must have happened.

Raymond, shaking his head and smiling, had gone back to the cards.

'Your family is so *uptight*!' he said casually to Fran. 'Take your old man. He was hung up for the whole ten minutes I saw him before that meeting. It's the old primal male instinct. He wanted to punch out the guy who is screwing his daughter!'

'That's not true,' Fran said miserably.

'Honey, some things have to be faced.' Raymond smirked to himself as he clapped one card down on top of another.

'And you're not screwing me!' she said hotly.

'So what were we doing last night?'

Fran groaned and looked away, her face hot with humiliation.

'I don't blame Dad at all,' Geraldine cut in. 'If I were him I'd want to punch you too.'

'Would you now?' Raymond looked up with a smile but his eyes were as cold as a snake's.

'Yeah. I would,' Geraldine said loudly. She looked

over to Fran who was glaring at her. 'For God's sake, tell him to go.'

'Geraldine,' Fran said in a small, determinedly calm voice. 'It is *you* that has come to this dinner uninvited! This is Amy's party, not yours.'

They all turned to look at Amy who was sitting quite still, looking at her hands. Raymond continued to put out the cards, still smiling.

'So, Amy, do *you* want us to go?' he said without looking at her. 'Are you of the same mind as your boring little bourgeois friend here?'

'You creep!' Geraldine spat at him. 'Don't you dare put it on Amy!'

Unable to stand the tension any longer, Amy suddenly jumped to her feet, let out a scream and stood there trembling. She wanted to go on screaming but the sound of her first cry had shocked her just as much as it had the others. She wanted to hit the guy, yell at Fran, at them all. She had a mother. *A mother.* After so many years she now knew her very own mother was out there, waiting for her. She couldn't stand it any more. A gust of something hot and terrible rushed up from the depths of her body. Within only a few seconds she felt herself become a huge dam; about to burst with all that boiling sludge inside her. The others staring up at her in shocked silence. Amy was lost. She didn't know who she was any more.

She crumpled suddenly. Her legs simply gave way and she fell to the floor in a flood of tears. Loud, terrible, tearing sobs that wouldn't stop. 'Oh God,' she wept, rocking herself, hands over her eyes. 'Oh God. Oh God!' All the tears that she'd never cried were suddenly there, waiting to be released, longing to get out.

'What is it, Amy?' Geraldine knelt down, putting her bright-pink-nailed hand on Amy's shoulder. 'Please don't cry like that! What is it?'

But Amy shrugged her away and continued to weep. 'Get away from me,' she managed to gasp between her sobs. 'The lot of you!'

'But Amy.' Geraldine hesitated, unsure what to do. Raymond was sitting at the table still, cleaning his fingernails with a toothpick, quietly chuckling to himself. 'Get out of here, you *bastard*,' Geraldine screamed at him. 'You bloody weirdo! You really get your rocks off on this, don't you? For God's sake, Fran, can you do one sensible thing in your stupid life and get him out?'

But Fran, standing now, watching, her face as white and tense as a ghost's, seemed to have become immobilised.

Amy's sobbing became louder, more desperate. Geraldine turned back to her. Putting both arms around her now, she began to rock with her on the floor.

'Come on, Amy,' she murmured. 'Don't cry. It's not that bad, honey! We're your friends!'

'No . . . no!' Amy moaned. 'Please, all of you. Please just ring up my aunts. I want to go home!'

The door swung open.

'Daniel is here, Amy, and . . .' Molly walked in, followed by Daniel. 'I thought I heard the bell and . . .' Molly stopped in mid-sentence.

The room was in disarray. The air full of smoke, dishes all over the table, Amy on the floor sobbing, with Geraldine kneeling, trying to comfort her. Fran was standing on the other side of the table, arms folded tightly over her chest, her face tense and white. The only person who looked vaguely calm was Raymond. His chair pushed back, he had one leg up on the table.

'My God,' Molly exclaimed. 'What in heavens is going on here?' She looked accusingly at Fran and then Geraldine. 'Girls, what's happening?'

'Oh, Mrs O'Brien!' Raymond cut in, laughing. 'This night has been truly superb. Congratulations. You have, whether you know it yourself, created a very subtle *work of art*.' He turned to Fran. 'Can you see it yet, my dear, sweet Fran? This is what it's all about. What I've been talking about all these months.'

But Fran wasn't listening. Or maybe it was his words that moved her suddenly into action. She lunged for the bread knife on the table and then, pointing it at Raymond, began to yell.

'Get out of here! Now. Or I'll kill you. I promise you. I will! I'll kill you!'

Raymond didn't get up from his seat, but put both hands up in an attitude of mock surrender.

'Now, Fran,' he said coolly, still smiling. 'There is no need to get excited. I merely said —'

Catching him completely by surprise, Fran lunged across the table at him with the knife, getting him with it just below the rib cage. Luckily the knife was too blunt to do any real damage, although the intention was obviously there. Nevertheless, Raymond doubled up, roared loudly in protest and then fell backwards off his chair. Molly and Geraldine let out shocked screams. Immobile with surprise in the doorway, Daniel saw that Fran was trying to climb across the table and repeat the action with more force. He ran over to her and began wrestling the knife from her grasp.

Amy lifted her head up to see what was happening

and was so surprised that she immediately stopped crying.

'Let me alone,' Fran panted as she struggled to fight Daniel off. 'I want to . . . get him. Daniel . . . you just leave me alone!'

'Sorry . . . but . . . you can't,' Daniel grunted. He had both her arms above her head now, pushing her back up against the wall, holding her wrists in one hand and trying to prize open her fingers with the other. 'Next time. Come on, Fran, stop this.'

'*You* stop it. Leave me alone!'

'No. You stop it!'

At last he had it. He threw the knife onto the floor and, panting with exertion and leaning against her, he waited for her to stop struggling before slowly releasing her arms. One at a time. From her angle on the floor Amy could see their faces in silhouette. Daniel's lovely mouth just above her nose. His hair dark and curly in the candlelight. One strong hand still on her trembling shoulder, the other still grasping the hand that had held the knife. Quietness descended around them. They were looking into each other's eyes. Amy stopped breathing. She could almost feel in her own belly the heavy bolt of attraction crackle to life between them, as real and fascinating as a flash of brilliant lightning. Then it was gone.

My God, she thought, hardly able to believe it. They'd been on the verge of kissing each other!

She watched Daniel move away, blinking a little, as though bewildered. And Fran standing there rubbing her wrists, breathing hard, still trembling slightly, looking at the floor. Amy smiled. It was funny really, seeing them both trying to disown what had just happened. The raw sexiness of what she'd just witnessed created a sudden swell of loneliness inside her own chest, making her insides heave with longing. Would something wonderful like that ever happen to her . . . or would it always be for other people? She sighed, feeling suddenly exhausted, trying not to be jealous, on the verge of tears again.

And then the knowledge came to her, very clearly. *You must at least go and see your mother.* She knew as she sat there on the floor, half-listening to the accusations, the slam of the door as Raymond stormed out, the cries of apology, the explanations, loud shouting and eventually the laughter that broke out around her like waves at the beach, that she would always feel an outsider. She would always be shut out from her own life until she found her mother.

It had been Daniel Readon who'd talked her into going finally. He'd called around a couple of nights after the disastrous dinner. The days were now longer and, having had an early tea with the aunts, Amy was doing some digging in the garden, and brooding over how it might turn out with her mother. Dressed as usual in his work clothes and boots, Daniel got out of the Land Rover and, grinning, walked over to her.

'How's it going, Amy?'

Within minutes she was sitting on the veranda with him and blurting out the whole thing.

'Listen, Amy,' he said, 'she sounds all right. You'd never forgive yourself if you don't at least give it a go. You never know, maybe she's as scared as you about it.'

'I'm not scared!'

Daniel looked at her wryly and Amy started to laugh.

'Well, maybe a little bit.'

That was the great thing about Daniel. He would often lighten her up when she was down, and he did things to build her up as well. (Like invite her to the Ballingo Ball in July when everyone else was going and as usual Amy didn't have a partner.) They'd had a great time together. Dancing, talking and horsing around. There was no other person in Ballingo her own age that she felt as close to. Their houses were close and on his way back from Ballingo he often dropped by for a chat. Both Kath and Harriet adored him for his good looks, manners and gentleness. Amy knew that they secretly wished for a romantic relationship to develop (in spite of the religious difference) and found it hard to believe that both Daniel and Amy considered their friendship platonic.

'So how are you?' she asked, nudging him. 'I've been raving on about myself non-stop for about an hour.'

Daniel smiled and looked down. 'I've got news actually.'

'What?'

'I've decided to go to university next year,' he said quietly. 'I mean, I'll come back to the farm eventually but . . . I need to get away and do some study.' He looked at her with another of his wry smiles. 'And learn a bit.'

The news hit Amy like a ton of bricks. Her one local friend and he was going to leave. She tried to keep her face from giving way to her feelings. 'What do you need to learn about?'

'History, politics . . . all kinds of stuff.' He smiled. 'I try to read but I get lost in it all. I think I really need to do a proper course.'

'But who will run the farm?' Amy said in a small voice.

'We'll get a manager in,' Daniel replied, a little

uneasily. His tone was matter-of-fact and to the point though. 'Of course Mum knows a lot as well but she won't be able to manage the heavy work. So we'll get someone in for a year or two . . . however long it takes.'

Amy didn't know what to say. She suddenly realised that she relied on Daniel. In fact her whole idea of herself as being happy working in this town was somehow dependent on him being around as her friend. It was devastating to think he wouldn't be there any longer. She opened her mouth to speak again, but nothing came out.

'I'll come home a lot,' he said gently, as though reading her thoughts. The kindness in his tone made her throat choke up. Damn it! She gulped and made herself swallow. She was turning into a complete sop lately. It would look so bad if she cried.

'How about I get us a cup of coffee,' she said suddenly, jumping up. 'And you can tell me more about it.'

'Sure.' Daniel sounded a little surprised as he followed her into the kitchen. 'But what do you think about it, Amy? Do you think it's a crazy idea or what?'

Amy was filling the kettle at the sink. 'If it's what you want,' she said, with as much conviction as she could muster. 'Then yeah, I think it's a good idea. When do you go?'

'Not till next March,' he said slowly, going to the window and looking out discontentedly. 'God! Now I've decided, I really can't wait.'

Amy was dying inside but what could she say? Why did everyone want to leave their town? Everyone young and interesting. All her friends. Soon there would be no one left. *My life amounts to just a succession of people leaving me.*

'Hey listen,' he said, leaning across and touching her hand briefly. 'There is something else I came about too.'

She looked up and saw that he hadn't guessed her mood at all. He was smiling at her confidentially, as though everything was fine.

'I wondered,' he said, colouring slightly, 'if you had Fran's address.'

'Fran O'Brien?' Amy said, surprised.

'Yeah.' Daniel was embarrassed.

'Yeah, of course I have,' Amy said. 'I'll go get it for you.' She moved to get out of her seat. 'Why? Are you . . .' And then she stopped, remembering the moment between them during the disastrous dinner. The raw attraction that had suddenly surfaced and the way they'd both been so keen to deny it. Her spirits fell another few notches as she tried not to mind.

'I'm going to Melbourne next week.' Daniel was self-conscious in trying to explain himself. 'To see about enrolling. I just thought . . . well . . . it was really good to see her again. In spite of the actual situation.' He grinned at Amy and then added hopefully, 'I thought I'd look her up. What do you think?'

Amy swallowed hard and said nothing.

'Do you think she'd be into it?' Daniel persisted.

Amy knew suddenly she was jealous. Terribly. Daniel was her friend. She hadn't been at all jealous when he'd told her about other girls. *But Fran?* This was different. It wasn't fair for that attraction to come alive now. On top of everything else, it just wasn't fair!

'I dunno, Dan,' she said evenly, furious at herself for being so mean-spirited but unable to stop the flood of ill-feeling that was coursing through her. 'The last thing Fran said to me on the Sunday after that terrible dinner was that she didn't want anything to do with men for a long time. She wasn't interested in going out with anyone.' *What a bitch I am, telling him this!*

But instead of putting him off, the information only made Daniel throw back his head and laugh.

'Well!' was all he said. 'That last boyfriend was a bummer, heh?'

Amy nodded and tried to smile. 'Yeah,' she managed. 'He was a creep.'

'So can I have that address?'

'Sure.' Amy sighed and got up. 'I'll get it now.'

We'd both long finished our pies. I was sipping my second cup of coffee, waiting for Amy to continue. Every so often she would peer around the shop to make sure it was still empty.

'So did you go up to meet your mother?' I asked eagerly. Why had she stopped talking? She was looking dreamily out the window as though she'd lost her train of thought entirely.

'Hmmm.'

'What was it like?'

Amy sighed then turned back to me with a grim smile. 'A complete and utter disaster.'

'Why?' For some reason I was shocked. I suppose I was expecting . . . a happy ending to it all.

'She was living on this commune about three hours from the nearest big town,' Amy replied, shuddering slightly as she picked up the paper bags, screwed them up and threw them in the bin. 'No running water or electricity. You might even think it would be fun to live back in last century until you've done it for a few days. There was no radio, or TV, no washing machine. One gas-burner for cooking. God, it was so primitive.'

'How many people?' I was trying to imagine it.

'About seventy!' Amy got up and started rinsing our few dishes under the tap. She snorted with laughter. 'They were all into astrology, massage, crystals, you name it! The men were anyway. The women did the work! Washing, cooking, growing the vegetables and looking after the children. But the worst of it was, they were so arrogant. They really thought they were doing something so incredibly wonderful.'

'But how did you get on with her?' I cut in. I was desperate to hear that she and her mum had hit it off after all those years of being apart. 'I mean, could you talk to her?'

'Not really. She was right into this alternative way of living and I . . . well, I think she'd taken a lot of drugs. I was too young to appreciate that she was just trying to find herself. I'd built up a picture in my head of who my mother was and when she didn't fit it, then kebang! I was very hard on her. I had no idea of her pain, if you know what I mean.'

I nodded slowly. This was moving into emotionally slippery territory but still, I wanted her to continue.

'I mean, relinquishing a child and all that,' Amy went on hurriedly, sensing my sudden unease. 'But I had my own . . . pain.'

'So do you . . . ?' I felt depressed suddenly. 'Do you see anything of her now?'

'Oh yes,' Amy said. 'We get on well enough. We write to each other. And I see her every Christmas. But it took a long time. It was a . . . long, slow rebuild.'

'How long did you stay up there on the commune?'

I was fascinated in spite of myself. Here was a person who'd experienced a real-life commune back in the seventies, just like the kind that Schmity used to talk about in history.

'Only three weeks,' Amy replied. 'She was devastated that I decided to return to Victoria. But I hated that place. I hated the squalid conditions and the fact that all day was spent just doing basic things to survive. And . . . I missed everyone. My friends, my aunts. I remember being so pleased that I had them to come home to, and that she had given me away to them.'

'But she was your mother,' I protested. 'And you were desperate to meet her. Surely it must have been . . . good on some level?' My voice died a little at the end of the question.

Amy was looking up at me wryly and it only took me a few moments to realise what that look meant.

Listen to yourself, girl.

Look at your own life!

How much do you miss your mother?

I found myself flushing defensively, hoping like mad that she wasn't going to hit *me* with questions about my own family because I wouldn't be able to handle it. It was what the small silence between us was begging for though, I knew that.

'So did Fran and Daniel start going together after that crazy dinner?' I jumped in quickly, thinking that it was up to me to change the subject.

'Oh God, no!' Amy laughed. 'Fran was so contrary in those days. They were absolutely right for each other those two but Fran had to spend about another five years finding it out. Drove everyone to distraction, including poor Daniel, who was such a *hunk*! Every other woman was after him and Fran couldn't see for ages just how gorgeous he was.'

I picked up the photo again and smiled. My aunt did have a very sassy, defiant air to her. I remembered my Uncle Dan as a gentle man. And I suppose he *was* good looking, in a broad, strong Aussie way – thick, muscly brown arms, huge feet and hands, nice deep-set blue eyes – but he was quiet. And I suppose as a kid I tended to overlook him. When everyone else was yelling and arguing around the Christmas dinner table – there was always a lot of laughter and joking, in spite of the Mum and Fran stand-off – Uncle Dan would be concentrating on his food, or looking around benignly, smiling, asking questions and listening to everyone else.

'So she really gave him the runaround?' I asked with a grin.

Amy nodded and got up. 'Fran is one of the most complex people I know, Sophie,' she said emphatically. 'Always was. Just when you think you've got her worked out she . . . surprises you.'

I nodded and got up to wash my cup. I had the distinct feeling that Amy was trying to tell me something, but although I was curious, I wasn't game to ask what exactly.

When the phone rang Amy got up to answer it and a couple of people came in for small items. I reluctantly left the little lunch alcove and went to serve them, thinking all the time about what Amy had told me and trying to piece things together so they made sense.

It was still raining, the gutters were rushing and gurgling, no one much was about outside. After the door closed shut on the last customer I went back to my desk near the window, got the letter from my mother out of the drawer and, without even hesitating, I chopped it up into tiny pieces. A few seconds of pure gladness as I dropped all the tiny strips into the wastepaper basket. Whatever she had written would now never touch me. After doing that I quickly slipped on my big raincoat and boots and walked to the door.

'Thanks for lunch, Amy,' I called.

'Oh, Sophie.' She looked up with a warm smile. 'You're welcome. Will you be right walking back in this squall?'

'Yep.' Hand on the door, I stopped, turned.

'What about Raymond?' I asked quickly. 'Do you know what happened to him?' The story of Amy and her mother had disturbed me and so I desperately wanted to get my mind on to anything else.

'Oh, Raymond!' Amy seemed pleased to be asked. 'Very much alive and well. He actually runs a very successful business, about four kilometres away from here.'

'You're kidding,' I said. 'Do you ever see him?'

'Occasionally.' Amy smiled. 'He comes in for some little thing like a packet of soap or golf balls every now and again. I think he really comes to check up on everyone. He's still the same. A busybody. Still interested in Fran. Calls her his "assassin". *And how is my assassin getting on?* Amy giggled. 'The only difference is, he wears loud ties and expensive suits now. And last time I saw him he was in a silver Porsche.' Amy met my eye, serious for a moment. 'But don't even mention his name to Fran, will you? She just loathes him!'

I took off up the hill. Then when I was almost home, opposite the house in fact, I turned around and went straight back down again. Everything was spinning around in my head. *Amy's mother, my mother . . . ?* My only hope was to try and get back on track with Mr Schmit again – into an old question-answer session, but for some reason I couldn't. I knew I'd go even crazier holed up in my room thinking about it. In spite of the weather, I walked out along the river to Ruby's Point. I also wanted to see Grandview in this drab, wet, grey light. When I was in fresh air looking at that place, the bridge and the sky, my head didn't seem to play so many tricks.

When Mr Schmit started sidling in for attention I pushed him aside.

Why does the name Paul Healey ring a bell in your head?

I don't know.

Think!

Some boyfriend of my mother's . . . I think.

Think harder. Lauren told you once that your mother had been engaged and . . .'

I can't remember any of that.

Can't or won't?

Get stuffed.

Hearing about Amy's birthday dinner all those years ago got me thinking of the one I tried to organise that Friday night after the beach trip.

I told my mother I was inviting Mihn.

'That's nice, darling,' was all she said. She walked out of the room to pick up the ringing phone in another room. When she came back she was frowning and I knew it would not be quite as easy as I'd hoped.

I think she was mildly disturbed by the idea of me having a 'young man' over for the evening, as well as curious. 'And who else?' she asked, casually flicking through her freshly washed hair with slow fingers. 'Who else will be coming on Friday?'

I almost lied but decided that the nearer I was to the truth, the more difficult it would be for her to catch me out or interrupt my plans. 'No one else,' I muttered. 'Er . . . he's just a friend.'

'I thought his sister was your friend,' my mother said lightly. God, she looked gorgeous that evening. It wasn't fair. She was nearly fifty, for God's sake! And on her way out to dinner with her tennis 'pals' and their husbands. After that there was a party at the casino. Her hair had been cut in this new style and she was wearing a beautiful little black lacy evening dress. Emphasis on little. Tight and short. Nearly fifty and she could still wear mini-skirts! Her long shapely legs were encased in fine black stockings and her feet in very high suede shoes. It made me sick to think that at seventeen I couldn't wear anything as tight, revealing or fashionable as that – without looking ridiculous.

'Are you going to cook?' she asked with a little mocking smile.

That's right. Put me down. But I didn't show my anger in case she decided to turn nasty.

'No, no!' I called on my way out of the room. 'We'll just order in a pizza or something. Maybe I'll make a salad.'

In fact I'd planned the menu right down to the last strawberry. And it certainly wasn't going to be pizza and salad.

Wouldn't you know it, my sister Lauren had to be

home that night. The first Friday night in the whole year and she was 'exhausted', absolutely 'had' to have an early night! When I heard this I immediately panicked and went searching for her upstairs. Having Lauren around would jeopardise all my plans. Luckily for her she was holed up in the bathroom taking a shower because my intentions were verging on murderous. 'You're never home on Friday nights!' I yelled at her through the door. 'So why this week?'

'What's it to you?' she called back snootily. I'd heard my mother tell her about the dinner I'd planned with Mihn so I knew she was faking ignorance.

'Because I'm having someone over!' I shouted back. 'As you well know!'

The shower turned off and Lauren gave a loud, exaggerated sigh.

'Look, I won't cramp your style,' she called through the door. 'I'm going to bed early. I'll stay upstairs. I promise.' I could tell she thought it was funny that I didn't want her around and that made me want to kill her. 'You don't have to cook for me or anything, Sophie. Relax, okay?'

'As though I *would* cook for you!' I snorted, storming off and muttering under my breath, *You scheming little* . . .

Of course, having her about did cramp my style. At least initially. When I was preparing the food (the one dish I knew how to cook – chicken with cashews) she was hanging about, making herself toasted sandwiches, and giving out comments. Where had I met him? Didn't I think that dish was just a little passé? What was I going to wear?

I barely answered her. Just grunted 'yes', 'no' and

'none of your business', where appropriate. The truth was, I was as nervous as hell and I didn't want her around because she was so beautiful. Even in her daggiest tracksuit – which she was dressed in this night – Lauren always managed to look gorgeous. I suppose I was scared that Mihn would fall in love with her on the spot and that somehow I'd find myself looking on at my own dinner party while those two sat gazing into each other's eyes.

Mihn and I had spoken twice on the phone since the beach and, if anything, things seemed to be more intense between us. I had great hopes for this night and I didn't want Lauren around to spoil them.

He arrived exactly on time. To the minute. I heard the bell and immediately panicked, rushing through to the laundry where Lauren was stacking her dirty washing into the machine.

'He's here,' I snarled. 'So get lost, will you.'

'Oh why don't you get lost, Sophie!' she said, faking world-weary exasperation. 'When I'm finished here I'll go upstairs, okay?' Then she turned her back on me and coolly went on with what she was doing. I fantasised for two seconds about grabbing that cute, little blonde pigtail and twisting it so hard that she'd scream for mercy, but the doorbell rang again so I ran back into the front of the house and, checking myself quickly in the hall mirror, opened the door.

'Hi, Mihn!' I smiled, motioning for him to come in. There was a moment there when we both almost kissed each other but it disappeared quickly in a rush of embarrassment.

He looked even better than I remembered. Dressed in a crisply ironed white shirt and jeans, his hair pulled back into a ponytail. He took my breath away actually. *Could it be . . . could it really be that this . . . this absolutely gorgeous guy has come to see me and not Lauren?*

'Are you hungry?' I asked as I led him into the lounge that I'd specially made ready for the occasion with soft lights and little plates of pretzels and dips on the glass coffee table. But he only shrugged shyly.

'Not really,' he said, looking around the room nervously. *Oh God.* My heart fluttered madly on its big dive downwards. What a stupid thing, inviting him around for dinner! He was so thin. He probably didn't even like food. We should have gone out to a movie. And this room! This room is too formal. We'd both just sink into these overstuffed chairs and disappear.

'Actually,' I said nervously, 'let's go out to the other room and have a drink.' I wanted to get as far away from those huge silk-covered couches, glass cabinets and antique tables as I could. God, why didn't I remember how simple and plain his own house was? Letting him even see in here might look as though I was showing off.

'Okay.' He followed me meekly into the kitchen/family room area of the house that was furnished in a far more relaxed style. (Even so, I began to surreptitiously mess things up a bit on my way into the kitchen.) The cleanliness and overall tidiness of the place was embarrassing.

'What would you like?' I said suddenly, feeling desperate. I could hear my sister still messing around in the back rooms. 'We've got beer and wine and whisky and . . .' I grinned at him in a way I hoped he'd find sweet and cheeky but was probably just forced, 'anything really that you'd like.'

'Just water thanks,' he said.

I couldn't believe it. *Water!* After all the trouble I went to, getting in Coke and tonic and soda and making sure there was every kind of spirit known to mankind within arm's distance.

'With ice?' I said hopefully.

'No thanks.' He shook his head, and leant down to pick up a medical textbook that my father had left lying on a low sideboard. *Water?* From the tap or bottle? Fizzy or flat? *Shit!* We had every kind of water there was in our house. From the Swiss alps to Hepburn Springs, in green, pink or clear bottles. I disappeared into the kitchen, not daring ask him what kind he wanted. I was terrified that he would be looking at our house and me, thinking, *Who is this fat, rich chick and how did I get involved with her?*

'Your father is a doctor?'

'Yes,' I said, apologetically. 'Unfortunately'

'Why unfortunately?' he said, frowning, flipping through the textbook.

'Well.' I smiled stupidly at his bent head, a glass of water in each hand, not knowing what to say. 'I suppose it's okay . . . I mean. It's just that . . .' my voice petered out. *What an idiotic thing to say!* It would take three hours to explain the problems I had with my family's attitude to medicine. So why did I have to bring that up?

He looked up and suddenly grinned at me. There was such warmth in his expression that I momentarily couldn't move. I wanted to walk over to him but I couldn't move. I stared back at him, blushing.

'So you hate dentists and . . . doctors?' He was laughing at me now. 'Who else?'

I smiled and suddenly knew it would be all right. I wouldn't have to talk my way out of it. Everything would be all right.

'Physiotherapists? Do they shit you up the wall as well?'

I was wearing my favourite blue dress and I could tell by the way he was looking at me that he thought I looked good. I'd agonised about whether to dress up or simply wear the casual look that I'd taken so much time with the Sunday before, for the beach. Jeans and a shirt, to pretend I thought it was nothing that he was coming around. But in the end I decided that I might as well look my best. I'd put on make-up and brushed my hair till it hung gleaming like two panels of thick wavy gold around my face. The dress was in two pieces, the outside transparent and floaty with a soft frill along the hem. And underneath was a fitted, silk slip in the same colour. Quite formal but it suited me. At that moment, when we were both standing at opposite ends of the table smiling at each other, Lauren decided to bustle in.

'Oh, Lauren,' I said immediately, trying to look happy to see her. 'This is Mihn.'

'Oh hi!' she said with one of her dazzling smiles, as though she hadn't expected to see him but was so incredibly thrilled that he was there at last. 'So pleased to meet *you*!'

'Yes,' Mihn said politely, taking the hand that she was offering, slightly bewildered by her enthusiasm, 'pleased to meet you too.'

Then much to my relief, he folded his arms and looked away self-consciously. So far so good, I thought to myself. He hasn't fallen in love with her yet.

'I'm just on my way to get a drink and go upstairs,'

Lauren said breezily, edging towards the kitchen. Then a quick sideways smile at Mihn. 'Early night tonight. I'm exhausted.'

He nodded and I followed her out to the kitchen to check the food.

'So are you going to piss off properly now?' I hissed at her under my breath. Her back was turned to me as she got the milk from the fridge. When she turned around I could see I'd seriously annoyed her.

'You are *sad*, you know that, Sophie?' she snarled. 'Sad! I actually feel sorry for you.'

Then she walked out.

Sad was I? Hmm. Well maybe. It took me a little while to get over that one because, of course, she was right. I was being pathetic. Still . . . why was it that she could always beat me? She was always superior, even when she was giving out insults.

When we sat down to eat, with Lauren safely ensconced in front of the telly upstairs, I began to relax. Candlelight flickered from both ends of the table – I'd carted in the big silver candelabra from the formal dining room – and my mother's Enya CD bathed us in gentle sound. Mihn ate very slowly but seemed to really enjoy it. That pleased me so much I thought I'd be able to eat something too. But all I could manage was to pick up my fork and let it hover over my plate, occasionally picking up a choice little morsel and then moving it to another position, as though I was playing chess. We were very quiet for awhile. Every so often we would look up at each other and smile.

'So . . .' he said softly after a few minutes.

'Yes?' I murmured in reply, looking up from my plate to see him watching me.

211

'Hmmm.'

I put my fork down and waited for him to continue but he just smiled at me happily, bent his head and took another slow mouthful. And that is how the meal progressed. Quietly and very slowly. I ate nothing and we hardly said a coherent word to each other and yet I had never enjoyed a meal so much nor been so happy.

The funny thing was there was so much I could have said. So many topics I would have loved to talk to him about. But when I finally got a first sentence together in my head, I found I didn't want to go to the bother of saying the words. After a while I could tell that the same thing was happening to him. He would smile at me and I would smile back and then he'd eat something and I'd move a fresh green bean or cashew to the edge of my plate and then we'd look up and smile again or maybe sigh. That was it. What there was between us seemed so delicate and fragile that somehow actual words were an intrusion.

All my sensations were heightened. I was intensely aware of everything giving me pleasure. My soft hand against the hard silver of the knife. My feet tucked into my best blue sandals. The way my hair swung against my cheek when I moved my head. I fancied at one stage that I could feel the blood pulsing right down into the little toe on my right foot. I wriggled it and then giggled just thinking about it sitting there, always at the end of my foot. I wondered (this is really sick) if sometimes it got jealous of my big toe, which got all the attention. When he looked up, I slipped off my sandal, lifted my foot up to let him see my toe wriggling and he began laughing too. So there we were, two morons laughing at a wriggling toe! Then I put my foot down and commenced moving the food around my plate again and he went back to his meal. After a while I became aware of my breath going in and out in the most exquisitely orderly way.

Not once during the dinner did we touch each other. Nothing needed to be said. We both knew that it would come later. I had put fresh pure-cotton white sheets on my bed, cream towels in the bathroom and even pinched a couple of my sister's scented candles. My parents never got home before 3 a.m. if they were at a party. Everything was in order, everything would be perfect. The dinner continued at a snail's pace with neither of us speaking a word. Yet it was wonderful. We smiled and smiled. We looked in genuine wonder at each other's hands and faces, and at different times burst out into delighted laughter for no particular reason.

At half-past eleven, with the bottle of wine between us barely touched and the coffee drunk, Mihn at last reached across the table and took my hand.

'I want to kiss you,' he said, with a soft, slightly wry smile. 'That's the only thing I want now. To kiss you.'

Perfect. Feeling the touch of his thin hand on mine after all these gentle hours of being together was like heaven.

'Yes.' I whispered, about to get up and move around to where he was sitting. 'That's what I want too.'

I got up and then stopped. There was some kind of knocking outside and then the sound of voices. *Oh no!* I couldn't believe it. My hand still in his, I turned my head to the door, waiting. Sure enough it was my mother's voice, now in the hallway.

'But she hasn't any right!' My mother was fuming loudly about someone. 'They have plenty of money.

There is no need for her to act as though she can't afford a skiing weekend!' The muffled tones of my father trying to calm her down followed.

I pulled my hand away from Mihn as the door into the family room opened and the light clicked on above us.

'Oh, I'm sorry!' my mother said, genuinely surprised. 'You're still eating! I *am* sorry. *Hello*, you must be Mihn.' She'd never met him before but that didn't stop her acting like they were old friends. 'We came home early, I'm afraid. I felt like I couldn't face a party.'

'Mrs Douglas.' Mihn stood up, ignoring me and smiling at them.

My father came forward to shake his hand just as I was thinking I'd like to string both of them up in front of a wall and shoot arrows at them.

'Sorry to interrupt!' Dad turned to me in his jolly, well-meaning way. 'Your mother wasn't feeling too well.'

'Okay,' I manage to mumble without meeting his eyes.

'No, no,' Mihn was being so polite. 'No problem. I was just about to leave.'

My Aunt Fran seemed to be in an exceptionally good mood that evening. I longed to know if it might have something to do with her work. Perhaps she had got up enough courage to begin painting. But I didn't dare ask. I dreaded her knowing that I'd been snooping around her stuff. When I'd eventually got home from the river that afternoon I'd let myself into her studio again for a poke around.

I was smoking in my bedroom, listening to music and thinking about what I'd seen in her workroom, and about Amy and her mother, when I heard her car pull up outside.

'Sophie,' she called down the passage as she came in the door, 'you home?'

'Yes,' I called back.

'I'd love you to come down and help me,' she said. 'I've just invited Amy and John, Jimmy and his daughter back for a meal.'

'Sure,' I called back, stubbing out my cigarette. 'I'll be down there in a minute.' I went to the bathroom and brushed my teeth and washed my hands to get the smell away, hoping that if she did smell it, she'd think I'd been smoking outside.

'So?' She smiled, looking up from where she was chopping onions at the table. 'How are you?'

'Oh, good thanks.' I took hold of a lettuce. 'Will I wash this?'

'Thanks!' she said. 'And there are lots of other salad things in the fridge. Could you make up one in that big glass bowl?'

'Sure.'

We worked silently for a while. But it didn't feel stiff. The radio was going softly in the background and I could tell that although she was frantic to get the meal ready on time, she was happy. Every time I'd see something I could do, I asked if I could take it over for her. It was enjoyable because I hadn't been in a kitchen or had anything to do with food preparation for months.

'So you've had a good day?' I said at last, trying to make myself sound bland and innocent.

'Oh yes!' she said, stopping what she was doing for a while. 'A good day, Sophie.'

Her warmth was sort of catching but it made me shy in a way, especially considering my sneaky activities that afternoon. What a dog I was! She was whistling and humming along to the music on the radio.

'What happened?' I said.

'Well . . . hard to explain,' she said, frowning as she chopped up the onions. 'But I think I got somewhere today, if you know what I mean.' She pointed at her head and I nodded. I had no idea what she meant but wasn't game to say so.

'Sophie, you can just trundle on for weeks at a time thinking nothing is going to change.' She laughed suddenly. 'That you're doomed never to achieve anything and then, hey presto, things do change. You make a little step forward and you understand something new.'

'You're talking about art?' I said shyly.

'Yep.' She smiled at me and tipped the onions into the hot oil in the pan. 'Today I just calmed down somehow. Sooner or later I'll start painting again. There is no point tying myself in knots about *when* exactly.' I nodded, pretending I understood what she was getting at. 'Besides, I did a nice drawing and had a couple of good ideas. What about you? How did the terrible addiction go today?'

'Okay!' I laughed, hoping she didn't mean cigarettes. 'I passed by the fish and chip shop twice and I wasn't even tempted.'

'Good for you,' she said happily. 'Let's have a glass of wine before the others arrive.'

I didn't drink wine all that often but I opened the bottle for her and poured out a couple of glasses. That was when the phone rang. My hands were all wet, I was peeling potatoes, so she ran to get it. The phone was just over the other side of the room, near the table, so I could hear who it was.

'Hello,' she said brightly, 'Fran speaking.' Then I saw her face drop and become tense. 'Ah, Geraldine! Did you want to speak to Sophie?'

The answer was obviously 'no' because Fran turned her back to me and lowered her voice. I gulped down some wine, glad that I didn't have to talk to her but suddenly insanely furious that she didn't want to talk to me! Although I strained to hear, I couldn't catch much. Fran seemed to be murmuring yes and no and my mother was doing the talking. Their conversation didn't go on for very long. My aunt was frowning when she put the phone down.

'My mother?' I said with what I hoped was the right amount of disinterest. 'What did she want?'

Fran went back to the stove to stir the onions.

'Not much,' she said, her back to me. 'Just to see you were okay. And . . . to make sure you got the letter.'

'So why didn't she ask *me*?' I said, louder than I'd planned because I really didn't want my aunt asking me about that letter.

'Well because . . .' Fran turned around slowly. 'She said it would be no use because you wouldn't talk to her anyway.'

I sniffed. True, but I wasn't going to admit it. I was quiet for a while. A good while actually, wondering what else they'd talked about but not game to question Fran further. Who knows what might happen if we really started talking about her! I was overwhelmed. My mother didn't want to speak to me. And if she had, I wouldn't have come to the phone.

Then it rang again. My aunt and I were still both working away in the kitchen. I was suddenly scared.

'It's Mum, I bet!' I whispered, pointing at the phone.

'Geraldine!' she said at exactly the same time. Then we both burst out laughing and let it ring a couple more times. Fran moved to answer it and I waited, breathless.

'James!' I heard her say, her voice full of warmth and surprise. 'Oh it's so good to hear from *you*, darling!'

I relaxed. I knew my cousin was in England and that she'd been longing to hear from him for ages. I began to chop tomatoes into neat little wedges and dropped them on the oily lettuce, thinking with relief that my mother could be shoved back into the 'closed off' section of my brain for a while longer.

Fran talked quietly to her son for perhaps ten minutes then put the phone down. I looked up eagerly, expecting her to look happy and animated. Instead she was crying. I didn't know what to do. I put the knife down and took a few steps towards her then stopped, not wanting to intrude. She was standing next to the window, her hand still on the receiver, the telephone cord wrapped around the other hand, tears running down her face. *Oh shit, don't tell me something has happened to him!* But when she saw my concern, she waved at me and smiled.

'It's not really bad news, Sophie,' she said. 'I've been worried about him over there on his own. He's so quiet and shy and now he's met someone.' She walked over to me and hugged me quickly and tightly. 'And they want to spend Christmas together. So that's good, isn't it? But . . . he won't be home.'

'Oh.' I gulped nervously, a little stunned but pleased too. It felt very strange to be grabbed like that. I could feel the skin tingling on my arms and back where she'd held me. 'But you'll have Peter and Damien, won't you?'

'No,' she said, 'they won't be coming either. Peter

has to work in the restaurant Christmas Day and Damien rang me yesterday, all apologetic, asking if I minded him spending Christmas this year mountain-climbing with a group of friends. What could I say?'

'I hate it the way everything is open on Christmas Day,' I said, stupidly, but not knowing what else to say. 'It means a lot of people have to work.'

'All the boys were so wonderful last Christmas, helping me with Dad,' she said sadly. 'I really can't begrudge them . . .'

'No,' I muttered, liking the way she was just rattling on to me.

'I'm such a sucker for Christmas,' she said, blowing her nose, 'that I continually have to remind myself that it often doesn't mean that much to others. How about you, Sophie? Does it mean much to you?'

I shrugged, suddenly shy. 'Well, er . . . sort of,' I mumbled. 'Not really that much.'

Christmas was . . . *Christmas*. Presents. Packing everything up in the car, coming up here to Ballingo to see the grandparents and . . . well, all that was over now. Where would I be this Christmas? It was only five weeks away. Would I be home by then? Back with zany, vibrant Mum and tense, kindly Dad, beautiful Lauren and cool, clever Peter? Sitting around our beautiful lounge room giving presents? Me apologising for upsetting their lives, for causing them all grief, for making this year such a horrible one for everyone? We could all then sit around together and decide my future. I shuddered just thinking about it.

Amy and her husband John, Jimmy and Blue. Fran and me. Six of us around the kitchen table tucking into home-made bread and avocado dip, then the chicken, potatoes and salad. I was on my second glass of wine and feeling good, a bit giddy I suppose. There was a lot of laughing and jokes between the others that I wasn't picking up on but I didn't mind. In fact, it was sort of enjoyable, just to be able to sit there quietly and listen to them poking fun at each other. I felt a bit shy.

There was the cool, stunning-looking Blue sitting right across from me in her tight white jeans, pink shirt, her sleek black hair pinned up with two Chinese sticks. She did seem a bit friendlier than when I last met her in the shop but I didn't trust her for a minute. After Alana I think I'll be wary of anyone who looks as good as that, probably for the rest of my life.

I liked John. He is one of those quiet, ugly men who come up with witty comments and dry jokes when they're needed. Apparently he's some kind of big name in the computer world. I don't know why, but when he spoke I kept remembering Schmity. Stupid. Because John is tall and thin and wears really thick old-fashioned glasses. Schmity is short and fat and doesn't even wear glasses, and yet there is a similarity that I can't quite work out.

My Uncle Jimmy in action is like one of those yapping little fox terrier dogs that fly out at you from behind fences. Edgy and quick in his talk and movements, and a great teaser. None of it serious. Every now and again he'd make some joke about my blue hair, then he'd have a go at Fran's cooking. *Hope you can paint better than you can cook, Fran.* Then he'd be off outside to have a smoke. I almost joined him once but thought it might turn out more embarrassing than fun. It was funny seeing his daughter sort of bossing him around and humouring him like he was a kid.

'Dad, just calm down, will you!' she ordered when he was holding the floor, raving on about some past government minister. 'Not worth getting yourself into a knot about it.'

And Jimmy immediately did what he was told. With this sheepish look on his face, he'd quieten down for about two minutes. 'Okay, Blue,' he would say, winking at me, 'you're the boss!'

It was Jimmy who started the dancing. We were all just sitting there talking, and hardly noticed when he left the table again. Everyone probably thought he was out for a smoke. I know I did. But no, he was in the other room organising the stereo. Suddenly Buddy Holly's 'That'll Be The Day' came blaring into the room and then Jimmy strutted back in, his jacket and shirt off, eyes closed, singing along to the song, arms holding an imaginary partner. Blue and I looked at each other and groaned. I mean, the music is so completely beyond . . . *anything*. But we didn't get a chance to pass comment. Jimmy suddenly made a grab for Fran who was sitting at the end of the table.

'No, Jimmy,' she resisted, 'I'm too old. Go on. Do your James Dean number by yourself and leave me alone!' But he wouldn't and she eventually got up and they started rocking together like they were really made for it. Fran was laughing. Jimmy spinning her around like she was his private play thing.

I was okay up to this point but then Blue and Amy started dancing in this really funky way and I started to panic. There was just me and ugly John left at the table. I avoided his eye, got up and started moving things over to the sink. When I turned around he had joined the others. God! For a moment I forget my panic.

He looked so funny! Like a praying mantis, all arms and legs twisting so awkwardly, dancing around the other two couples. I slumped down into the end chair, as far away from the others as I could while still being in the same room, put my feet up and poured myself more wine, pretending that everything was cool and that I really did just want to sit there and drink. I knew what was coming but I tried to ward it off for as long as I could.

'Come on, Sophie!' Fran yelled right on cue from the other side of the room. 'Get up and dance!'

I tried to smile and shook my head. 'No thanks.'

Thankfully the track finished. I was praying that they were all going to come back, sit down again and resume the conversation. But Jimmy disappeared into the next room.

'Put on something decent,' Blue yelled after him. The others laughed. Fran walked over to me.

'Sophie.' She held out her hand. '*Your* Mum, *my* sister, Geraldine was *the* champion of the dancefloor when we were young. And I bet you are, too.'

This odd, freezing feeling started to crawl over my skin and I knew the others were watching me, even though I wasn't looking at them or my aunt. I got up slowly. I was either going to be sick or I was going to hit someone.

'I remember Geraldine,' I heard Amy telling Blue as I lurched drunkenly for the door, 'she was such a joy to watch.'

'Excuse me,' I said, 'got a headache. Have to lie down.'

I brooded on my bed for an hour or so, hoping the little dinner party in the kitchen wouldn't hear my loud House music. At the same time hoping that they would. Part of me wished they believed that I really was bored with their company. Anything else was too humiliating. I was nowhere even remotely near sleep. I smoked a couple of cigarettes then climbed out the window into the back garden for a while to look at the sky, trying to keep myself from thinking. But it was still cloudy and the nippy wind that had me shivering in my tee-shirt made me feel worse. Nearly the end of November and there were no stars to speak of. In the end I realised that I was so churned up that there was nothing for it but to go back inside again, lie on my bed and try and work it out.

So what was going on in there?

Oh God, Schmity is back again. In my head. Prying. Looking for answers I don't have. Nothing is clear about any of this.

I don't dance. Full stop. That's the thing. For years. Well, from the time I was a kid anyway. I just don't dance.

What do you mean, you don't dance?

Okay. When I turned thirteen Mum and Dad gave me my first teenage party. I'd been going to a few before that. Very innocent affairs. All kids my own age. No alcohol, drugs or cigarettes. But held at night, with boys and music. I didn't really want one but Mum insisted. I was dreading it so when it actually got going, and all the kids arrived and seemed to be having a good time, I was so relieved that I started to have a good time myself. All very cute. Low lights, loud pop music and everyone dancing, including me. The girls were all from school and the boys were their brothers and cousins. There were equal numbers. Mum was very good about working out that kind of stuff. Lauren was seventeen then, in her last year at school and still doing some ballet, although she'd decided not to take up the offer of a place at the Victorian College of the Arts. That night she was helping Mum.

Anyway, I had to go out to the kitchen for something. Some boy had spilt his drink. My mother was standing at the fridge hauling stuff out. Lauren was filling the dishwasher. Both with their backs to me.

'Doesn't Sophie look a scream dancing!' my mother said to Lauren.

'Oh yeah.' Lauren was squatting down, fiddling with the control. 'Like a little Ewok!' And then they both did a slow mimic of me dancing, some awkward, clumsy, jerking movements before dissolving into giggles.

So that's it?

I suppose it's nothing. But I wanted to kill them both. I remember wishing I had an axe to chop off both their heads! I decided that I would never dance again. They would never be able to laugh at me again like that.

Did they see you?

No.

So you never danced again?

I don't want to get into that. Let's just drop it.

Did you ever dance again?

I can't bear to even think about it.

You have to.

Why?

You know why.

Of course I danced again. With Mihn. In April this year. Just before . . . before . . . *a few days before . . .* Oh shit, this stuff is crap. It means nothing. I can't see the point of raking through this.

You can!

Okay. Our school held a full-evening-dress, formal dance for the final year and we were all allowed to invite partners. Everyone was there dressed up to the nines. Alana and Jess, all the girls from school. I'd just turned seventeen. Mum didn't approve of Mihn – I think she blamed him and Mai for my falling out with Alana and Jess – but she did let me have a new dress for the formal. It was a navy-blue crepe, fitted, with spaghetti straps and a low sway-back. Three sizes bigger than my sister's but I didn't care that night. The colour set off my eyes somehow and my hair. I'd never bared my shoulders before. But in this dress, under the evening lights, my skin was smooth and glowing. I felt confident for once. After the disastrous dinner, Mihn and I had finally got it together and I was on top of the world. He was all I wanted.

I was proud too of Mihn being a little older than all the other girls' partners. We didn't have to be driven by parents.

He came with Mai and her partner, a cousin of theirs from Footscray, to pick me up in the little second-hand car he'd just bought the week before. He was so rapt to have it. Had been saving for a year. He turned up at the door dressed up in a hired dinner-suit, his long hair slicked back, his lovely, fine-boned face smiling. I was so proud that when I walked out of that house, it was as though I was walking on air.

The music started and I just got up. I found, after all that time I thought I couldn't dance, that it was easy. It felt like . . . I was flying. *My mother is not here, Mum and Lauren are not here and I'm dancing!* It didn't matter at all that we were just shuffling around the floor at first. I didn't care if Alana and Jess were looking at me. In my heart I think I'd finished with them by then. If they were resentful that I was with Mihn, I didn't care about that either. For a while we danced in a foursome. Mai and her cousin, Mihn and me. After a little while Mihn and I stopped shuffling about and really got into it.

Then, as we were going into the nearby room for supper, Mihn got a call on his mobile phone. I didn't even know he had brought it so I was immediately wary. Since his brother had got out of jail a couple of weeks before, Mihn was always getting calls but didn't often tell me what they were about. In fact he'd got himself the phone so he could take calls from his brother. Truc wouldn't risk the humiliation of ringing home because his parents didn't want to know him. I saw this look pass over Mihn's face and I immediately knew something was up.

'It's my brother,' he whispered to me. 'I'll have to go.'

My heart dived.

'Where is he?'

'He's outside.'

'What?' I was immediately panic-stricken. Truc terrified me. He was the one thing about knowing Mai and Mihn that wasn't good. I went to see him once with Mihn when he was in jail. And he was so unfriendly, so edgy, so angry that I left thinking it must have been the place. Once he got out he'd calm down and be different. But it didn't happen like that. He didn't like me. Just the idea of his little brother — that's how he thought of Mihn — having an Australian girlfriend infuriated him. A crazy form of inverted racism permeated his whole outlook.

But it was the effect he had on Mihn that really had

me worried. Mihn was so keen to keep him off the streets, and away from the crowd that had got him into trouble eighteen months before, that he was willing to do anything for him. He got him a place to stay, bought him some new clothes and was even trying to get him a part-time job. And it wasn't as though Mihn had a lot of money. He had to work hard for every cent, as well as study. His parents didn't pay him anything like award wages. But Truc wanted more. He was always ringing up and demanding Mihn meet him somewhere for something: money, information, even food. I was just beginning to realise that there would be no end to it. Truc actually wanted Mihn *with him* – as an everyday part of his life. He didn't respect that Mihn had chosen a different course altogether.

Truc sneered at the whole idea of university but anyone could see that he was actually jealous. Except Mihn. He couldn't see anything. He simply wanted to do what he could to keep his brother away from criminals and drugs.

'What does he want?' I whispered.

'He wants my car,' Mihn replied. 'He's in some kind of trouble. Someone is after him.'

I knew then, at some intuitive level, that Truc was back with those people, the crowd that Mihn had told me he'd gotten away from. The ones who dealt in drugs and stolen goods, the ones he'd been with when he'd landed up in jail. He was stringing his brother along with all this talk about getting it together with a proper job. But I didn't say anything.

'Hey. Don't look like that!' Mihn smiled at me. 'I'll be back in a few minutes. Okay? I'll just give him the car and we'll have to get a taxi home.'

'Okay,' I said.

I joined Mai and together we watched Mihn disappear, both of us worried. I spent the next ten minutes eating a bit of supper, trying not to worry, talking chit-chat to other girls from my class. Out of the corner of my eye I could see Alana and Jess's little group standing around laughing and acting cool, even felt their eyes on me a few times, and I almost went over. But at the last moment I chickened out. Then the room started to buzz.

Fight! Fight!

There's a fight outside!

Someone's got a knife.

Some Vietnamese dudes outside . . .

A fight! Yeah? Outside . . .

Cops . . . outside.

The word took about two minutes to circulate before the whole crowd of nicely brought-up private-school kids was doing a stampede for the doors to see what was going on. *Oh God. Please don't let it be Mihn or his brother*, I pleaded, but I knew my prayers were useless. When I got outside the police were already there. There was a round flowerbed set in the middle of the concrete carpark and Mihn's little car was parked across it, the doors wide open. Another car had skewed to a halt just behind it. I could smell burnt rubber. Maybe Truc had tried to flee in Mihn's car. Maybe anything. There was shouting and screaming as two guys, one of them I guessed was Truc, were being pushed up against the side of a paddy wagon. Around them about two dozen Vietnamese guys in separate groups were looking on. *Who were they? And when had they arrived?*

I began to push my way through the crowd, trying to

find Mihn in the harsh light. He was over on the other side of the police car, standing quietly in his dinner-suit, being interviewed by a couple of policemen. Damn it. I didn't know what they wanted with him but I was going to make sure they knew he was with me.

'Can you see what's happened?' It was Mai behind me. We clutched hands as we pushed our way through the mesmerised crowd. Everyone was looking on like it was a drama unfolding on TV, everyone hungry for details.

See that guy. He was at the formal.

Who with?

So who are the others?

I heard my own name being bandied around a bit but I took no notice of the whispers and stares. The back of the police van slammed. *Had they put anyone inside?* I couldn't see.

'Would everyone please come inside now!' Teachers were moving through, trying to usher the students back into the hall. 'Come on now, everyone. All the excitement is over.'

I think Alana and Jess deliberately moved into position so that I'd have to pass them on my way over to Mihn. They looked me up and down as though I had somehow amused them.

'Wow, Sophie,' Alana said, meeting my eye, giving one of her glassy, high, little laughs. 'Your new friends seem really nice!' There were bitchy twitters and it was all I could do to stop myself smashing my fist across her perfectly painted, pretty little mouth.

Well, you'd been asking for that!

What do you mean?

Think! No one likes to be dropped without warning. And that is what you did to her and Jess.

I . . . hadn't seen much of them, it's true.

You dumped them.

Okay. I got a bit slack . . . I'd met Mai and got involved with Mihn and . . .

Exactly.

But none of that was any excuse for what they did to me later!

Well . . .

There was a small tap at the door. I pretended not to hear as I lay there in the dark, close to tears. Sometimes I can write my diary and sometimes I just can't. After thinking I was getting somewhere up in this hole of a town, with my aunt and her friends, away from all of them back there, I was suddenly back to square one. I felt unbelievably depressed.

I'm this ugly, gloomy, completely unsuccessful person that rudely stomps out of pleasant social occasions and snoops into other people's private places. How low can you get?

I threw the book across the room, turned the light out and turned up the music.

'Sophie,' my uncle's voice called, 'let me in.'

'The door is open,' I called back, hoping like hell he wouldn't come in because I didn't feel like talking to him or anyone else.

'So what is going on in here?' Jimmy came marching into the room, shut the door behind him and stood leaning against the wall, looking down at me.

'Not much,' I snapped shortly.

'Aren't you cold?' he said, looking at me incredulously.

'No,' I said. In fact I was and had just been thinking about getting under the blankets but I knew I needed to clean my teeth first and go to the toilet.

'So,' he said, looking around in this almost disinterested way, 'you're a smoker.'

I didn't say anything. Wasn't it obvious? I hated making conversation for the sake of it.

'Aren't you worried about your lungs?' he joked weakly, sitting on the end of my bed. This from someone who'd disappeared at least three times during the dinner to have one himself.

'No.'

'Be careful, won't you. This place would go like a box of tinder.'

'Okay,' I muttered sourly. My aunt had said the same thing about six times.

'All the wiring is shitty too,' he added.

I nodded. When would he just leave me alone? But when he did get up, instead of going to the door he walked slowly over to the window, pulled it open and let in a fresh gust of air. I sat up in surprise. Two totally different reactions were colliding inside me like tankers. I couldn't help admiring his nonchalance – *cheek* really. At the same time I was furious that he thought he could just come in and invade my space like this. This was my room. I didn't care if he *was* a psycho war veteran. It was no excuse.

'Do you mind?' I said coldly, through gritted teeth. He merely cleared his throat and leant out the window, drawing exaggerated deep breaths.

'Hmm . . . ah God. I just love this place,' he mumbled to himself. 'Don't you?'

I didn't trust myself to answer. I was on the point of telling him to go get stuffed because I wanted to go to sleep, when he edged his way back into the room and turned to face me.

'Want to go for a ride?' he said.

'A ride?' I repeated stupidly. I was still half-sitting on the bed, staring at him.

'A horse ride,' he said impatiently. 'It's not an ideal night but we could go out along Jackson's Lane. No pot holes out there. Anyway, I've got this powerful torch.'

'You mean *now*?' I said, looking over at the fluorescent hands of the clock near my bed which showed 11.15.

'Yeah, now!' He switched on the overhead light and grinned at me. 'You're like me. I can tell. Never sleep before midnight.'

I shook my head and blinked wildly, waiting for my eyes to adjust. I hate people doing that!

'Where . . . I mean,' I stuttered, thoroughly confused, 'I mean, where can we get horses from?'

'Haven't you seen Pride and Joy,' he said, genuinely surprised, 'in the vacant block behind the pub?'

'No.'

'Do you ride at all?'

'No,' I said again, thinking that I hadn't been for a ride on a horse since I was ten. And that had been half an hour on a little pony so old it was about to drop dead.

'You'd better have Pride then,' he said thoughtfully. 'She's as quiet as a mouse. Won't give you any trouble at all.'

Pride and Joy? Oh Jeez. You are a whacko.

'You really called them that?'

'Oh come on!' he said ignoring the question. 'The others are so boring. Amy and John have gone. Fran's tired. Blue wants to go to bed.'

'Couldn't we . . . er, go tomorrow?' I was actually

warming to the idea. But somehow picking up my rid-ing career in the middle of the night seemed a little too much like pushing my luck.

'I've got the gear,' he said, as though able to read my mind. 'Helmets and stuff. Come on, Sophie. It's just magic at night. I promise you won't be sorry.'

'Okay,' I said.

'We'll drive back to the pub,' he said, giving my knee a hard, triumphant slap, 'saddle up the hacks and take off. Put on a thick jumper though. It'll be bloody cold.'

Jimmy was right. It was magic. The sky even cleared for us. A fat, yellow half-moon kept poking out of the blackness like a piece of ripe cheese, illuminating the road and the sky, bathing everything in soft, pale magi-cal light. We rode along, mostly silent, watching the clouds whip past, sometimes plunging us back into darkness and then out into light in a matter of seconds.

The quietness, the clopping of the horses feet, their snorts and heavy breathing, was intoxicating – around me the darkness and the swaying shapes of trees on either side of the road. We didn't talk much at first. He didn't ask any questions about my walk-out at dinner.

'How come you called your daughter Blue?' I called to him at one stage.

'Ah, that is a long story,' he said laughing, 'but a good one. I'll tell you some time.'

After about half an hour we came to a sharp bend in the road.

'Want to go look at the river?' he said, pointing away from the road. 'There's a good little spot just down there, through the bush.'

'Okay,' I said. The idea of leaving the track and traipsing through bush in the middle of the night was intensely unappealing, but I didn't want to be a spoilsport. 'If you know where you're going,' I added nervously.

'Of course I do!' Another burst of his loud laughter, unreal at that hour, in that place. We got off our horses and I followed Jimmy slowly into the darkness. I felt nervous suddenly. What if the torch gave out? We'd be stuck out in the middle of nowhere in pitch blackness. And all I'd ever heard about this uncle of mine was that he had crazy turns. What if he was in the middle of one now and he was luring me down here to murder me?

'You okay?' he called back a couple of times.

'Sure,' I muttered, pretending to be more easy than I felt. 'How much further?'

But before he could answer we were there. And it was, as he said, a good place. The moon was out the moment we pushed through the bush and on to a small grassy bank that led down to the wide river. Jimmy got me to hold the torch while he tied up both horses to a tree, then we climbed down the bank a little way to sit and look a while.

'What do ya reckon?' he asked, putting the torch between us and lying back on the grass, hands behind his head.

'It's great,' I said softly, very glad that I'd come. Glad I wasn't back there smoking or sleeping or grumping about in my head with Mr Schmit. 'How did you know about it?'

'Oh, I've been riding out along here since I was a kid.'

We talked on a little more about nothing much in particular. When I asked how organisation for the local school fete – to be held a week before Christmas – was going, he groaned. He'd promised his mate, the head-master, that he'd organise the art-craft stall but the stuff people said they'd contribute was only dribbling through. There were only a few weeks to go.

'How come you're so involved?' I asked. Somehow, what I knew of my uncle didn't fit with the dagginess of a school fete. 'I mean is . . . was it your old school or . . . ?'

'You're kidding.' Jimmy laughed. 'No way. I went to St Pat's with all the Micks. So did Phil Ryan. He's now the head of the secondary college.'

'Oh,' I said, thinking I understood the connection at last. 'So he's an old school friend?'

'Something like that,' Jimmy said with a sigh, turning away from me.

'What do you mean?'

'Well, he was a good mate to me when I came back from 'Nam. I was completely stuffed. I guess you could say I owe him.'

A million questions immediately crashed into my head. There was stuff I suddenly wanted to know about my uncle, about his time over there, his failed marriage and his supposed craziness. But the way he'd turned his head away as he spoke stopped me. I shut my mouth and let the questions sit there in my head.

'We were hoping Fran would get involved,' Jimmy said at last, turning back to me. 'But she ain't keen.'

'If I'm still around I'll help on the day if you want,' I said lazily. 'Standing behind a stall selling crap to old ladies would be just my style.'

'It makes at least ten grand every year, you know,' he said defensively, 'and that gets really important stuff for the school. People come from miles around. It's really well known.'

'Oh right,' I said apologetically. 'That is a lot of money.' I didn't add that I'd always avoided getting involved in those kinds of money-raising things.

'What about you make us something?' he said slowly.

'What kind of thing?' I was wary.

'Oh I dunno, anything,' he said airily, waving one arm at the sky, 'anything that would sell.'

'Well . . . I wish I could,' I said, meaning it, 'but I can't sew or knit or cook and I've never done any artwork.' I'd decided then and there that I liked my Uncle Jimmy. I would have been glad to help him out a bit. After all, I didn't exactly have a lot on.

'You should be artistic.' Jimmy sat up, gave me a thoughtful smile. Picking up the torch, he shone it in my face. 'Your aunt is a bloody artist. You should be able to paint or draw or do . . . *something*.'

'Yeah,' I shot back at him, 'I *should* be able to dance like my mother and paint like my aunt, play soccer like my brother *and* cut out cancer from people's guts like Dad! But I can't do any of it. *Sorry!*'

It wasn't even funny. Or maybe it was a bit. But Jimmy collapsed back on the grass laughing.

'Okay,' he said, after he'd calmed down. 'You don't have to make anything.'

I suddenly remembered the pottery wheel in my aunt's studio.

'Actually I *can* make pots.'

'*Pots?*' he said, 'What do you mean?'

'You know, with clay,' I explained, 'but I haven't got a

wheel. Or for that matter a kiln to bake them in so . . .' I didn't dare tell him I knew where a wheel was. What if he let on to Fran that I'd been snooping around in her studio?

'You mean, sugar bowls and . . .' Jimmy hesitated, thoughtful. 'That kind of crap always goes down *really* well at fetes.'

'Yeah,' I said, grinning at him, 'I was the star of the pottery class at school about six years ago! The only one who could really do it. But I'd need a wheel and a kiln.'

'Listen, if we can get hold of a wheel,' he said, 'then I reckon I can get access to a kiln.'

'Really?' I said, now interested. 'Where?'

'Oh, there's this whacko guy I know. He owns that huge ceramics business a few miles out of town. *Flying Duck* it's called. Really successful. He's loaded. He's pretty obnoxious, but who cares? Sort of okay in his own way.' Jimmy grinned at me. 'I reckon he'd let you fire your stuff in his kilns.'

'But four kilometres out,' I said, warming to the idea. 'How would I get it out there?'

'Me,' he said simply, 'or Blue. She can drive.'

'We'd have to buy clay and glazes and shit.'

'That's the thing though,' Jimmy said enthusiastically. 'We'll give old Raymond the hard-luck sob story. You know, the old this-is-for-the-poor-old-local-school number, and he might just give us some of the stuff you need, free!'

'Raymond?' I repeated stupidly, thinking I'd heard wrong.

'Yeah, Raymond Watts,' he said matter-of-factly. 'He owns that joint. Why? You met him? He used to go out with Fran years ago.'

'Not really,' I said, slowly thinking how weird everything was getting.

'You got any objections to at least trying?' Jimmy asked, getting up and brushing down his jeans and heading over to untie the horses.

'Not at all,' I said, suddenly really liking the idea. 'Let's try it.'

'You never know.' Jimmy smirked wickedly at me in the dark. 'We might be able to pair him up with Fran again. She needs a fella.'

'You think so?' I said. The thought hadn't crossed my mind.

'Course she does!' Jimmy said. 'Real bad.' He winked at me. 'If we're smart, we might be able to kill two birds with the one stone.'

Going back into town Jimmy and I were mostly silent. By the time we finally reached my aunt's house it was after 2 a.m. It felt like I'd just come back from a two-day trek. At the front gate Jimmy reached for my reins and I slipped off my horse, glad that he couldn't see my legs almost buckle beneath me.

'Thanks, Jimmy,' I said, giving the quiet little mare's soft nose and sweaty neck a pat. 'It was great. Thanks a lot.'

'You're right,' he muttered, moving off again into the darkness. 'See you tomorrow.'

'Yeah.'

I walked around the side of the house and, before letting myself in through the back door, I stopped for a moment, aware of the soft, velvet quality of the darkness surrounding me. For the first time I felt the quietness of that little town and was not bored or irritated by it.

We went out to see Raymond the next day. Just Jimmy and me. I didn't say anything to Fran about it because I didn't want to upset her. The whole thing might not work out anyway. It only took us about ten minutes to get there on the highway that goes back to the city.

Jimmy turned off to the right into an impressive brick gateway just a few metres in from the road. 'Watts Flying Duck Ceramics Pty Ltd' big gold letters spelled out on a deep-blue background, and then underneath, in smaller writing, '*Wholesale Terracotta Sales to Australia and the World*'. Wow. I smiled to myself, thinking back to the story Amy had told me, wondering if I'd be game to ask him if he actually did manage to herd those other ducks into the Melbourne Club back in 1970. So, after all these years he was still into ducks!

Jimmy had rung him that morning to ask if we could come and talk. Raymond had agreed to see us at eleven, and we were a bit early. We got out of the car, leant against the bonnet and watched groups of people coming and going through the gate that led into a big saleyard. Piles of terracotta plant-pots, fountains, wall-reliefs and general knick-knacks in various shapes and sizes were lying out in rows in the sunshine.

'Let's go and have a bit of a geeza,' Jimmy said after a while.

There was plenty to look at. The yard was flanked by two huge brick buildings. One housed the kilns and work areas and the other was a showroom and offices. After wandering around the outside yard for a while, we gravitated towards the showroom.

Inside I was suddenly deeply interested. There were all kinds of beautiful earthenware pots, dishes and sets of crockery, some of it in bright glazed colours, other pieces subtly done in hand-painted designs. I wandered around touching things, marvelling at the gleaming polished finishes, loving the simplicity of a set of very fine ash-grey plates. On each one a beautiful leaf drawn as though in black ink. I stood in front of those for some time, my heart sinking.

'I can't do this kind of thing,' I said to Jimmy. 'No one will buy my crappy stuff from the fete when they can get this kind of thing.'

'Bullshit,' he said immediately. 'All this stuff is so expensive. Have a look at the price-tags. If you can make some simple little sugar bowls and pots to stick plants in, people will buy them. We'll keep them cheap.'

'Maybe,' I mumbled, uncertain what to think. I picked up the price-tag of a particularly beautiful blue jug. One hundred and ten dollars! Wow! He was right. But at the same time I longed to make something as beautiful as the jug and the huge oval-shaped platter that went with it. And all those fine plates with delicate markings.

'I'm finding this kind of wonderful,' I admitted to Jimmy at one stage, shyly. 'Just looking at this stuff makes me feel . . .'

Jimmy put his arm around my shoulders and gave me a squeeze, smiling.

'What?'

'Like slapping some clay about myself,' I said. 'I really want to get my hands dirty!'

'Good,' he said warmly.

'Well, hello!'

Jimmy spun around from the cabinet he was peering

into. 'G'day, Ray!' he said, holding out his hand. 'How are ya?'

I almost laughed as I waited to be introduced. He was exactly as I imagined he'd be. Tall, thin, with silver-grey hair, olive skin, and flashing, deep-brown eyes. And incredibly cool in his expensive designer-wear. Light jeans, silk shirt and a leather jacket that was just so chic.

'And this is the niece, is it?'

He held out his hand and I took it, expecting his eyes would immediately slide off me and on to something more interesting, but they didn't. In fact they stayed intently on my face, as though he was really interested.

'Sophie,' I mumbled, feeling shy under his gaze. 'Pleased to meet you.'

'I'm pleased to meet *you*, Sophie,' he said, pumping away at my hand. 'I heard you were around. Glad to meet you at last.'

I couldn't help laughing a bit. *Jeez! What an operator!*

'So how long are you staying?'

'I'm not sure.' I shrugged, then looked over at Jimmy, who was grinning. 'As long as they'll have me.'

'Hmmm.' Raymond frowned. 'We're having a little rest from Mum, are we?' he asked with droll good humour.

'Er, yeah, we *are*, I guess,' I mumbled, wondering what the hell else he knew about me.

'Fabulous woman your mother,' he said suddenly, with real feeling. '*Fabulous* but formidable. *Very* formidable! She still dancing?'

'Er no,' I said, a bit stunned.

'So.' He grinned, waving his arms around at the showroom. 'Have you had a look around?'

'Yeah,' Jimmy said for both of us, 'some bloody fantastic stuff here, Raymond. Real top quality.'

'Isn't it fabulous?' Raymond said proudly. 'You know I've got eight full-time potters working for me at the moment. I mean, just on this classy ceramics ware, and I'm thinking of taking on another.'

'That's pretty good.'

'All that stuff outside is the bread-and-butter of the business,' he explained, 'but this is what really interests me. Come up to my office and we'll talk.'

We followed him up the polished wooden stairs into a large plush office with a tinted window that overlooked the saleyard and the big kilns. On our way up we passed the 'classy' potters workroom and I peered inside curiously. There were only a few people working in this huge sunlit room. Each at their own table, some with wheels, others constructing the clay with their hands. Just the smell of the place made me feel weak at the knees with envy.

'Sue, can we have some coffee and sandwiches?' Raymond called out to a middle-aged woman who had passed us on the way out of his office.

'Of course, Mr Watts,' she replied breezily.

There was no question of having to talk Raymond into it. He obviously liked Jimmy and the whole idea of my wanting to make pots and use his facilities seemed to please him.

'Of course you can!' he said, turning to me, as soon as Jimmy broached the subject. 'I've got clay here. Glazes. Have anything you want. I'll introduce you to Leanne and she'll show you where everything is. We'll fire your stuff with the small precious loads.' He smiled at me. 'Don't want it to get lost.'

I was suddenly embarrassed, hoping he didn't think I was going to come up with anything wonderful. I wasn't even sure if I'd be still able to use a wheel! It had been about six years since I'd tried.

'I'll only be doing simple crappy stuff,' I said. 'Just for the fete, you know.'

'My dear girl,' he said quite seriously, moving forward in his chair, 'do what ever you want. Come and work out here if you want to. We can make space for you in that room downstairs.'

'Might be a good idea, Soph,' Jimmy said enthusiastically. 'Then you'd be near everything and I could run you out every day.'

'Er no, thanks, but,' I said hurriedly, 'I'd prefer to work back at the house.' I could picture my fumbling efforts in front of all those trained, gifted people only too well.

'Just as you like,' Raymond said. 'Do whatever you like.'

'Mission accomplished!' my uncle yelled, once the car was heading back to Ballingo.

I slapped the hand that he was holding out for me and laughed. 'Yep,' I said, winding down the window and putting my head out, 'aim achieved.' I'd really enjoyed meeting Raymond after hearing about him as the jerk twenty-five years ago. And the whole thing of going out there with my uncle had been great.

'Now, we've just got to find a wheel,' Jimmy said thoughtfully, 'and then you're in business.'

'Hmmm,' I said guiltily, 'exactly my thoughts.'

'You know,' he said suddenly, 'I've got this feeling that there is a pottery wheel in Fran's studio!'

'Well!' I tried to sound surprised. 'That would be handy.'

'We'll ask as soon as we get back there,' Jimmy declared, offering me a smoke. 'She won't mind.' I nodded. 'So what do you reckon about old Ray?'

'I dunno.' I smiled at Jimmy. 'Pretty cool.'

'I reckon we should fix him up with Fran.'

'Jimmy,' I said, warily, 'Amy told me she hates him.'

'Oh hate . . . love.' Jimmy shrugged, and flicked his ash out the window. 'Same thing in the end.'

'Oh yeah?' I looked over to see if he was serious. 'Since when?'

'Leave it to me,' he said with another crooked grin. 'You just concentrate on the pots, okay?'

'Okay.'

What is happening here? In a matter of ten days my house has been turned into an industrial site. No. It only looks like that. The back veranda, which was virtually bare when I moved in here, has been partitioned off from the weather by tarps and is now more or less a bloody potter's studio! Mum's old laundry, just off the veranda and shut up for years, has been opened so they have access to running water. Bloody hoses running out all over the place. A couple of tables from the shed are lined up near the wall, covered in plastic bags of clay. There are buckets, trays of finished earthenware pots, bottles of glazes, tools. My niece is going full-bore at that old wheel all day, as though her life depended on it, and Jimmy and his daughter are here at least twice a day, collecting trays of pots and delivering them back baked and ready for glazing.

The conversations are all about whether they'll fill them with lollies or pot-pourri and how much they'll get if they fill them with chocolates or lemon butter. There is a lot of calling out about firing times, shouts for someone to make someone else coffee, arguments about whose turn it is to pack the car. And laughter. So much gusty, spontaneous laughter that from my studio it sounds like there is a perpetual party going on out there. Oh, and I forgot the music. After an hour of that terrible mechanical thumping sound on the first day they set up, I ran out of the studio pulling at my hair like a mad woman.

'Turn that noise off or I'll go crazy!' I yelled. I'm glad that Jimmy and Blue were there so Sophie didn't have to take the full brunt of my wrath. 'This is my house and I'm trying to work.'

'Shut up, Fran,' Jimmy called back. 'It's not your house any more than it's mine.' Then he looked at Sophie. 'Let's just play classical.' She shrugged and I crawled back into the studio to lick my wounds. And from then on the air outside was filled with Bach and Beethoven and Mozart arias! Oh my God . . .

I can only marvel at the plans I had for a quiet, contemplative private life up here in this old house. How did they get so thoroughly overturned?

Oh hell! I suppose I'm exaggerating. No one interrupts me. They don't dare! And I *am* managing to get some work done. In so many ways I'm pleased. Apart from anything else it is all so funny. Jimmy strutting around like he's organising World War Three. He doesn't actually *do* anything much but give orders. When I pointed this out to him the other day over lunch he said, 'I'm the ideas man, Fran,' as though that explained everything. I said, 'Oh righto, Jimmy,' trying to keep a straight face.

Blue is there a lot of the time, trying to calm him down while she actually does the work: arranging the lollies and dried flowers into the pots, wrapping them up into pretty paper to sell as gifts, storing them in boxes. I think Jimmy's job is to price them but of course no one agrees with what he decides so there are arguments about that. Then Amy troops in with her contribution – magazines full of ideas for what Sophie can make next! Even that damned dry-stick of a headmaster, Phil Ryan, came around one afternoon to spend a couple of hours on my back veranda. (He looks exactly the same as he did a quarter of a century ago, except for a few lines around his eyes.) 'Hello there Fran,' he says, folding his arms as though he's the overseer at the local factory and I'm the unit manager. 'Just came around to see what's what.'

And there is Sophie. The girl is coming alive before my eyes. The pots she's making are ordinary enough. Nothing wrong with them, but basically just plain dishes and simple little vases and things to put plants in. A few plates. Jimmy acts as though they are the most beautiful things he's ever seen. And he's genuine.

'Oh, Soph, you've outdone yourself here, girl!'

'What about making six like this one and we'll flog 'em off as a set of fancy goblets?'

'Jeez, this glaze is superb, isn't it?'

He stands around fingering her work, real wonder in his voice. Sophie knows they're nothing that special but I can see she's touched by Jimmy's high praise. And the *glazes* are superb. That old fox out there at Flying Duck wouldn't have anything that wasn't the best.

She is improving, I think. The tray-load I saw yesterday, all finished in blue and terracotta shades and white, were really quite lovely, in a rough kind of way. When I told her that I thought she had a feeling for colour she was so pleased that I felt ashamed I hadn't shown more interest in them before.

I'm going to have to get on to her about the smoking

though. I've been putting it off. I was down that end of the house this morning and it smelt like a bloody crematorium. The smell is starting to seep into the rest of the house. How do I know she's not smoking in bed? I said as much to Jimmy this morning.

He nodded seriously, then grinned at me. 'Good luck,' he said and I didn't dare ask what he meant by *that*.

I must get someone in to check the wiring too. When I pulled out the iron the other day I was almost electrocuted! My problem is, I've spent all my married life *not* paying the bills, *not* ringing up plumbers and electricians and handymen, *not* haranguing bank managers and *not* carrying out the garbage. Daniel did it all. Now that I'm on my own I find it difficult to even contemplate some of the stuff that needs to be done, much less do anything about it.

Oh, enough of it all!

Tonight, getting ready for bed, I began thinking of Vincent Van Gogh just before his twenty-seventh birthday. Approaching thirty and he'd still not made anything of himself. His father wanted him to be a banker, his brother, Theo, thought he'd have success as an art dealer, then when he'd failed at both he tried theology and failed again.

In March 1880 he walked from the French border city of Valentines to Courieres – about thirty miles. He wanted to visit the studio of Jules Breton, one of Europe's leading painters, and show him some of his pen and charcoal drawings. But he was too shy to go in. He stood outside Breton's studio simply too scared to knock on the door. After hanging about for an hour or two trying to summon up his courage, he gave up and wandered into the town's church. Titian's painting

Burial of Christ was hanging there. Moved by the beauty of the painting he looked at it for some time, then walked the fifty miles back to his home in Cuesmes, Belgium.

Three days and three nights in the beginning of March in wind and rain without a roof over my head, he wrote. But during this journey he realised he was a painter. Although he never explained to anyone why or how this happened.

From that moment everything has seemed transformed for me.

Oh Vincent! How my heart goes out to you. Being too scared to knock on that door! I wonder how someone like you would go at the end of *this* century, when panache and style are considered essential to getting *anywhere*. So many people on the make, so many wannabes, so many fakers! Maybe it has always been the case, but I don't think so.

I lie in bed trying to remember everyone I know in the art scene. All the exhibitions I've been to, the articles I've read. I try to fit into that scene a very poor, shy young man who is too scared to knock on a door. But no, I am forced to decide. I don't think Vincent would get very far today.

I remember my own dark night of the soul and, I'll admit that I imagine it was a little like Vincent's! I reckon he never spoke about it because he wasn't actually sure what was going on. That's how it was with me anyhow. All I can say is that in the morning I was different. I just knew what I had to do. It wasn't a matter of wanting to do it. (Being a painter is sometimes the last thing I want!) But having to do it. Of feeling like I'd be smothering myself if I didn't at least try.

It was in March too. After Dad's funeral. Back in this house for the first time in a year, on a boiling hot day. So many people had come back to the house for the wake. Hundreds. Relations and old friends, acquaintances from every conceivable corner of Dad's life. Of all our lives. It was like everyone the family had ever known or come across had crawled out of the woodwork for the occasion. My sisters and aunts were like a small army, feeding them and washing up. Somehow I kept myself apart from all this. Not that I consciously decided to. But I did have the right to step back, I knew that. After my months of looking after Dad I knew that no one would judge me for not being part of the catering team. (Except perhaps Geraldine!) And it wasn't as though I was absenting myself from people. I talked and smiled and even cried a few times. But inside I was hanging about on the edges. I felt emotionally remote.

That night I stayed in the old house on my own for the very first time in my life. No one wanted me to. Everyone was telling me to come back with them, to the city, or if I wanted to stay in Ballingo, there were any number of spare beds. It seemed every house had at least three and they were all made up for me! But it was as though I had no choice. I knew I would be staying in the house by myself, and I knew that although I was mentally and physically drained, something big was brewing.

When night fell I went out walking down by the river, over near Grandview, back and forth a few times over the bridge. When I got back it was midnight. I played music. Tchaikovsky's violin concerto, over and over again. I ate leftover food. I turned out the lights and sat alone in the dark. I was restless, churned up and confused. I began drinking and crying and so I pulled out all the old Bob Dylan albums. *Blood On The Tracks* I think was one I played over and over. And Joni Mitchell. I began to talk to myself. To my dead father, and to my mother. To Vincent Van Gogh, to Edvard Munch, to Ernst Kirchner, the German painter I loved so much, and to Dorothea Lange, the American photographer. Carson McCullers. Rauschenberg. I had conversations with all the artists I'd grown to love over the years. I felt they were there with me, even though I knew the thought was ridiculous. They were there and I was choking in front of them.

What happened? Where did my drive go? Perhaps my talent was only small. So what? There are enough great paintings in the world after all. I'm not interested in success anyway. I certainly don't want to be famous. It's more that I want to know. I want to make sense of my life. I want to understand. And the only way I know how to do that is by making images on paper and canvas . . .

Eventually I fell asleep on the back step, resting my head against the door jamb. I had a very strange, vivid dream of walking in the snow for miles and miles. So odd to actually feel cold in a dream when the weather around me was still warm. But there I was, trudging through snow, everything about me in black and white. I was desperate to get to the end of my journey because I had the feeling that then, and only then, everything would at last become clear. My feet were bare and numb with the cold. Bleeding too. That was the only colour. I remember looking back at my tracks in the snow and there were little dots of blood on each footprint. Eventually I did reach the end. I came upon a huge precipice. When I looked down I was very frightened because there was nothing but rocks below. Then I very calmly reasoned with myself. I didn't want to walk any further, so I would have to jump, even though I was frightened. So I did. It was while I was falling that I woke up, very startled, gasping for air.

It wasn't yet fully light. Some stars were still visible. The trees were shivering with a very still, almost unnatural silver light. It was all around me. It seemed, in my confused state, to be sticking to my skin, to my arms and legs. I actually tried to brush it off as I sat there shivering in the warm air.

But I had a plan. It had come to me unannounced in my dream. I would begin painting again. And I would not go out again to the exotic landscapes of the outback or the centre. I would begin it here, in this old family home in the little town where I'd been brought up. It wasn't really as though it seemed like a *good* idea. Only that it was something I had to do . . . if I was to stay alive. That was last March.

Through the next few months I organised my life around this central plan. I packed up my house, got my younger boys Peter and Damien settled into a flat near their university, and I told friends and business acquaintances. James was already settled in a place with friends. Secretly I began to feel as though my health and the health of my children actually depended on my going. There was a hot voice in my ear, driving me forward. The deaths would continue if I didn't go. Fate would continue to snatch away those near and dear to me if I didn't fulfil my destiny. I had lost my darling Trish through that long, slow, horrible disease of breast cancer; my mother simply dropped dead soon after, probably with exhaustion.

Then Dan was electrocuted while trying to help one of the neighbours – another reason why I wanted to leave the house for a while. I really didn't like seeing those people every day, even though I knew they felt terrible about the careless, makeshift electrical wiring in their garage, the wiring that killed my husband. They had gone to great pains to offer me support. And then my old dad. Weak and dying for nearly ten months. Missing Mum to the end, he finally dropped off the twig.

What else could happen? Anyone might ask. *Who else could go?* Well, there were my boys for a start. Eighteen-year-old Peter. Nineteen-year-old Damien. And James, nearly twenty-one and planning to go overseas.

I just wanted . . . I needed to pick up where I left off in my mid-twenties. I wanted to do what Kirchner said he wanted to do – find form for inner experiences – or die.

It is my own inner landscape of meaning that I am trying to find. I want to paint my own landscape until I simply exhaust myself. This town, these smokey-blue hills, the people, the big wide sky and all we've lived through. Not in any literal, realistic sense. Oh, God, why don't people understand this?

I think of Fred Williams and my heart skips a beat. The terrible forlornness of his landscapes, the exquisite blinding blue of some of his skies. People are so off the mark if they think he was just painting dirt and sky, rocks and scrub!

By capturing one small moment I will make the meaning leap into the heart of whoever is doing the seeing . . . that's the plan anyway.

If it is so important to me, and I'm not trying to

impress anyone, why am I afraid to pick up a brush? It is not as though I'm not thinking about colour all the time. I am. These last couple of weeks up here have made me feel as though the blindfolds are coming off at last. I'm *seeing* as I haven't for years: three chooks out at Amy's farm this morning, white blobs threading through strands of green, making their way down to the river; the faded blue of the veranda poles fore-grounded against a white, miserable, cold sky; the dense red of that woman's coat in the street yesterday. Standing in front of the grey bricks of the old bank, I could have sworn it was a splash of blood!

I was sitting stringing beans at the kitchen table, asking Sophie about the horse-ride she went on the night before with Jimmy and Blue. She'd been out three times now, and although she was complaining about how stiff and sore she was, I could tell she was excited by the whole thing and dying to go again.

She picked up a magazine and moved over to one of the comfortable chairs near the fire. I busied myself setting the table. The spinach and cheese pie was in the oven and it needed another twenty minutes. I began to wash the rice at the sink, a little churned up inside. Would it hurt to say I'd have her for Christmas? She'd asked me earlier that afternoon when I'd come to check over the latest batch of pots back from the kiln.

'Oh Fran,' she said casually, 'are you planning on being here at Christmas?'

'Yes,' I said, warily. I suppose I knew what was coming.

'Do you think I could stay till then?' she asked, not looking at me. 'It's . . . three weeks away.'

'Well, I don't know, Sophie,' I said. 'I'll have to think about it. What about your parents?'

She just shrugged and pretended to go on with her claywork but when I looked back at her from the window of my studio, her shoulders had slumped and I knew she was disappointed.

I took secretive little glances at her as I settled the saucepan on the stove. She really hadn't been that much trouble so far. And she was looking so much better. I could actually see the girl who'd been here months ago. The ripe peach who had stood smiling at me outside the church was beginning to show herself again. I suddenly felt rather proud. Of course Jimmy and Blue and Amy were more responsible than me. Still, I'm buggered if I'm not going to take some of the credit! Imagine my sister's surprise when she sees her daughter next. Then again, you can never bet on Geraldine's response to anything. She rang again a few days ago and when I told her that Sophie was making pottery for the school fete, she just sniffed.

'Well, I suppose that's something,' was all she could manage. 'At least she isn't just lying around.'

I'm telling you good news about your daughter! I had wanted to scream.

'So were you close to the girl, Mai?' I asked Sophie. Sometimes I stun myself with what comes out of my mouth and this was one of those times. *Don't ask questions and don't pry*, I'd decided three weeks ago, and here I was plunging into deep water without even thinking about it. Her head jerked up a fraction at the sound of my words and then her whole body settled into a kind of studied stillness. She didn't turn around to face me but continued to stare down at the magazine.

'Yes,' my niece said, 'she was . . . my friend . . .

and . . .' Her voice dropped away. She turned her head slightly so that I couldn't see her face.

I almost got up and went over to her but I forced myself to stay put. 'And you blame yourself,' I said softly, 'because you were driving?'

She nodded her head, still not looking at me. At that point I did get up. I went over to the chair on the other side of the fireplace and sat down. Then, when I realised she didn't want me to see her face, I squatted down to poke the fire, my back to her. I was waiting. Quietly waiting. Something I'm very good at. I have a natural talent for listening.

A couple of years back I met up with a fellow who'd been at art school with me. He'd become quite a successful painter. He chewed my ear off all afternoon, telling me about his life and work (without asking me one question about myself!), and then he told me that I should honour this talent I had for listening. I remember laughing bitterly on the way home in my car. Bitter because I knew in my bones that although I might have a talent for listening, my natural talent for painting was greater than his. In fact, at art school he'd only been mediocre. Yet he'd had the tenacity to make the most of it. Something I'd been unable to do myself. Damn, damn!

Since then I've often been aware of these two talents of mine being at war with each other. The caring, helpful, loving, non-judgmental Fran is at loggerheads with the self-centred artist who likes to be alone, who is tough and cerebral, hardly needing other people at all. It is part of why I didn't want the girl to come and live with me in the first place. I intuitively knew she would call on the side of me that I wanted to submerge. That side is exhausted.

And yet . . . I can't help myself. I'm watching out for her all the time. Noting the odd smile, the looser clothing, the clearer skin, as though she is my own daughter.

Oh stop it, Fran! You are, you have always been, your own worst enemy!

'It was . . . the worst thing,' she said. 'When Mai died.'

'Yes,' I said. What else could I say? I believed her.

'I still can't believe it,' she whispered blankly, almost without expression, holding herself across the chest with both arms tight, rocking herself a little as she spoke. 'Sometimes I still wake and this shudder goes through me and I think, no! It can't have happened. It just can't have because . . .'

'Because?' I encouraged her. *Get it out girl, get it out. The first step is to put it out in the air so you can at least look at it . . .*

When she did speak it came out in a rush.

'I talked her into it. She didn't want to come. She was younger than Mihn, my age almost exactly. And she felt loyalty to her parents. You see, their brother, Truc, was trouble. Always in trouble. He'd rung Mihn and asked him to come down to this town in Gippsland to pick him up. He'd been in trouble with the police down there. And Mai didn't want to come. She didn't like going against her parents, who'd disowned Truc. Also, she had an assignment that she wanted to finish. I can see her face, her saying, "No . . . I have to get it finished." And me saying, "Oh come on, Mai. You need to get out more."'

'So she agreed to come?' I said, anxious to keep her talking.

'That's what I said,' she went, not hearing me. 'I can

remember it word for word. If she hadn't been there she wouldn't have got killed.' Sophie looked up to face me.

'You see, I spent time with them. With the family. Just before this happened we were really close. Mai and, er . . . her brother Mihn and me. I mean. I was . . . happy. I loved Mai. And . . . I saw how they all depended on her, how they all loved her.'

'And you talked her into coming to pick up the other brother with you?' I said.

'Yes I did. I thought it would be fun for us all to go together to the country. Also . . . I dreaded the trip home with Truc. I thought if Mai was there, it might be easier.'

I waited a bit, but she didn't say anything for a while.

'And did you have a licence?'

'I was on my L plates.'

'So it was legal?'

'Yes . . . those parents!' She burst out with a heavy, hoarse sob. 'They were starved and beaten. Nearly killed by pirates. Risked so much to get their family out of Vietnam. All they wanted was a new life. They did all that only for me to . . . me to . . . to kill their daughter!'

I wished that I could take it away from her. Such a bitter cup to have to swallow from, at such a young age. But I knew I couldn't. I edged over nearer to her and put my hand on her knee. No one could take it away from her. We sat together in quietness for some time. Just the muffled sounds of her crying mixing in with the soft sounds of the log burning, of flames and ashy sticks collapsing and disintegrating.

'I've done things like that, Sophie.'

'But you haven't caused someone's death by doing it, have you?' she gasped back sharply.

'No . . . that's probably right,' I said, trying to think back to the time when I was young and in love in that desperate kind of way. Knowing I'd done some terrible things and not being able to think of the right one then, when I needed to.

'All Mum could say to me was,' she said passionately, '"It's not your fault." It's not your fault! It's nobody's fault! But it was . . . it *was* my fault. I mightn't have meant it but it was still my fault!'

'Yes,' I said.

Her head jerked up and she gave me a sudden hard look.

'So you agree?' she whispered.

'Of course.' I shrugged. 'You were driving. There was probably something you could have done differently. Did you go to the funeral?'

'No,' she sighed, 'I wanted to . . . everyone in my year went.'

'So why . . . ?'

'Suddenly everyone loved her once she was . . . dead,' Sophie went on bitterly. 'Everyone loved her after I killed her.'

'Why didn't you go?'

'I couldn't face it. I knew everyone was . . . they'd all be blaming me.'

'How do you know that?'

'I was told.'

'By who?'

'By . . . my two best friends.' She gave a sad, mirthless laugh. 'My *ex*-best friend, Alana, told me that his family didn't want anything to do with me. Ever again. I was the one who talked Mai into coming and I was the one driving the car.'

'Why did they turn on you?'

'What . . . do you mean?'

'Your friend, Alana? His family? Mihn? Why did they all turn on you?'

'Well, I was driving and . . .'

'And a truck came up behind you, right?' I cut in sharply, I'd heard the details from Jimmy. 'The driver hadn't slept. He was going too fast. He lost control of the truck and hit the oncoming vehicle and . . . your car was caught up in the crash. Maybe you should have seen him coming. Maybe you should have pulled off the road before he began passing you. Maybe you shouldn't have been driving at night in the first place. *But why did your friends turn on you?*'

She opened her mouth and then closed it again. She might have whispered something but I wasn't sure. I decided not to ask her to repeat herself. I didn't want to push her. I got up and walked over to the stove. The pie smelt as though it was ready and the rice was nearly done. I took the dish out and set it on the table. Guilt never just disappears as soon as you learn to see something from a different angle. Words can't erase it. Only time and distance and . . . oh, I don't know, *some kind of new life maybe?* This niece of mine . . . this little girl was on one of those steep learning curves that made me feel giddy just thinking about it. I was standing by the table. The food was cooked; we might as well eat it. But I continued to stand.

I remembered then what I really wanted to tell her. I took a deep breath.

'I told Dan to go next door and help them with some problem they were having with their renovations,' I said sharply. 'He wouldn't have even known about it except for me. They came in to ask for some tool or other. I went out to the shed and gave it to them. When Dan came home from work I told him to go over there and help . . . *help them out Dan* while I finish getting the dinner!'

I could feel the fury building as I spoke. Amazing that there was still so much left. Almost as fresh as the day it happened. Still there underneath, waiting to explode to the surface. I longed to sweep every damn thing on the nicely set table onto the floor and hear it all smash.

'I didn't even kiss him goodbye, Sophie!' I spat at her aware that my voice had gone down an octave or two. It seemed to be coming from the pit of my stomach. 'I sent him next door to his death without a word of goodbye!'

Then, suddenly exhausted, I sat down and put my head in my hands.

'Are you hungry?' I moaned through fingers, motioning with one hand towards the pie that was steaming on the table between us. I didn't lift my head. There was no answer.

'Are you hungry, Sophie?' I asked again, sitting up slowly and picking up the bowl of rice, wondering if I'd gone too far. She was staring at me, stunned, sitting there with her hands on her lap. Neither of us had served ourselves anything to eat yet. She gulped and shook her head.

'Not really,' she whispered miserably, eyes on her plate. I put the bowl of rice down again.

'Why don't we just put it all back in the oven,' I said suddenly. 'Let's go for a walk down to Ruby's Point. You and me. Maybe go via Amy's. We can eat when we get back. Let's just piss off. What do you say?'

One of those smiles broke out on her face and it was as though the sun had come out in the middle of a bleak afternoon. Lovely wide mouth and those eyes, no longer blank, lighting up too. I suddenly saw her mother in that face. Her mother, Geraldine, my older sister, probably about the same age, sixteen or seventeen, standing in this very room, dressed in high heels and a tight, short mini-skirt, laughing her head off at something Jimmy had said.

'Yes, okay,' Sophie said, 'I'll bring Amy the little vase she wanted.'

'Good. Let's go.'

So we put on our coats and boots and walked down the hill to Amy's place. I told her all the details about Dan's death. She hardly said a word.

We were out for a long time last night. Amy, my niece and me. The three of us walking along together. All the heaviness somehow just lifted and melted away into the crisp night. We walked along the river, right to Ruby's Point and then along the little dirt track for a couple of kilometres. A lot of it was under bushes and trees. But every so often the trees thinned right out and, the night being clear, with a bright moon, we saw the river before us, huge, gleaming and alive. Each time we saw it I was filled briefly with an intense joy. The sound of the water was so quiet yet powerful, like an old man breathing.

I woke in the middle of the night, wondering about guilt. Hers, mine, the way it stretches and pulls and eats away at the inner being like an infestation of maggots. I do know the *feel* of it very well but what about the colour? Eventually I dozed off again, telling myself that when I found the right colour for guilt, I'd begin painting again.

Daniel's eyes were the most lovely, unusual brown. Flecked with light. Sometimes I used to look at him and think he actually had sparks in his eyes. I can see him at our wedding, in a purple bell-bottomed suit that he'd borrowed from his brother, a white, ruffled shirt with purple trim (the photos are hilarious), his hair long and, as his mother so rightly sniffed, *completely unkempt*. I remember him standing there, making a speech about me.

Fran is bold and brilliant, beautiful and brave, he said, *and that's why I'm marrying her today.*

I'd been arrested the week before at an anti-Springbok demonstration, had given up my teaching job the week before that, and was off on my own to the Northern Territory for a painting trip. No one at the wedding could believe it. *You mean you're not having a honeymoon?*

Three months . . . and you aren't going together?

'That's right,' I said coolly. 'I gave up my job to paint, not to live a quiet suburban married life!'

Oh God, I think of him lying on his belly on the floor, near the fire, reading stories to the boys, and I miss him so much that I want to go into the bathroom and slit my wrists!

I came across this wonderful wreckers' yard this morning. I was walking back from a two-hour hike I'd taken along the northern end of Ballingo's national park. I was only about a kilometre out of town. There were all these clapped-out old bombs around a plain little wooden house. Someone was living there – there was washing on the line. An even row of flapping nappies against the black-green of the hedge. I stood there filled with wonder. Just to the right of the nappies were eight flattened cars piled on top of each other! Stunning. Each was rusty but a different colour. They seemed so absolutely indifferent and *finished*. At the same time so full of what they had been. Behind the house, in the distance, were six tall pencil pines.

A perfect composition. The dark vertical shapes in the background, directly above the flat horizontal slabs of colour that were the cars, and to one side the white flapping shapes of the nappies – like so many flags of surrender. And in the foreground was a little girl of about four. Black tangled hair and red rubber boots. She was jumping around in the puddles, singing to herself, completely oblivious to everything. I sat down across the road from her and pulled out my sketch pad. My mind was going berserk. Oh this world! I kept thinking. This bloody world! The beauty of it. What can I do with it? This terrible, unfathomable world of squashed cars and little girls in red rubber boots! I rushed home, my heart racing and light.

I stayed in the studio for about four hours straight, just working on the one idea, completely immersed.

I want people to look at my paintings and feel a frisson of recognition. *Perhaps I have seen this image before*, they think. But no. The image has simply reached out and touched *who they are* under all the layers of bullshit. It doesn't matter if they don't find pleasure and solace in my work, as long as they find something *true* to take away into the rest of their lives.

She didn't set the world on fire, they will say. But neither did she waste her talent completely in the end.

At two o'clock I came out to make myself some

lunch, still deep in thought about what I'd seen. Seeing Sophie alone, I stopped before opening the door.

'Want a sandwich?' I called out. But she didn't hear me. I hadn't seen her since the night before. I walked over, thinking that I'd ask again.

She turned around and that's when I saw what she was doing.

A half-finished exquisite little figure in clay. An angel, I suppose. But not sweet or sentimental or any of those other attributes people normally associate with angels. This was a real person who happened to have wings! He had ears that stuck out a bit too, a frowning face, perfectly made hands that folded in front of him, and two big feet sticking out from under a rough tunic. Standing at about half a metre, he was simply perfect. My mouth fell open and then I started to laugh.

'Oh, Sophie,' I said, hardly able to believe it. 'He's absolutely beautiful!'

'You think so?' she said shyly.

'Oh God *yes*!' I breathed the word again, '*Yes*.'

She loosened a piece of cloth covering a large fruit box and gently pulled out three more of these figures, setting them out on the table for me to look at. Each of them very different. One, an Asian girl with cropped hair and a sweet expression, was only half the size of the other two. They were taller, thinner. But the differences were not only in size. One really lovely one was quite fat, with what looked like a pair of jeans under his angel's tunic, glasses on his nose and hob-nailed boots on his feet. Each of them absolute individuals, rock-solid, and yet there was something ethereal about them too.

'These three are dry,' she said, matter-of-factly. 'I'm going to take them out to fire this afternoon when Jimmy comes.'

'What gave you the idea?' I whispered, truly amazed. *What a stupid question.* I of all people should know there is never a satisfactory answer to it. But I was flabbergasted. And so curious too. They were superb. Delicately finished with such detail, and yet raw. Way beyond cute. Sophie handed me a mud-encrusted craft magazine that Amy had brought her a few days before.

'I started off with this,' she said shyly. 'Then sort of branched out when I got bored.'

Make Your Own Angel For Christmas was the heading. But there was nothing about Sophie's figures that was even remotely like the sickly-sweet illustration.

'Did you actually make one like this?' I laughed, pointing at the illustration.

'Well I did,' she replied. 'But then I got excited thinking about other possibilities. So I mashed it up and started again.'

'Are they angels?' I asked carefully, not wanting to intrude.

'Well . . . sort of,' she said, pointing to a stooped, thin, old figure. 'This one is modelled on Grandpa. Remember how bony and thin he was?'

I stared at the figure she was pointing to, and saw that it was indeed like my father. A sudden lump rose in my throat. I swallowed and, not knowing what to say, I grabbed her arm and pointed at the little Asian girl.

'And is this one . . . your friend? The girl who died?'

'Yeah, but I'm not happy with her,' Sophie replied

calmly. 'She was one of the first I'd made. I'd like to do her again. Different this time. This one is too sweet.'

'The real girl wasn't sweet?' I asked.

'No way,' Sophie said emphatically. 'Once I got to know Mai I found out that she wasn't sweet at all. Or demure. She was really sparky.'

Sparky?

I smiled immediately, liking the description. 'Are you going to glaze them?'

'I don't know.'

'Talk to Raymond about it,' I said. 'He'd be good to advise on this.'

'Yeah, maybe.'

The first four of her figures came back from the kiln a few days later, looking even better. Raymond had advised her very well. They were glazed but only faintly. A transparent wash of black ink in the joints and crevices and tinges of gold on the wings and hands. The whole effect, an almost imperceptible enhancement to the natural quality of the baked clay. Simple but expensive, I guessed. From my art-school days I knew that gold glaze was heaps more expensive than the other glazes because it contained real gold. That old fox was being very generous for some reason.

'Did he like them, Sophie?' I asked, running my finger over a fine gold-edged wing.

'Yeah,' she said, very pleased. 'He wants me to make more. Says he'd be able to sell them through his special-product division to big stores like Myer and David Jones for Christmas.'

'*Really?*' I couldn't help being thrilled. 'And you want to do that?'

'I dunno.' She shrugged, flushing a little. 'I guess . . .
I'll decide after the fete.'

'So you're going to give all these away?' I said, thinking that they really were far too good for a little
country town fete. Raymond was right. They could
easily sit beside other beautiful handmade goods in
exclusive sections of prestigious stores. Or in a craft
gallery of course.

'Yeah.' She seemed surprised at my question. 'That's
why I'm making them. For Jimmy's art-craft stall.'

'How do you find Raymond?' I asked casually.

'Oh,' she said, smiling, 'he's been just great.'

'Well . . . that's . . . good,' I said, disconcerted by
her enthusiasm. 'I knew him, you know . . . years ago.'

'Yes.' She looked down at the figure I was running my
hands over and continued shyly, 'He said that he *wasn't*
surprised by these. He'd been expecting me to come up
with something exceptional because of you being my
aunt.'

'Oh.' I smiled at her then turned away. 'That's nice.'

That *flatterer* par excellence!

Of all the people in the world it had to be Raymond
who was the first person I ran into at Jimmy's party.

I hadn't been to a party for ages. Initially when
Jimmy told me he was giving one, I told him I wouldn't
be coming. I'd never liked parties much and I was too
busy with my work. Since Dan had died I hadn't felt up
to socialising anyway. But Jimmy wouldn't accept any
of my excuses.

'Fran,' he said, pulling a chair out for me, 'sit down.
You've been hiding yourself away since you got here!'

'Well,' I protested, 'that is, *was* the whole idea!'

'There are heaps of people in this town who want to meet you.' He went on as though I hadn't spoken. 'Good people who knew Mum and Dad. You've been here for a month and you've hardly been out of the house. If it goes on for much longer they'll think you are a snob.'

'Oh, God.' I laughed. So now my brother was teaching me good manners! *When I think of all the times in the past I've bailed him out of places, dead-drunk and abusive, looking for trouble!*

'I'm giving a party for the people working on the fete *and* to welcome you back to the town,' he said sternly. 'You have to come.'

'Okay,' I sighed, 'as long as I don't have to dress up.'

'Of course you have to dress up,' he roared. 'You and Sophie. This is a serious, formal *dress-up* party.'

'Jimmy!' I cut in. 'I don't think I've worn a dress since Dan died.'

'Too bad!'

So dress up we did. In fact, that was the best part of the whole night, dressing up for the bloody thing! I dragged out a fitted dark-green lace dress that I'd had for over twenty years. It was probably too formal but I didn't care. I felt good in it. It still fitted well. The colour against my skin, combined with the rich fabric, had me feeling excited. I went down the street and bought myself a packet of dark rinse for my hair, thinking that I might as well go the whole hog and get rid of the grey while I was in the mood.

But the most fun was in getting Sophie an outfit she felt happy in. She'd lost quite a bit of weight but not enough to fit into any of my old dresses (some of which she liked). So we went down to Amy's shop and rummaged around all afternoon, trying on and discarding about a million combinations, eventually settling on a bizarre concoction that Amy devised. (It never ceases to amaze me that Amy, such a conservative dresser herself, has such an amazing flair for dressing up other people!) A long black satin and lace nightie or petticoat (no one knew which it was) over purple leggings and a tight mauve long-sleeved tee-shirt. Purple high heels of mine, a wide silk black belt with shells on it, belonging to Amy, and a twisted purple and green scarf around Sophie's half-blue hair. With the rings back in her nose she looked absolutely fantastic.

As soon as I saw Raymond coming over to greet us, I immediately wanted to go home. The truth was I'd never really got over my desire to kill him.

'My dear, *dear* Frances Mary Kathleen O'Brien!' he said, wry as ever.

'Hello, Raymond!' I gulped. 'How are you?' God, he still had those wonderful flashing eyes. I loathed him but couldn't help admiring his style.

After accepting Raymond's kiss, Sophie moved off easily into a group of young people I didn't know.

'Young potters from my business,' Raymond explained, reading my surprised thoughts. 'She gets on very well with them, you know. Wonderful girl.'

His obvious familiarity with Sophie disconcerted me.

'Well . . . good,' I mumbled. 'I suppose.' I looked around for anyone else I knew. But although Jimmy's bistro was full of gabbling, well-dressed people, all smiling and drinking and calling out to each other, there was no one I recognised immediately. I felt panicky as I gripped my handbag, wishing I could just leave straightaway and go home.

Mercifully, Amy buzzed by with a tray of champagne glasses. I took one, gulped half of it down very quickly and, as it hit the bottom of my empty stomach, I decided that it might, with a bit of luck, be possible after all to have a good time. By the time the second glass was empty I was feeling definite about it.

'Your niece is very gifted, I think,' Raymond said a few minutes later, exchanging my empty glass for a full one from a passing tray, without taking his eyes off my face.

'Yes,' I said, 'aren't those . . . things she makes just so wonderful!' I could hear the gushiness in my voice but didn't seem to be able to stop myself. 'I'm so proud of her.'

'I don't think her mother will be pleased though,' Raymond said, frowning thoughtfully.

'No.' Again I was disconcerted. How come this old fox knows everything? He was probably right though. It would be hard to get Geraldine to admit that within the space of a few weeks her daughter was looking a lot better.

'So, Frances,' Raymond said, 'how long is Sophie staying with you?'

'Well, I'm not sure.' I knew my voice was slurring slightly but I refused to feel embarrassed about it. 'Christmas soon and I suppose her parents will want her home.'

'It is just that I would like to make her a proposition.'

'Oh.' I giggled fatuously (I'd had nearly finished my fourth glass of champagne by this stage). 'You were always so good at propositions, Raymond!'

He smiled and I felt such a fool.

It got worse. I did escape Raymond from time to time

during that party. Sometimes for up to thirty minutes. But somehow, just when I thought I was free, there he was at my elbow with something to eat, a witty comment, another drink. I spoke to a lot of other people that night. I know I answered questions and gave my views on all manner of subjects but I was steadily getting completely blotto. I didn't mean to. I just kept drinking as I glided around from group to group, meeting up again and again with Raymond and getting steadily drunker.

At around eleven the lights dimmed, the music became louder and people began to dance. Wild and carefree at first. I looked around for my brother, my great rock-and-roll partner since we were teenagers, thinking that I was either going to have to dance wildly for the rest of the night or curl up in a corner and sleep. But instead of Jimmy there was Raymond holding out his arms to me.

'Shall we dance, Frances?' he said softly. In my drunken state he suddenly looked wonderful. Tall and handsome and, most important of all, *male*. So cool and debonair and so successful in his Italian suit, silver hair and shining slip-on shoes. Why not? I thought. I had hardly touched a man for eighteen months. I moved forward easily, into his arms, and begun to dance with him. He was very good and in spite of my intoxicated state I managed to dance well, too. Within a few minutes we were both puffing and laughing.

After a while the lights became even dimmer and the bright rock music gave way to slower, romantic numbers. A few warning signals began to bleep inside my thick brain then but I was well past heeding them. By the end of the first slow number Raymond was holding me close, running his hands up and down my back, murmuring in my ear that he still fancied me, that he'd never forgotten me and that now at last, after all these years, we should *catch up* with each other properly.

I remember snorting with laughter because he'd managed to make that innocuous little phrase, *catch up*, sound so lewd. I also remember Jimmy passing by with this huge grin on his face, and it suddenly occurred to me, through the thick fog of alcohol, that this had been Jimmy's plan all along: to get me together with Raymond. *The bastard!* Luckily (or unluckily) the thought passed away into the place where all my other sensible thoughts had parked themselves for the night.

So instead of slapping Raymond's face and pushing him away, I was laughing and letting him fondle me in front of a room full of people! The cream of Ballingo that Jimmy had invited to that party to meet his sister, the artist, were standing about watching me being fondled and pawed by a leading local identity under a strobe light. These were people I was going to have to live with for the next year! Friends of my mother's. People who knew Daniel. The doctor, the local real-estate people. A whole group of Flying Duck employees . . .

I think I passed out in the toilets but I can't remember much about it. Amy got me home in the end. When I got inside the house I know I was groaning and Amy was telling me not to worry. And Sophie was there too, taking off my shoes and helping Amy take off my dress. What appalling behaviour for my niece to have to witness! I went off to sleep, my last conscious thought was to thank God that I *did* pass out. The image of myself waking up next to Raymond Watts in (what I'm sure would be) his plush king-size bed in that two-storey palace out on the Flying Duck estate was just too horrible to contemplate.

I woke at midday feeling absolutely terrible. Sour and bitter and looking for someone to blame. Why had Jimmy insisted I came to his blasted party? What business did he have trying to match me off with someone I'd rejected twenty-five years ago? How come Amy kept plying me with fresh glasses of champagne instead of taking me aside and telling me I'd had enough? Amy and Sophie had been laughing last night when they were helping me undress. *How dare they!* The whole episode was so humiliating. I wanted to get up and swear at someone but I could hardly move. My head throbbed and my throat felt as dry as a gravel track on a hot day.

Eventually I stumbled to the bathroom, found some aspirin, downed four, then crawled back to bed to let them do their work. I must have gone to sleep again because when I next noted the time it was four in the afternoon and I was beginning to feel better.

I wandered out into the backyard, surprised to see that the sun was shining because the house was still quite cold. There was a slight breeze making the peppercorn tree that hung over the far end of the studio quiver. The fronds were almost caressing the building.

My head felt thick and terrible but I went back inside for the studio key. I wanted to check on some of those sketches I was doing the day before, just to convince myself that what I was doing was on the right track.

The key wasn't in its usual place . . .

'What the bloody hell!'

I stood at the door of the studio, still in my dressing-gown, and simply stared in open-mouthed fury. 'What do you think you're doing, Sophie?'

'Oh I . . . I just came in here . . . looking for something,' she stammered, her face immediately heating up.

What could she say? I'd found her in my studio, my inner sanctum. Not only that, but I'd caught her in the act of reading my personal journal! There was nothing she *could* say.

'You came in here to poke through my things,' I hissed, slamming the door behind me. I strode over to where she was standing, snatched the big black book from her and snapped it shut. She cringed as though she was expecting me to hit her over the head with it. I have to admit that the thought was very tempting.

'How dare you!' I yelled. 'How bloody dare you?'

'I'm really sorry, Fran,' she whispered, on the verge of tears. 'I just –'

'You just *what*?' I snapped. 'You deliberately came in here to snoop on me. It is such a . . . *shitty* thing to do!'

She nodded and gulped.

'Is this the kind of thing you do to your mother?' I demanded nastily. 'Snooping around her things?'

'No.' She looked surprised at the suggestion. 'I just –'

'If it is,' I cut in cruelly, 'then I don't blame her for finding you a bloody handful. I mean . . . God! I'm starting to have real sympathy with her!'

Shut up, Fran. You are right out of control.

I exhaled sharply a couple of times, trying to calm myself down. But my head was throbbing again.

'Listen,' I said very coldly, turning my back on her, 'just get out of here, will you!'

She almost ran for the door.

'And, Sophie!' I called after her. She stopped in the doorway, awaiting my next onslaught, 'I thought I said no smoking in the house!'

'It was just in my bedroom,' she said weakly. 'It's a long way from the rest of the house.'

'It is part of the house, isn't it?' I screamed, stamping my foot. 'So don't make stupid excuses and . . . don't lie to me!'

With that she fled.

I was so furious that I stomped around the place, swearing and muttering. How dare she abuse my trust! After all I've done for her! As though I needed her to come and live with me!

Then Amy rang and I told her the story in all the shocking details – catching the girl red-handed, the look on her face telling all. My disbelief. My fury. Amy said nothing for a couple of moments and that should have warned me. But I was so heated I decided she couldn't have quite understood and instead of asking what her silence might mean, I started ranting again.

'What a little . . . *cow*, to abuse my trust like that!'

'Oh calm down, Fran,' Amy said impatiently. 'What does it matter?'

'She's read my diary.' I wailed. 'My inner-most thoughts. That is just *unforgivable!*'

'I remember you once telling me all that you'd read in Monica's diary,' Amy said mildly.

I was speechless for a minute, because this was true and I'd forgotten all about it. Not only had I read the whole damned thing, I had told Amy everything I'd read as well. That was terrible of me. Monica's first Christmas home after leaving the convent and her diary was full of angst and secret, heartfelt desires. Her relationship with God, the other nuns. The way she'd been in love with some man for over two years without ever having said a word to him about it. It had been so intriguing that I'd simply been unable to stop. Bad enough. But imagine me thinking it was all right to tell my best friend!

'I was just a kid!' I countered defensively, deflated.

'So is she,' Amy said quickly. 'In fact you would have been older, I think.'

'Oh but Amy,' I blurted, 'can't you see that this is just what I don't need? Why I wanted, *needed* to be on my own!'

'Oh, just pretend it never happened, Fran,' Amy said lightly. 'She's probably feeling so damned humiliated right now at being caught. She won't do it again.'

'Well . . . that makes two of us.' I sighed deeply. 'Humiliated, I mean . . . about last night.' A nauseous wave ran right through my body. Had I really been standing in the middle of the dancefloor kissing Raymond Watts? There was still part of me that didn't believe it had happened. 'Oh, Amy, what am I going to do about that?'

'Fran,' she said, 'forget it. Listen, go sleep some more and we'll talk tomorrow. And, regarding your studio, just . . . take the key with you next time you go out.'

I lit a fire and Jimmy rang.

'Sorry, Jimmy,' I said, abruptly, when he asked how I'd enjoyed the night before, 'not up to talking about it.'

'You want me and Blue to come around with a few beers?' he suggested breezily. 'Hair of the dog and all that?'

'Definitely not!' I shuddered at the thought. 'Look, I've had a bit of an argument with Sophie.' I forced myself to sound light. 'She's gone off. If you see her could you please tell her I've calmed down and she's not to worry . . . She's welcome back and we'll say no more about it.'

There was an immediate wary silence from Jimmy. 'What did you fight about?' he asked suspiciously.

'I caught her reading my diary,' I replied bluntly, 'in the studio.'

'What did you say to her?' Jimmy demanded. 'I hope you didn't . . . that kid is pretty vulnerable, you know.'

'Oh never mind what I said,' I snapped, 'and while we're on shitty actions, you set me up with that creep, didn't you?'

'Who are we talking about, Fran?' He was all innocence but I could hear the laughter in his voice.

'You know!'

'You didn't seem to think he was a creep last night,' Jimmy said.

I took a deep breath. Sometimes I just want to grab Jimmy around the neck with my bare hands and squeeze the air out of him.

'Jimmy, I'm going to put the phone down now,' I whispered, 'because I *never* hang up on anyone. Okay? Except obscene phone calls. But if you keep on with this I'm going to have to break that rule. Or else come around and break your neck.'

'Get a grip, Fran,' he said impatiently. 'What are you crapping on about? You got a bit pissed and got friendly with a bloke who is very keen on you. He's no idiot that guy, you know. Rich too. Everything going for him. He's been bloody fantastic to Sophie . . .'

I put the phone down very gently while Jimmy was still talking.

I heated up the soup I'd made the day before, cut the bread then went to check if Sophie was back. It was after nine at night, and almost dark. I was quite calm at that stage, if still feeling a little fragile. But I felt bad at how harsh I'd been with her. Over the meal, I'd apologise. Maybe we'd be able to have a laugh about everything.

Including Raymond. Amy was right. Why take everything so seriously? Up to this point I'd grown to really like my niece. I was genuinely excited by the emergence of her talent, too.

I knocked on her door, but there was no answer. 'Oh, Sophie,' I called, thinking she might be in there feeling too guilty to come out, 'are you home?' I gently pushed open the door. Apart from the mess of clothes strewn everywhere, the room was empty.

I slept badly that night. I realised when I woke that I'd been half-listening for her to come in during the night and every little noise had disturbed me. I got up quickly and went to her room again, hoping I'd see some sign on the way of her having arrived home. A bag or a coat dropped maybe, or a cup used in the kitchen. But there was nothing. When I pushed open the door, the room was exactly how it had been the day before. A spurt of panic ran through me but I managed to throw it off. Silly to worry. She was a talented, sensitive girl, probably very hurt by what I'd said. She must have decided to stay away for the night to give the whole silly thing time to blow over. A sensible idea, I told myself. Figuring that she would have gone to stay the night with either Jimmy or Amy, I waited a couple of hours before ringing them. I didn't want to be too pushy, hassling them all before breakfast.

But neither Amy or my brother had seen her or heard from her at all.

Amy came by in the early afternoon and we sat down together to think seriously about where she might have spent the night.

'Oh God, I hope she hasn't gone back to her parents!' I groaned. 'It would be so silly.'

'Well, it might be better than sleeping out,' Amy said, frowning.

Amy's sombre comment immediately alarmed me. 'You think something terrible has happened to her?' I asked breathlessly.

'No, Fran.' Amy smiled and put a steady hand on my arm. 'But until we find her, we just don't know, do we?'

I nodded. In truth I was starting to feel very bad about it all. This was my fault. She was just a kid and a vulnerable one at that! By three o'clock there was still no news of her and I rang Jimmy again.

'Jimmy.' I was trying not to sound overly dramatic. 'It has been nearly twenty-four hours since I've seen her.'

'Okay,' he said immediately, 'I'll come over.'

'Should I ring Geraldine and Robert to see if she's there?' I asked, hardly able to ask the question, I was dreading the whole idea so much.

'She won't be there,' Jimmy said emphatically. 'Let's not get them worried and hyped up before we have to.'

I breathed a sigh of profound relief.

Jimmy was right. Back home to Brighton would be the last place she'd go. I was sure of that.

Jimmy and I went out looking for Sophie while Amy stayed back at my house in case she rang. We were out for at least two hours, searching up and down the streets of Ballingo, into all the shops, checking her favourite walking tracks along the river and out along the main highway towards town. No luck. No one we spoke to had seen her. Most people knew her on sight and promised they'd keep their eyes peeled.

'You're very quiet,' Jimmy said as we wound our way back home.

'I was really nasty,' I said in a small voice. 'She is only seventeen and . . . I virtually told her to get out.'

'You did?' He seemed surprised.

'I didn't mean it!' I cried defensively. 'I just meant for a little while. I was furious and . . .'

Jimmy shrugged and said nothing. I watched his handsome, frowning profile as he drove, wondering what he was thinking.

'How about all those kids she was friendly with at the party?' he said suddenly.

'Yeah,' I said, 'worth a try. But I didn't get to meet them. Did you?'

'Ray will know.' Jimmy looked at me meaningfully.

'Oh God, Jimmy.' I looked at him pleadingly. 'I just couldn't face talking to Raymond.'

We got home and Jimmy was about to ring Raymond when there was a gentle knock at the front door. A flood of relief swept through me as I watched Jimmy go to answer it. *It would be Sophie. She'd forgotten her key. She was home. At last!*

I resisted the impulse to jump up and wrap my arms around her as soon as she walked in. She'd probably be feeling a bit strung-out too . . . But Jimmy was alone when he came back into the room, in his arms a huge bunch of red roses. He dumped it unceremoniously into my arms.

'For you,' he said, disinterestedly, 'from Raymond.'

It was as much as I could do to get up and put the lovely things in water.

By the middle of the next day, Amy and Jimmy were as worried as I was. No one we'd spoken to had seen Sophie. It hardly seemed possible that someone could just disappear like that, especially in a country town, where people noticed others all the time.

'Do you think we should call the police?' Amy said softly. We'd just come back from looking through the town and down at the river again.

'I've already told them,' Jimmy said, pouring himself a whisky.

There were only two policemen in the town, so it wasn't as though they'd be able to do much on their own anyway.

'What did they say, Jim?' I asked, my heart sinking.

'If she's still not found by tomorrow,' he said with a sigh, 'they can call in reinforcements from nearby towns. Drag the river and all that stuff.'

A chill of pure horror went through me. Amy saw it and quickly put her hand over mine.

'Now, Fran,' she said softly, 'don't jump to conclusions. Jimmy doesn't think anything terrible has happened, do you?'

Jimmy shrugged and looked out the window. I returned Amy's smile but I was panicking inside. *Not another death. Oh please. Not a beautiful young girl of seventeen. Not my niece who I'm meant to be looking after. Oh God . . .*

We were all sitting in the kitchen, having just got ourselves a very light meal of bread and cheese.

'I think we'd better call Geraldine now,' Jimmy said matter-of-factly. 'They should be told.' He looked at me. 'Want me to do that, Fran?'

'No,' I said, getting up, 'I'll do it.'

'What do you mean, she's *missing*?'

I had told Geraldine only the bare bones of what had

happened. That I'd been hung-over from the night before. That Sophie and I had had an argument. And that she hadn't been seen since. I was sitting back now, rigid, waiting for her reaction.

'How long is it since you've seen her?' Geraldine's voice was icy. For once I was actually in deep sympathy with her. Since I'd had my children I'd dreaded getting one of these kinds of phone calls.

You son is missing . . . presumed dead.

Your son has been in a fatal accident on the highway.

Your son was one of the victims of a melee that got out of control.

It was the stuff of my worst nightmares. I had never imagined that I might one day be the one telling another parent bad news.

'She hasn't been seen for over two days,' I repeated.

'So why didn't you call me straightaway?' Geraldine asked. 'I mean, after a . . . few *hours*?'

'Well . . . we thought . . . we didn't want to worry you.' I knew I didn't sound very convincing. 'Jimmy and I. We honestly thought she'd turn up.'

'You and Jimmy,' she snorted, contempt oozing out of her voice, 'didn't want to *worry* me!'

'That's right, Geraldine.' I tried to reply calmly.

'As though Jimmy is even *able* to make a sensible decision!'

'Geraldine . . . you've got the wrong idea about Jimmy.'

'Oh have I?' She laughed.

'Yes!' I said, close to tears. It was really ridiculous that she still thought of him as some kind of invalid. 'He's doing really well. He runs that pub beautifully . . . you really should come and have a look.' *As though I'd want to even see her in this town.*

'Look, could we just leave Jimmy out of it,' she cut in sharply. '*You* didn't want to worry me!' Then she gave a short, guttural sob, 'Oh God, Fran! How could you have thought that . . . that I wouldn't want to know? About my own daughter!'

'Well —'

'You've never had any respect for Rob or I, have you?' she shouted wildly.

'Oh please, Gerry!' I pleaded.

'*Please what?*' she screamed at me.

'Please can we keep all this for another time?' I said, forcefully. 'I'm worried sick . . . about Sophie. And I know you are too, so please let's work together on this.'

'I could never work with you, Fran,' she returned icily after a tiny pause. 'I don't trust you.'

'Right then could we —'

She cut me off. 'Let me speak to Jimmy please.'

I handed the phone over to Jimmy and rushed from the room to be violently sick outside. It was only after I was washing my hands that I thought how weird it was. She despises me so much and yet she sent her troubled daughter up to me. It didn't make sense.

When I got back inside Jimmy and Amy looked strangely at me.

'She's coming tonight,' Jimmy said.

'What?' I had no idea who they meant. 'Who is coming here?'

'Geraldine,' Amy said, lowering her eyes. 'She'll be up here later on tonight. In a few hours. As soon as she can.'

'Oh.'

We sat, the three of us, quietly around the kitchen table, all bone-tired, desperately racking our brains about where Sophie might be. *If only she was hiding out somewhere and not* . . . Terrible images came to me with sickening speed and then disappeared: her body lying by the side of the road. Run-over, attacked, raped . . . *drowned*. Oh God, what if . . . The worst-case scenarios were playing themselves over and over in my mind. At nine, Amy listlessly cut some cake she'd brought with her and made us yet another cup of tea.

My grandparents got the news about Ruby in this very house. I could almost see the two policemen coming to the door in 1924.

Could the lad leave the room please, Missus?

Grandma had known then that something terrible had happened. My father was only ten but all his life he remembered those policemen coming to the house. Stern, pale faces, blue serge uniforms and brass buttons. The formal way they'd stood in the doorway. He remembered listening, his ear at the keyhole. *We are sorry to inform you that your daughter Ruby has been found drowned in the river.*

Was history going to repeat itself?

'Come on, you two.' Amy's voice interrupted my morose meandering thoughts. 'Try to have something to eat before your sister arrives.'

But none of us could eat. I tried to imagine how I was going to greet Geraldine. What was I going to say to her? What would she say to me? I couldn't imagine how I could possibly go on with my life if my niece didn't come back.

'What about Ruby's Point?' I said dully.

'Been there,' Jimmy said, 'twice.'

Half an hour later Jimmy got up and went for his jacket hanging on the door.

'Jimmy.' I was immediately alert. 'Please be around

when Geraldine gets here. I just couldn't face her on my own.'

'Of course I'll be back,' he said sharply, feeling in his pocket for the car keys and mobile phone. 'I'll only be an hour.'

'Where are you going?' I asked.

'I've just got this hunch,' he said. 'It's probably nothing. But I want to go out along the river again. But . . . don't get your hopes up. If anything comes of it, I'll ring you on my mobile straightaway.'

Make sure the back-door is dead-locked. Close the upstairs bathroom window and the door into the den. Keys? Phone? *In handbag.* Enough cash? *Should do.* Petrol? *Yes.*

Thank goodness the BMW had just been serviced and the petrol filled up. Rob had seen to that last week. It would be a pain having to stop and do all that as well as contend with the afternoon peak-hour traffic leaving town. It was a three-hour trip.

Geraldine hurried down the wide maple stairway of her open-plan home, dumped the tightly packed tote bag on the floor under the hallway mirror, and took a quick look at herself. Short cream linen shirt, deep-maroon wide pants that ended mid-calf, and high-heeled sandals. Discreetly elegant as usual. The thick gold chain around her neck matched the watch that Rob had given her last birthday. Nearly fifty, and she looked easily ten years younger. She ran her fingers through her thick bob of damp, curly, dark hair and stared into her own clear blue eyes, telling herself not to panic.

My daughter. My youngest daughter Sophie is missing . . .

287

It would be just like Fran to drink too much and fly off the handle for no good reason! That was Fran. Always impulsive, always reckless . . . Geraldine picked up the bag and walked to the phone, willing herself to calm down. There was no point jumping to conclusions about anything . . .

Geraldine could feel a headache beginning at the back of her right eye. *So how does this play out? We find her, I bring her back here and . . .?* Bang! Back to zero. Back to Sophie holed up in that room. *Back to me going out of my mind.* She would have to ring Rob's secretary to let him know where she was going. And then Peter. And leave a note for Lauren. They'd all be worried.

As she punched in the number and waited, she turned to the window. Virtually the whole front wall of this house was window. And on a calm day like this, the view over the bay below was dazzling. A wide blue sky dotted with tiny fluffy clouds, the water itself as clear as a blue Chinese plate, dotted with the white sails on the boats. A light breeze was coming in from the sea. She watched small groups of people strolling along the water's edge, could even hear ever-so-faint sounds of people calling out. Two children zig-zagging after each other up and down the beach. A rush of envy hit. How long had it been since she had a few carefree hours, felt the scrunch of sand beneath her toes? None of those people down there had impossible daughters. Or crazy brothers. *Or sisters who . . .*

Get some outside interests, her new doctor had suggested. Some friends. Re-establish old friendships if you don't feel comfortable with the set you and your husband have acquired together. Maybe it is time to think of some part-time work to keep your mind off things.

Well maybe, Geraldine thought as she heard the phone being picked up at the other end. *Maybe he was right*.

'Oh, Anne! Geraldine here. Good thanks. Is Rob around? Oh, he's still in theatre? Okay, could you leave a message for him?'

What was so galling was that Fran had been applauded for her impetuousness from the time she was little. Dad had been so strict and terse with his three eldest, Monica, Trish and Geraldine. They were rarely indulged with stories or ice-creams, much less the right of reply. There were rules about eating what was in front of you and rules about going to bed at certain times. Rules about doing homework straight after school and rules about no friends over during the week. And those rules were very rarely broken. He was a good father, but distant and stern. At least in those early years. Any fun they had came with Mum, and usually only when Dad was out of the house.

Then, after a three-year gap, Jimmy had been born and Fran soon after. Well, Jimmy was *the boy*, wasn't he? So everything was different for him. And Fran? She was the youngest. Never as pretty as Geraldine, Monica or Trish. But very strong-willed. One of Geraldine's earliest memories is of Fran, only about three, stamping her foot at her father when he told her that she had to come inside for bed, then screaming 'no!' when he'd insisted. But the amazing part was that instead of getting a smack around her legs for such naughtiness, he'd only laughed and told her she could stay out another few minutes. At eight, Geraldine, who'd been smacked for far less, many times, had been filled with an acute sense of the injustice of it.

Even years later, with all the political trouble she got

herself into, Fran had delighted her father. It seemed that the more violent her outbursts, the further she diverged from his own political views, the more he was interested in what she had to say. Or so it appeared to Geraldine. Fancy building a seventeen-year-old a proper artist's studio because she said she wanted to be a painter! It was ridiculous then and, thinking about it now, it still was. Especially considering the fact that they had no money to spare. And it wasn't as though Fran had even used it properly. She'd done her art training in the city and after that had never really lived at home for more than a month at a time.

Painting had proved only a short-lived thing with Fran anyway. Sure, she'd had a few moments of fame in her twenties. But when commitment for the long haul was called for she'd dropped away. She didn't have it in her. She'd married and had a family like everyone else and lost her drive. Of course it was nice for her to make a bit of money on the side with her children's-book illustrating. But all that so-called early promise had come to nothing. If anyone needed proof about how things had been in their family back then, they only needed to look at that blasted white-elephant of a studio sitting in the backyard.

Geraldine shrugged and tried to think of something else. It made her uncomfortable to realise that she got such a fierce sense of satisfaction thinking about what a disappointment Fran's artistic career had turned out.

She pressed a button and the garage door slid up, then bleeped her key ring and the car door opened for her. What else *could* she do but go up there? Wait for Sophie to turn up? It all seemed a bit unreal. She hadn't seen or spoken to Sophie for nearly a month. *My own daughter, only seventeen years old, and I haven't spoken to her in a month!* The car slid smoothly down the driveway to the street. She turned around and headed north towards the freeway. With a bit of luck she might miss the worst part of the peak hour.

My daughter, my daughter Sophie is missing . . .

Off the freeway now and making her slow way through the miles and miles of outer-suburban shopping strips, trying to make it sink in. Camping gear and furniture, clothing and footwear, take-away food and liquor outlets by the dozen. For this last month she'd been trying to remember all she could about Sophie as a very little girl. She'd pulled out the old photo albums, the report cards and childish drawings. (All these had been saved and filed away meticulously.) But she couldn't actually remember much at all. Not like the way she could remember Lauren and Peter.

Sophie? The whole two years after her arrival were still a kind of miserable daze. Every doctor she went to sat her down and told her seriously (as though he'd just had some kind of revelation) that she wasn't well. As if *she* needed to be told that! She'd been the one experiencing the crazy mood swings, the headaches and sense of utter helplessness. But nothing any of them gave her had helped. It had been time, and time alone that had healed her. Just the passing of the days and months and the constant reassurance of a good husband and a few kind friends. The misery had eventually worn itself away, like the smoothing out of a stone in the wind and rain.

Sophie. My daughter Sophie is missing. What has happened to her?

The anxiety-headache was getting steadily worse.

Geraldine pulled over to the side of the road, put her head back against the rest, closed her eyes and tried to calm herself. Everything would come out all right. Why worry before you knew there was something to worry about? But Fran had sounded seriously worried. And it was that edge in her sister's voice that was fuelling her own panic. She rummaged around in the glove box, found a packet of Panadol and downed a couple with the help of a few slurps of mineral water. Then she started up the car again and pulled out into the traffic. Once she got past the suburbs she would feel better.

How dare Fran act so superior about Jimmy! As though she could claim any special relationship with him. When Jimmy was going through the worst time in his life, Fran was nowhere to be seen. Too busy with her political activities, too busy with her groovy, arty friends! Too selfish to come home when Jimmy really needed her. Apart from Mum and Dad, who hadn't really known what to do, Geraldine had been the only one who'd been there for him.

Oh God, she could see them now. Jimmy and that gorgeous young fellow! Both of them just out of the army only a few days. In jeans and short-sleeved, checked summer shirts with ultra-short haircuts, standing at the door smiling. Dad had just brought them home from the Watsonia Barracks. Jimmy so dark and lean and wiry. His friend pale-skinned with red curly hair and light-brown eyes. Both of them so handsome.

'Surprise, *Jimmy*!'

With her three sisters, she'd jumped out from behind the door. 'Welcome Home!'

Trish, Monica, Fran and herself, brought together again for their brother's first night back home. Trish was married with a two-year-old and was expecting another. Monica had just left the convent and was still wearing a scarf around her head to cover her cropped hair. And Fran? Geraldine could picture her standing there in a purple caftan, defiantly wearing the silver peace sign around her neck that both her parents had asked her to take off for the occasion. Geraldine had been only recently engaged to Rob. The lovely sapphire engagement ring still felt new and exciting on her left hand.

All of them moving forward to hug their brother.

'So, Jimmy?' Laughing, Trish began feeling his arms and shoulders for missing parts. 'All in one piece?'

'Yep.' Jimmy had laughed, then winked at his friend. 'I think so anyway.'

'Mum!' Jimmy's arm was around his mother, 'I'd like you to meet my mate, Pete Drysdale.'

'Well hello, Pete!' Mum had immediately put her arms out to the young man she'd never seen before, and kissed him warmly. Everyone had laughed at that.

'Hey, Mum!'

'A bit fresh!'

'And my four mad sisters!' Jimmy said, dragging each of them forward. 'Trish, Geraldine, Fran and Monica.'

'But don't call him Pete,' Jimmy added, grinning around at them all. 'Everyone always just calls him Blue.'

'Pleased to meet you, Blue!'

'Welcome, Blue!'

'Well thanks!' the young man said, looking at each one in turn. There was something warm and serious and watchful in his expression. At the same time you had the feeling that he might burst out laughing any minute. 'Great to meet you all!' Geraldine shivered as she remembered his easy manner and the clear, slow speaking voice.

What a great couple of days they'd had. Geraldine couldn't remember ever having as much fun, either before or after that time. It was like a sunniness had entered all their lives. The bitching between her and Fran disappeared. Trish stopped feeling sick and weighed down by the demands of her pregnancy and two-year-old. Monica stopped worrying about what she was going to do with the rest of her life. Mum and Dad had their only son back, alive and seemingly not much the worse for what he'd been through. It was like they were all suddenly on holiday. No one wanted to be serious any more.

And there was no talk of the war. That's what they'd all dreaded. Fran and Jimmy at loggerheads about it all. And everyone else being frozen out. Fran, to her credit, stood by her promise not to bring it up if no one else did.

Within a few minutes of sitting down to the lavish meal that they'd all helped their mother prepare, Blue and Jimmy were cracking jokes and everyone was laughing. Blue fitted in like another brother. It was as though they'd known him all their lives. Within an hour he'd got up to help with the washing-up, played cricket outside with Trish's little boy, Brendan, and asked Geraldine if she would teach him the rumba. From there the night developed into an impromptu party that didn't end till after midnight.

Geraldine had been competing in ballroom-dancing contests for almost six years by this stage. She'd fully expected Blue to have two left feet like most of the other young men his age. Her fiancé, Rob, couldn't dance at all, but it didn't matter, they still had fun when they went out. But within the first half-hour of teaching Blue the rumba, she knew she'd met her match. He was a natural. In fact, twenty-five years later she'd doubted if she ever met anyone who could dance like Blue. How they'd hit it off! The newly engaged nurse of twenty-five and the young returned soldier of twenty-two. It was like they were made for each other. Compared to Blue, her dance partners, who she'd been perfectly happy with until then, seemed stilted and wooden.

Long after the others had gone to bed, Geraldine and Blue stayed up dancing together in the semi-dark. Hardly speaking between numbers. Just reaching for each other as the music began, locked in the formal rhythms of the foxtrot, waltz, tango and rumba, gliding and swooping around the room together like birds. Deadly serious. No chatter, no laughter. His hand on the small of her back. His lovely mouth only inches from her ear. Why had no one thought it strange, her staying up to dance with this young stranger? Even while it was happening part of her wished that someone would come in and tell them that it was late and they both should go to bed. She didn't seem to be able to stop it herself. But her father, last to bed, about 1 a.m., had just poked his nose in casually and wished them good night. At nearly 3 a.m., both almost dropping with exhaustion, they'd quietly parted for bed. But not before he'd stopped her at the door, pulled her back into the room and, without a word, kissed her as she stood there in her dainty white cotton dress and bare feet. In the creaking darkness, the beautiful engagement ring felt heavy on her finger. She hadn't protested but returned the kiss with equal passion, wildly disappointed when he pulled away from her.

Asleep for only a couple of hours, she'd woken with a jolt at 5 a.m. Have to go to the toilet, she thought, but then the ache immediately returned when she remembered the dancing and the kiss. On the way back she thought she saw a pin-prick of red light outside. Although still half asleep, she took a look out the window. It was him, Peter Drysdale, *Blue*, sitting with his legs over the back veranda, smoking, looking out into the dark night that was filled with stars. She suddenly longed to join him out there. What would be the harm in it? He was just a boy. They could have a chat and a smoke. But she stopped herself. There was something about the shape of his shoulders, his profile in the dark that held her back. *And she was engaged to Robert Douglas,* she told herself sternly. Robert Douglas, brilliant young surgeon and lovely, trustworthy man. How could she possibly go out and sit with that boy? Someone she'd just met.

Geraldine lay awake trembling. Waiting for the sound of Blue's footsteps coming down the hall, past her room, to the one he was sharing with Jimmy. But they never came.

In the morning over breakfast she decided to joke about it.

'So the bed no good, heh?'

'The bed?' Pete said, spreading jam on his toast. 'What do you mean?'

'I saw you having a smoke last night.'

'Oh yeah.' Pete brushed it off. 'Most nights I can't sleep much.'

'Why not?' she asked innocently. He just stopped chewing and looked at her, and she felt her question hanging there in the air, heavy as a piece of rock. Then all the feelings of the night before came rushing back and she was immersed in panic. Where were the others? When she'd come in for breakfast, Jimmy and Monica had been sitting with Blue drinking tea. This was ridiculous. Her brother and sister had somehow disappeared without her noticing. It was just Blue sitting opposite her now.

'I'm okay till about two or three,' he said softly, 'but after that the whole bloody . . . catastrophe . . .' his voice faded away as he reached over for the packet of cigarettes. She snatched them up before he could get to them, and pulled one out quickly. Without meeting his eyes she put it the wrong way around in his mouth. He laughed and switched it around. *What am I doing?* she wondered, *flirting with this boy?* But again, she didn't seem to be able to stop herself. She was so used to men who took charge, pushed themselves and jostled for her attention. The fact that he did none of these brought out something bold in her. This young man, who simply looked at her as he fumbled around in his pocket for the flash gold lighter he'd bought in Bangkok, was fascinating.

'Sometimes I think if I could just sleep . . .' Blue said quietly, almost to himself, turning away, 'then everything would . . . *come good again*. Know what I mean?'

She nodded. Not really understanding. She'd never had difficulty sleeping.

'Tell me more?' she said softly after a while.

'No,' he said unexpectedly, smiling at her. 'I don't think I will.'

She sought Jimmy out for information later that day. A picnic on the river was planned for that evening and Blue and Monica had gone down the street for some beer. Jimmy was lying on his back in the backyard, under one of the peppercorn trees, his hands behind his head, eyes closed.

'What's Blue's story, Jimmy?' Geraldine asked as casually as she could. 'Where does he come from?'

'Why don't you ask him?' Jimmy said. Not unkindly, more as though he'd prefer to talk about something else. But Geraldine persisted. She really wanted to know.

'He won't say anything,' she said impatiently.

'That would be right,' Jimmy murmured, staring up at the clouds.

'Oh come on, Jimmy!' she said, poking him in the ribs. 'Tell me.'

Jimmy told her about the first day he'd met Blue properly. He'd been aware of him before this. Most people were. It wasn't just the red hair and the smart mouth. It was the way he looked at anyone who was talking to him. Like he was interested. Like you had something important to tell him and he was really taking what you had to say on board. Three weeks in at Pucka and they'd been marching around in the hot sun for over two hours. The sergeant in charge was giving them hell. A real little Hitler. Standing in the shade himself, screaming out these dumb orders that were the staple of army life and that no one had got used to yet.

'Attention!'

'Eyes right!'

'Private Jenson doesn't know right from left, so that means another half hour for everyone!' Sarcastic bastard.

'Halt! Jenson.'

'Yes, Sir.'

And the poor kid would be hauled out in front of everyone, humiliated and abused. Standard procedure for any minor mistake.

Jimmy had blisters on his feet from the boots and his throat felt raw with thirst. This stuff was shit. He didn't want to be a friggin' soldier. He wanted to fix cars. He marched and wheeled and saluted just as he'd been taught, thinking all the time that he'd run away, that night. It would just be a matter of hitching a ride. Changing his identity. New Guinea, that's where he'd go. He knew a bloke there. Go and work on his coffee plantation. Shit. Being a slave would be better than this. With the sergeant's back turned for just a minute, Jimmy turned slightly to the red-haired guy standing next to him in line.

"Mum said this would be good fun,' he whispered in a little kid's high-pitched whine out of the side of his mouth. 'And it ain't!'

It wasn't even funny but he could tell that the guy was having trouble holding back his laughter. Jimmy could hear the choked-back chuckles and so he started grinning himself. The sergeant turned around in time to see both of them laughing. He came over, made them stand out from the line and roasted them. But in spite of everything he screamed at them neither could stop laughing.

They paid for it of course. Latrine duty for a week. Extra kitchen duty. Another hour of parade every day when all the others were having a break. No swimming for the next five days – most of them reaching 40 degrees Celsius. But they both agreed it had been worth it. Laughing in that idiot's face. And after that they were mates. When Jimmy thought about it, a lot of their time together had been spent laughing about something or other.

Geraldine lay down next to her brother, listening and smiling to herself. Trying to imagine it all. Once started, Jimmy now seemed to want to go on.

Pete Drysdale had been highly recommended for three separate bravery awards, he told her. It was almost unheard of for an ordinary infantryman. The army courts had already started to take evidence from eyewitnesses and Jimmy was expecting to be called himself any day. Jimmy had seen with his own eyes what his mate did, so he knew it wasn't bullshit. He'd seen Blue crawl out from cover into a swamp to rescue little Tim Matheson who'd had both legs blown off beneath the knees. Tim, the platoon's clown, who had joked the night before in the mess about the quality of the spuds, was lying there, screaming, bleeding to death as he lay half drowning in a foot of water.

They were in enemy territory, snipers all around. Blue had gone out for Tim, even as the others tried to hold him back, telling him not to be so damned stupid, such a fool, the medi-chopper was on its way. He'd gone out, and had got himself hit too, in the leg. Hospitalised in Vuong Tou for a month afterwards. But not before he'd dragged Timmy back in time, stopped the bleeding with his shoelaces. No feet and legs left for Tim, but alive. And after months in hospital, still alive.

'But I don't know much about his family,' Jimmy went on casually. Geraldine's heart had been racing as she listened to her brother talk. She sat up, slightly giddy. It was as though . . . as though she knew it all already. That she could tell he was special by the shape of his hands, the way he held himself while they danced. The others were coming back now, through the front gate. They could hear Monica telling Blue about how the hens had to be locked away every night because of foxes.

'His old man owns some kind of big electrical business,' Jimmy went on. 'They're loaded.'

In the morning they all stood outside the front gate to wave Blue off. He'd kissed Geraldine like he'd kissed the others. On the cheek, a warm, friendly smile and a tight, brief hug. Nothing special for her. She was relieved at the same time as feeling helpless, as though she'd been thrown into a deep pit of disappointment.

'Hey, thanks for everything,' he said, smiling at them all.

With the others Geraldine watched Jimmy walk with his friend to the car, her heart suddenly thumping in her chest. *What can I do?* She'd wanted to call out to him. Tell him she'd be prepared to call off her engagement if he'd take her dancing. If he'd kiss her again. *Anything!* But she stayed silent.

'So I'll see you at the end of the week, mate,' she heard Jimmy say.

'Right.' Blue slapped his shoulder, before getting in. 'Look after yourself, O'Brien . . . and listen, thanks for having me.' He turned around at the family waiting at the gate and waved again. 'You're lucky, you know . . . you mad bastard,' he added, for them all to hear. Jimmy must have grimaced in reply because Pete spoke quite seriously.

'I mean it.'

'Yeah . . . yeah.' Jimmy sighed.

'Your sisters . . . your mum,' Pete said, grinning at Jimmy. 'They're all great . . . even your old man.' He laughed. 'He's a bloody character!'

'Yeah, well.' Jimmy grinned sheepishly. 'Thanks for giving them such a good time! They love you, Blue.'

'So they bloody should!' Pete waved, slammed his door shut and started the car. 'Bye mate.'

'See ya, Blue.'

Just before taking off, Blue looked over to where Geraldine was standing at the edge of the little group. He smiled and blew her a kiss. Then he was gone.

Three a.m. two nights later and the phone was ringing. Geraldine stumbled out of bed and pulled on the nightie she'd found too hot in the middle of the night. The thing was screaming through the house like a bloody alarm. Better get it before it woke everyone. But when she got out to the kitchen she saw that her brother, in only his underpants and singlet, had beaten her to it.

'Hello,' she heard him croak as she turned around and headed back to her bedroom. 'Who is this?'

It would probably be a wrong number. She smiled to herself as she crawled back into bed, thinking that her brother would probably give whoever it was an earful. She had to go back to work in the morning. Better get some sleep.

She was first up as usual. Showered and already in her nurse's uniform by 5.30 a.m. She came out to the kitchen, turned on the overhead light and found her brother sitting on the floor in just his underpants and a singlet, his teeth chattering loudly, hanging onto the phone, the black cord wrapped around his wrist and his face drained of colour. She had never been one to panic and she didn't panic now. He was in shock. She knew that, and with hardly a word she went over and gently took the phone from his grasp, unwound the cord, then, straining mightily, helped him up from the floor.

His arms and legs were very cold, but his forehead felt clammy with sweat. Positioning his right arm around her shoulders and putting the other one around his waist, she slowly helped him limp along back to the bedroom. It was only when he was under the warm blankets that Geraldine dared to ask, very quietly, what was wrong. Jimmy stared back at her as though he hadn't heard. As though he wasn't seeing her face but something else altogether. So she reached down and pulled out one of his cold hands and, rubbing the fingers gently in her own, asked him again.

'What is it, Jimmy?'

'Blue's dead,' he replied in a low, rasping whisper. 'Last night. He shot himself through the head.'

Geraldine was not one given to displays of emotion. She didn't laugh loudly or raise her voice very often, and she hardly ever cried. But she cried that morning. She simply sat there kneading her brother's hands, rocking back and forth, letting the tears flow, a slow, even rush of sobbing that made her dress wet and her eyes swollen and sore. She didn't even try to stop.

Jimmy didn't cry. He lay on his back with his eyes closed for a while and then curled around on his side, breathing heavily, facing into the wall, letting her pat his shoulder and touch his hands. The noise of her own crying seemed to be coming from a great distance. He turned over and sat up a little when the dawn eventually broke. They sat there holding hands, and looking out the window as the dark sky turned into a mottled mass of gold and pink. They watched the pretty streaks of coloured light flutter and play on the far wall and all the time Geraldine thought, over and over, *I can't believe this. I just can't believe it.* But she didn't say anything and nor did Jimmy.

Eventually she went out and told their mother. Fran had gone back to the city the evening before, and Trish and her little boy and Monica had returned to their homes too. So Geraldine rang them all with the news. Then she rang the local hospital were she worked and told the matron she wouldn't be in for a few days, that something had happened and she didn't care if she didn't get paid.

Later, Jimmy told her he could hardly remember what they did over the few days before the funeral. Only that it felt as though he was walking around in a fog. Long, silent, sharp blades of pure grief and anger slid in between his ribs every so often – but only inter- mittently, just to wake him up, keep him on his toes. Mostly it was just a fog of incomprehension. And a strange, deep feeling of having *missed out*. His best mate had gone somewhere and had forgotten to invite him along. Geraldine listened. She didn't pester him with questions or comments, just kept him company when he needed it. As the shock gave way to grief, Jimmy needed it very much. Mostly he needed to talk and Geraldine made sure she was there. They became very close over those few days, walking along the river and sitting out in the back garden.

Trish and Monica phoned every day. And both made a quick visit as well, at different times, just to show their concern. Fran did not come home again nor did she phone.

A few army guys came to see Jimmy. Benny Meltzer, with Max Greene, on the first day after the news. And then little Timmy Matheson in his wheelchair, with Packer, one of the more popular officers. Geraldine and her mother made them tea and sandwiches and Geraldine sat with them some of the time, too, out on the veranda as they talked about Pete in between long silences. All about the different times they'd had with him. The jokes he'd told, some of the times they'd been scared together. They talked about his courage under enemy fire, the way he held firm when others around him were losing it; hardly able to shoot, much less think.

Jimmy listened but he didn't join in. He told Geraldine later that he knew these guys meant well but their talk was useless. It didn't even get close to Blue, or to what it had been like over there.

'Scared out of your brain?'

'No, Geraldine,' he'd shouted. 'That doesn't do. It's not adequate. They keep using phrases like that and it makes you forget what it is really like!'

Geraldine nodded. They were in the kitchen washing up together. Mum and Dad were off at some church picnic. They were alone in the house.

'So what was it really like, Jimmy?' she'd whispered, not really wanting to know but feeling his terrible need to tell.

'*Scared out of your brain* is for when you're a kid and you go on the big dipper,' Jimmy tried to explain. 'Or when you know you're in for a belting . . . it just isn't . . . adequate for Vietnam!' Geraldine nodded. 'For the jungle, I mean,' he went on heatedly, leaning up against the bench, staring out of the window. 'For traipsing along in the damp heat wondering every time you put your foot down on that bit of dirt or this pile of leaves if you'll be blown to smithereens!'

Geraldine stood watching him. Her brother's youth was ebbing away in front of her eyes. Blue dying like that had done it. She was sure. Somehow, within just a couple of days, the incredible spark and energy that was her brother had drained away. He was a very different young man to the one who'd come home only the week before. And, of course, a *very, very* different one to the boy who'd left for Vietnam eighteen months before. *Oh, Jimmy!* she wanted to howl. *Jimmy, I loved him too!* But she didn't say it. It would confuse things too much.

'Watching for every noise,' Jimmy went on, almost dreamily, 'for any movement in the trees and then this tearing, ear-splitting explosion, followed by two, three or six rounds of enemy fire and . . . the guy in front of you is in pieces.'

Geraldine shuddered, wishing he'd shut up. How come she was the only one around for him to talk to? It suddenly felt like such a burden. Having to listen to all this stuff. Where were his parents, his other sisters?

Oh, Jimmy . . . Jimmy . . .

Then the letter came. Three days after they'd heard the news of Blue's death. Geraldine had gone down the street for something and when she got back her mother told her that Jimmy had received a letter in the mail, that it seemed to upset him, but that he wouldn't tell her who it was from. Nor had he come out of his room since getting it. Geraldine put down her groceries immediately and went to knock on Jimmy's door. When there was no answer she gently turned the handle and let herself in.

Her brother was lying curled up on the bed, his back to her. She could hear the unmistakable sounds of his sobs and it confused her. Two days ago she'd been wishing that her brother would cry. He had been walking around like a tightly wound-up spring, ready to snap. Rigid and almost expressionless. He needed some kind of release. But these wrenching sobs were too much. They came from too far down inside. Geraldine had to fight very hard just to stay there with him. All her instincts told her to run. Get back to her own life. To Rob and her friends. To warmth and gaiety. To all the exciting marriage plans. To the future, which promised to be so full of good things. She fought down the urge and tip-toed over, sat on the bed and put a hand on his shoulder.

'Who wrote, Jimmy?' she asked.

Without looking at her, Jimmy pulled the envelope out from under the pillow and handed it to her. Then he turned away again, lying on his side, legs drawn up, both hands pressed flat under his face.

'He must have written it before he knocked himself off,' he mumbled hoarsely. 'You read it.'

Geraldine took the envelope and slid out the single piece of paper. The note was written in huge, unwieldy letters as though the writer was either drunk or out of control, in a great deal of distress anyway. Geraldine began to shiver as she read it, because she was opening a message from a dead person.

Sorry mate! Sorry, sorry! What else can I say? You are a good mate, O'Brien. The best. Thanks for everything. I just can't see my way through this. Everything is blurry. Thick and dark. I've tried. I try thinking of all the good things . . . but the rest of it just comes crashing in . . . like someone throwing rocks. You know what I mean. I know you do.

Listen O'Brien, you're stronger than I am. In spite of all that bullshit over there. Saving little Timmy Matheson etc. etc. . . . that was all easy shit. I didn't even think about it. I hope you have a good life. Get married. Have kids. Take them on the river. Play cricket. All that stuff.

So much else to say, mate, but I haven't got time.

Tell Monica from me to keep on going after what she wants until she gets it. That girl is special, even though she's decided to give up being a nun. Tell Trish good luck for the new baby and get little Brendan a cricket bat for his birthday with the money I'm leaving you. Tell Fran to keep painting and fighting wars and all the rest. I reckon she'll achieve a lot. (Scare the shit out of all the old mongrels anyway!) And tell Geraldine she is the best dancing teacher ever, okay? Tell her to keep at it and she might end up famous. That bloke she is marrying is a lucky bastard. Tell her that from me.

Say that I've just gone away for a while and that I'll see them again one day.

There is a heap of money (over $200 000) from my grandfather's estate that I was entitled to collect when I turned twenty-one. (We both know where I was that day, heh?!) I haven't touched any of it. I'm leaving it to you, O'Brien. There is no one else. Use it to buy your own business, or whatever you want to do. I made a will and left it with the solicitors in Ivanhoe (Barnes and

Milikin), and so everything is in order (just in case my family try to pull some kind of bullshit on you). I'm very clear about this, O'Brien. I want you to have that money.

There's not much else to say, so, see ya mate. Well . . . guess I won't be doing that, so, goodbye.

From your friend,

Blue

PS Thanks for Binh Ba.

Geraldine read the letter through a few times, feeling the now-familiar prickles starting behind her eyes. She must have cried more in the last few days than in the rest of her adult life. And here the tears were again. Slow at first, but within a minute or two they were streaming down her face.

'So what was . . . Binh Ba?' she'd asked. Jimmy immediately groaned as though in pain and curled up further. Geraldine tightened her grip on his shoulder.

'Don't tell me, Jimmy,' she said fiercely. 'Just forget I asked, if you want to let it be.'

He told her though. It took him a few days but eventually it all came out. Spasmodically, like dirty water from a clogged-up tank. *Thanks for Binh Ba*, Blue had written. Oh shit. They'd both had bad times before but Binh Ba was crunch-time, for both of them.

He told Geraldine that, on the plane coming back to Australia, he and Blue agreed they would never talk about it, that they didn't even want to hear the words or even see them written on paper. Binh Ba was no man's land. Start remembering it and they would go crazy.

Oh Blue . . . Blue . . . you bloody idiot. We were gonna do so much, mate. We had plans! Remember our plans . . .

They held the funeral five days later at the All Saints Anglican church in Ivanhoe. Just two streets down from the Drysdale family home. A warm, bright day, with thin white clouds in the sky and a fresh breeze. There had been a special request for privacy from the immediate family. The parents wanted a small funeral with only family and very close friends in attendance. *A minimum of fuss*, was how Blue's mother put it to Jimmy in a cold, perfectly controlled whisper when she rang to ask him to let people know her wishes. He wondered halfway through the conversation if she was drugged. The voice was so flat, so icy and restrained. Geraldine thought it might do him good to meet up with mates. She encouraged him to stay a while, have a talk over a few beers. But Jimmy didn't want to see anyone. He didn't have any mates except for Blue. So they drove straight back to Ballingo when it was over.

Binh Ba was bodies. The bits of them all over the place. The shouting, the tanks, the flying mortars coming down. From house to house. The scrambling old women, the kids running to get away. Blue and Jimmy, running like madmen from hut to hut, the tank behind. They threw the grenades, followed up by a few bursts of machine-gun fire. *Hey! No more hut! No more people!* Looking for trapdoors and air-raid shelters. Open up, chuck a couple of grenades down and on to the next one, blasting away at anything that moved. All the smoke and the screaming and the terror. It was a massacre really. Over a hundred nogs dead at the end of it – no one knew if they were the enemy or not – strewn over the bleak village square like broken dolls, bits of them up trees, in

310

ditches, not a hut left, every pig and chicken slaughtered. And they were the slaughterers.

And Blue's face when it was all over. His face ashen with fatigue, eyes like burnt holes. 'I've had it, mate,' he said. 'This time I've had it.' Jimmy had almost just shrugged and let him walk off. *Hadn't they all had it?*

Jimmy felt too wretched himself to roll a cigarette. But there had been something different in Blue's voice. Something cold, blanked-out, something final. So Jimmy had followed his mate around to the back of a tank and when he saw Blue reloading his rifle he knew instinctively what he had in mind. Almost without thinking he'd jumped on his friend from behind, pulled the gun from his hands, kicked it away, pushed him onto the ground.

It was hard keeping him there. Blue was bigger, probably stronger, but Jimmy had surprised him and, on this occasion, had the inner-strength and purpose needed. Still, it took all he had to hold him down, ignoring the shoves, the groans of 'Get off me, ya bastard!' The tears and the curses.

'Don't be a bloody fool, Blue!' Jimmy had panted. 'Don't be a fool. We've only got a few months left. We'll get home. One day this will be nothing but a memory!'

Gradually Blue's struggling body went limp. Jimmy got off him. They sat together in the dirt, not looking at each other.

'It'll just be a memory, Blue,' Jimmy said again, waving loosely at the smoking devastation and death surrounding them, his own voice sounding distant even to himself, as though the words he was speaking were being sung into his mouth by some old person a long way away. 'One day all this will just be a memory . . .'

'Yeah.' Pete was staring down at his trembling

hands. 'You're right.' he whispered. 'One day . . . it will be gone. It'll just be a memory.'

Silence descended. Jimmy looked up at the sky and the slashed, shelled rubber trees, all of them with splintex sticking out of them. They didn't even look like trees any more. More like oversized kids toys – freaky and dangerous. And he wondered if the last few hours had really happened.

There was smoke rising from the remains of burning huts and noise from the men who were dragging the bodies over to the centre of the square, even laughter. Someone was yelling about calling in more men to help dig the hole to bury the bodies. But those noises were peripheral. What he was most conscious of was the heavy fog of still, deep quietness that had opened up between him and Blue. He looked at his watch, suddenly aware that he not only had no idea of what day of the week it was, but was hazy about what month it was. June or July? He had no idea why he was where he was.

'What day is it today?' he asked at last.

'It's the sixth,' Blue whispered dully.

Jimmy was surprised, 'How do you know that?'

'My birthday,' Blue muttered.

'That a fact?' Jimmy tried to smile but he couldn't quite manage it. His mouth didn't seem to be working.

'Yep.' Blue got up slowly, like an old man, brushing down his clothing, walking over and picking up his gun. 'Twenty-one today.'

Geraldine wiped the tears from her eyes with the back of her hand and took another swig of mineral water, watching the road ahead. The countryside sped past in a blur. She checked herself in the rear-vision mirror: her mascara had smudged and her eyes were red. She slowed down, letting the traffic pass as she fumbled around in her bag for a tissue. How long since she'd thought about Blue? About Jimmy and herself back then? About when they came home that first night? The laughter? The dancing? That kiss by the door? *All that crying after . . .?* Whatever Fran said about Jimmy being okay now, Geraldine knew he wasn't. Not deep down. She knew her brother had been fundamentally wrecked by the death of that kid.

For months after Blue died, Geraldine often dreamt of him sitting out on the veranda. It was uncanny. Sometimes the dreams were so vivid that she'd have to get up and make sure they were dreams – that he wasn't actually out there waiting for her. After checking, she'd always gone back to bed feeling as though she'd been hit in some way. There was no other word for it. As though someone had come up behind her and sliced her open with a blunt little machete. Like the ones Jimmy told her about finding down the Viet Cong tunnels.

It was the same for Jimmy. After she told him that she saw Blue in her dreams, he told her that he did, too. The veranda was his place somehow, they both agreed; a small part of Blue must be still hanging around there, waiting, or maybe watching out for something. Jimmy admitted that he often had the sensation of his guts oozing out, seeping out the ends of his trousers and onto the floor. After dreaming of Blue.

Had he wanted to talk that night? Would it have made any kind of difference if I'd gone out and interrupted him? Kissed him again? Asked him what he was thinking about?

Fran chose to believe that Jimmy was okay because life would be easier if it were true, Geraldine thought bitterly, blowing her nose.

313

Geraldine felt that the quiet tranquillity on both sides of the road was almost an affront to the deep turmoil of her life; cows in their paddocks, sheep huddled under the shade of trees, the sleepy, little towns with people sitting around as though everything had always been the same and would continue to be. At the halfway point between the city and Ballingo, she stopped to stretch her legs and get a coffee. Evening was closing in; she still had another hour and a half to go and she didn't want to go to sleep at the wheel.

She checked her phone. There were four messages. She knew she should listen to them and ring people back – Rob would be worried and so would Peter and Lauren. But she decided to wait a while as she sat drinking her coffee. Better to have a plan to tell Rob about when she spoke to him next.

She sat in the diner, watching the light fade outside, both hands wound around an empty coffee cup. She was infused with a deep desire to stay exactly where she was. She didn't want to go back to her beautiful house in Brighton and she didn't want to get to Ballingo that night. She was caught in a strange midway point between the past and the future, and it seemed suddenly very sensible to stay right where she was. What would be waiting for her at home but more terrible worry, whether her daughter was found or not. And up in her childhood home? What ghosts and dramas would be lying in wait there? For the last twenty years she'd done her very best to eliminate things in her life that did not fit the plan she and Rob had worked out very early on. A happy, stable family life for themselves and their children and the best of everything they could afford. He was a great planner and so was she. It was one of the many reasons why they'd got on so well. They'd had their disappointments like any couple, but what had got them through was a mutual agreement not to *dwell* on the negatives or on the past. Rob was always enthusiastic about the next day, and that was the thing that endeared him to Geraldine more than anything.

Until this year, until Sophie crashed so spectacularly and brought everyone down with her, and before their home-life became stressed and wretched beyond belief, that outlook had worked brilliantly. Geraldine shivered. It was crazy to be going alone. At the very least she should have Rob with her for support.

When she went to pay for her coffee, she had a sudden, terribly intense feeling of dread, that she was about to be sucked right back into the past.

When Fran heard Geraldine's car pull up outside she got off the chair where she'd been sitting impassively for over two hours and went into the front room. Through the window she watched the car lights flick out and heard the engine cut. Although she couldn't see the car she knew it was Geraldine. The journey from the city took three and a half hours, allowing for a half-hour coffee break. Fran had timed her sister down to the last five minutes. Jimmy hadn't come back. Amy had been called away. Fate had conspired to make it happen like this. Fran knew she was being punished. By who she wasn't sure. But with her niece's disappearance and now left alone to face Geraldine, she was sure that was what all this was about. Punishment.

She was beyond exhaustion. Her head was going around in ever more crazy circles. At odd times over the last few hours she thought she could actually feel herself being slowly dismantled, piece by piece. What was she really? Just a body trunk, a collection of limbs with a round thing on top they called a head. And underneath that was a whole lot of blood and bone and tissue. *Made up of?* Mainly water, she'd been taught in school. Billions and billions of molecules, spinning around. All inside seven layers of very thin skin that could break open any moment. And when that happened, whatever it was that was essentially *her* would just spill out onto the carpet. Through the wooden floorboards and onto the grass and dirt, to disappear forever. No great loss, if you thought about it.

The outside light was on. She watched the dark shape of her sister come through the gate, wondering if they'd been alone together in the same room for more than five minutes in the past twenty years. Probably not. Both of them had studiously avoided even the possibility. Her stomach began to lurch crazily as she walked over to unlatch the door.

'Hello, Geraldine,' she said, and stopped before asking how her sister was. Geraldine was standing on the doorstep, one arm raised, about to ring the bell. Her face in the yellow light looked fraught. All the usual gold jewellery, crumpled linen, nice hair-cut and shoes were there but her sister seemed to have shrunk and there were huge shadows under her eyes.

'Fran,' Geraldine said coldly, meeting her eye briefly and then looking away, past Fran and into the lit hallway, as though she expected someone else to materialise. 'Any news on Sophie?'

'Nothing . . . no. I'm sorry.'

'Oh.' Geraldine nodded. Fran motioned that she should come in.

They went through to the kitchen. About to offer her sister a seat, Fran realised suddenly that it was Geraldine's family home as much as it was hers. It would be presumptuous of her to play the host. It would probably give offence.

'Would you like a drink? A glass of wine or . . . ?' she asked. Geraldine shook her head and slumped onto the old moth-eaten easy chair near the window. 'How about coffee or tea?'

'Well, yes . . . a cup of tea would be good,' Geraldine said curtly. 'Thank you.'

Relieved because she had something to do, Fran went to fill the kettle.

'So what do *you* think has happened to Sophie?' Geraldine suddenly asked accusingly. Fran turned around. Her sister was pulling at the threads in the old chair, eyes downcast, her face closed.

'I wish I knew,' Fran said, a feeling of sickness rising in her throat. She gulped it down, and then said, before she could stop herself, 'God, I'm so sorry about this, Gerry. I should have told you sooner . . . I really shouldn't have lost my temper, I have . . .'

Geraldine made a small slapping movement with her hand on the arm of the couch, got up abruptly as though she couldn't bear listening to the sound of Fran's voice for one moment longer, and walked to the window, her high heels making impatient little scrapes and clicks on the polished floorboards.

'Never mind,' she said sharply, folding her arms and turning her back on Fran. 'You weren't to know. I . . . I sent her to you after all.'

'Yes but . . .' Fran stopped. Her sister's bent head and rigid back did not invite further confidences.

'So what is the situation with the . . . police?' Geraldine said quickly.

Fran watched her rub the back of her neck with one hand as she looked out into the darkness. Her polished nails, dark hair and gold rings gleamed in the light.

'Detectives from Beeton are coming in the morning, at about ten,' Fran said dully, looking down at her own rough artist's hands and non-existent nails. *To think that I thought I could absent myself in some way from people, from this family . . . to think I thought I was an artist.* 'They'll set up a proper search party if . . . if she hasn't turned up by then.'

'They'll dredge the river and . . . ?'

'Yes . . . and the lake.'

'So let me get this straight,' Geraldine cut in again, pulling up the sash on the old window, letting the cool, dark night air spill into the room in a rush, making Fran shiver. 'This will be her third night out. Is that right?'

'That's right.' Fran poured the tea. Not daring to actually hand it to her sister, she placed it on the table. 'Tea is ready,' she said shortly. 'I should tell you, too, that the police *don't* think anything terrible has happened.'

'Oh?' Geraldine turned around, her eyes suddenly alive for the first time since she'd arrived.

Fran went on, heartened by Geraldine's fleeting enthusiasm. 'They told us that teenagers disappear all the time. That they're always going missing and they . . . just about always turn up.'

'Really?' Geraldine seemed to be weighing up this information carefully. 'But what do they think about Sophie's particular case?'

Fran could only shrug. Seeing the cup of tea, Geraldine came over and stood at the edge of the table, picked up the cup and took a few quick, scalding sips. Fran sat down the other end of the table.

'Did she say anything about what the Vietnamese

boy wrote in his letter to her?' Geraldine asked Fran suddenly. 'Maybe he upset her.'

'I didn't even know he wrote.' Fran frowned, trying to remember. 'Are you sure?' As far as Fran knew Sophie had never collected the mail from the box. There had only been one letter for her since she'd been there, and that was from Geraldine herself.

'The day it arrived at my place,' Geraldine explained, 'I'd just written to her myself, so I put his letter in a big vanilla envelope with the note I'd written. It should have arrived a couple of weeks ago.'

'Oh, yes,' Fran said, relieved. 'I gave that letter to Sophie myself. So she definitely got it.'

'She didn't say?'

'No,' Fran said, 'she didn't say anything to me about either his letter or yours.'

They were both still for a few moments, sipping their tea and not looking at each other.

'Could I see her room?' Geraldine said, getting up.

'Of course.' Fran's surprise immediately turned to confusion. Did she even have the right to let Geraldine loose in her daughter's room? How would Sophie feel about it? She had gone in there herself the day before to look for clues. Any kind of clues. And found the girl's diary and had read a few pages. What she'd said about her mother had been terrible. Well . . . maybe it was just ordinary teenage stuff. But what if she *didn't* come back? What if she was dead and all Geraldine had of her daughter was this document stating how much, and in how many ways, she loathed her? Geraldine must have seen the confusion on Fran's face because she gave a sudden, odd little apologetic smile.

'Don't worry,' she said, 'I won't be snooping through

her things. I just want to . . .' She stopped, shut her eyes briefly and clenched her fists. Her face crumpled up and tears welled in her eyes. 'I just want to . . . breathe in, *smell* her again,' she continued, gasping a little, 'in case she . . .'

'Oh God, Gerry!' Fran took one step towards her sister and stopped. An arm around her sister's shoulders was out of the question. Geraldine wouldn't want it. It would be awkward for both of them. Even so, just standing there on the other side of the room watching Geraldine in tears felt awful. It brought home just how estranged they were.

This is my sister, Geraldine! The one who gave up hours of her spare time to help me pass French in my last year at school. Geraldine, who, when I was twelve and she was seventeen, snuck me in the back seat of the car so I could see a film at the drive-in that Mum and Dad thought unsuitable . . .

'Sophie was . . . *is* . . . a great girl, Geraldine,' Fran managed to say at last. 'You can be proud of her, you know.'

'Please *don't* tell me that, Fran!' Geraldine snapped furiously. She went over to her handbag and began rummaging through it for a tissue. 'It is not what I need to hear. You didn't know her when she was holed up in that room, screaming at me and looking hideous! She was *not* a great girl then!'

'Well, no, but . . .' Fran floundered. 'I didn't mean that . . .'

'You'll be satisfied to know that I'm feeling very guilty right now about Sophie,' Geraldine went on, blowing her nose. 'Very guilty. I favoured my other children above Sophie. I know that. Compared to them

I found her . . . difficult. Over this last year in particular she became this boring, mutinous, sullen lump of a girl. Absolutely impossible! I know my attitude made it worse for her. When the thing happened earlier this year, I mean the accident where the little Vietnamese girl died, I was dreadful. I didn't want to deal with it and so I refused to let her deal with it. I refused to see that it was a big . . . a terrible thing for her . . .'

'Yes.' Fran had no idea what to say. It was so odd. Her sister was confessing her faults in this low, angry voice. Yet at the same time she was so closed-off, so impossibly aloof.

'*But . . . I do love her!*' Geraldine said forcefully. 'I hope you understand that, Fran. She's my daughter and I love her above anything!'

'Of course I understand that,' Fran said shakily. 'Listen, Geraldine, we all make terrible mistakes with our kids . . . I –'

'You didn't!' Geraldine jumped in angrily. 'Your three children are all well-adjusted and doing well. Don't patronise me, Fran. I've got enough on my plate.'

'I'm not patronising you!' Fran said weakly.

How come I'd forgotten? Of course, everything she'd ever said to Geraldine was misinterpreted, thrown back in her face. Every apology, every kind comment, every single overture. 'So you want to go see Sophie's room now?' Fran said sharply.

'Yes. Thank you.'

Fran left Geraldine in Sophie's bedroom and went back to the kitchen fuming. Let her snoop. Let her read the bloody diary if she wants to. *Why should I care? How am I going to be able to stand being in this house with her for the next hour? Much less tonight . . . tomorrow. Oh*

God, nothing else matters but that the girl gets home safely.
Poor Sophie! Where is she?

Somehow Fran had lost the ability to even imagine
Sophie walking back through the door. It didn't matter
how much she willed it with her body and soul; the
fact was, she couldn't picture it happening. The girl
had disappeared into thin air. Fran had the feeling that
Sophie was no longer even part of the ordinary scheme
of things. She had entered into a new life where no one
could get at her. It was easier for Fran to imagine
Sophie sprouting wings like those on her own little
clay angels than walking back into the house. But these
were wild, crazy thoughts and she knew she shouldn't,
she mustn't trust them.

She tried the pub again and managed to get on to
Jimmy's daughter.

'Hi, Blue.' She was being short but couldn't help herself. 'Any word from your dad? . . . Nothing? What do
you think has happened to him?'

But Blue didn't know. And she was busy filling in
for her father in the front bar so couldn't speculate. She
promised to call the moment she heard anything.

It was not a particularly cold night, but Fran lit a little
fire, more for comfort than anything else. When her sister came back into the room it was blazing away brightly.
Fran saw the look of surprise on Geraldine's face but
couldn't tell if she approved or not. She didn't bother
asking. Let her go sit somewhere else if she didn't like it.

They waited together all evening. In the kitchen,
near the phone, in two easy chairs near the fireplace.
But the phone stayed dead. At one stage Geraldine took
a call from Rob on her mobile. If it hadn't been so
fraught, it might have been funny. Just the two of

them. How bizarre to think of her and Geraldine being tied to each other for a whole evening in this way when they'd avoided each other for twenty years!

Amy came in just before eleven and took the edge off the tension a little. She made cocoa and small-talked a little with Geraldine. Fran was grateful for Amy's wonderful ability to breathe normality into all kinds of strange situations.

Even so, the hours crawled by. After an hour, all conversation between Amy and Geraldine petered out and a soft, tight silence reigned. At different times they each nodded off. Fran's head thrown back onto the headrest of her father's old green fake-leather smoking chair. Geraldine on their mother's settee, legs tucked under her. Amy simply curled up on the floor in front of the fire like a cat, with a little cushion under her head. All waiting for the phone to ring. Three middle-aged women, Fran thought to herself grimly. *Frozen in time.*

At one stage the forced passivity of the situation got to Fran so much that she was on the point of asking Geraldine to come out with her. Surely it was ridiculous to just sit there. Better to do something!

'Come on, Gerry,' she imagined herself saying brightly. 'Let's go looking for her. We could go walking through the streets like we did when we were young girls, then down along the river.'

But it was useless. She and Jimmy and Amy and the two local cops had searched everywhere around the town over the last couple of days. And there was no way she and Geraldine could ever be like they were when they'd been girls. Too much had happened.

At 2 a.m. Fran woke. She looked at the kitchen clock, realising that she must have been asleep for over an hour. She wondered at the sound that had woken her. There was muffled gasping behind her somewhere. She peered around her chair and saw that Geraldine was sobbing. Amy was squatting down nearby, one comforting hand on her knee.

'She might be out in the cold,' Geraldine was whispering through her tears, 'alone and afraid. Someone might have hurt her.'

Fran listened to Amy's soothing noises and felt increasingly remote from her sister's distress. The longer Sophie stayed away, the more unlikely her return, was what she was thinking. What happened in most cases was beside the point. This was Sophie and she had her own good reasons for leaving.

'All I can think about,' Geraldine said, sobbing, 'is what a terrible mother I've been to her.'

Amy murmured a protest but Fran didn't hear what she said.

'I wasn't what she needed,' Geraldine whispered, blowing her nose and then bursting into a fresh flood of tears, 'and what I had to give she didn't need . . .'

Fran let herself drift off into sleep again, half-listening to their whispers, feeling excluded, wondering if it was ever possible for two people to start afresh with each other. How did people wipe the slate clean and begin again?

An hour later Fran woke with a start. Someone was at the back door. Had she locked it last night? She changed position in her chair, aware that both her shoulders ached and her left leg had gone to sleep. She was cold too; the little fire had gone out and the rug she'd crawled under wasn't enough. She really should get up and walk around a bit but she was so tired. She shut her eyes against the watery light coming in through the curtains.

Jimmy came into the room and then, before Fran could even sit up, Sophie appeared behind him. They were both totally dishevelled. Jimmy's hair was covered in dust and his clothes were spotted in dried mud and ash. Sophie, completely dazed, looked even worse. One sleeve of her jacket was torn. Her hair and skin were grimy. Her boots and jeans were muddy and there was a long, blood-encrusted scratch across her cheek. Fran gave a sharp cry and jumped up. Geraldine and Amy woke too, staring blankly at the newcomers for a few moments, as though they might be apparitions.

'Sophie!' Fran shook her head, utterly shocked.

Then Geraldine gave a low moan and scrambled to her feet. She didn't move towards her daughter but covered her eyes with both hands, bending over, as though she had stomach cramps, and crying softly.

'Thank God,' she groaned into her hands. 'Oh thank God.'

'Yes. It's me,' Sophie said, but didn't smile.

Fran held back from moving forward to hug her. Something in the girl's stance warned her off. It didn't matter though. Relief was coursing through her veins, like soft rain on a warm day.

'I'm so pleased to see you.' Fran's voice choked slightly. 'We all are.'

Sophie nodded, looked briefly and blankly at her mother and frowned.

'What are you doing here, Mum?'

'You were missing,' Geraldine said softly. To Fran she sounded unbearably vulnerable.

'I wasn't away that long, was I?' Sophie said, frowning, as though she was seriously trying to work it out.

Geraldine shook her head and looked away, on the point of more tears, not trusting herself to speak.

'Nearly three days,' Fran replied. No one else said anything. 'I bet you feel like a shower?'

'Oh yes.' Sophie nodded, a faint smile touching her lips. 'I think I need one.'

'Could I just . . .' Geraldine whispered, 'hold you for a minute?' She was standing staring at her daughter, her face bright and confused, eyes wet with tears. 'Just want to make sure you're actually here!'

Sophie nodded and when her mother moved towards her, arms outstretched, she accepted the embrace, stood there, let herself be held, although she didn't return the hug with any enthusiasm.

'Go and have a shower, Sophie,' Jimmy ordered shortly. 'I'll tell 'em everything, okay?' He looked at the others. 'She needs to go to sleep for a while.'

Sophie slipped out of her mother's grasp, past Amy and her aunt, and disappeared from the room. Geraldine went into another room to ring Rob and tell him the good news.

'So where did you find her, Jimmy?'

Within a few minutes of Sophie leaving the room, Jimmy was at the sink pouring four slugs of whisky into little glasses, quietly grinning to himself as Amy, Geraldine and Fran all began firing questions at him. The wait was over and they were weak with relief and exhaustion. Jimmy brought over the glasses and gave them one each.

'Under the bridge at Ruby's Point.'

'But you looked at Ruby's Point before,' Fran exclaimed as she took a sip and then slumped down on the nearest seat. 'Twice.'

'Yeah, well, she only got back there last night,' Jimmy said. 'She'd walked along the river all the way around to Beeton, before turning back. I had this idea that she might be getting hungry.'

'That's about fifteen miles,' Amy observed.

'Sorry I didn't call you last night,' Jimmy said. 'But I'd left my mobile phone in the car and that was about two miles away by the time I got to her. She was in a . . . pretty bad way.'

'What do you mean?' Geraldine cut in quickly, her face immediately alert and tense with worry.

'She was confused. Didn't want to come back,' Jimmy said. 'I had to talk her into it. We talked about . . . a lot of things actually.'

'What kind of things?' Fran asked curiously.

'Everything,' Jimmy said vaguely, letting out a long satisfied sigh as he took a deep smell of the whisky, 'and nothing.' He grinned at Fran mischievously.

'*Jimmy!*' Fran laughed and looked at Geraldine, wanting to share her amusement in Jimmy, who had always loved being enigmatic. But Geraldine remained grim and didn't meet her eye.

Jimmy diffused the moment by lifting his glass and smiling at them both. 'Here's to it!'

'To Sophie.'

'To lost children everywhere.' Amy said softly.

Fran and Jimmy smiled, and lifted their glasses.

'We'd better ring the police and tell them,' Fran murmured.

But they all sat where they were, silent for a few minutes.

'Well, she's certainly lost some of that weight,' Geraldine said, at last taking a sip of her drink.

Fran closed her eyes and tried to pretend she hadn't heard her sister's comment. She was exhausted and weepy. This wasn't the time to nit-pick. But she was irritated beyond belief and couldn't help herself.

'Oh, yes, well . . . the most important thing, of course!' she groaned, taking a hot, strong gulp of whisky. 'As long as she's getting *thin* then everything is sure to be okay, isn't it!'

'Fran!' Amy said warningly. But the accumulation of worry and stress, the lack of sleep for the last few nights, plus the last few hours with Geraldine had taken their toll.

'Well, really!' Fran gulped down the rest of the whisky and reached for the bottle. 'I mean *really*!'

'I don't have to put up with this, Fran.' Geraldine stood up, her face completely closed off. 'I'll wait down at the pub for Sophie to wake up, if that's okay by you, Jimmy? I really don't think I can sit here and –'

'Oh sit down, Gerry,' Jimmy said, impatiently. 'Come on, you two. Stop the bickering. Don't you want to know how I found her?'

To Fran's surprise her sister gave in immediately. She sat down and the three of them listened with rapt attention to Jimmy describing his trip. The search along the river and then the hunch that his niece might have made her way eventually back to Ruby's Point. He described his relief at finding her, next to the remains of a little fire under the bridge, looking tired and cold but otherwise none the worse for her three days away.

'Did anything happen to her?' Geraldine wanted to know. Jimmy shrugged.

'I don't think so,' he said slowly, 'She was pretty spaced out but I think that was about her spending those nights alone.'

'You were sitting with her from ten,' Geraldine persisted. 'Did she give any hint that she'd been hurt or . . . troubled by anyone?'

'We were talking about all sorts of things,' Jimmy said shortly. 'She didn't say anything about even *seeing* anyone.'

'Yes,' Geraldine snapped irritably, 'but what about . . . what were you talking about?'

Fran and Amy exchanged a brief uneasy glance. Geraldine's manner was so sharp that Jimmy might very well decide to cut her off completely. But they were both deeply curious, too.

'Well.' Jimmy made a encompassing movement with his hands. 'About the old days mainly. Dad's sister, Ruby.' He looked at Amy. 'I told her all about your aunts being best friends with her. And about my old mate, Blue . . . she wanted to know about him so . . .'

'You mean . . . Peter Drysdale?' Fran watched the colour drain from her sister's face. 'Surely she's troubled enough without hearing about all that?'

Jimmy shrugged and took another gulp of whisky. Fran shifted in her seat, making the old chair squeak. She simply couldn't bear another minute of Geraldine's superior, narky, *you-all-owe-me* attitude. Her sister, within the space of half an hour, made her feel more irritated and furious than she'd been in ten years.

'Oh for God's sake, Geraldine,' she snapped with an impatient slap of her open hand on the table. 'Grow up!

The girl is seventeen. She wants to know things!' The censoriousness. The repression of feeling. The coldness! Geraldine was enough to send anyone barmy.

The full blaze of Geraldine's furious glare shifted onto Fran. 'Like you, Fran?' Her clenched voice was as light as whipped cake-frosting. 'All grown-up like you?'

Well . . .' Fran shrugged. She knew she should shut up. She was getting into hot water. Even so, it was too hard to keep her mouth shut. 'Do you think things just go away because you don't talk about them?'

'No, I don't think that, Fran!' Geraldine said in a hot, low, very controlled voice, a deep flush beginning on her neck. 'But everyone has their own way of coping. And I need your fatuous remarks like I need a hole in the head!'

'Do you think that I don't know that you were in love with that boy, Blue?' Fran cried suddenly. 'We all knew it. Mum, Dad, Jimmy, Monica and me! We knew you were mad for him! We knew that if he'd given you one hint . . .'

Geraldine jerked upright in her chair as though she'd been hit. 'How dare you mention that?' she whispered furiously. 'What right have you to bring up business that you know nothing about?'

Fran shrugged, got up, went to the fridge and pulled out bread, eggs, butter and cheese, and almost threw them onto the table. She knew she was behaving like a seventeen-year-old brat herself, but too bad! She was tired and old and she'd had an incredibly tense three days. Also, she was starving. It was Geraldine who brought it out in her. She would make some eggs and toast and fried tomatoes. It wasn't as though she had anything to lose anyway. Geraldine would disappear from her life after this day, for another twenty years most likely, so why even care?

'Anyone else want scrambled eggs?' she said, her voice sounding brittle even to herself. 'I'm hungry.'

Geraldine simply turned away. But Jimmy and Amy nodded like stunned mullets.

'Yeah. That would be good.' Jimmy groaned rather than spoke. 'I'm pretty famished. You too, Amy?'

'Yep. Thanks.'

'If you remember, I also loved Paul Healey,' Geraldine said very coldly, reaching over for one of Jimmy's cigarettes and lighting it with a small, trembling hand. Fran felt as though she'd been standing on the brink of a sharp edge and that Geraldine's words had somehow *pushed* her off into the air. *Falling.* They were both now in thick, muddy water. Would either of them ever wade out again?

Fran made herself look at her sister. So this is where Geraldine wanted to go? Well, they were in there now. Geraldine's hostility had made her wilt many times in the past, but after believing that she might never see her niece again, Fran felt giddy and light. What was there to worry about, really? After all, she was a woman in her forties! It was ridiculous to be so intimidated by all that had happened so long ago.

'Can I ever forget I had my first love affair with your *ex*-fiancé?' she began boldly, beginning to break the eggs into a glass bowl. *Four, five, six . . . eight . . . ten.*

'Enough, Fran!' Jimmy said.

Fran looked up at him, hoping he meant the eggs because she hadn't finished with what she intended saying. She looked first at Jimmy, then Amy, and then made her eyes rest on her sister's face. 'Or does everyone expect me to carry the guilt around with me till I die?'

Silence. Fran poured a slug of milk into the eggs and began to scramble them up with a fork. 'I'm making these for everyone,' she said shortly, 'so I hope you're all hungry.'

So here we are again. Back to the same thing. Why do we have to be stuck here when other people move on? Other people would be able to laugh about it twenty years on! But of course I can't say that because I'm the guilty one. The sinner. No matter how much I apologise or try to explain!

'Geraldine,' she said loudly, suddenly, 'I was *eighteen*!' Geraldine winced, shook her head and looked away, her mouth determinedly shut. She didn't want to continue the conversation. 'Then I met Daniel and married *him*! Remember? And all of it so long ago.'

Fran looked down at her hands, so rough and gnarled and ugly compared to her sister's, and felt unbearably weary. She should forget about the eggs right now and just crawl into bed and eat in the morning.

'I was a complete innocent from the country, lonely and confused,' she continued, close to tears. 'This very handsome 25-year-old pursued me. He was *not* engaged to you at the time. Even so, I didn't feel right about it . . . because I knew he'd hurt you badly.' She banged her fist on the table, making them all jump. 'Geraldine, he wasn't worth all this, you know! He wasn't worth twenty years of this!'

Geraldine winced again, then stubbed out her cigarette. 'How dare you, Fran,' she said, her words more forceful now. She got up and collected her bag and coat from behind the door. 'But then you always *dare*, don't you? You just say whatever is convenient at the time. Without any regard for the truth.'

'What is that supposed to mean?' Fran said.

Geraldine was at the door now, one hand on the knob, the other holding her coat and bag.

'That same man just happened to have broken my heart. And don't pretend you didn't know it.'

'Of course I knew it!' Fran shouted. 'But it wasn't my fault!'

'No?' Geraldine looked back coolly from the door.

'No,' Fran said emphatically.

'You're a liar, Fran,' Geraldine continued icily. 'You lied to me and you lied to your husband. I know that your relationship with Paul Healey didn't finish after a few months. It continued on and off for . . . *years*. For all I know, it's probably still going on.'

Fran was so shocked that her knees literally gave way. She couldn't keep standing. Pushing away the bowl of eggs she crumpled down heavily onto the nearest chair. This was too . . . absolutely horrible. Geraldine's words had put a knife right through her. She lifted one hand to her flaming face. Amy and Jimmy were staring at her opened-mouthed, in shock. *How could she possibly know?* No one – *no one* knew about her and Paul through the years. There was silence as each looked to the other, waiting for someone to speak.

Fran gulped, opened her mouth and then shut it again. She felt as though her chest had been uncovered and a raw, septic wound exposed for everyone to poke their fingers into.

Fran and Paul had married different people, but the feeling for each other had never gone away. They only ever met once a year, and always in a strange city or a very secluded hideaway, and only for a couple of days. They were both so determined that their relationship should not impinge on any other part of their lives that it was sometimes two years before they met up again. He was a prominent politician now, a real mover and shaker in the Labor Party, with a pretty wife and four gorgeous daughters. The complete opposite to her darling Dan, who was so gentle and unassuming. Over the years she and Paul had been so careful. So proud of being able to conduct this relationship over the last twenty years without hurting anyone.

Oh God!

'The thing that I can't stand about you, Fran.' Geraldine gave one of her freezing smiles from the doorway. 'Is that you always made out that your marriage was so wonderful. That you and Daniel were so happy together.' Geraldine held her head high.

She looks like a queen who has made the judgement to chop off someone's head. Mine, Fran thought. *Mine.*

Fran hardly dared meet her sister's scorching look. She felt as though all the stuffing had been knocked out of her. An odd, empty feeling, as though she might be filled with straw or paper or some other flammable stuff that would disintegrate at the touch of a match or a fist.

'We *were* very happy, Geraldine,' she whispered dully. 'You might not understand it, but we were very happy.'

'No, I suppose I wouldn't understand it.' Geraldine gave a bitter laugh and took a step closer. 'I wouldn't understand because I think honesty and integrity are important. Let me tell you something, Fran.'

Fran looked away, suddenly filled with dread. Whatever it was, after this, it would be too much.

'I ran into Daniel one day outside a bank in the city.' Geraldine went on relentlessly. 'Only a year before he died. We had lunch. He was . . . upset, Fran. At the end of the lunch he said he'd found a letter. Asked me if I knew anything about it. By that stage I'd seen you and Paul together once myself.' She smiled again, rigidly. 'Since you'd supposedly *broken up* at nineteen! And then I became friendly with Paul's sister through my tennis club or . . .' Geraldine shuddered with distaste. 'At least she became friendly with *me*.'

Fran began to shake. *God I can't bear this. I just can't bear what she is going to tell me . . .*

'Apparently she was the one person Paul confided in about your little once-a-year *understanding*.' Geraldine's voice was so cold and sarcastic, so full of hate that Fran couldn't stop shaking. 'But who knows? He might have told other people! Certainly she probably did! I'd known her for only a couple of years when she confided in me. I was so devastated when she first told me that I —'

'Oh,' Fran moaned involuntarily, putting her hand over her eyes. ' I'm so sorry, Gerry!' The apology was out before she could even think of how it might affect her sister. 'There was no intention in the world to hurt you. The opposite in fact —'

'Don't you apologise to me!' Geraldine said shrilly. 'I just want you to *know*. Through the years that woman, *his sister,* made it her sneaky, cruel business to ever so discreetly let me know that it was still happening between him and you. As soon as I'd feel my life coming together with my own family and friends, I would somehow meet up with her again. Over dinner, at tennis. Our damned daughters went to the same school! I never liked her. But of course I let her do it to me. I couldn't help myself. I wanted to know. I was fascinated, even though it was wrecking me!'

There were a few moments' silence. Jimmy and Amy stared at the table. Fran simply stared at the floor.

'Anyway . . . I told him,' Geraldine said quietly. 'I told . . . your husband.'

'You told Daniel?' Fran repeated and then shut her eyes. The sensation again was one of falling. This time into darkness. Down a mine-shaft. Red dots sailed in from the sides, like hot coals sent especially to mock her. She couldn't bear looking at her sister a moment longer. She didn't want to see anybody. Not her brother, Amy, or her sister. She wanted to block out all thought and go blind. 'God!' she sobbed, standing up suddenly. 'That was so cruel, Geraldine! So spiteful!'

Oh Daniel. Dan . . . Darling, why didn't you ever say something? I would have stopped it. I wouldn't have hurt you for the world. I thought . . . I thought . . . I could have both . . . as long as . . .

She saw again her sister coming to the door of the student-house she had shared with some other art student, all those years ago.

'I'll never forgive you, Fran,' Geraldine had screamed, then slapped her face. 'Never!'

Twenty-five years ago she'd said she'd never forgive and she hadn't. *God, she hadn't*. She'd been as good as her word. Fran began to rock back and forth, arms across her chest, hunched up.

'So you let my husband go to his death knowing that . . . I was betraying him?' she said, not looking at her sister. 'You wanted to hurt him . . . and me that badly?'

'I didn't know Daniel was going to die!' Geraldine replied vehemently. 'Of course I didn't know that. I also didn't know that he would choose not to confront you with what he knew. It was weak of him not to.'

'Don't you criticise him!' Fran screamed furiously. 'You cold vindictive bitch!' Then, completely without premeditation, she picked up the bowl of eggs and flung it as hard as she could straight at her sister's head.

At the last second Geraldine saw what was coming and dodged sideways just in time, bumping into the old dresser, banging her elbow and head. The glass bowl shattered onto the floor. Most of the slimy yellow liquid sloshed out around the broken pieces of glass but some of it flew up onto the door and walls. Momentarily shocked, the four of them were still for a few moments, staring at the puddles of egg spreading out around the broken glass on the floor.

'Ah shit!' Jimmy groaned softly and got up. 'This has gone far enough. Cut it out.'

As though activated by his movement, Amy got up too, picked out a couple of old tea-towels from a drawer, went to the sink and put them under the tap. Trying to step around the spilt egg, Geraldine gingerly opened the door.

'Where do you think you're going, Gerry?' Jimmy demanded loudly. Geraldine stopped, halfway out of the room, and turned to face him.

'I'll just go for a walk,' she replied weakly. Her face was a white mask. 'And when Sophie wakes, I'll take her home.'

'It's after two in the morning,' Jimmy snapped.

Geraldine shrugged. 'I can't stay here.'

'Well, you're just bloody going to have to,' Jimmy shouted impatiently. 'The pub is booked out with a tour bus tonight. Sophie needs to sleep for a few hours. And so do you. We've got this fete on tomorrow.'

'What?' Geraldine replied weakly.

'Listen.' Amy was kneeling on the floor gingerly

picking up the broken glass and placing it on spread out newspaper sheets. She stood and looked first at Fran and then at Geraldine. 'I'll clean this up. But let's just call a truce, heh? You two *must* go to bed.'

'No,' Geraldine said in a small voice, tears in her eyes.

'Geraldine,' Jimmy said gently, going over to her, taking one hand and putting an arm around her shoulders, 'there is a spare room right next to Sophie's. You'll want to be there when she wakes, won't you? Talk to her about going home? How about just going and getting some sleep?'

Geraldine covered her face with her hands. Jimmy looked at Fran.

'That's okay, isn't it, Fran?' he asked.

'Of course,' Fran whispered.

Fran woke with a start just before five, a strange smell in her nostrils. She looked at the clock near her bed and groaned. Less than two hours' sleep and she was awake already. She lay there very still, trying to remember what she'd been dreaming. Something horrible. Something about Geraldine. The smell must be from the dream. What had they been doing? Making biscuits or bread, maybe? Cooking something. Something had gone wrong as usual and they'd been screaming at each other. She snuggled back down into the bedclothes, loving the warmth and the fact that she was alone, and then it all came crashing back.

Don't start thinking! If you start you'll never be able to get to sleep again! But . . . oh Daniel . . . you went to your death knowing I had . . . another life, that I wasn't to be trusted . . . but darling, I didn't. Not really. My life with you was my real life . . . you and me and the boys . . .

The last time she'd been with Paul was six months before Dan's death. There was an illustrators' conference on in Sydney and she'd said she'd be staying with an old friend who was the only person on earth – on her side anyway – who knew about her continuing liaison with Paul. When she got to the hotel room he was already waiting for her, watching TV in his rumpled, fancy, dark suit. He stood up. The politician's grin was at once knowing and innocent. He'd always reminded her of those old pictures of JFK: tough, idealistic and tender. He would be prime minister before the decade was through. Everyone was betting on it.

'G'day, babe!' He always made her feel like she was still nineteen. 'Come here.' He picked her up and carried her over to the bed. 'The committee on reconciliation is meeting in just over an hour.'

'Paul, you have to go to it!'

'I've rung in sick.'

'Can I have a drink first?'

'No.'

And then afterwards.

'Can you sign a book for my daughter?'

'Of course.'

'*Mincemeat* is her favourite drawing ever.'

'*Millicent*, you complete . . . tosser!'

They'd dissolved into laughter; so easy and warm and full of friendship.

'You're a liar, Fran,' her sister had said. She was right. It wasn't true to say that Paul wasn't part of her life. Her meetings with him kept something important alive in her. A tiny, burning coal that said she would not be contained or confined by anything or any person, that

340

she was her own woman; free and unencumbered. An artist. The liaison with Paul had kept her wired up for her vocation throughout the years.

So what would be the point in telling people about the stone that had lain in my heart throughout these last twenty years? The stone that would wake me in the middle of the night, sometimes for hours. The knot of frustration in the gut. The longing to work on a big canvas, to use colour again. But more than that. Much more. A longing to get out on my own and face the cold and inexplicable. To pull out every blasted thing inside myself, turn it over, poke it, and then sift it through my brain and hands onto a piece of stretched, primed cotton.

Why would I tell anyone? I never even told Daniel. It didn't seem fair somehow. It wasn't Daniel who'd insisted on my having children or working for the East Timor Association. It wasn't him who told me to be a kids' book illustrator when I really wanted to be a painter. It was no one's fault. I'm not blaming anyone and . . .

And how can I possibly say that I'm sorry for any of it? That I made all the wrong decisions? How could I be sorry that I loved? That I cared? That I eased someone else's pain? All through the years, Dan and I had kept open house for East Timorese refugees. Frightened families. People who'd endured the most terrible things. I'm not sorry. In so many ways I'm glad. But deep in my heart I know that all of this has kept me away from the thing I wanted to do most.

The night of her father's funeral, when she knew that it was at last time to go back to her gift, she also knew that she would not see Paul again. Terrible to say, but the truth was, he had fulfilled his purpose. It was all over between them. She'd rung and told him, and although he'd protested, he had accepted it in the end too.

Sophie pulls the blinds down and snuggles into her bed. Sleep. She really needs some sleep. These ordinary, cotton sheets and warm blankets seem unbelievably luxurious. She wonders what she is doing back in the old house, and then wonders how she could ever have left it. Its creaks and groans, its ghosts of Ruby, her grandparents, her mother and aunts, her Uncle Jimmy and that guy Blue, all sneak up and surround her like a comforting cloak on a bitterly cold day.

Her mother and aunt are back out there arguing in the kitchen. She can hear their raised and angry voices but she has heard enough. She heard some of what they were saying when she went back down the hall to get a clean towel.

Do you think I didn't know you loved that boy?

She wonders if Fran is talking about Paul or Blue or someone else but she doesn't stay to listen. She is too tired. *Does Dad know I'm safe?* She will go to sleep for a few hours and then get up and . . .

He just happened to break my heart. That was her mother's voice. So her mother has a broken heart too!

If only she'd told Sophie that. *Maybe everything . . . things might have been different.*

Then someone must have knocked something over because there was a loud crash of some sort and after that, quietness.

Just before she goes to sleep she thinks of Mr Schmit. There is something she wants to ask him but she can't get her head around the right way of putting it. Something he once said about not being content with just one way of seeing things. Of things not being what they seem. She wishes she had him nearby to explain the last few days. She knows there are things he would want to ask her, too. But her sleepiness is making his voice muffled.

Oh, Schmity. If only you could have seen me, out on the river alone at night, thinking every swaying tree shadow was some murderer coming to kill me. At first I was so fearful. *There are brave men and women in every epoch*, I remember you once saying. *They overcome their own personal fears to contribute to the greater good.* Tough, resilient . . . I wanted to see what I was made of. You once spent a whole lesson on those guys who plotted to kill Hitler. I wanted to see if I had any of those qualities in myself.

So why did you leave?

I couldn't *not* leave. When Fran caught me I just felt so . . . bad. So worthless. Like all the things I'd grown up thinking about myself had all turned out to be true. I knew I couldn't stay.

Were you afraid?

Yes. That first night out was . . . But I was more fed up and angry than afraid. The fear was secondary.

So what did you think about?

I thought of my great-aunt, Ruby, throwing herself off the bridge. And I wished I knew why. But I felt like . . . and this will seem funny . . . *like I got close to her.* I felt that I understood her. I have the same kind of hair as her, you know! In a weird way I felt that I *was* her.

So you wanted to die?

I did. At first anyway. I fantasised about how peaceful it would be, going down into this deep, long, dreamless sleep. There were times when I could almost feel the chilly water surrounding me, feel the air leave my body in a row of bubbles hitting the surface, getting smaller and smaller until they stopped altogether. I could picture myself, twisting and turning through the murky water like a fish. Weaving past plants and rocks that had been there forever. My body slowly disintegrating, bits of it just wafting off. It wasn't frightening, more a . . . *comforting* thought.

So why didn't you?

What?

Jump off the bridge?

I wanted to see some people one more time. Mihn. I wanted to see him. Even just from a distance. I couldn't bear the idea of not seeing him again. And . . . *this I don't understand* . . . I wanted to see my mother.

Your mother?

Yes.

So when you found your mother here . . . what did you think?

I was surprised but not all *that* surprised. It was like I'd been thinking about her and . . . hey presto, there she was, like a magical extension of my thoughts.

Were you pleased?

No.

Why did you want to see your mother?

Hard to say, but something to do with maths.

Maths?

That side of my brain anyway. I've always been good at maths. I like seeing a problem through to the end.

So your mother is . . . a mathematical problem?

Maybe an historian wouldn't understand! Everything is so completely *unfinished* between us. There is part of me that wants to see it through to the bitter end.

Whatever that end may be?

Whatever that end may be.

Sophie drifts off to sleep dreaming of herself down by the river. She sees the sunlight playing on the carpet of dry leaves and undergrowth. The early morning sun spreading pink and gold across the flat expanse of water. She pictures herself waking up cramped in the little dry ditch she'd dug to sleep in, keeping her eyes closed as the scent of earth and the leaves mingle in her nostrils. Listening for small sounds; slithering, rustling, chirping sounds of lizards and snakes and birds. A breeze makes the leaves shudder and whisper above her. She pulls from her pocket a piece of frayed, thick rope that she found. She will keep it with her always because it feels like Mihn's hair in her hands. Just as dawn breaks she thinks she actually hears time going past, very slowly.

'I love these kind of nights,' she remembers saying to Mihn, staring up into the sky, mouth open, smiling in wonder, spinning him around with her on the footpath. 'Don't you?' Standing together on The Esplanade in St Kilda, lights of cafes and restaurants way behind them on the shopping strip.

Mihn looks up into the bright, star-filled night, and she realises with a sudden pang that he does. Yes, he loves these kinds of nights too. Like her. So they are together in this, as well as in so much else.

'Hmmm,' he says, then he pulls her towards him. 'But I love you more.'

Like her aunt, Sophie woke with a start at five but instead of snuggling back down into her bed she sat up and sniffed, alert in spite of her tiredness. Some kind of horrible smell had invaded the room. Then a word begun to knock at her consciousness. *Fire* . . . Sophie gasped as the penny dropped. The smell was actually smoke! *Oh God!* She jumped up, turned on the light, threw on her dressing-gown and pulled open the door.

She could barely see. The hallway was filled with smoke. No flames but thick, cloudy white smoke. Sophie immediately panicked. What to do? She ran blindly down the hallway and across to the kitchen, gagging against the acrid taste in her mouth and throat, her eyes streaming. She grabbed the phone on the bench but then didn't know who to ring. The triple zero number was only applicable in the city. Wasn't it? *Oh shit! Not this house. No! Please not this house!* Her hands were shaking. What a fool she was. She didn't know the first thing about what to do in an emergency. She called Amy's number because it was the only one she knew. But after about four rings there was no answer and she gave up and dialled Jimmy's pub. The number was printed on a little card above the phone.

Much to Sophie's relief, Jimmy answered almost immediately.

'It's Sophie here,' she yelled.

'What's happening?'

'There is a fire in the house.'

'Where in the house?' he asked, his voice urgent and low.

'I don't know,' she wailed. 'Can't see flames, just smoke.'

'Are you all safe?'

Sophie said nothing. For a couple of moments she was amazed to realise that she had actually forgotten about her aunt lying asleep just across the hallway. Then she was immediately suffused with dread. *What about my mother? Was she in the house?* Her mother had been there when she'd arrived back with Jimmy but she'd felt too tired and strange – too *out of it* – to talk to her or even show surprise. Oh, why had she come? Someone please tell me this isn't happening!

'Is Mum here, Jimmy?' she asked.

'Yep,' Jimmy barked back. 'She's down in the end bedroom next to yours.'

'I can't go back down there,' Sophie yelled, beginning to sob. 'There's too much smoke!'

'Look, I'll be there straightaway,' Jimmy said quickly, 'and I'll ring the fire brigade.'

'Okay.' Sophie's voice was shaking. 'Thanks . . .'

'And, Soph.' Jimmy spoke very slowly, as though to a child. 'Just get yourself out, okay? Bang on Fran's door on your way out the front. That's all you have to do. That's all that matters. I'm coming, okay? We'll . . . get your mum. Just get out safely yourself.'

'Right.'

The phone slammed down in Sophie's ear. Get out. Get out now, Jimmy had said. But how could she leave her mother? Panicking, she began to sob loudly as she tried to make her way back into the hallway, sobbing

347

with fear but also anger. Her mother had no right to come. Fran hadn't wanted her. And *she* didn't want her either. *But what if the fire started in my room?*

From a cigarette. Fran had told her not to smoke! Had she been smoking? Couldn't remember. God, this was impossible. Hard to breathe. Still no flames but she could hear a deep kind of rumble. The flames were somewhere, and not far away. She turned back into the kitchen, coughing and spluttering.

Anger gave way to complete fear. If the smoke was that bad in the hall, then it was likely to be worse in the back bedroom where her mother was. She might be asphyxiating right now. Sophie ran out the front door, then, remembering what Jimmy had told her, ran back to Fran's room, banged loudly on the door and shouted for Fran to get up. As soon as she was sure that Fran had heard, Sophie ran around to the side of the house. Somehow she'd have to try and get to her mother from the outside, through the window.

When Sophie got around the side of the house, only metres from the room her mother was in, she stopped. The sight before her was almost mesmerising. Quite beautiful really. Bright orange flames were pouring from the roof, out of a hole the size of a doorway, into the black night air, licking greedily at the eaves. Some part of the wall must have caught fire and already it had burnt all the way through. She stood there for a couple of moments. *My mother is in there. Burning. My hateful, tight-mouthed mother who never wanted me, who always has made me feel worthless . . . Why don't I just . . . stand here and watch?* But then she thought of her aunt, of her grandparents, and finally of Mr Schmit, who was going at her full bore.

So you're going to watch?

Well . . .

You think your mother being dead will rid you of your troubled childhood?

No!

Then why?

What do you suggest?

That you get on with your own life.

How? When she's around . . . I can't do a thing . . . I . . . ?

You're already doing it.

I am?

Of course you are.

You mean *now*? This is it?

This is it.

'Mum!' she screamed, galvanised into action. 'Are you in there?' But her only answer was the dull, hot roar of flames going about their business. Sophie remembered the back window. Looking around frantically she spied the metal garden rake standing by the fence. The only thing remotely suitable. She ran over and grabbed it, then began smashing in the window.

Mr Parks, the old man from next door and her grandfather's dearest friend during his last years at home, suddenly appeared at her side. Pulling off his dressing-gown, he gave it to her.

'Put it on the window,' he yelled, 'so you don't cut yourself on the glass.'

'Thanks.' Sophie threw the woollen gown onto the window and begin to climb in through the bits of jagged glass still attached to the window-frame. The flames had lit the room so she could see a little through the thick smoke. Just the wardrobe, the little dresser, and the shape of her mother sitting up crouched against the bed-head near the far wall. Geraldine saw Sophie and began to scream. Sophie was crying herself with fury and pain. Despite the gown her leg was cut, but she didn't have time to stop and check how badly. *Oh thank God! She is here. And alive!*

'Come on!' she yelled. The heat was in her mouth and throat and the smoke stinging her eyes.

'But what's happening?' Geraldine was in shock, cowering into the corner, as though a ghost had come through her window. 'What is . . . happening . . . Sophie, is that you? What is . . . ?' She was gagging and coughing and rubbing her eyes, still not moving from the bed. Sophie grabbed both her shoulders and shook her frantically.

'Fire!' Sophie gasped, pulling at her. 'Can't you see? Come on, we've got to get out and get Fran, too.'

Geraldine suddenly mobilised. She grabbed her daughter's hand and, stumbling together, they made their way blindly for the window.

'Hey Sophie, Geraldine!' It was Jimmy's voice outside. He was climbing in to help. 'You in there?'

'Don't come here,' Sophie yelled at him. 'Go make sure Fran is okay!' The foul taste of smoke, the grit in her eyes and throat was getting too much. Every second breath she had to spit and she was having difficulty suppressing the need to vomit.

'Go on,' she gasped. 'You first.' There was nothing for it but to climb over the broken glass. Either that or choke. Sophie pushed her mother roughly out the window, and when she heard Geraldine drop into the blackness, she began to edge out herself . . .

'Here, take my hand!' Geraldine's coughing and spluttering voice came from outside.

'Thanks.' Sophie felt her leg scrape painfully against another sharp edge as she slipped through. They stood for a few moments just looking at each other, gasping, then around at the crowd that had formed. A team of perhaps twenty neighbours were out with buckets and hoses trying to put out the flames.

'Sophie!'

She jerked around to see who was calling her. Jimmy came around the corner clutching Fran. 'Oh thank God!' Fran spluttered, clutching both her sister and niece's arms. 'Shit! Are you both okay?' They nodded numbly.

'Where the bloody hell is the fire brigade?' Jimmy suddenly yelled. 'That's what I want to know.'

Now out of immediate danger themselves, they all turned to stare at the house. The hoses and buckets were having no effect at all. The fire had taken hold. Hungry flames spurted wildly out from all the windows and lit the surrounding air in an eerie orange glow. Smoke was billowing from the roof of the front lounge. The roaring and crackling noise had become deafening.

'I reckon we've got about five minutes, tops,' a young man called to Jimmy, on his way back to the garden tap for more water, 'if those buggers don't get here soon.'

Sophie's heart fell as she watched Fran run after Jimmy and clutch his arm in desperation.

'Don't let the house burn, Jimmy!' her aunt was yelling. 'We have to be able to do something!' She was jumping up and down, completely agitated. 'Have we got another hose? Where is the fire brigade?'

Please. Let them get here in time to save this house.

Sophie prayed, moving away from her mother and back behind the team of neighbours who were shouting to each other as they poured the buckets of water onto the flames. Sophie sat down on a patch of grass and, drawing her legs up, put her head down on her knees. *I have done this. This is my fault. Along with killing Mai . . .*

Fran

When Fran heard a series of loud explosions down the front end of the house, and saw the huge spurt of flame rise up into the night sky like something from an industrial accident, she knew it was all over. The gas stove, she guessed. The heater perhaps . . . Immediately after the flame died away, a shower of bright gold stars rose up in its place like fireworks, then it too was gone. The house was literally going up in smoke.

Fran edged over near the side fence, away from everyone.

This lovely, simple old place . . . our home . . . with all its secrets and memories . . . All my plans, my hopes for this year.

Someone was putting a blanket around her shoulders and someone else was squatting nearby, trying to calm her gasping sobs, but she didn't notice who it was. She watched as though it were a film, as some woman she didn't recognise knelt down and wrapped strips of old sheet around her niece's leg. The girl was sitting a few metres away on her own. Part of Fran wanted to go over and comfort her, but somehow she couldn't move. The left wrist had become very tight

353

and sore. When she moved into the light of a torch she got a fright. The wrist had swollen to at least twice its usual size and was throbbing terribly. Must have done it when she'd tried to shift Dad's little desk out of the lounge room. In the end there hadn't been time, so the desk had been left to burn, along with everything else.

But the pain in her wrist was not really connected to her. It belonged to another person. I'm in shock, she kept saying to herself. I'm not crazy. I'm in shock. People were muttering about hospitals and doctors although she couldn't make out exactly what they were saying. In the distance she heard the wail of the fire engine and it made her groan. Too late. Too late . . .'

Ten minutes.

She heard the men around her talking.

That's all it took from go to woah.

No one was even trying any more. The fire was like something alive with a will of its own. Everyone stood well back because the heat was so intense. Tin crashed down from the roof into the bright coals. Walls tilted and then subsided gently into the flames as though they were no more substantial than pieces of cardboard. Sparks spat and flew into the night air like tiny, angry creatures bent on revenge.

Ten minutes. That's all it took.

Two fire trucks pulled up and six fully outfitted men jumped out, pulling with them two enormous hoses. Within about thirty seconds they had two hard jets of water pounding the flames. Fran wanted to cry out for them to stop. The house was beyond saving, why couldn't she at least have the weird and terrible pleasure of watching those bright, greedy flames going about their business? But she didn't have the energy to call out.

354

Within half-an-hour it was all well and truly over. The fire was out. The only parts of the house still standing were some bits of the back veranda and steps, a few half-collapsed door jambs and the still smouldering criss-cross of roof beams at the front of the house. Their shapes against the slowly emerging dawn sky reminded Fran of photos she'd seen of European cities after bombing raids.

The firemen had not been tardy or negligent, it turned out. The town only had two trucks, and when they'd got Jimmy's call they'd been coming back from fighting a fire ten kilometres out of town. They'd come as quickly as they could but it hadn't been quick enough.

The crowd had become bigger. Maybe fifty people now, standing around staring and talking in low, sombre tones. Half hiding down the back garden, Fran could see more people arriving through the smoke and grit. It was bizarre to watch them walking through the front gate when the fence was destroyed and the house gone. She edged herself further back. She didn't want to talk to anyone.

They came to find her though. One at a time, respectfully, as though they understood what she was feeling. One with an old man's dressing-gown and slippers, another with a blanket and kind words, and someone else with tea and some honey sandwiches. Fran surprised herself by eating four. Eventually Jimmy came over with a half-full Vegemite glass of whisky.

'Come on, Sis,' he said kindly, handing it to her, 'don't take it too hard.'

'Leave me alone, Jimmy,' she mumbled.

'Yeah, right,' he said, then squatted down next to her. 'At least it didn't get your studio.'

Fran looked over at the studio with complete disinterest. 'What use is it without somewhere to live?' she replied dully.

'All your work is in there, isn't it?' he said. Fran shrugged. 'At least it didn't get destroyed,' Jimmy added.

'Now is not the time for me to start looking on the bright side, okay?' Fran snapped.

'Okay,' he said, and sighed as he took a sip, 'fair enough.'

They both watched as someone dressed in a heavy coat and protective boots walked into the black, sloshy remains of the house. The image, surreal in that early morning light, was riveting. A dark, roving figure moving in and out between the charred roof beams and piled-up debris, bending down low every now and again to fossick or pick something up.

'Who is that?' Fran asked wonderingly.

'Sophie,' Jimmy replied.

'Oh.' Fran took a deep gulp of whisky and shuddered. 'Sophie.' She put her head on her brother's shoulders and let the fresh lot of tears leak out of her smarting eyes. 'Was the bloody fire caused by her cigarettes?' she asked dully.

'Nah,' Jimmy said, 'apparently the fire started in the room Geraldine was in.'

Fran stopped crying, sat up, and looked at her brother.

'*What*?' she said incredulously.

'The neighbours are all positive about that,' he said. 'That's where the flames were first spotted.'

'Was *she* smoking?' Although Geraldine had the occasional cigarette, Fran couldn't imagine her ever smoking in bed.

'No,' Jimmy said, 'but she put on a heater to warm up the room and then fell asleep. The wiring in that section of the house was really old.' He looked intently at Fran. 'You know that. She should have been told not to use anything but the light.'

Fran groaned and turned away abruptly.

'And of course Geraldine couldn't put up with even three minutes of being just a little chilly!' she snapped sarcastically. *God! Am I to be dogged by faulty wiring all my life?*

'Come on,' Jimmy said, touching her arm, 'don't be hard on her. She's feeling really bad about it now.'

'Good,' Fran snapped, 'I'm glad about that, at least. So where the hell is she now?'

Jimmy pointed to the two policemen and the small, neat figure of Geraldine wrapped in a blanket standing by the back step. Fran felt a wash of something like anger pass through her but it didn't really take hold. She was too wrecked. Too tired, too absolutely devastated. Geraldine turned around right at that moment and caught Fran's eye. They were maybe ten metres apart. She made a small, apologetic gesture with her hands, before turning back to the policemen. Fran sniffed furiously.

Oh never mind, Geraldine. I didn't really want the house anyway. Thank you for saying you're sorry!

There was no way she was going to say it was all right. It wasn't all right. It never would be. So much had been lost. All her plans were ruined. And if her sister hadn't meant to cause the fire, then so what? She'd done it, hadn't she?

When the policemen wandered off and Fran saw that her sister was standing alone and about to walk off, too, she called out. 'Oh, Geraldine, is *this* enough?'

'Fran!' Jimmy muttered warningly under his breath. 'Cool it, will you?'

'What do you mean, Fran?' Geraldine replied stiffly, taking a few steps towards her then stopping. Fran could see she was too nervous to come over and it brought up the savage bully in her.

'What I mean is,' Fran went on bluntly, pointing to the blackened remains of their old home, 'are you satisfied now? Is this punishment enough? Or can I expect more?'

Geraldine hesitated, on the brink of storming off. She held her ground.

'I . . . I didn't mean it, Fran,' she said, her voice strangled. 'I'm terribly sorry . . .'

A few people were watching now, including Sophie, who was standing in the middle of the remains of the house, staring at them both. Her mother and her aunt. The two sisters. So different. And yet . . . anyone look-ing at them would know they were sisters.

Sophie watched as her mother walked quickly over to where Jimmy and Fran were sitting. She stood in front of them rigidly, as though she was awaiting sentence, but Fran wouldn't look up. Her hands were nursing the drink Jimmy had given her and she was staring down into its depths, feeling like getting completely drunk. What other sensible option was there in the circumstances?

'I really am so sorry, Fran,' Geraldine said again. 'This house meant a lot to you. I was cold and I thought I'd just warm the room up. Thought I wouldn't sleep in a million years but . . . obviously I did. I fell asleep.'

Fran nodded sourly. So much of her wanted to get up and hug her sister, beg forgiveness for her own actions over the years. But she couldn't bring herself. She was still too raw. Only a few bloody hours ago, this sister of hers told her Daniel knew about Paul and . . . how was she going to be able to live with that? *And now this!* Her whole life had gone up in flames. She was still in shock, too. Part of her, even now, thought she might be dreaming. Had they all really gone to bed, only about five hours ago, inside the blackened walls of that soaked mass of smouldering wood and tin in front of them? Was all this even possible?

'Hey! You two!'

Sophie was holding something.

'See!' she cried. 'I've found it!' Geraldine turned around and Fran looked up, sighing. Sophie was holding out the river painting for them to look at.

Fran stared at the painting that she'd done so long ago. It was covered in grit and the Ruby figure in the left-hand corner had been burnt out almost entirely. Most of the surrounding bush was also destroyed. Parts of the sky were still there, but the river's surface was a different colour entirely to the one she remembered painting as a seventeen-year-old girl.

'Is it salvageable?' Sophie asked anxiously. Fran shrugged and then looked up at her niece, dressed in a heavy coat and boots. The cut along her cheek looked so sore, but her eyes were eager. 'You think it could it be fixed, Fran?'

Oh sweet girl. Was it really only hours ago that I seriously imagined you jumping in the river? Lost for ever.

'Sure,' she said shortly. 'I'll see what I can do, okay? Then you can keep it.'

'You mean that?'

Fran groaned, then gave a short, sad laugh.

'I do. It's yours. I don't want it. And someone should get something that they want out of all this mess.'

Sophie

After the fire Mum and my Aunt Fran managed to sort out a kind of a truce. They didn't become best buddies, but they started talking a bit. The jury is still out on how far it will go. Even after three years they can still get jumpy around each other. I don't particularly like being in the same room with them because either one is likely to fly off the handle over the least thing. But on the other hand, I've seen them having a laugh together and I really like it when they start reminiscing about things that happened to them when they were kids. So you could say there has been a definite improvement.

Jimmy reckons that if Geraldine turns up to Fran's exhibition next month, there will be no stopping the thaw-out.

'They'll be as thick as thieves in a few years.' He winks at me. 'Mark my words!'

I didn't like to say that I thought the odds of Mum coming were pretty remote. She's always hated any social occasion where she can't at least shine a bit, if not dominate. But her style is too sharp and classy and rich for Fran's bohemian, arty friends, so she tends to avoid them. I've seen it happen.

When we get together, Jimmy and Amy and I entertain ourselves for hours talking over the ins and outs of all this family stuff.

Truce isn't the right word actually. That implies a kind of stand-off, and it wasn't like that. It was more that things had evened out. They'd each stolen the one thing the other wanted most in the world. Fran took Paul and Mum destroyed the old house. Unwittingly of course. Neither of them intended hurting the other, but neither did they take enough care not to. Anyway, that's Jimmy's theory; the fire cleaned out a lot of the rubbish they were both holding onto. Jimmy has great theories about the need for cleaning out rubbish. On the other hand, he is the first to admit he's not all that good at doing it for himself.

The day after the fire was bizarre. I don't think I'll ever forget it as long as I live. For a start we had no clothes. Everything had been burnt. We were, all of us, so spaced out and exhausted and shocked that we didn't know what was going on. Except for Jimmy, who was determined to carry on as usual. And that meant going to the fete. After the shock of realising he was deadly serious, I decided that I actually did want to go, even though I was still half off my head.

All the stuff I'd made was down there, and I wanted to see if anyone would buy it. I think Fran initially said she wanted to go so she could get away from Mum, but then Mum said that if everyone else was going then she might as well go, too. So in the end we all went.

Jimmy brought us down to the pub for breakfast and showers and Amy organised clothes for us. A red-and-white checked cotton summer dress for me, with a belt around the waist. It was the sort of dress that in normal circumstances I would never look at, much less wear or buy. (I hardly ever wear dresses anyway.) But when I put it on, it felt good. Light and comfortable for a hot day. I'd lost some weight and the cut and the colour suited me. It was old-fashioned but in a cool, off-centre kind of way. I can't remember what Amy found for Fran, only that when my aunt came back from the doctor's (with her sprained left wrist tied up in a sling), she looked good in something white.

She gave my mum this completely plain, bright-blue short shift, with matching flat sandals. With Mum's eyes and dark curly hair she managed to look as classy as ever.

Looking back, I don't think Mum knew what she was doing there. We hadn't really spoken. I think she would have preferred just to bundle me up and head straight back to the city, but she didn't dare even suggest it. No one talked about insurance or what was going to happen to the block of land that belonged to them all, or to Fran's studio. In an odd way, once we got down to Jimmy's pub it was like the fire hadn't happened at all.

The secondary college grounds were crowded when we arrived. It was like a market. Hundreds of people wandering around the different stalls set up under the line of peppercorn trees that lined the playground. Balloons and streamers were tied to every tree. Kids' rides, games and races were being held on the oval. The big gym at one end of the playground was set up like a restaurant. All kinds of different foods laid out on trestle tables and heaps of people milling around, laughing and talking, calling out to each other as they ate.

We wandered around together at first, in a daze.

Amy and Fran, Mum and me. Not saying much, just staring at everything as though we'd landed on Mars. Then Fran excused herself. Said she wanted to grab a coffee and sit under a tree. Her wrist was hurting. So then it was just Amy and Mum and me.

Underneath I suppose I was really hanging out to see my stuff, but of course I didn't mention it. Part of me was wondering if it would still look okay. Perhaps Raymond and Fran had been humouring me. Carrying on about how good it was to encourage me to do something. Within the fifteen minutes it took to circle the various stalls my confidence slipped away quickly. It was all going to be so embarrassing when the three of us saw how ordinary it was.

The art and craft section was set up against the back wall of the gym. My cousin Blue was behind one of the tables, with a couple of older women, selling stuff. They'd done a great job displaying it all. There were six brightly papered trestle tables, three of them crowded with my pots and vases and plates. Decorated in gold and red paper, the whole effect was very Christmassy and festive. There were lots of people hanging about looking and buying. But back a little way from the rest, on a separate trestle table against a backdrop of beautiful gold and red velvet, were my angels.

I felt this sudden lurch of recognition in my chest when I saw them sitting there. As though they were old friends, alive in some way. I stopped dead, my heart in my mouth as Mum and Amy walked on ahead, blocking my view. I almost called out for them to stop because just the idea of them getting up close and looking at those odd, familiar things made me feel totally exposed. And wary as hell. Ridiculous, but I felt at that moment completely within my mother's power. Like I was some little helpless insect she might swat.

'Hey, Geraldine!' Blue called over to my mother. 'What do you think about what Sophie's been doing?' Then she smiled at me. 'Be proud, Sophie! They look fabulous, don't they?' I nodded mutely, wanting to thank her for going to all the trouble to display them so well but I couldn't speak. 'Sold two to the local priest,' she prattled on happily. 'He said he's going to put them in the church's nativity scene.'

'Wow!' I managed a smile at that.

My mother didn't turn around. I think she called out something to Blue in reply but she didn't turn around. From the back I could see her head was bent and one hand was touching the head of one of my angels – the new one I'd done of Mai. Squat and tough and . . . the face very realistic. Mum was obviously examining it very closely but I couldn't stand the strain of waiting for her reaction so I simply walked away.

Once out of her sight I calmed down. Why was I being such a cretin? The angels were good, everyone said so. I'd just seen them myself and . . . I was proud of them. *Yes I was*. Why should I care what she thought?

'Hi, Sophie.' I looked up and saw Patrick, one of the younger potters from Flying Duck, a really nice guy of about twenty, smiling at me.

'You okay? I heard about the fire.'

'Yep,' I sighed. 'I'm okay.'

'What's with the dress?' He was eyeing me up and down with this amused look. I smiled. He was dressed as usual in his overalls and tee-shirt. The only concession to it not being a work day was that the overalls were clean. Together we went over to the food section and bought ourselves hot dogs and cans of soft drink.

'Is Raymond coming?' I asked. We were sitting together under a tree, and I was trying to eat what I'd bought without the sauce and mustard dribbling onto the dress.

'Oh yeah.' Patrick grinned at me. 'Every year he does some kind of surprise.'

'What do you mean?'

'Last year he got hold of an army tank and painted it all these bright colours and then rolled it through the gates over there.' He pointed to the wide gates leading to the front of the school.

I smiled, trying to imagine it.

'You should have seen the headmaster's face,' Patrick went on. 'I'm going to have another of these. You want me to get you one?'

'No thanks.'

I'd caught sight of my aunt sitting by herself on a little grassy knoll behind the scones-and-jam tent, so I excused myself and walked over. I was still so spaced out that I hadn't even begun to make any connection between myself and the fire, the fire and Fran's work. Of course I know now that if it hadn't been for me disappearing the way I did, my mother would never have had to come up, and so the old house would still be standing. By the time I began, I knew that, as rotten as the outcome was for Fran, she wasn't going to hold it against me.

I sat drinking soft drink with my aunt for a while. Then, when we heard cheering and shouting, we got up and followed the crowd over to the road. From a distance it looked like this amazingly tall, thin, wildly coloured creature was ambling up the road. A cross between a praying mantis and some kind of dragon, with a long bouncy tail that fell right down to the road before curling up into a circle. As it got nearer I could see it was someone on very high stilts, dressed in red and gold. Very gorgeous and weird.

It was Raymond, of course. And he was surrounded by ten guys, all done up in red and gold velvet suits and playing carols on flutes. A whole crowd of kids clapped and cheered as the strange procession made its entrance through the school gates. Although his face was virtually unrecognisable under all the bizarre paint and feathers, I caught glimpses of his flashing eyes and that wide mocking smile. What a character! He saw us too. About to head over to the oval, he suddenly turned and loped straight toward us. Being approached by someone three metres tall is a bit frightening but we held our ground.

Only a few metres from Fran and me, Raymond bowed very solemnly from his amazing height and, reaching into a pocket, picked out a flower and threw it at Fran. She blushed and the crowd whooped and whistled, then he turned around and made off for the oval.

I risked a quick look at Fran and saw she was laughing to herself and shaking her head.

Not long after that, I think it was at about three o'clock, I felt like I was going to faint so I went back to the hotel and crawled into one of the freshly made beds.

When I woke it was midday the next day and I felt completely disoriented. After lying in bed trying to work out what day it was, I went down to the kitchen for some coffee and toast. I'd started wondering where my mother and aunt were when Jimmy rushed in from the front bar and told me that Mum had left for the city early that morning.

I think my mouth fell open because Jimmy added hurriedly, 'Oh, she just wanted to get into her own clothes and see your dad. She said to tell you goodbye.'

'Oh,' I said warily. *Jeez, already? We'd hardly said two words to each other.* 'So when is she coming back?'

'I've invited them all up here next week for Christmas,' Jimmy said, pouring himself a cup of tea and lighting a smoke at the same time. 'Your mum, your dad, Peter and Lauren.'

'And . . . er, are they coming?' I asked, thinking it was pretty unlikely. After Grandpa died, Mum said she'd never go near Ballingo again, if she could help it.

'Yeah,' Jimmy said nonchalantly, as though it was nothing. 'Monica will be here too. And you two, and Gavan and the kids.'

'Oh. Right.' I had a spurt of joy thinking that he was associating me with Fran instead of my mother. 'And did Mum say anything to you about . . . *me*? I mean, when she wants me back or what she wants me to do next year or . . .'

Jimmy shook his head, looking at me quizzically through a cloud of smoke.

'Not a thing.' He frowned. 'But you'll work all that out, won't you?'

'Oh yeah,' I mumbled, embarrassed, 'I guess so.'

'Course you will.'

In truth I was relieved I didn't have to face my mother that day. A showdown was in store and I wanted to put it off for as long as possible.

What would I do next year?

When, if ever, would I finish my final year?

Where was I going to live?

It wasn't until later that night that I found the note she'd written me.

'Have you got that painting?' Fran said, walking into the kitchen. She was bleary-eyed, her wrist still in a sling, and dressed in Jimmy's old silk dressing-gown. She shrugged grumpily at Jimmy who only grinned and pointed to the teapot. Fran nodded and groaned as she sat down, the weight of the world on her shoulders.

'It's up in my room,' I said.

'We could have a look at it today, if you want.'

'Okay.' It pleased me very much that she'd remembered.

Fran and I trudged up the hill to the old house, me carrying the painting under one arm, hardly speaking at all. I think we were both secretly hoping that the house would somehow be there when we reached the top. But there was just the burnt-out shell, actually sadder and more completely *gone* than in the half-light of early morning. We both stopped and simply stared.

'I thought if I didn't say anything . . . somehow it would come back!' Fran said eventually, clutching my arm, tears running down her cheeks.

'Me too,' I gulped. 'I thought I might have been dreaming!'

We walked through soot and charred ruins to Fran's studio.

The studio was barely affected by the fire. Just a few scorch marks on the outside. Everything was exactly how it had been a few days before, when she'd found me in there snooping. Even the milk in the little fridge under the bench was sweet. Strange to discover that, when so much else had happened.

I went about making us both some strong coffee while she set up the damaged painting on the easel. I could see it was difficult for her, with one hand out of action.

'Can I help?' I asked, bringing over her coffee. She flinched a little and I knew that my voice had startled her. She was staring at the painting, her head cocked and with that totally concentrated look on her face that I'd seen before when she was working.

'Oh no . . . thanks,' Fran mumbled. 'I'll yell out if I need you.'

'Okay.'

I sat down the other end of the room at the big table, pretending to read an art magazine, but I was watching my aunt most of the time. Firstly she made up some kind of solution in a small jug and it was only after I saw her dipping a sponge into it and dabbing the painting that I realised she was washing it carefully. After that she dried it with a noisy electric hair-dryer then went to the big cupboard under the window, pulled out a wooden box and put it on the big work bench. From the box she slowly chose a few tubes of paint. A huge white one first and others, different blues, a bright yellow and a deep red. Then some brushes and turps, some old rags and linseed oil. All very methodical. When at last she squeezed out some of the paint and began to mix it into patches of colour on her palette, I looked at her face. She wasn't smiling exactly but I could feel her intense enjoyment of the whole process.

First she roughly washed in some background. Dabs of blue and green for the tree foliage, patches of pale pink and slate-blue for the sky and water.

'Does your wrist hurt much?' I asked.

But she didn't hear me.

'Just get on a first layer,' she muttered to herself, ''till you get the feel.' Then, as she reached for a couple of tubes of red, 'Might do Ruby first.'

I watched, oddly awed as she began to painstakingly paint the swirls and folds of Ruby's dress. Even with one hand she was so deft. The hands and face, the hair and feet were still only washed-out shapes but it was amazing to see that red dress slowly come back into existence. I found myself thinking of Jimmy down by the river when I asked him to tell me what he knew about Ruby. The conversation had been intriguing but in the end I was left with as many questions as when we'd started.

'No one really knows the full story,' he had said, lighting a cigarette. Then he grinned at me across the little fire we'd made in the picnic grate and handed me the flask of whisky. 'Although there are any number of people around who will tell you they do. This town is full of Ruby experts!'

'Why?' I said, taking a quick nip of the fire water, shuddering as I felt it roll down my throat. 'I mean, why is it no one knows for sure?'

'There was no proper post-mortem,' he replied, taking a deep drag of his cigarette. 'There should have been but the family were too distraught. They didn't want it. They were too upset. The terrible shame of suicide was something they just couldn't deal with. In those days the authorities weren't so strict. The official death certificate says she drowned – death by misadventure.'

'So how do you know that it isn't true?' I asked.

Jimmy squatted down near the fire, warming his hands, the cigarette still in his mouth. He grinned at me suddenly. 'Amy's Aunt Harriet was best friends with

Ruby. According to her, Ruby was in love with a guy called Harry Readon. Fran's father-in-law.'

'*What?*'

Jimmy laughed at my disbelief. 'Yep. Your Uncle Daniel's father. This is a small town, girl. Get used to it.'

'And . . . ?'

'Well, he was older than her,' Jimmy went on, 'in his mid-twenties. Both families were dead against them marrying. There was the Catholic/Protestant divide then and . . . he'd returned from the First World War wrecked. Like a lot of 'em, he couldn't settle down to farm the big property that the family owned. And she was only seventeen so no one was keen on them marrying.'

I couldn't quite work Jimmy out. He looked like he wanted to get right along home as quickly as possible, but he was also acting like he was settling in for the night. He stared behind his shoulder into the rustling trees behind every now and again, as though he was expecting someone to appear any minute. He was frowning, too, as he talked, tapping both his feet edgily.

'Really?' I said, keen for him to continue. 'Couldn't they have run away together or something?'

Jimmy nodded slowly. 'They planned to run away and get married after Harry had saved some money. He got a job shearing about seventy-five kilometres away, at a place called Buxton. Ruby apparently wrote to tell him that he should come and get her after the Ballingo Ball the following month. She was adamant that they run away then. He didn't answer her letter and when he didn't come for her that night of the ball she . . . must have despaired.'

'But *why*?' I was puzzled. 'Did she know for sure he wasn't coming or didn't want to marry her?'

'No no.' My uncle shook his head. 'On the contrary, he *did* want to marry her. He was absolutely distraught when he heard that she was dead. Cried on her grave. The lot. He just didn't get the letter. Ruby gave the letter to Harriet to post. You know Amy's aunt?' I nodded. 'Well, Harriet's mother, who was a real old tyrant, found the letter before she could post it, and Harriet never got to tell Ruby that she *hadn't* posted it because she got sick with measles. Her mother kept her home from the ball where she'd planned to tell Ruby about not posting the letter –'

'Oh God,' I burst out disbelievingly. 'Couldn't she have *rung* her?' I felt genuinely outraged that such dire consequences could result from a couple of simple mistakes.

'Harriet's family didn't have the phone on,' Jimmy replied mildly, 'and they were about five miles out of town, and of course Harriet didn't know how important the letter was to Ruby or she would have snuck out from her sick bed . . . done anything to let her know. Poor old Harriet! She still blames herself for Ruby's death after all these years.'

Poor old Harriet. I shuddered and wrapped my parka more closely around me. *Guilt*. Scratch the surface and everyone had stuff to be guilty about. The few times I'd met that old aunt of Amy's I'd thought how simple her life must be. No husband, no children, living out on a little farm all her life, first as a kid with her parents and then with her unmarried sister. Bringing up Amy together. The fact was, she'd caused the death of her best friend by getting measles. And she blamed herself, still. I shivered. *Just like me. I was driving the car and so* . . . It was weird, trying to imagine that old woman as a young girl, defying her mother, running around with secret letters.

I licked my lips. My mouth was dry and I wanted to go down to the river and get a drink but I also didn't want to risk interrupting Jimmy in his talkative mood. Conversations about Ruby tended to dry up too quickly for me. Why was it? I wondered. Did people feel guilty or bored or scared with what happened to her? Damn that! My stomach rumbled again. He had brought me some sardines in a can and some dry biscuits but they were all finished. I hadn't thought I was hungry until I'd finished eating them.

'Why did she give the letter to Harriet in the first place?' I asked, still fuming at the stupidity of it all.

'Because she was the only person Ruby really trusted,' Jimmy said simply. 'Ruby sneaked the letter to Harriet during mass one Sunday morning but Harriet didn't have a chance to post it that day. She figured that she would the next. Then her mother found it in her coat pocket and Harriet got sick . . .'

'Why didn't Ruby wait until she at least heard from the guy?' I asked.

'Well . . .' Jimmy threw his cigarette butt into the flames. 'She was probably pregnant. Don't know for sure but it sort of figures. Her being so frantic to bring forward their running away . . . so she didn't see any way out.'

'Oh,' I sighed, trying to fend off the shaft of sadness that suddenly and unexpectedly lodged itself inside my chest with his words. *Pregnant.*

'So Ruby came home from the ball,' Jimmy continued, 'and she probably waited till morning for Harry to turn up and when he didn't she came down here and threw herself off the bridge.'

'Shit!' I groaned. 'Not fair at all. What *putrid* luck. Everything was conspiring against her!'

Jimmy smiled. 'We were worried you might have had the same thing in mind,' he said, the smile giving way to an anxious flicker around the corners of his mouth. 'We were all bloody worried, Soph. Your Aunt Fran, Amy and me . . .'

I shrugged, embarrassed to think that I had actually toyed with the idea of following Ruby into the river.

'Ah no.' I said. 'You shouldn't have worried.'

The sadness of Ruby's story suddenly left me. In its place came a profound gladness that I was still around. It would have reverberated right across the different strands of family, down into the next generation and then further still. Like the long, waving arms of an octopus, it would suck out joy and life and energy wherever it could. The whispered secret, the half-understood mystery, the fascinating, sad truth that pulled at the wellbeing of future generations for the next hundred years. God! If I'd followed Ruby over the bridge into that cold watery grave it would have lived on in other people's lives for ever.

'Have to admit I thought about it.' I grinned at Jimmy. 'But then I thought my family were psychotic enough. They'd all turn into complete cot-cases if I pulled that one on them!'

Jimmy laughed. 'What do you say we get going now?' he said, getting up and stretching. 'The car's a bit of a hike, you know.'

'Okay.' I got up too. I was hungry and sleepy and glad to have been found. I would wait until I felt better before I asked about Ruby again.

Fran smiled without looking up from painting the super-fine white frill around the bodice of the red dress.

'You know, Sophie,' she said, 'Ruby was a real beauty that night of the ball. Full of fun, Dad said. Dancing with everyone. She even sang a song.'

'Did she actually wear a red dress that night?'

'Oh yes,' Fran said softly. 'My father found her. He and two other boys around his age found her lying face down in the backwater. She was still in the red dress that she'd worn to the ball. She even had her shoes on.'

Poor Grandpa!

'And your father-in-law was . . . ?'

'Yes.' Fran sighed, in an absent sort of way. 'Harry was her lover.'

I would have loved to ask her more about her father-in-law. Did he ever talk about Ruby? When, if ever, did he get over her death? But I didn't like to. Fran seemed so intent. She worked steadily on the painting for about three hours in all, gradually and painstakingly building back the layers of paint that had been burnt away or scorched. Every now and again she relaxed a bit and occasionally asked me what I remembered about a particular colour.

'Was that gum tree more blue than green?'

And when she came to the final layer of paint for the dress, 'How about Ruby's dress, Soph? Was it a soft red or a brighter kind of . . . ?'

I answered the best I could but I was not used to thinking about colour with the kind of distinction she wanted. Red was red. Blue was dark or light as far as I was concerned. Watching her work made me realise there was a whole world inside just one colour. As complicated and varied as all the different kinds of wine, say, or the different ways there are of playing the one tune, or . . . *the million different feelings you could have when just one person died*.

It was something I vowed to talk to Mr Schmit about, if I ever saw him again. Variations on the one thing. I peered forward and saw that her palette had at least five different tones of blue. That might be a good place to start the conversation with old Schmity. The colour blue, and all its variations. A gut feeling told me he'd like talking about that.

That river painting was never the same when I looked at it. Sometimes the sky had seemed like gun-metal blue, at other times a bright, searing blue. Then at other times it had almost been pink. I told my aunt this and she just laughed.

'The light coming from the front window always makes a difference,' she explained, 'light is never the same.'

When we got back, Raymond was out the back of the pub talking to Jimmy. I could tell he was on his best behaviour. So circumspect. It didn't suit him at all. I also realised that he liked Fran a lot and that was why he was being so subdued. He had come to offer her a small, unoccupied cottage that he owned near the river, only a quarter of a mile from the old house.

'Please take it, Fran,' he said a number of times, 'you would be doing me a favour. It would only take a day to clear out all that's there. I could have it ready for you next week. You could simply walk from there up to your studio every day.'

She nodded and pretended to think about it but I could see she didn't want to be indebted to him.

I suddenly had the idea that I should take Raymond aside and tell him he'd have more chance with Fran if he remained his true outrageous self. Instead of saying that no one would interrupt her, he should have been telling her that he planned to sing outside her house every night! Something like that anyway. I wished I could have told him about the smile she had on her face when he threw that flower from his stilts. But I didn't dare.

The next morning Fran was missing. Damien rang to speak to her about the fire but no one could find her. I looked in her room then rang Amy. When it seemed that no one knew anything of her whereabouts, Jimmy suddenly lost his temper.

'Where the bloody hell is she then?' he roared. 'Does she think I've got nothing better to do then go searching for her? I've got a business to run. How come everyone thinks they can just piss off?'

'Okay, Dad. Be quiet,' Blue said matter-of-factly. Then she looked at me. 'What about the studio?' I nodded and Jimmy, still fuming, stomped out of the room.

'I'll go and look now,' I said hurriedly. 'Won't be long.'

As soon as I got to the site of the old house I knew Blue's guess was right. Fran's old coat was on the back step and the light was on. I took a quick look in the window and saw that she was working down the far end of the room on a big canvas – and that she was completely preoccupied. I also knew she'd hate to be disturbed. But I was filled with an intense curiosity, and glad too that I had a good excuse to disturb her. Fran would want to know about Damien for sure. I knocked on the door.

'It's open!' she called out gruffly, so I walked in. That smell of turps and linseed oil. The rich, secret smell of paint! She turned around to face me, frowning, dressed in paint-splattered loose pants, boots, and with a big shirt over her tee-shirt; her hair pinned up roughly into a bun. Her hands were covered in paint. Her face, completely devoid of make-up, was lined and tired. She was struggling with some idea, I could tell by the expression on her face. I felt proud suddenly. *I know what that feels like.* Then a sudden rush of excitement filled my head. *I want to work like this . . . This is what I want too.*

'Sophie?' Fran smiled distractedly, waiting for me to speak. I looked over at the canvas she was working on. A big, surreal landscape, mountains, sky and winding roads leading nowhere, all in tones of chilly, desolate blue. Only watery colour at this stage. Down in the right-hand corner a heap of muted red and dirty yellow wrecked cars lay on top of each other like dead insects. A shiver went through me.

'So you've started?' I said in awe. Even though the painting was only just begun I could feel its magic already. It was drawing me in to its central force, to the swirling chaotic mass of tracks leading outward, to every far-flung corner of the canvas, and ending with the crushed cars. My aunt grinned, threw the brushes down onto the work bench, ran her hands down the front of her shirt to wipe off the excess paint, then reached out and pulled me towards her, hugging me.

'Yep!' she exclaimed, 'I've been here since six this morning! And I'm like a pig in shit!'

'Wow.' I was delighted.

'I really think the house needed to burn down,

Soph.' she laughed, 'I needed to hurt my wrist. It was all exactly what was needed!'

'So you reckon you'll stay here?' I asked. 'I mean, in this town?'

'Well, why not.' She frowned, then went over to fill the jug at the sink. 'You want a coffee?'

'No thanks. I don't want to hold you up. Jimmy's in a temper about not knowing where you are. And Damien rang. Wants you to ring him. Someone told him about the fire.'

Fran nodded, quite unconcerned. 'I'll find another little house and I'll come up here every day and work,' she mused thoughtfully. 'Of course it's what I should do. Simple really.'

'It's going to be fantastic,' I said, looking at the painting.

'Well . . .' She smiled, then, looking away, she began clicking her fingers nervously along the edge of the sink. 'It's a start anyway.'

So what did I do in that week between the fete and Christmas? I can hardly believe it, but the truth is I made a baby out of clay – Jesus in his crib and a Mary and Joseph figure, too. I fired them and then glazed them in the same style as my angels.

I am not a religious person. Never have been. I suppose because I wasn't brought up with it. My father is simply disinterested but my mother has always been vehemently anti-religious. (She loathed the convent school she went to and was always telling us about the ridiculous *mumbo jumbo* that she'd been brought up with.) But there I was, breaking my neck to get them finished in time for Christmas Eve. The local priest had come around to the pub two days after the fete, crazy about the two angels he'd bought, and virtually begging me for a full set.

'As many angels as you can manage, my dear,' he said on the way out. 'They'll look absolutely beautiful set up in front of the altar at midnight mass.' He was a nice enough guy, in his fifties, with grey hair and thick glasses. 'And the holy family, too, of course,' he added.

The holy family?

I didn't know what he was talking about. But I was flattered, I suppose, said I'd do it, then didn't have the faintest idea how to begin. So I sat down and read the bible story for the first time in my life; looked at some pictures and tried to think about how to begin. I didn't tell the priest that the angels he'd bought weren't exactly Christian. They'd been inspired by Mai's story of how her family had survived at sea, so, if anything, they were Buddhist. But then I thought, Stuff that, why worry? An angel is an angel, isn't it? A messenger from God. The whole idea of them appealed to me. In fact, after reading some of the bible stories I found myself envying people who lived back then. How cool to have someone come and tell you what you should do in a dream! My dreams, the ones I can remember anyway, are either just complete freakouts where I wake up sweating and crying, or a whole lot of mixed-up stuff that doesn't make sense.

I wish God (if he or she exists) would send an angel down to me in a dream occasionally, with an important message. *Any* kind of message would do actually.

It surprised me to find out that Aunt Fran didn't feel at all the same as my mother about religion, and in the end, it was after a couple of talks with her that I found

I could begin. She encouraged me to steer away from the sweet, idealistic interpretation I'd seen illustrated in books.

'The reason why Father Peter likes your work is because it's not sentimental,' she said, 'so make Joseph a hairy, gutsy kind of fellow.'

'Hairy and gutsy,' I repeated stupidly, not really knowing what she meant.

'Sort of a cross between Ned Kelly and Daniel Day Lewis,' she suggested, then as an afterthought, 'but a bit Jewish too.'

'What does that . . . ?'

'Oh you know! Put a good nose on him. And make him intelligent.'

'Okay.' I grinned. I was getting the drift.

'And make Mary young and strong and not too pretty,' she went on sharply. 'A sort of country girl that you might find cleaning people's houses in the city.'

'Can I give them wings?' I asked hopefully.

'No way!' she said emphatically, then laughed. 'Those two are not angels.'

'What are they then?'

'They're . . .' She shrugged and then waved an arm as though it was suddenly all too much. 'Oh never mind. You can do it, Sophie. I know you can. Make a young couple and their baby in a crib. You can make them, they'll be good. I know they will.'

'Okay,' I said, unbelievably pleased with her confidence in me, 'I'll give it a go.'

I walk along the street with this jumpy, slightly bilious feeling in my chest. Every five minutes I think I've got to find a toilet or go over to the gutter and be sick. But that's not the problem. The problem is . . . well, the problem is I'm terrified.

It is raining. Summer, but the breeze coming in from the sea is fresh, with an odd bite to it. The weather report said showers that morning, so why didn't I bring my waterproof jacket? Was it an unconscious desire to demolish my position before I even opened my mouth? I am making a mistake. I'm convinced of that now. A *big* mistake.

I ran out at Flinders Street Station thinking I was going to miss the tram going up Elizabeth Street. Now that I'm on it I wish I *had* missed it. The thing in the box has been wrapped up carefully but it is awkward and heavy to carry. I'm sorry I bought it. Maybe I will dump it in the nearest rubbish bin. But when I get off the tram I see there is no bin big enough along the street. I'm going to feel like such a fool handing the bloody thing over.

Nothing ventured, nothing gained . . . Better to have risked . . . Blah! Blah!

It doesn't matter how many times I mouth off those pat little truisms, they don't give me comfort at all. Even though I'm chanting the words over and over to myself like prayers. *Mumbo jumbo.* Mum is right. *Bloody mumbo jumbo.* Who needs it?

If at first you don't succeed, then try, try, try again!

I walk along Victoria Street wishing I was one of the squat blank-faced ladies in front of me, pushing shopping trolleys. Head filled with nothing more important than the price of beans and potatoes at the market this week. What brought me here? Into this street? On this particular day? It feels so weird. I smell the fish from the open doorways into the market and I want to be sick again. Inside the vendors are calling out.

382

'Whiting only twelve dollars a kilo!'

'Fresh snapper for tonight only!'

I see myself that night. Was it only ten days ago? Gleaming. Silvery and sleek as a wet fish in the new tight white dress. My first ever midnight mass. I'm standing between Fran and Jimmy. Next to him is Blue. My mother, father, sister and brother are standing in the pew in front of us. Mum and Lauren both look so glamorous. Everyone in that church keeps taking surreptitious little peeks at them all the time. I realise that I am not at all jealous and it pleases me. I look over to the other side of the church and there is Amy and her grey-haired hippie mother standing next to the two ancient aunts. A first apparently. After twenty-five years the aunts and the mother have finally deigned to have a Christmas together. As though she can feel my eyes on her, Amy looks over and smiles. I'm glad to see she is so happy.

I can hardly believe my mother is actually there, in church. But it was Jimmy who insisted. 'We've all got to go,' he said when they arrived late in the afternoon. Trish's husband and kids, Monica and her friend, all of us. 'In memory of Mum and Dad and the house. Everything okay?' he went on. My mother opened her mouth to protest but before she could speak, Jimmy jumped in hurriedly. 'Anyway, there is Sophie's work! You want to see them all set up, don't you?'

Mum closed her mouth again and gave me a nervous smile. 'Of course,' she said, 'okay. Midnight mass it is.'

The church was so packed that when the service started and people begin singing, I felt as though I was going to faint. So many bodies packed in so tightly around me, breathing in the same air. But I kept my head up high and I was all right after a while. Right in front of the altar were my holy family and angels set out on a low table. Gold glittering on the tips of the angels' wings and around the edges of Mary's dress.

I wish now I'd had time to do some proper animals: a horse, a donkey, and an ox. As it is we had to make do with a background of paper cut-outs. Still, my figures look good in the flickering candle-light. I'm particularly pleased with Mary. The apprehensive expression on her face seems just right. She's kneeling in front of the cradle like she's just had a quick delighted look at her new baby and then realised the whole thing could get completely out of hand if she doesn't watch out.

The baby in the crib is a bit of a disaster – I couldn't get a shape that even remotely resembled a new baby – but even though I sweated on it all week, it doesn't seem to matter. Everyone around me nudges me and compliments me and I feel exceedingly pleased with myself. Maybe I will stay in the town as Jimmy and Fran suggested the other night. Live at the pub with Jimmy, go to the local secondary college for my final year. I could keep working out at Flying Duck in my spare time. Raymond said I could have a job out there if I wanted it. Then I wonder if I'm part of his plan to win Fran over. Even if it's true, it doesn't worry me. There are all kinds of possibilities.

The service commences. I understand nothing that is going on but I like the atmosphere. Sort of secret and joyful with all the music and candles. A well-dressed, tall man with reddy-brown hair, accompanied by his pretty, blonde wife and four daughters, walks in late. I know it is Paul Healey before anyone tells me. Jimmy told me earlier in the night that he'd seen him that day in town. He'd brought his family up to see his parents for Christmas. He parks himself just across the aisle from me and I keep looking at him and thinking about Mum and Fran and all that happened years ago.

But it is outside, in the semi-dark, with everyone milling around in the warm, starlit night, that things sort of come together for me. By this stage I've seen Raymond and some of the Flying Duck employees and everyone is calling out to one another, greeting each other with kisses and shaking hands. And laughing. They're talking about how hot it is going to be the next day and whether they can be bothered cooking turkeys and puddings. Someone shouts that they're taking their family down to Ruby's Point for the day. Sit under the trees and jump in the water when it gets too hot. I talk to people who think they know me because they knew my grandparents. I don't mind.

I watch my mother greet Paul Healey for the first time in twenty-five years, and I am suddenly filled with admiration for her. My mother is so dignified and friendly and Fran in contrast seems to go to pieces. I almost start to laugh as I see her greet Paul and his wife and then scuttle hurriedly away to another group. Obvious to anyone in the know that she was as uncomfortable as hell! But Mum introduces Dad to Paul and then Peter and Lauren. I can see she is genuinely proud of her family. She pulls me over, introduces me and tells him about me making the nativity scene. He says all the right things about it being really different and artistic, then all this stuff about how talented I must be. No mention of Fran. No mention of taking after my aunt. The man has class, I can see that. Still handsome too.

There are no theatrics. My mother moves easily away holding Dad's arm and I am left wondering if I imagined half of what Jimmy told me.

The buzz of friendly talk mixes somehow with the soft light coming from the little candles the kids – all dressed up as shepherds and angels – are holding. I look up at the star-filled night then at the crowd around me. Half of them neighbours, the other half either close or distant relations. *So this is it*, I say to myself. Not even quite sure what I mean, but the feeling of separate pieces clicking back together inside me is so precise that my heart begins to thud and my breath becomes short for a few moments. *Oh, so this is me . . . !* The realisation comes like a delightful surprise. A hard squirt of cold water from the hose on a stinking hot day. Almost a bit much but welcome anyway. *Okay. So now what?*

And that's when I decide that I've got to do it. That I've got to stick my neck out, I've got to at least try to . . . *finish* the equation off in some way. Otherwise it will haunt me forever. It was that feeling outside the church on Christmas Eve that put me *here* . . . in this North Melbourne street at the end of a wet working day. Walking towards a shopfront that I thought would stay forever a place of nightmares.

I've planned this as intelligently as possible. Close to five o'clock. They'll be there, getting things ready for the opening of the restaurant. But what if they don't live here any more after . . . ? Maybe they went back to Vietnam. Perhaps they've gone to another suburb. Or on holiday? These thoughts fill me simultaneously with hope and dread. After all, it is January. Most businesses close down for a few weeks. *I'd be off the hook then, wouldn't I?* Then I remembered Mihn laughing at me when I asked him once when his parents took holidays.

'My parents don't have holidays,' he said. 'Just being in this country is a holiday for them.'

'Oh really?' I'd said.

Oh God. There it is. The outside of the restaurant. The thin red dragons curling up either side of the black lacquered front door. I take a deep breath and make myself hurry. If I think any more about this then there is no way I'll go ahead with it. I don't even try the door handle although I know the door would probably be open. Instead I bang the big showy brass knocker. The noise is deafening. Like the hard crack of bullets firing into the damp evening air. Nothing for a few moments, although I hear some noise, a little scuffling, and then some people talking inside. It is still not too late. I could still run.

I reach up to try again and the door opens. It is Mihn's mother, Mrs Duong. So squat and round. She doesn't recognise me at first. She just smiles blandly, and then she squints up into my face and I see the recognition begin in her eyes.

'Sophie,' she says softly at last in her funny staccato accent, wonderingly, as though she has been presented with a puzzle. I nod. Feeling ever so nervous, I push the box over to her. I will give it to her and leave. But she doesn't take it. Instead she reaches out and puts one of her little hands on my arm. 'Sophie,' she says again, not looking at me. Her eyes are filling with tears and her mouth is trembling, but she is squeezing the flesh of my arm with her fingers. Actually hurting me a bit, although I don't mind because I know she doesn't mean to.

'Mrs Duong,' I whisper.

She kicks open the door behind her with her foot.

'You come in,' she says gruffly. 'Too wet. You come in.'

She leads me into the restaurant. It takes a while for my eyes to adjust to the darkness. I see the younger kids sitting at the end table. They have stopped folding the red napkins around the plastic chopsticks, and are now staring hard at me. There is a sudden sound of footsteps coming down the stairs and the beaded curtain is pushed aside. First Truc and then Mihn emerge from behind it, but stop in their tracks as soon as they see me. Dead still. Truc is unrecognisable. No longer dressed as a gangster, his hair is short and neat and he is wearing dark pants and a blue-and-white checked shirt. Behind him Mihn looks the same as ever. Tall, gangly and long-haired. They are all now staring at me expressionlessly. No one smiles. I put the box down on the nearest table.

'I brought something,' I manage to say at last. 'A present I made . . . for you all. A kind of angel.' I smile, feeling as foolish as I knew I would, and began to back slowly towards the door. 'It's just something . . . you don't have to keep it if you don't want it.'

I am at the door now. All of us, the five Duongs and me, still staring at each other. I wonder where the father is, then suddenly can't bear it any longer. I drop my gaze and stare at the floor. I wish they would say *something*. Even 'get out and don't come back!' would be better than nothing. I tentatively reach behind my back for the door knob, still without looking up. This is so odd. I hate being where I am and yet I don't want to go.

'Sophie.' Mihn is standing in front of me. His thin

hand reaches out and covers mine, stopping me from opening the door. 'Don't go yet,' he says. 'You don't have to go yet.'

'But I'd better,' I mumble, not daring to look up. 'I'd better go.'

'Hmm.' I hear the smile in his voice, so I do look up then and I see he is smiling a little. His almond-shaped eyes are as bright and warm as I remember them. 'What took you so long?' he asks, softly, so the others don't hear. 'You didn't answer my letter. I've been waiting for you to come. What took you so long?'

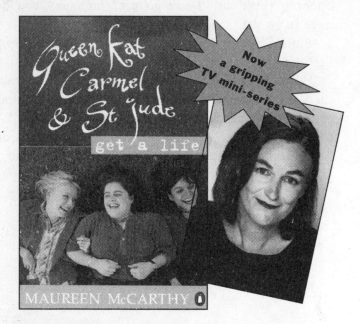

**A powerful story of friendship, families, betrayal
and love, and a tumultuous year in the lives
of three unforgettable young women.**

*Shortlisted for the 1996 Victorian Premier's Literary
Awards and the 1996 NSW Premier's Literary Awards,
and a Notable Book in the 1996 CBC Awards.*

'A multi-layered story that will have the reader laughing
and crying, probably at the same time.'

West Australian